FIRE WHEN READY

WAR OF THE SUBMARINE: BOOK 3
R.G. ROBERTS

Copyright © 2023 by R.G. Roberts

All rights reserved.

No part of this publication may be reproduced, distributed, or transmitted in any form or by any means, including photocopying, recording, or other electronic or mechanical methods, without the prior written permission of the publisher, except as permitted by U.S. copyright law. For permission requests, contact R.G. Roberts at www.rgrobertswriter.com.

The story, all names, characters, and incidents portrayed in this production are fictitious. No identification with actual persons (living or deceased), places, buildings, and products is intended or should be inferred.

Also published on Kindle Vella as season 3 of *War of the Submarine*.

Cover designed by MiblArt.

This one is to Erin, who helped me build the world and dream in it. Also, because there's more Bobby O'Kane here, and she likes that.

Contents

Epigraph	VII
Prologue: The King of the Seas	1
1. Achieving the Impossible	9
2. Moving Upstairs	21
3. With Friends Like These	37
4. Who Needs Enemies?	51
5. Woe Begotten Talents	65
6. Clash of Titans	81
7. The Good Idea Fairy	95
8. Who Needs Enemies?	107
9. SOS	117
10. Tilting at Windmills	133
11. Casanova	145
12. Rules of Engagement	155
13. That Rock and a Hard Place	169
14. Cold Reminders	183
15. Letters from Beyond	197
16. Not a Moment Too Soon	213
17. Good Old-Fashioned Greed	225
18. Chaos	241
19. Punching Bags	255

20.	Shots Fired	265
21.	Necessary Risks	275
22.	Battle Plans	289
23.	Hide and Seek	303
24.	Playing Chicken	315
25.	The Destroyers	327
26.	Smart Pirates	339
27.	Vanguard	353
28.	The Early Bird Gets the Worm	367
29.	Turnover	381
Epilogue		393
Some Fun Notes		398
Also By the Author		403
About R.G. Roberts		405

"You may fire when ready, Gridley."

Commodore George Dewey at the Battle of Manila Bay, 1 May 1898

George Dewey was expelled from Norwich University in 1854 for drunkenness and herding sheep into the barracks—chaotic and unpredictable behavior in keeping with many fine Norwich traditions.

Prologue: The King of the Seas

20 January 2039

The Amazon Confederation (underwater station), 268 nautical miles from the Cocos Islands

Captain Jules Rochambeau, French Navy, could hardly believe how easy this conquest had been.

"Are they stupid or just careless?" he asked his second-in-command, Commander Camille Dubois.

She shrugged her beautiful shoulders. "One never knows, *mon capitaine*. With the Grand Alliance, I find one should never blame circumstances when sheer incompetence will suffice."

Jules snorted. "It is good we are leaving soon, then. I grow tired of this 'station hopping' and wish to return to our true profession."

"We must do as we are needed." Camille shrugged again, seemingly unconcerned.

But Jules was not satisfied. A tall, swarthy, and dark-haired man, he was the commander of the finest attack submarine in the world and despised being a glorified ferryman. Yes, French victories were sweet—particularly when they beat their ally, India, to prizes such as the Amazon Confederation. This underwater station was rich in oil and flew an independent flag, which meant no nation on *either* side of the broiling world war would fight to free them. France, meanwhile, would gain much-needed riches and resources.

They'd also threaten the Alliance's flank at Christmas Island. Once a minor Australian possession, Christmas Island had already been the site of three battles, and Jules had no doubt that it would be the site of many more. It was one of the few forward bases the Grand Alliance of the United States, Britain, and Australia had...and Jules looked forward to taking it from them again.

It would certainly be more interesting than transporting marines this way and that. He'd had his fill of underwater stations a year ago on Armistice Station. Why must the admiralty send their most successful submarine commander to play this silly little game again?

Sighing, he returned the quarterdeck's salute as he crossed back onto *Barracuda*. His beautiful submarine was tied up against the northern TRANSPLAT, or TRANSportation PLATform of the Amazon Confederation. His operations officer met him before he could head below.

"We have orders, sir," she said, smiling.

"Tell me I will like them, Sophia."

"We are ordered to depart within the hour and hunt for a British submarine," Lieutenant Sophia Moulin replied. She was too professional to wiggle with glee, but Jules could tell she wanted to.

His heart thundered in his chest. "*Gallant?*"

"No, *mon capitaine.* HMS *Ambush.*"

"*C'est bon.* It is about time." Jules waved a hand to push aside his disappointment. Ursula North was apparently not ready to be found. That was fine. He would hunt and kill her countrymen—and some Americans for good measure.

Jules Rochambeau knew he was the best submarine commander in the world. He had the kills to prove it, and in ten months of world war between the Freedom Union and the Grand Alliance, no one had been able to stop him.

He did not think anyone ever would.

Fogborne Research Facility

Red Tiger Station, 33 Miles (800 feet deep) off the Coast of Taiwan in the South China Sea

"You get that code done yet?"

The question interrupted the incessant clanking of a keyboard; Ning Tang liked her keyboards large, loud, and colorful. She looked up, brushing black hair out of her eyes, and sighed.

"Yesterday. I finished it yesterday. And I debugged Sam's mess he calls a program."

"I knew I could count on you." Doctor Kimberly Leifsson grinned. A tiny, graying woman, she was the head of the Fogborne Research Team and—technically—Ning's boss. Not that Ning noticed most of the time.

Kim stood in the entryway to Ning's cubicle in the Fogborne Research area. It was almost an office, except it didn't have a door, but Ning had this closet-shaped area to herself. She liked the silence; it let her think of weird things no one else considered. Besides, she was three feet from the door to the reactor space.

"I know you'd rather be calculating temperature curves—"

"Did that yesterday, too." Ning stuck her tongue out, and Kim laughed.

"I bet you did. Sam says you watched the containment test, too."

"Hey, if we're making history, I want to *make* history." Ning pushed back from her computer, double checking that her work was saved first. Forgetful geniuses were *so* last century.

"We're definitely making history." Kim grinned. "The French at the Experimental Reactor Team might've beat us to the first fusion reactor, but that thing is the size of a football field. Yours is much smaller."

"You mean it's *useful*." Ning tried not to flush with pride. She was used to being smart. Dummies, or even normal people, didn't graduate from M.I.T. at fifteen and get a PhD before they could vote.

Ning knew she was a genius. She also knew she was a little weird; she loved a riot of bright colors, followed anime cartoons obsessively, and raced underwater speeder subs every chance she got. Her hair was short, spikey, and black striped with purple, and she wore a rainbow of glasses she didn't need. But twenty-three-year-old geniuses who were almost done designing and implementing the first submarine-sized nuclear *fusion* reactor were allowed to be as wild as they wanted.

Nuclear fission had been the name of the game since nuclear reactors started providing practical power in the early 1950s. Fission was the act of splitting the nucleus of an atom into two or more smaller nuclei. It was more accident prone than fusion, which mashed atoms together instead of separating them, but easier to achieve.

Fusion had been the holy grail of scientific engineering for decades. Everyone wanted it. No one managed.

Then Christophe Girard at ERT made a breakthrough and built a sustainable, working reactor in Marseilles, France, a few years earlier. It was a big beast, but it generated more power than it needed to run. Finally, the world celebrated—safe, nuclear power generation was here!

Unfortunately, Girard was a selfish bastard who didn't like sharing his designs. It took three years before anyone else built a comparable fusion reactor, but that sucker was big, too. And not terribly efficient. Girard also proved incapable of scaling down his design, which was why Ning Tang was now a millionaire.

Pulsar Power LTD got wind of her half-finished project three years ago, buying the Fogborne team lock, stock, and barrel. They set them up with this cozy little research facility on Taiwan's biggest underwater station, in more comfort and with resources Ning had only dreamed of. Red Tiger was three-quarters the size of Armistice Station—and would probably get bigger now that Armistice Station had done and got stolen by the French and Indians and was no longer a haven for crazy-ass freestyle capitalism. Ning liked working there. She was also well on her way to powering the entire station with a fusion reactor, and wouldn't that be cool?

The only problem was that the value of real estate in the area was starting to drop, what with the four-way—or was it five way?—Chinese civil war ongoing.

"You think we'll meet the testing schedule?" Kim asked.

"I think you should brace yourself for a million-dollar bonus." Ning grinned. "We'll be ready next week."

Three days later, *Barracuda* picked up *Ambush's* track. Their intelligence was solid; the British *Astute*-class boat was escorting a pair of supply ships, one American, one British. All three steamed along like there were no threats in the area.

Jules' lip curled. Ursula would never be so careless, but whatever dunce they gave *Ambush* to was not in her league.

"This is a plum target," he said to Camille.

She grinned. "Someone at the Admiralty likes you."

"I almost feel sorry for them." Jules cocked his head. "They have made it so far—across much of the Indian Ocean from Diego Garcia. I am certain the ships or submarines in Perth need these supplies."

Camille giggled. "Do not jest, *mon capitaine*. You do not feel sorry for any of them."

"*C'est vrai*," he replied. *That's true.* "They are fools to only have one escort."

"Fools or desperate."

"Sonar, confirm that *Ambush* is our only underwater target," Jules ordered.

"Confirmed, *capitaine*. Three contacts on sonar. Range approximately fifteen nautical miles. Their course one-one-zero, speed twenty knots."

"Is *Ambush* ahead or astern of the supply ships?" Jules stroked his chin.

"Astern, sir."

"What are you thinking?" Camille asked.

"We might as well have some fun with these three." Jules chuckled. "Calculate an intercept course for thirty miles ahead of their projected course and proceed at best silent speed."

"*Oui, mon capitaine.*"

Jules was not concerned with being heard. *Barracuda* was an Advanced *Requin*-class submarine and one of the quietest submarines in the world. The arrogant Americans—and their British friends—still hadn't figured out that the *Requins* were more dangerous than their own boats. More fools, they.

Barracuda was just three years old, but she'd been in the war from the beginning. At three hundred and thirty-two feet long, she was about the same size as the British boat she hunted, but she was almost twice as fast. The F21 Artemis torpedoes she currently carried were slower than British torpedoes. Unfortunately, the newer F27 Rafale torpedoes hit a production bottleneck back home, and Jules shot off all the first bunch he'd been given.

Still, his F21s were faster than *Ambush*, so they would do the trick...particularly if Jules could line up down the throat shots.

He had three targets and six tubes. This would line up perfectly. All he would have to do was wait.

Four hours later, the sun started setting topside and *Ambush's* sailors were changing the watch.

"Any contacts?" Lieutenant Nigel Barrington, the oncoming officer of the watch, asked Lieutenant Olivia Evans as he relieved her.

"Nothing for days and miles, unless you count those two topside." She rubbed her eyes. "Bloody boring."

"A few more days and we'll be in Perth. It's nice there this time of year," he replied. "And I hear the beaches are lovely."

"They'd best be. I could use some sun and relaxation," Evans said. "Anyway, she's all yours. Try not to let the wheels fall of, will you?"

"I'll do my best," Nigel said, trying not to smile as she left. Evans was a character, but a good friend—one he'd be happy to go to the beach with when they finally reached Perth.

Ambush had drawn the short end of the convoy escort stick, catching three back-to-back jobs without respite. Their commodore had promised the crew some liberty in Australia, however, and Nigel was looking forward to it. This was his first deployment to this part of the world, and war or no war, he wanted to see a little bit of the southern hemisphere.

"How we looking, navigation?" he asked the quartermaster to his right.

"Spot on track, sir. Steady at fifteen knots, holding course one-one-zero. We'll stay on this course for another two days."

"How exciting."

"Ours is not to reason why, sir."

Nigel laughed. "You know, I've—"

"Torpedo in the water! *Multiple* torpedoes in the water, bearing one-one-zero!" the sonar watch said. "Range—rechecking, this can't be right—range...two nautical miles?"

Ice dropped into Nigel's gut. "Hard left rudder!" He could not spare a thought for protecting the two precious supply ships; a torpedo that close would rip *Ambush* into pieces. "Snapshot tube two, bearing one-one-zero!"

Ambush's action stations alarm screamed as the submarine rolled into her turn.

"Ahead flank!" Nigel ordered, seconds too late. The F21 Artemis Torpedo had a maximum speed of fifty knots. Combined with *Ambush's* speed, that provided a closure rate of seventy-five knots and gave Nigel only one minute and thirty-six seconds to react.

The sonar watch had cost him precious time when they did not believe their data. Now, *Ambush* had less than a minute to outfox a torpedo that was sixteen knots faster than her and less than a mile off her heels.

Nigel did everything right. He dropped noisemakers, corkscrewing *Ambush* away from the pair of incoming torpedoes *Barracuda* fired like a wet cat evading a bath. But there wasn't enough time. Rochambeau had placed his submarine right in the Alliance ships' path...and waited until they were daringly close to fire.

Ambush's captain made it to the attack center in time to hear both supply ships exploding as the torpedoes targeting *them* struck true. She did not arrive in time to do much else.

Five minutes after the torpedoes were fired, one struck *Ambush* forward as she twisted into another starboard turn. The other missed, but *Ambush* crashed into the bottom, anyway.

Luckily for her crew, she landed on a rise in the ocean floor just beneath her own crush depth of fifteen hundred feet. Unluckily for those who survived the impact, her emergency buoy failed to launch. No one realized *Ambush* and her two supply ships were missing until they missed a scheduled comms check twelve hours later. USS *Hampton Roads*, a cruiser, was sent to investigate, and she reached the site of the sinking three days later.

There she recovered the survivors from the two supply ships, found bobbing in their life rafts. No rafts were found for HMS *Ambush*, and she was assumed lost with all hands.

Unable to use most of their systems—including communications—with the front half of the submarine flooded, *Ambush's* survivors died five days after the sinking.

The day after that, Jules Rochambeau sent out a tweet:

Captain Jules Rochambeau
@JulesRochambeau
Another one down. Dear Ursula, will you not come out
 and meet me? Should the best not compete with the
 best? @RoyalNavy send Captain North and HMS Gallant
 to meet #Barracuda. No one else is worthy.
#submarines #war

Chapter 1

Achieving the Impossible

2 April 2039, Fogborne Research Facility—Red Tiger Station, the South China Sea

"Load transfer complete!" Sam Yeung pumped his fist in the air. "Yes!"

Kim Leifsson squeezed Ning Tang's shoulder. "Well done."

"I'm *so* buying my own submarine with this bonus." The words slipped out before Ning could stop them, but she grinned anyway. Four months of testing, of slowly ramping up the pressure and the power output, and they were finally there. The Fogborne Fusion Reactor was powering Red Tiger Station.

Of course, the old systems were online and configured for emergency backup power. No one trusted a brand new—and small!—fusion reactor to do the job by itself. No one but Ning and her fellows.

The team of five sat in the bowels of Red Tiger Station, the largest independent underwater station in the South China Sea. Their reactor room was close to the ocean floor, because station management—no matter how well paid—were afraid of a new nuclear reactor. But Pulsar Power, Ltd. had believed in them and provided the funding to create this high-tech control room, where floor-to-ceiling screens showed the status of every reactor indicator.

Plush green chairs—Ning's choice, given their almost bottomless budget—were at every one of the six consoles. Two were staffed with operators, hired off the U.S. Navy and re-trained by the Fogborne Team. The others were for the Reactor Team to monitor the reactor.

Their reactor. Ning was still giddy. She'd known it would work, but watching the reactor take the load like a champ was almost better than the bonus they'd receive.

Sam laughed. "Better be a fast one. Better yet, design one and stick a fusion reactor in it."

"Don't get overconfident, Sam." Kim peered over the rims of her glasses at the pair. "Powering the station for an hour is a small step. Powering it for *months* through successful stress testing…now that's the victory."

"Yes, Mom." Ning rolled her eyes. "Thanks for spoiling the party."

"We can start testing now," Sam said.

"You know better." Kim wagged a finger at them. "Stable load first. Then bonus. *Then* the next tests."

"You really think we're going to have time for more tests?" Sam asked, sounding a little more serious. "It's getting kind of hot outside, if you know what I mean."

Like Ning, Sam had relatives in nearby Taiwan. In his case, it was most of his family. His mother held dual American-Taiwanese citizenship, as did Sam, but she lived in Taiwan. She was an electrical engineer, and her connections got him the job with Fogborne when the team was first stood up as a joint Taiwanese-American project.

Ning was recruited straight out of M.I.T. by their first parent company, partially for her Taiwanese roots, but mostly because she liked to design nuclear reactors in her free time. But she had one set of grandparents on the island, as well as three aunts and two uncles. She didn't get to see them often—Ning couldn't remember the last time she'd seen the sun, let alone a relative—but she video-chatted with them as often as she could.

So far, Taiwan remained largely untouched by the wild civil war engulfing China. But the three-sided fight between the Communist government, pro-democracy Chinese forces, and Taiwan—which was sometimes on the side of the pro-democracy forces, but tended to disavow their more extreme tactics—had already spread to the South China Sea.

And the South China Sea was literally their front yard. And back yard. Sides, too.

Ning grimaced. "No one wants to pull an Armistice Station here, right? Red Tiger works with everyone."

"Including a few terrorists who are based out of here, if the last news reports are accurate," Sam said.

"I hope they're not." Ning shuddered. Wild though she was, she didn't understand why people resorted to violence. Couldn't they talk about this like rational adults?

Who wanted communism, anyway? China'd been creeping toward democracy for ages, or at least toward capitalism. Couldn't they find some happy medium that didn't involve invading Taiwan? As usual, that was what set everything off. Idiots wanting more territory.

"I've been in communication with the home office," Kim said. "If things get any worse, they'll pull us out of here and base us elsewhere."

"What're they going to do with the reactor, box it up?" Sam's laugh was high-pitched.

Ning chewed her lip. "I could probably break it so that no one could use it again."

"I think Pulsar assumes that we'll have to abandon it. Their likely plan is to sell it to Red Tiger Station, assuming the power is stable enough. If you can pull *that* off—for the reactor to be the station's only source of power, you're looking at many more millions."

"Hey, if I'm going to buy my own subracer, I'm going to need all the millions I can get."

Thinking about the sweet little sub she wanted to buy—or maybe design, because yeah, it would be super cool to have *her* reactor in her submarine—was a lot nicer than thinking about the war happening next door.

But no one really wanted to bother Red Tiger. Ning was sure of that.

South of the Maldives (Occupied by India)

"Spying is boring, but if the excitement over in crippie corner is anything to go by, it's productive as hell," Commander Teresa O'Canas said to her executive officer, Lieutenant Commander Sally Weber.

The normal quiet hum of energy in USS *Douglass'* (SSN 811) control room was louder than usual, courtesy of the three watchstanders and two officers clustered around two consoles in the starboard aft corner. Their screens usually showed drone feeds from either a spy drone in the sky or a souped-up underwater drone that replaced *Douglass'* standard Unmanned Underwater Vehicle, but today they had both operating.

Sally grinned. "Hey, as long as no one shoots *Douglass* out from under us, I'm all for spying."

"Particularly since it comes with the opportunity to break some shit on the way out the door?" Teresa laughed.

Normally, spying was a mission she would abhor, even though it was right in her toolkit as an officer who'd been trained in the prewar days. Back then, creeping in a few miles off an adversary's coast—they didn't say enemy in those days—was the most excitement you could get. Now, however, with a weapons room full of torpedoes, Teresa burned to do a bit more to the Indians than *listen*.

But she couldn't deny the usefulness of good intelligence, even if she hated sitting still.

"I'm a simple woman, Captain. I like breaking things and blowing shit up."

"You and me both, Sally." Teresa glanced over at the cryptologists again. Despite her Top Secret clearance, she didn't have a need to know what they were listening to, and she couldn't speak Indian, anyway. But she hoped it was good.

Douglass wasn't exactly optimized for this mission. She was one of the last Block V *Virginia*-class boats, which meant she had spy gear installed, but she hadn't been built from the keel up as a spy submarine, either. They'd had to onload a lot of equipment and personnel for this particular mission, which left Teresa feel like her submarine was a can and her crew the sardines.

Being packed in like this left her feeling stir crazy all the time, and sitting still for days on end didn't help. Two more days of spying and they could finally get out of here. Then they could lope down to the target-rich environment near Port Maritus and maybe pick up some French merchant ships. Then *Douglass* could pay back the French for sinking so many American-allied merchants, at least a little.

Teresa shook herself. She needed to get rid of some of her nervous energy. "I think I'm going to go work out. Mind the shop?"

"You got it, ma'am."

Teresa had one foot outside the control room hatch when the sonar operator sat up so fast his neck cracked. "OOD, new contact to port. Bearing approximately three-five-two, range twenty-one thousand yards. Blade count sounds military. Computer is chewing on ID."

"OOD, aye," the officer of the deck replied.

Teresa yanked her foot back inside control and dogged the hatch shut. "Bottom your underwater drone," she ordered. "We have a contact."

"Captain, we're onto something—" Lieutenant O'Reilly, their borrowed cryptologist twisted to look at her with pleading eyes.

"And we all like living. Bottom the drone."

"Crypto, aye." O'Reilly tapped one of the seated watchstanders on the shoulder. "Do it."

Teresa turned back to sonar. "What d'you got, Rivera?"

"Ma'am, you're not going to believe this, but I think we've caught an *Akula* underway from the Maldives." Rivera grinned. "Computer says ninety percent match with K-165, *Sindhudhvaj*."

"I'm impressed you could pronounce that." Teresa chuckled. "I'm not even going to try. Weps, set up on our new customer, K-165."

"Weps, aye!"

A chill ran down Teresa's spine. This wasn't her first engagement—far from it; she'd squared off with a Russian in the North Atlantic and then danced with the French all the way through the South Pacific. People liked to forget that the French still owned *French* Polynesia and New Caledonia. The latter was only seven hundred fifty miles off Australia's east coast—a stone's throw in a war like this. Only the desire *not* to drop bombs or missiles on civilians' heads kept the proximity of New Caledonia and Australia from turning into a deadly shootout...but it hadn't stopped the maritime tug-of-war for the waters between them.

Douglass had spent almost three months in those waters, hunting French surface ships when they got too big for their britches and the odd *Scorpene*-class submarine. They'd bagged a Russian *Yasen* on the way north, too, crossing through supposedly neutral waters that once leaned toward Japan and were now...interesting.

Now, however, Teresa was at the crossroads between orders to remain undetected and a rapidly approaching Indian fast-attack submarine.

She turned to Sally. "Thoughts?"

"These new *Akulas* aren't too quiet, but they pack a pretty good punch." Sally's eyes were on her tablet, where the *Classified Jane's Addendum* was open to the page on the Indian-built version of the *Akula III*. "Weapons room holds forty torps or missiles, eight tubes, single screw with a max speed of approximately forty-two knots. The threes have a towed array, though he's probably not using it in this shallow of water."

"Thanks, XO." Teresa hated memorizing little details—even useful ones—about enemy submarines, so she was always grateful when Sally covered for her little lapses in memory. This wasn't the first *Akula III* that *Douglass* had faced off with, either, but it was good to have fresh information in her mind when she made decisions that could kill them all. "Likely carrying TEST 83 torpedoes?"

"That's the best the Indians have right now. Rumor says they're trying to buy the Futlyar off of Russia, but no one's selling yet. Personally, I don't think the Russians can make enough to afford to export them."

"Don't we know how that is." Teresa shook herself. "All right. Good to know that their torps are only about thirteen knots faster than we are."

"Better if we don't get shot at, ma'am," her weapons officer put in with a grin.

Teresa hooted with laughter. "You know, I never thought of that. Good call, Weps. Let's shoot this guy before he realizes we're here."

"Captain, that'll make us break stealth," Lieutenant O'Reilly said.

"Only if he gets a message off."

"Or if someone else is nearby and hears," O'Reilly replied. "Torpedoes can be stealthy, but explosions aren't."

"True statement." Teresa shrugged. "You're right, they're going to know we're here the moment we put a torp in this guy, so you've got"—she leaned over to check the plot—"two hours to finish gathering your intel. Then I shoot this guy and we get the hell out of Dodge."

"We were supposed to have two more days!"

"Welcome to the war, Lieutenant. Nothing goes according to plan."

Teresa's words were oddly prophetic. Her plan of shooting the *Akula* didn't go the way she wanted it to, either. Forty minutes later, the Indian sub suddenly turned in their direction and increased speed—not, Teresa suspected, because they'd spotted her boat, but because they were leaving the Maldives on a mission.

But they were still on a collision course with *Douglass*.

"Enemy speed now four-zero knots. Range twelve hundred yards. Closest point of approach two hundred yards in nine minutes."

"I guess that's that. Firing point procedures, tubes one and two, track 7088," she ordered. "Make both tubes ready in all respects, including opening the outer doors."

"Firing point procedures, tubes one and two, track 7088, aye," Weps said. "Making both tubes ready in all respects, including opening the outer doors."

Teresa strode forward to turn the firing key by the weapons console. "Key is green!"

Now *Douglass* could shoot anyone who came at them, including this Indian who was blindly charging in their direction. The range wound down as Teresa's sailors worked, checking the system solution manually, just like they'd been trained to do.

The wait seemed interminable, even though it was only about two minutes. Hugging herself, Teresa struggled not to pace. There was nowhere to do it in the cramped control room, and her crew would think their captain was crazy. But standing still was beyond her, so she bounced on her toes until Sally elbowed her gently.

"Solution ready!"

"Ship ready."

"Very well." Teresa took one last look at the boat's integrated combat systems picture. The *Akula* was only five nautical miles away now and closing the range quickly. She couldn't afford to hesitate. "Fire."

Weps' hand slapped down on the firing buttons. "Two fish away, running hot, straight, and normal!"

"Very well." Teresa squared her shoulders. "OOD, come right and start opening the range. Make your speed—"

"Captain, torpedo in the water bearing three-four-one! Now two torpedoes, same bearing!"

"Hard right rudder!" Teresa ordered. "All ahead flank."

Numbers whirled through her mind as the deck trembled beneath her feet. *Douglass* twisted into the turn, leveling out on an eastern course away from the Maldives and sprinting for her life. Teresa was no math whiz; she'd hated nuclear power school but gutted it out because she always wanted to be a submariner. But she still knew that the TEST 83 torpedo had a maximum speed of fifty-five knots. Combined with its maximum range of thirteen nautical miles, and that meant it had a runtime of just over fourteen minutes.

Douglass was a Block V *Virginia*-class submarine. *Her* top speed was forty-two knots, but the nuclear reactor back aft meant she could maintain that speed indefinitely, unlike a torpedo running on battery. With a five nautical mile head start, and the torpedoes' overtake speed of thirteen knots, those fish chasing her boat would need twenty-three minutes to catch up with her.

Teresa smiled. "They're going to run out of gas before they can get us."

"I just did the same math." Sally grinned. "It's nice to be on the side of speed for once, isn't it?"

"Tell me about it." Teresa hadn't waited for the Indian to be close because of their intelligence mission. She'd waited because *her* torpedoes were just as slow as the TEST 83. The only difference here was that the *Akula* was moving toward her torpedoes in the perfect down-the-throat shot.

She watched the plot as the *Akula's* captain threw their rudder over, desperately trying to generate velocity in any direction other than toward the torpedoes. But submarines didn't turn that fast, particularly Russian-designed ones. *Akulas* were built for speed, not maneuverability. The big beast over there out-massed Teresa's submarine by three thousand tons, and it showed when she tried to turn away.

By the time the *Akula* was on her new course, the American torpedoes were on her tail and homing in.

The Mark 48 CBASS was not a new torpedo. In fact, the sub force had spent the entire war complaining about how slow it was. At only fifty-five knots, like the TEST 83, the CBASS was slower than a lot of the enemy submarines it was designed to kill. It was also slower than the newer Russian and French torpedoes sent out to kill *American* submarines.

But it was faster than an *Akula III*. Like Teresa's *Douglass*, INS *Sindhudhvaj* was designed in a different era before underwater colonies proliferated and undersea technology took giant leaps forward. The CBASS did have one particular advantage, too: its range was almost twice that as the TEST 83 torpedoes USS *Douglass* was playing tag with.

Ten minutes later, two American torpedoes slammed into INS *Sindhudhvaj* and the *Akula* broke up, exploding twice before hitting the ocean floor.

Teresa ran the Indian torpedoes out of gas, crept back to collect her drones, and decided to take the risk of completing her mission. After all, what Indian in their right mind would expect an American sub to stick around after they'd announced their presence? It went against all tenants of American stealth doctrine.

Teresa wasn't sure if it was the smartest decision, but her boat stayed on station for three more days without discovery, and it sure made the cryptology team happy.

8 April 2039, Port of Malé, Maldives (Occupied by India)

Vice Admiral Aadil Khare was still a vice admiral, which was, admittedly, a disappointment. But this news was not.

"Are you sure this is accurate?" He sat back in his chair and tried to get comfortable. Even the flag cabin on *Rajput* was a cramped affair, but destroyers were built to take the battle to the enemy, not to sleep admirals in luxury.

At least *Rajput* was a newer destroyer, a *Kolkata II*-class commissioned just seven years earlier. She was one of the fiercest ships in the fleet, and a good flagship...even if he wanted more.

Khare was ambitious. He would not lie. And he'd been on a straight-line track straight to the top of the Indian Navy until his seizure of Armistice Station—the largest independent underwater megastation in the world—went awry. It wasn't a *failure* in that the French-Indian alliance still captured the station, but precious intelligence assets had slipped right through their fingers. Several naval officers, including one admiral, escaped, led by one no-name commander, Alex Coleman.

Khare still hoped to meet him in combat someday, but as far as he could tell, the Americans buried him somewhere. Perhaps their sources were wrong, and Coleman was not a submariner. Perhaps his specialty was decidedly more...shady.

Captain Kiara Naidu, his chief of staff, beamed. "I received the information from intelligence this morning, sir. I thought you would want to hear right away."

"You're very right about that." Khare sipped his tea and forced himself to forget Armistice Station. "Fusion reactors—*working*, usably sized fusion reactors—would be priceless to the war effort. And you say they're being developed by a civilian company?"

"Pulsar Power Limited." Kiara's beautiful face was serene. "They part-own a platform out in the South China Sea, right in the middle of all the chaos."

"Hm." Khare pursed his lips. "That's an interesting problem."

"Isn't it?" She cocked her head. "On one hand, I imagine no one will notice if we wander in there and take what we want, not with that three-way—or is it four-way?— Chinese civil war going on. On the other hand...one never knows who might *shoot* at us there."

Khare grimaced. "And we remain chronically short of missiles."

"Unfortunately."

"Yet capturing the team who created the reactor, if not the reactor itself, would be an incalculable boon to India. Having the first usable fusion reactors would guarantee our future as a world power."

"As a superpower, I would think." Her brown eyes met his, and Khare was glad—not for the first time—that he'd added this brilliant and ambitious woman to his team. Kiara wanted to go straight to the top. But she was more than a decade his junior, so Kiara was content to follow him and reap the benefits of their combined successes.

"Indeed."

He sipped his tea again, mind racing. The problem was the underwater station in question. Pulsar Power Limited was a predominantly American-owned company with strong Taiwanese ties. No one would mind if he attacked them, not with America arrayed against the Freedom Union. But getting there *was* a thorny problem.

"Do we know exactly where the station is?"

She nodded. "We do. We have a spy inside on the security team."

"Could that spy deliver the plans to us?" As much as Khare would like the coup of capturing the *entire* research team, he would settle for the plans. India had an excellent research and development establishment, after all.

"So far, no. But there always remains a chance." Kiara frowned. "A slim one, though."

"Let us try that first. Meanwhile, we will wait for more missiles—and for our collective embarrassment over the Second Battle of Christmas Island to fade."

"You do not want revenge?"

"It was not my loss." Khare waved a hand. "Admiral Devi was fortunate to die in that disaster. She should have seen that attack coming."

Kiara laughed. "Did you expect the Americans to use land attack missiles against a fleet at anchor?"

"No, but I was not in charge of the contingency planning, now, was I?" Khare had been furious not to be chosen for command at Christmas Island, but now he thanked his lucky stars that the admiralty had passed him over.

Now Devi was dead. That meant there was one less competitor in the field.

"Contact your friends in intelligence," he continued. "I will call my cousin, who works in research. She will know what to do with those plans if they make it into our hands."

"Aye, sir. And if intelligence cannot steal the plans?"

"Then we will steam into the South China Sea with our task group and *take* this"—he glanced at the briefing on his tablet—"Fogborne team."

"I look forward to it, Admiral."

Chapter 2

Moving Upstairs

10 April 2039, the Western Indian Ocean

Commander Michelle Wollstonecraft hated her submarine.

Perhaps that was a little harsh, but it was true. Having been promised a brand-new *Cero*-class boat—an Improved-*Cero*, no less!—a detailing snafu instead found her inheriting *Utah* when its commanding officer went right off the deep end. She'd been in command for six months now, and she still didn't feel at home.

Damn Adam Rampichini. If he hadn't gone and overmedicated himself with alcohol and sleeping pills, he wouldn't have ended up on the fifth floor of Balboa Naval Hospital, and Michelle wouldn't be commanding *Utah* instead of him. Instead, she'd be on a boat that was nineteen knots faster and, she reckoned, far quicker to respond to the helm.

It wasn't that *Utah* was ancient. She was a newish *Virginia*, a Block IV boat commissioned in 2025. But that meant she was fourteen damned years old, and Michelle imagined the boat squeaked and creaked at the worst times. The poor sonar operators' ears were probably bleeding.

Or they'd already gone deaf. With her halfway-to-delinquent crew, who knew?

"Are we in position yet, XO?" She shoved her glasses up her nose and turned to face her second least favorite person in the universe, Lieutenant Commander Arnie Hoagland.

Her second-in-command smiled. And that was the problem with

him—he was *always* smiling. Executive officers weren't supposed to be that cheerful. He was supposed to be the bad guy so that *she* didn't have to be. The crew *liked* Hoagland.

"We're creeping in now, Captain. Should be in range in...five minutes." He glanced down at the navigational display, furrowing his brow like a competent warfighter.

The thing she hated most about him was that he *was*. Hoagland didn't seem to have faults. He was smart, affable, and damned good at his job. It set Michelle's teeth on edge.

"All tubes ready in all respects, with the exception of opening the outer doors."

"Thank you, Weps." Not grimacing was hard. Lieutenant Sharon Getz was *Utah's* weapons officer, and while she was also capable, she was another bubbly, cheerful personality.

There was also the matter of a complaint to the navy's inspector general that Michelle was *certain* had come from within the weapons department. Getz claimed not to know anything about it, but Michelle knew she was lying. Getz wanted to protect her sailors, but there was no reason to protect whichever little liar told tales about their captain. Getz's *job* was to support her captain, not shield hell-demon sailors from their just desserts.

Michelle sucked in a breath and banished those thoughts from her mind. A good kill would make everyone on *Utah* feel better. Commodore Banks would be pleased, too. It was time to get to work.

Stepping forward, Michelle glanced at the plot. *Utah* had executed a good—if long—stalk of her prey, a relatively new Indian *Requin-E* class submarine. Michelle wanted this kill so badly she could taste it; as far as she knew, no Alliance captain had sunk one of the French-built, *Requin-Export* class submarines. Such a feather in her cap would help her move out of this dingy submarine before she died of old age.

Then, of course, the enemy changed course and speed, turning their five-minute stalk into a novel's worth of delay. Four hours of intense boredom later, they were nearly in range, so Michelle ducked out of control. Just for a few moments. She needed to herself to freshen up and get her head on straight before potential combat beckoned.

She knew some captains preferred to stay in control for the entire hunt, but she believed that one perk of being the boss was the ability to grab a few minutes of peace. Now she was back, refreshed, and smarter than anyone who'd spent hours staring at the plot with no breaks—and able to spot things they didn't."

Her eyes narrowed. "We're at fourteen thousand yards, XO."

"Yes, ma'am. I was reading Captain Dalton's patrol reports about how shooting from too far out led to enemy submarines outrunning his torpedoes. He recommends shooting from inside ten thousand yards."

Michelle crossed her arms. "Is Captain Dalton in command of this submarine?"

Hoagland flushed, which made his freckles stand out and his red hair seem bright orange. "No, ma'am."

"And what do our standing orders from the squadron say?"

"Not to close enemies more than fifteen thousand yards." He stared at his feet.

Over by the helm, the chief of the boat twitched. Michelle shot her a *shut the hell up* glare before looking back at her rebellious XO. "Exactly. I cannot believe that you willfully disregarded squadron orders. I thought better of you."

She hadn't really thought better of him, but it paid to let the video data recorder see and hear her say it. Michelle learned early in her career to play to an audience. Particularly when that audience would judge her later.

"I apologize, Captain. I thought you were eager for the kill."

Oh, that was a glint of defiance in Hoagland's gaze, wasn't it? Michelle narrowed her eyes and gave him her nastiest smile. "I'm eager to do this the *right* way, XO," she said. "Officer of the Deck, decrease your speed to fifteen knots."

"OOD, aye. All ahead standard."

"All ahead standard, aye. My engines are ahead standard for fifteen knots." The chief of the boat was still throwing those warning looks Michelle's way, but she ignored her.

"Now, let us kill this enemy correctly. Fifteen thousand yards is close enough. I have no intention of risking the boat—and therefore your lives—while our torpedoes are capable of hitting targets from more than twenty-one nautical miles away." She crossed her arms. "Trust our technology. It's the best in the world."

Hoagland stepped away from the plot to stand by her side, speaking in a whisper. "Captain, intel says that the *Requin-E's* top speed is around fifty-two knots. They can outrun our torpedoes if we fire from too far away."

"Nonsense. There's no evidence they know we're here. Get back to your station with the tracking party. I want you checking our firing solutions quickly."

"Yes, ma'am." He deflated again and walked away.

Michelle raised her chin. "Weapons officer, firing point procedures, tubes one and three, track 7015."

"Solution ready," Getz replied.

"Ship ready." Damn Hoagland for his customary efficiency; the annoying little bastard was fast.

"Very well. Fire tubes one and three."

"Firing!" Getz's hands slapped down. "Tubes one and three fired electrically."

Moments later, the report came from sonar: "Conn, Sonar, two fish running hot, straight, and normal."

"Conn, aye," Michelle took the report herself, not trusting anyone else. Lord only knew what else they'd do to screw this up. She turned a glare on Getz. "Don't cut the wires. I want to guide these torps all the way in."

Getz flinched. "Do you want to change course so they can't trace back to our position, Captain?"

"Of course I do." Michelle rolled her eyes. "Officer of the Deck, come right fifteen degrees. Match speed with the *Requin*."

She paid the OOD no mind as her orders were obeyed. Lieutenant Ali was one of the few officers on board who was on her side all the time. Then a voice blared out of the speaker to her right.

"Conn, Sonar, target is increasing speed. Computer has tonal match for S-89, *Vela*."

"Oh, we're chasing Avani Patel." Michelle laughed. "She's supposed to be India's best. That won't last long."

It would be nice to have her name mentioned alongside John Dalton's. Maybe sinking India's shining star could even get her a better boat. Dalton was a full-blown captain, and *he* had a brand-new Improved-*Cero*. Maybe she could get one of them!

Michelle let her mind wander back stateside. Electric Boat was due to commission six *Ceros* this year and eleven next year. This year's boats had captains assigned, but *Perch* was due to commission in January. She'd take *Perch*. Or *Billfish, Burrfish,* or *Devilfish*, all of which followed before next April. A year to spend time in the shipyards—where crews worked hard and captains got a break—would be just about right.

"Conn, Sonar, *Vela* is up to fifty-two knots. Range still fifteen thousand yards. Torpedo range to target...fourteen thousand yards."

"Damn, they were quick to put the pedal down," Hoagland said.

Michelle stabbed a finger at him. "A little less commentary, please, XO."

Hoagland looked away but was silent. Just the way she liked him.

But he was right, damn him. Michelle did quick math. The Mark 48 CBASS torpedoes she fired had about twenty-two minutes of runtime at fifty-five knots. With a closure rate of three knots...they'd need over two hours to catch up with *Vela*.

Those torpedoes didn't have two hours of gas.

Michelle wiped suddenly sweaty palms against the legs of her coveralls as an icy wave of panic washed over her. This had to be Hoagland's fault somehow. Or Getz's. She couldn't have hosed this up on her own. She'd write it on her patrol report so that they were blamed. All she had to do was say the right things for the cameras.

She'd be fine.

No one dared speak as minutes ticked by. Michelle knew the chase was pointless, but she wasn't a quitter. She couldn't afford to look like one, either. What if something changed? A reactor casualty could slow the enemy down.

Pigs could fly, too, at least in the stupid cartoons her brother still liked to watch.

"Captain, I can't match *Vela's* speed," the officer of the deck said after ten minutes passed. "Do you want to cut the wires?"

Michelle groaned. Her torpedoes were useless, just like her ancient deathtrap of a submarine. *Vela*, that shiny new submarine the French sold India, was outrunning them by fourteen knots. "Very well. Weps, cut the wires. Our torpedoes aren't fast enough to catch them, anyway."

She'd have to take that tact. John Dalton, damn him, already opened the door, at least. Blame the torpedoes when you couldn't kill the enemy. No one said Dalton wasn't a canny operator.

"Cut the wires and close the outer doors, aye," Getz said. Michelle clenched her fists. Did she have to sound so chipper? Was she *happy* they couldn't kill the enemy?

Grinding her teeth was bad for her, but it made another few minutes pass.

"Conn, Sonar, target is dropping noisemakers!"

Michelle blinked. "Why would they do that?"

"That's...weird," Hoagland said, again moving over to stand next to her by the navigation plot. They watched together as *Vela* jinxed and turned, spiraling around her base course.

"They guessed we cut the wires," she snarled as both of *Utah's* torpedoes spun out to the east, well clear of *Vela*.

The Indian submarine continued in her turn, looping around to the west. But Michelle didn't see it, because her head snapped up when Hoagland said:

"Shit."

"I do not have time for your profanities, XO!" This time she stabbed him with that pointed finger, just to get the point across. "Keep them in your head."

Hoagland dared glare at her. "Ma'am, I respect your rank and your orders, but that doesn't give you a right to lay a hand on anyone on this crew."

"Excuse me?"

"Conn, Sonar, target is continuing her turn—transients, torpedo in the water, bearing two-niner-seven! *Two* torpedoes in the water, bearing two-niner-seven and two-niner-niner!"

Michelle froze.

Critical seconds ticked by while everyone stared at her, but words wouldn't come.

"Hard left rudder!" Hoagland snapped. "COB, stand by your noisemakers." He leaned into the intercom. "Sonar, Conn, torpedo characteristics?"

"Torpedo tonals match TEST 83, Indian design. Max speed five-five knots."

Michelle felt her submarine rolling starboard, turning and sprinting for all she was worth. "Those torpedoes are seventeen knots faster than we are," she whispered.

And she'd let *Vela* turn and shoot when *Utah* was running straight at them.

Hoagland met her eyes. "All we can do is run, ma'am. And then hit the roof and try to save everyone we can."

---

9 April 2039, Virginia Beach, Virginia

The SUBMISS/SUBSUNK message came in a few minutes before midnight, but Admiral Winifred Hamilton was still awake. She wasn't in the office—she wasn't such a masochist—but she checked message traffic before bed.

There was almost always bad news these days.

She sank into a chair at her bedside, tucking slippered feet under herself. Freddie lived alone and didn't need much space; her two-bedroom apartment was nice but not too spacious, though she had spoiled herself by moving to Virginia Beach instead of nearby Norfolk. Here she could be by the beach and watch ships and subs sail down the Thimble Shoals Channel on a clear day.

Freddie read the message with practiced eyes, sighing. Another one lost. She wished she was surprised.

Then she steeled herself. Every SUBMISS/SUBSUNK message was accompanied by an automated video upload from the sub's VDR, or video data recorder. That showed the video of the sub's control room, and Freddie backed it up until *Utah's* stalk turned sour.

Watching the video made her stomach heave. But she didn't vomit. As Commander, Submarine Forces (and Commander, Submarine Forces Atlantic, since the jobs went hand in hand), Freddie forced herself to watch *every* VDR upload of every boat that sank. Every American submarine that sailed was her responsibility. So she'd seen captains freeze before, though most weren't such unmitigated bags of self-importance as Michelle Wollstonecraft. Freddie had never met Commander Wollstonecraft, and a traitorous part of her hoped she never would. She pushed that thought aside.

Wollstonecraft didn't freeze for long. Much good it did her. She and her XO worked together to try to outrun the TEST 83 torpedoes *Vela* fired, but math was math. When *Utah's* countermeasures failed, they had no way of escaping. Not after they'd driven their boat right into a perfect *enemy* firing solution. At least Wollstonecraft did the right thing and drove for the roof, which meant some of her crew—and maybe even her pompous-but-generally-competent ass—got off alive.

What made Freddie's blood boil wasn't Wollstonecraft's behavior. It wasn't even the fact that *Utah's* buoy failed to go off at crush depth. No, it was the fact that *Utah* executed a good stalk and fired two torpedoes that were *too damn slow to hit their targets.*

The Mark 48 torpedo had been a staple of the U.S. submarine community for longer than Freddie had been in uniform. Continuously updated since 1972, every American submariner had assumed that the Mark 48 would be the best torpedo in the world *forever*. Its most recent evolution, the CBASS, was a solid torpedo...but it was slow.

And slow torpedoes were getting American—and Australian, since they used the same torp—submariners killed.

Fortunately, there was an answer. Last December, Freddie helped push through production of a new torpedo, developed jointly by

British and American companies as the child of the Mark 48 married with the British Spearfish. The Mark 84 Advanced Spearfish Variant was a good torpedo, maybe not as fast as some of their enemies', but fast enough to kill the enemy submarines.

Lazark, the American company responsible for its manufacture, was working around the clock to make them. And Freddie *knew* that the bulk of the torps had been sent to COMSUBPAC in Pearl Harbor, Hawaii.

She also knew Vice Admiral Brown had left them sitting in a warehouse.

She put her message tablet down and grabbed her phone. The recipient answered on the third ring.

"Freddie, it's after ten," the chief of naval operations said. "I hope this is good."

"I apologize for the late call, sir, but I needed to follow up with you about Vice Admiral Brown," she said. "We just lost another boat because they fired torpedoes too slow to catch the enemy."

"You're certain that's the cause?" Admiral David Chan, known to friends and colleagues by his aviator callsign of "Scrap," asked.

"I can forward the VDR video if you want. It's clear as day, even to an aviator."

"Easy, there. You're salty tonight."

"Sir, I'm losing boats because they shoot at the enemy and can't kill them. We're *losing the war* because Doug Brown is hoarding torps and you won't let me fire him. Fuck politics. This is important."

She could hear Scrap sigh on the other end. "What do you mean hoarding torpedoes?"

"There's a warehouse in Pearl with seven hundred forty Mark 84 torpedoes inside. None have been sent to boats on patrol." *I sent you that in my last memo,* she didn't add.

Freddie tried to dial back her anger. Yelling at the navy's senior admiral wouldn't get her what she wanted.

"That...that's worse than I thought."

"My info is old. There may be more now."

"All right. Fine. I'll clear the way with SecDef for you to fire the man. Do it gently, all right? I'll get him a staff job somewhere. We can't afford more flack in the media than we already have."

"That's fine by me, sir. I'm not out to make enemies. I just want to give our boats the best chance they've got," she replied.

"You have a replacement in mind?"

Freddie grinned. "You bet I do."

10 April 2039, the Western Indian Ocean

Commander Alex Coleman was getting better at pretending convoy escorts didn't bother him. It took practice, but he had a lot of that, and Convoy 687 was no different. This one was in route from Perth, Australia, to the Red Sea and then the Suez Canal; from there, they'd head across the Mediterranean Sea and the Atlantic, carrying precious ores and oil from Australia to the U.S. Fortunately, USS *Jimmy Carter* (SSN 23) would only have to take them as far as the Gulf of Aden; the shallow waters after that weren't friendly to America's biggest attack submarine. But she'd likely pick up another convoy on the way back.

Alex's newly relaxed frame of mine was helped by how much he genuinely liked the officers in his wardroom. The fact that Lieutenant Commander Kirkland, his XO, had taken to eating lunch right when the wardroom galley opened and then fleeing didn't hurt, either. Alex felt guilty for not enjoying his XO's presence, but George was the wettest blanket he'd ever met—the man didn't even like *comedy*, which was what *Jimmy Carter's* officers were watching over lunch today.

"You think the USO can get Billie Ro out to do a tour, Captain?" Lieutenant Maggie Bennet, his navigator, asked. A slender woman, she was built like the gymnast she'd been in her youth, with curly black hair that tried to escape her control every chance it got. "She seems like the type who might like a trip to Australia."

"Even if they did, we'd never see her." Benji Angler, the weapons officer, sipped his watery orange juice and shrugged. "We're barely ever in port. It's a miracle the captain's wife still talks to him at all."

Alex chuckled. "My wife understands being in command. She's not in port much more than we are, though I'll admit her jobs are a tad more exciting than our carousel of convoy escorts."

"Wish she'd talk to my girlfriend." Benji slumped. "Ex-girlfriend now."

"You had a girlfriend?" Maggie's eyebrows shot up.

Alex hid a smile. To say his crew had a rocky start was an understatement; poached from every odd corner of the submarine community, *Jimmy Carter's* crew was an assembly of odds and ends as much as the crew of a functional warship. The navy hadn't put much thought into manning their eldest attack submarine when they'd decided not to decommission her, which meant Alex did everything from trading spare parts for sailors to borrowing a corpsman from a friend's boat and never giving him back, albeit with permission.

Most of them hadn't been excited to come to *Jimmy Carter*. Hell, *Alex* hadn't; he'd felt gutted when he got this assignment coming out of the commanding officers' course at the sub school. After working his tail off to graduate first in his class, he found out that Admiral Hamilton's enmity for him stuck like a bad smell, and *Jimmy Carter* was his reward for the trifecta of disobeying orders to stop a crazy captain, going to Admiral's Mast, and then saving a bunch of civilians—and Hamilton herself—from the Indians at the beginning of the war.

But he'd come to love his creaky boat and colorful crew. They were good people, even if...not what he expected. Take Benji, whose full name was Benjamin Winthrop Angler IV, and whose father was Senator Benjamin Winthrop Angler III, the man who'd pinned the navy to the wall in the Angler Hearings early in the war. Benji, however, was apolitical to a fault, loved animals more than people, and was a damned good officer.

"For three whole patrols," Benji said. "My mom would've hated Caroline, which was one of the reasons I liked her. Local gal, worked out at the aquarium, helped get that sea lion off *Bluefish* when it fell down her aft hatch. Didn't mind that I'm navy. Did mind that I'm never around."

Maggie cringed. "Ouch."

"Yep. Here's to Caroline. May she find someone who can call her at night and isn't stuck in a metal tube." Benji toasted with his juice before downing it.

A knock on the wardroom door interrupted Maggie's response.

"Come in!" Alex said.

"Sorry to interrupt your breakfast, Captain, but the OOD said you'd want to see this right away." The radio operator of the watch extended the message tablet.

"As long as it's not another sea lion." Alex grinned. "Thank you. Send Lieutenant Alvaro my compliments and tell her I'll return the tablet soon."

"Aye, sir." The radio operator made herself scarce.

"Don't tease Elena too much about that sea lion, Captain," Benji said. "She got some great video of them hauling it off *Bluefish* with

FIRE WHEN READY: A MILITARY THRILLER　　　31

a crane."

"You're just sad you missed the fun," Maggie said.

"I wouldn't say I *missed* it." Benji laughed. "I had a pretty good time myself that night."

Alex tuned them out the moment he spotted the top message header. SUBMISS/SUBSUNK ICO USS UTAH SSN 801.

"Jesus Christ."

"Captain?" Maggie and Benji both jumped.

"*Utah* sank two days ago, but her buoy only just activated. We've got orders from COMSUBPAC to head for her last known position at best speed. Guess someone finally decided we're the rescue pros."

"Only took them two dicey rescues to figure that out," Benji said.

Jimmy Carter had pulled the survivors of two fellow submarines out of the water in the last seven months, as well as fishing four pilots out of the drink.

"What's our range?" Maggie asked.

"Only about twenty miles." Alex quickly forwarded the message to Maggie's onboard account. "The convoy's skirting right up on where her buoy launched. Cook up a course and head us there right away."

"I'm on it, sir." Maggie was out of her chair like a shot.

"They sure she sank?" Benji scratched his chin. "If the buoy only now activated, could it be a mistake?"

"Apparently the VDR footage makes it pretty clear that she ate a torp." Alex skimmed the message as fast as he could, ignoring the growing headache. "But she was near the surface, so the likelihood of survivors is high."

"I'll find the XO and let him know to get the rescue and assistance detail ready."

"Thanks. Then get your ass to control. Whoever shot *Utah* might still be around."

Jimmy Carter's top speed was better than that of the sunken *Utah*; she was older, but like her long-decommissioned sisters of the *Seawolf*-class, *Jimmy Carter* was designed with one true purpose: to hunt and kill other submarines. She was built with every bell and whistle the pre-2000 U.S. Navy could dream of, and it turned out that those were still damn good toys.

More importantly, *Jimmy Carter* spent her life right on the tip of the spear as America's spy submarine, which meant she got the best of new technology the moment it was ready. If she hadn't been so damned old that every flag officer avoided her like she had leprosy, she would've been a good warfighter. Alex knew that in his bones.

It only took his boat twenty-six minutes to cross the nineteen nautical miles to *Utah's* last known position at flank speed. Not sprinting and drifting was a risk, but Alex didn't want to leave American sailors in the water any longer than necessary.

They'd already been there two *days*. Wasn't that long enough?

If their life rafts didn't deploy, and *Utah's* sailors were in the water…many of them were probably dead. A lump rose in Alex's throat, but he didn't say that to anyone. Hypothermic tables were second nature for him since he was a trained diver. Most of his people would need longer to do that math. Hopefully, they'd find the survivors, first.

"Weps, be ready for anything," Alex ordered as *Jimmy Carter* slowed. "There's no knowing if we have company around here and we just blundered into the china shop."

Benji winked. "My finger's on the trigger, Captain."

"Sonar, Conn, go active three-sixty. I want to know the underwear size of anyone watching us," Alex said into the intercom.

"Sonar aye, going active three-six-zero degrees."

Unlike the movies, there was no bonging *ping*; a real sonar ping was more like an annoying little whistle. The sound was a submariner's worst nightmare when it was aimed at them—but it was also the most surefire way to know if another submarine lurked nearby.

The whistle whipped out, but nothing came back, including an enemy torpedo with their name on it. Alex watched his watchstanders slump in relief. "All right, people. Let's shift to rescue mode. Officer of the Deck, surface the ship."

"Surface the ship, aye." Maggie jumped to the periscope and went about her business.

Damn, it was good to have people he trusted. Relaxing without George around was a guilty pleasure, but at least running the rescue and assistance detail was something the XO was *good* at. Having him fretting here in control when someone might shoot at them was, well, less than optimal.

I guess the good thing about not going into combat is that I don't have George hanging like a lead weight around my neck. The thought made Alex smile crookedly, but he banished the thought as *Jimmy Carter* rose through the depths to the surface. He listened with half an ear as Maggie cleared the way and then scurried up the ladder after the boat was stable.

"Got something to port, sir." One of the lookouts pointed.

Alex hefted his binoculars. There they were, two rafts rolling against the swells, not too far from his boat. "So you do." He lifted the sound-powered phone. "Conn, Bridge, this is the captain. I have the Conn."

"OOD, aye," Maggie's slightly mechanical-sounding voice replied. "Left standard rudder. Ahead one third."

"Left standard rudder, ahead one third, aye. My rudder is right fifteen degrees, no new course given. Engines are ahead one third for five knots," Master Chief Morton, his chief of the boat, replied.

"Very well."

Alex checked the swells. The waves were worse than he'd like for this kind of evolution, but this wasn't the worst *Jimmy Carter* had handled for a surface evolution. Seven- or eight-foot seas were...doable.

The bridge radio crackled. "Captain, XO, I don't like the look of these seas."

Alex grimaced and picked up the radio. "They're within rescue range, XO."

"I'm worried we'll lose someone overboard, sir. *Again*."

Alex grimaced, not wanting to be reminded of the day a willfully blind douche of a surface officer ordered his submarine to resupply another ship *on the surface* in a goddamned monsoon. They'd lost two sailors overboard that day, and it still ate at him.

He shook himself. Captains couldn't afford to drown in grief; he had his own crew to worry about, and *Utah's* sailors needed him at his best. Besides, Alex knew his business rescuing people. Not only did he have more practice doing this than any other sub CO in the navy, but he was also a qualified rescue swimmer.

"Have them all tie off and triple check their lanyards. Pop 'em in life vests, too. We'll be okay." Alex's practiced eye watched the sub's bow swinging left and calculated how long it would take to stop. He lifted the sound-powered phone again. "Steady as she goes."

"Steady as she goes, aye. Steady course two-two-four."

"Very well."

George hadn't stopped talking during that exchange; Alex just stopped listening. "Sir, if we lose someone—"

"XO, Captain, we are trained for this. And we are not leaving those people in the water." Alex hated cutting people off. Particularly with both lookouts staring at him with such wide eyes. Because yeah, they could hear this stellar conversation. There was no privacy in the phone booth-size sail, and it wasn't like he could send them below.

"I'm not saying we should, sir. Just that we could pick them up later." George sounded like he was pouting, so Alex shuffled around the small opening at the top of the sail to look down at where his XO stood aft of it. Those hunched shoulders of George's were an entire *novel's* worth of protests, weren't they?

Alex bit back the harsh reply on the tip of his tongue. Somehow, *suck it up and drive on* just didn't feel like it would ring true for George, no matter how many Norwich University grads took it to heart. He shook his head and spoke as gently as he could.

"XO, Captain, the longer we are on the surface, the greater risk we face. And how do you think those sailors will feel if they see rescue come riding toward them, only to dive and hide until the weather is better?" he asked. "No, we rescue them now. Is your team ready?"

"Yes, sir." George glanced up at him as he spoke, misery etched into his features, but at least the man could still follow orders.

"Excellent." Alex made himself smile, more for the lookouts' benefit than his own. He'd spent too much time on George, however, and now he had to drive his submarine again. "All stop."

"All stop, aye. Engines all stop."

"Very well." Alex put down his intra-ship radio and lifted the bridge-to-bridge radio used to communicate with other ships and submarines. "Salt Lake, this is Killer Rabbit, calling you on channel one-six, over."

A long pause came before a female voice answered: "This is Salt Lake Actual, roger, over."

"Good to hear your voice, Salt Lake Actual. I estimate I will be alongside you for rescue in five mikes. My crew is standing by to assist, over."

Another pregnant silence came before *Utah's* CO finally replied: "And my crew will be grateful. Out."

Well, Alex had certainly rescued more *pleasant* people, but he supposed waiting two days to hear a friendly voice would put him in a bad mood, too.

Marco Rodriquez had just got out of the shower when the outside line phone in his flag cabin on USS *Fletcher* rang.

One of the few privileges of being an admiral was having said outside line phone to himself. Another was the ability to prance across his cabin buck-ass naked because he didn't have a roommate. He didn't have to prance far. Even a flag cabin was cozy on board a destroyer and barely twelve feet across. Compared to most staterooms on the ship, it was a veritable palace, but it still had slick, plastic-like floors, which made him slide his way to the phone. How inglorious.

Marco grabbed the phone in one hand and his towel in the other, rubbing his hair until it stuck up like a sea witch's. "Rodriquez."

"I do believe security protocols say that you're supposed to answer the phone a little more formally than that," Freddie Hamilton said from the other side of the world.

"Three star admirals concerned with protocol shouldn't be calling me herself. Don't you have a fucking aide for that?" he asked.

"She's busy." He could almost hear Freddie shrug. "I need your help, Marco."

"Conversations like this always end up with me in a metric shit ton of trouble." Marco put the phone on speaker and started drying off. The deck was slippery enough without making it wet, and he'd look like a damned idiot if he slipped again and broke his fool neck in his own cabin.

"This one'll be no different." She sighed. "Vice Admiral Brown was sitting on a goldmine of over seven hundred Mark 84 torpedoes. I fired his ass for not getting them out to the sub force. I want you to replace him."

"*What?*"

"You heard me."

"Pretty sure I didn't." Marco dropped his towel to stare at the phone like Freddie might crawl out and grow an extra head. No, two. "No one in their right fucking mind wants me to be COMSUBPAC."

Freddie's laugh sounded brittle. "Well, then color me crazy."

"You okay over there?"

"Of course I'm not okay. We've lost *twenty-five* boats since the war started, and I find out that the man who was supposed to be getting boats what they needed was instead hoarding high speed torpedoes like a damned dragon. I need someone with the guts to make a difference, Marco. I need you."

Marco blinked rapidly, feeling like someone'd just punched him in the face. "No way will Congress go for this."

"You let me worry about Congress. Your record speaks for itself."

"Fuck me, Freddie."

"No thanks." Finally, her laugh sounded almost normal. "You're not my type."

"Yeah, you neither."

She might've been if things were different. But instead, they were best friends, and that was more than enough for Marco Rodriquez.

Marco had spent the war in surface ships so far, and he'd done pretty good commanding fleet actions despite being a submariner. He'd wound up here almost by accident but had figured he'd stay—hell, there were worse places to be, and he had good people around him. But his heart was in submarines, because that was where his guts, blood, and dreams had always been.

Him. COMSUBPAC. The legendary job of "Uncle" Charlie Lockwood in World War II, the man who commanded the likes of Mush Morton, Dick O'Kane, and Eugene Fluckey.

He was just a skinny kid from Puerto Rico who squeaked into the Naval Academy on a scholarship.

What the hell was the world coming to?

Chapter 3

With Friends Like These

"*I am* senior to you." Commander Michelle Wollstonecraft wasn't even the type to say it in private; no, she was trying to stare Alex down in *Jimmy Carter's* attack center, in full view of twenty of his crew.

Alex snorted. "By about five seconds, sure. But this is my submarine, Commander, and you are a guest on board." *A not very welcome one.* He didn't say the words out loud, but he was pretty sure she got the message.

Michelle Wollstonecraft looked at him like he was a bad smell under her nose, and that imperious look did nothing to enhance her likability. She was a tall and good-looking woman, with blond hair, green eyes, and freckles that made her look younger than her age, but five days after rescuing *Utah's* crew, all of Alex's fantasies revolved around throwing her captain back in the drink. He was pretty sure the rest of *Utah's* people were good sailors, but they were quiet and jumpy.

He tried to give Michelle leeway for that, to offer compassion and friendship, but she was on his last nerve...and he wasn't sure that her crew wasn't more traumatized by *her* than by the loss of their boat.

Even better, today was the one-year anniversary of the war's start, and they were no closer to its ending—or to *Jimmy Carter* doing much more than pull survivors out of the water. And rescuing people like Michelle Wollstonecraft just didn't feel like a victory.

"Yet the senior officer present has responsibility for everything that happens under her purview." Michelle's smile was poisonous.

"The senior officer present is on board *Bougainville*." Alex gritted his teeth. *Bougainville*, whose captain commanded the convoy, was an amphibious assault ship, a lumbering big deck helicopter landing ship. She was less than half of *Jimmy Carter's* speed and her CO had no idea how to properly employ a submarine, but a full-fledged captain was one hundred percent senior to the prickly glory-grabber he'd fished out of the water.

Michelle crossed her arms and glared.

Alex met her eyes and tried to ignore a blossoming headache. Was it too late to hand her and her crew off to *Bougainville*?

"I still think you should be shadowing the convoy on its right flank." Michelle tossed her head.

"Your opinion is noted, thank you." Part of Alex wanted to crawl in a hole and hide, but he'd be damned if he'd let *anyone* chase him out of his own attack center.

Raised voices interrupted whatever response Michelle had cooking. Whirling, Alex headed for the sonar room.

Wilson—it was always Wilson, the troublemaking sailor who his command master chief had traded for spare parts—sat at the console, scowling up at a chief from *Utah*. "So, yeah, our stuff's crap, Chief. It's older than me, doesn't work with any modern software, and it's got some idiosyncrasies that make me twitchy as a dying fish. But it's what we've got."

The chief—a skinny guy who probably weighed half as much as Wilson on a good day—crossed his arms. "Seems like you're falling down on the job if you're not pushing for upgrades."

Wilson's broad shoulders twitched. "I'm not really sure what business of yours that is since you're a ship rider right now."

"I know who you are, STS1." The chief glowered down at Wilson. "My brother is on *Bluefish*, and he told me *all* about that trainwreck of a sonar operator who just can't keep his mouth shut or his liquor down."

"Hey, I don't barf much on liberty." Wilson's laugh sounded forced. "Or I didn't. I don't drink these days."

"Yeah, right."

"You might even say I'm turning over a new leaf."

"The fuck you are. I know your type. You're a disgrace to the navy. You and everyone else on this death trap ought to—"

"You might want to think real hard before you finish that sentence, Chief," Alex said.

The chief spun to face Alex, all color draining out of his face.

His nametape, now that Alex could see it, read *Oates*. He swallowed noisily. "My, um, apologies, sir."

"I realize *Jimmy Carter* is a great deal older than *Utah* and isn't your idea of paradise." Alex smiled coldly. "But we're all in this together, and since it looks like you'll be with us for the next few weeks while we finish this convoy escort, I think it might be an excellent opportunity to cross-train some *Utah* sailors to this ancient equipment Chief Oates is so fond of. Do you agree, Commander?"

He turned an innocent look on Michelle, knowing he'd cornered her. But she'd tried to boss him around on his own boat, and her crew—or at least one of her chiefs—was just as bad. Alex was done playing nice.

"It sounds like a great way to pass the time." Michelle's answering smile promised retribution, though whether she was furious at Alex or Chief Oates, no one could tell.

"Set up a rotation, will you, COB?" Alex didn't turn to look at Master Chief Morton. He knew the older man was right behind him.

Good chiefs of the boat were like that.

"I'm all over it, Captain."

Alex's smile felt natural for the first time in days. "Thanks, Master Chief."

Admiral Aadil Khare stood on the *Rajput's* bridge wing and contemplated the beautiful view. He *could* move his flag ashore. His star was rising once again; now, he was in command of the entire Maldives operating area, in addition to his formidable task group. But he thought remaining on board the destroyer was a better message.

Even if those gorgeous beaches beckoned.

"You made an excellent kill, Captain Patel," he told the lovely woman at his side. "India is grateful for your service."

Captain Avani Patel smiled. She was a tiny woman, fierce and with dark hair and glittering eyes that made fools of many a man. Fortunately, Khare's ambitions were greater any attraction than he felt—and besides, women didn't interest him. How *little* they interested him was something he kept to himself, since India's military regulations still prohibited anyone not identifying as heterosexual from serving, but at least it kept his mind clear when faced with a stunning beauty like Avani Patel.

More men should have such problems, in Khare's opinion. It

would probably make their navy better.

"Thank you, Admiral." She flashed him a smile. "I aim to serve."

He chuckled. "And you hope to eclipse that French peacock."

"Why not?" Patel shrugged. "He is a despicable human being and a womanizer on top of that. I do not wish him dead merely because he aides our cause."

"For now." Khare's smile was thin.

"Do you think we will eventually not need our French allies, Admiral?" Her bright eyes turned on him. "Will we betray them when it comes time for peace?"

"Our relationship with Britain—and her other former colonies—is fraught with history, but we *do* have common ground," he said. "That is more than we can say for their old enemy, the French. And Russia…well, the less said about their recent brutal and expansionist history, the better. If we move first, we will have the best chance at making a more profitable peace."

"I see." Her fingers steepled. "And will our continued actions against them harm that future peace?"

"I think not. It is war." He gestured at the islands not far away. "We will not get to keep these islands, of course. We will look gracious when we return them. But underwater stations are not homelands with centuries of emotional ties for people. They are equipment on the ocean floor. And those killed in uniform…we all agreed to take our chances, didn't we?"

Patel smiled. "Some more than others."

"Indeed. I have another mission for you, if your crew is ready."

"We are at your command, Admiral." She straightened.

"Work your way toward the South China Sea. We have interests in that area, a specific station with technology we wish to take," he commanded. "But on your way, I wish you to hunt USS *Idaho*. Intelligence says she is operating in the approaches to the Strait of Malacca while our American friends prepare for another attempt to break our blockage."

"*Idaho* is one of their best."

"And we know the United States will not make peace until their morale breaks." Khare bared his teeth. "Hammer them, Captain."

Patel's eyes gleamed. "As you wish."

"You know, if I was an absolute raging dumbass, I'd have called you ladies my harem months ago. But while I might be a foul-mouthed, inappropriate son of a bitch, never let it be said that I am stupid. And since it's now too late for that particular *faux pas*, I'll just say that I'm going to miss the shit out of this ship and her crew." Admiral Marco Rodriquez grinned like the unruly urchin he was, sitting back on the couch in USS *Fletcher's* wardroom with a mug of coffee in hand.

Nancy Coleman, commanding officer of the destroyer, laughed. She was a rangy and unflappable woman, with dark hair and eyes that proclaimed she'd never heard of the word *quitting*. She and her husband had that in common. "We'll miss you, too, sir."

She hadn't expected to like this too-colorful, too-competent submariner of an admiral. He was crass but brilliant, a quick learner and a great boss, and Nancy really was sad to see him go.

She also wasn't sure what *Fletcher's* future would hold without him.

Captain Tanya Chin, the admiral's chief of staff, chuckled. "Every time I think I have you under control, Admiral, you go and say something like that."

"Hey, I was specifically *not* saying something so numb-nutted as that." Rodriquez stuck his tongue out.

"Aren't vice admirals supposed to be, I don't know, more dignified?" Nancy bit her lip to keep from laughing. Before meeting Rodriquez, she would've thought *all* admirals more formal with their subordinates.

Pity she was sure Rodriquez broke all the rules, and she'd never have another boss like him. She'd just gotten used to his wild and wooly methods.

"That's what they tell me," he said. "But apparently results matter more in war. Who'd have fucking thunk it?"

"It only took us a year to figure it out," Tanya muttered.

"Be fair. They did promote Freddie Hamilton months ago," Rodriquez replied. "I'm pretty sure some politician thought it was great optics to put the first ever woman in as COMSUBLANT, but she's the finest strategist I know and a mean hand with a submarine. They picked the best person for the job, even if it was by fucking accident."

Nancy pursed her lips and kept her opinions on Admiral Hamilton to herself. She'd only met the woman once and found her an angry and small-minded bully. While Nancy loved the idea of a woman at the top of the sub force, she didn't enjoy the way Hamilton had it in for her husband.

Particularly since Alex—despite his inability to keep his trap shut—had been the only reason one Commander Chris Kennedy *hadn't* killed a bunch of innocent people and maybe tipped the U.S. into war months before the shooting actually started.

"Something wrong, Captain?"

Damn. Rodriquez's perceptive eyes were on her; Nancy shrugged.

"Just thinking about how I hate change." No way was she opening the can of worms that was Alex's career here and now. Rodriquez was obviously friends with Hamilton, and Alex would murder her if she meddled.

They long ago agreed that the only way to stay sane—and happily married—was to stay out of each other's careers. His boat was his concern; her ship was hers. End of story. Even if she thought he deserved better than exile to the oldest boat in the fleet where he got ignored.

Rodriquez snorted. "I'm an old elephant about it. Even worse, I *despise* Pearl Harbor with every fiber of my being, and I'm going to be stuck there for God knows how long. Maybe I can shift my flag to Australia."

"I think history says otherwise, sir." Tanya's smile was thin.

"Well, at least I can free you up to cruiser command, Madam." He waggled his eyebrows at Tanya. "I intend to leave the lot of you with glowing fitness reports and every medal I can lay my hands on, too." He held up a hand when Nancy opened her mouth to argue. "Don't be stupid. Admiral's prerogative. There's a war on, so you all get chest candy."

Nancy just shook her head and smiled.

She really hoped Rodriquez was as kick ass at being Commander, Submarine Forces Pacific as he was at being her admiral. If not, the navy'd gone and made another really dumb personnel move.

It wouldn't be the first one of the war.

North Stonington, Connecticut

"He should have called." Bobbie Coleman crossed her arms, a scowl marring her face. Although she'd inherited her mother's chestnut brown hair and outgoing nature, her stubbornness was all their father's, and that scowl said she wasn't going to let this subject go any time soon. "Mom called."

Emily sighed. They'd both spent plenty of time furious with their parents for leaving them at home during a war, but her anger was almost worn out. It had been, anyway, before Bobbie's team somehow managed to eke their way into a victory in the soccer championships. Their father hadn't called for that, and then Bobbie got the brilliant idea to go to the flipping Naval Academy for revenge.

Now she was pissed off, *again*, because Dad hadn't called for their normal Wednesday family Zoom. It was like opening the same old can of worms over and over again and hoping for something different than rot and wiggly crap to come out.

"Mom's on a destroyer." Sounding reasonable was hard when her sister knew these facts better than she did. "Big difference from a submarine. Lots more phones. Fresh air. Satellite connectivity. All that jazz."

Bobbie flopped in her chair with enough force to rock it backward. "I bet he got my email, and he still didn't call."

"Bobbie..." Emily heaved a sigh. Why did she have to be the mature one?

"Shut up, Emmy. I don't want to hear it."

Her eyes snapped into slits. Bobbie didn't have the right to go all older sister on her and then treat Emily like a five-year-old. Not right after Bobbie had finished a good, old fashioned, two-year-old-style tantrum. "Don't call me Emmy!"

"I'll call you whatever the hell I want to!"

She knew better than to rise to the bait, but a year of war and stress and loneliness made it so hard. "Fine, *Roberta*."

"Jerk." Bobbie reached out and yanked her blond ponytail.

"Hey!"

Bobbie bared her teeth. "Don't call me that, munchkin."

"Then don't call me Emmy, you big— Ow!" The words cut off in a howl.

"Language, Emmy." Bobbie pulled her hair again, cutting off whatever Emily had been about to call her sister. Even she wasn't certain what words she would have chosen, but Bobbie was right about one thing. It would have been dirty.

"You're not my mother!" She slapped Bobbie's hands away.

"Damn straight I'm not! I'd have drowned you at birth."

"You—"

"Girls!"

The new voice made both whirl to face the now-open door. Neither had noticed Grandma Roberta standing in the doorway of

Bobbie's room, but now two sets of eyes went wide, caught in the crosshairs of their grandmother's glare.

Emily gulped. "Sorry, Grandma."

Roberta Petretti was a tiny woman with steel gray hair and glasses. She even liked to wear paisley. But when she crossed her arms, she looked more like a demoness sans battle axe rather than a kindly old woman. "Now, what was that all about?"

"Nothing," both teens said.

Neither wanted to talk about it. They both knew the fight had nothing to do with childish nicknames or hated real names. No way were they going to talk about how much they missed their parents or how much they worried.

Even with their parents gone, they didn't live far from Groton *or* Newport. Both their classes at school were full of kids whose parents were gone. Hardly a week went by without some friend or acquaintance losing a parent or a sibling.

They'd been lucky so far, but with both parents deployed, how long could they beat the odds?

Fogborne Research Facility—Red Tiger Station, the South China Sea

"The news says there's a naval battle going on five miles from here," Sam Yeung said as he and Ning Tang bent over the design specs for the fusion reactor, working to scale their fully functional—and still secret—reactor down to something that would fit in a submarine. "Looks like the Chinese are rolling the dice and trying to invade again."

Sam was taller and wider than her, with a bit of extra width that came from spending too much time on computers and not enough time doing whatever medical types thought they should do for exercise. Like Ning, Sam was Taiwanese-American, though they hadn't known one another before he was hired as part of the Fogborne team a few years earlier.

His PhD was from CalTech, which she mostly forgave him for.

"Really?" Ning scowled. "Sounds kind of stupid in the middle of a three-way civil war."

"Four way. There's that new group, the Socialist Democratic Union of China," Sam said around the pen in his mouth and then shrugged. "But it's just as stupid as the pirates who tried to take this place over last week. Pulsar Security cut them to pieces."

"Yeah."

Ning tried not to shudder. Generally, she managed to ignore politics, the war, and the outside world. She didn't much *care* about any of that stuff. She just wanted to design her reactor, spend her money, and be left in peace.

But nine people died when those pirates rammed a remote mini-sub into the south end of Red Tiger Station. One of them, Guiying Ng, was a fellow sub-racing aficionado caught in the wrong place at the wrong time. Guiying and two others drowned when the automated watertight doors in the sub hanger failed to close in time, and Ning hadn't been able to bring herself to even look at the sub racers since then.

Six more died when the pirates tried to shoot their way onto Red Tiger's east TRANSPLAT, or Transportation Platform. Pulsar Power LTD's security forces took three casualties fighting them off, but at least Ning didn't have to use that TRANSPLAT every day. There were five others.

"You don't think it's going to come here, do you?" she whispered and then hated herself for asking.

"Even a battle directly overhead wouldn't matter. Unless a ship sank on top of us." Sam laughed. "That would suck."

Ning swallowed. "No kidding."

"Relax. I'm sure navies aren't that dumb."

"Really? It's not like the smartest tools in the shed join up." She snorted. "If they did, we wouldn't be at war because someone shot at the wrong someone and then no one could figure out how to stop."

Sam sighed. "Yeah, it'd be nice if they could all stop shooting and we could just get back to work."

---

28 April 2039, Perth, Australia

"So what do they have you doing these days, anyway, Tommy?" Teresa O'Canas asked as the trio dug into their second round of beers.

Alex needed them. A long apology to his daughter left him exhausted and a little winded. He knew his boat's shortcomings technically weren't his fault, but Bobby *needed* to hear that he wanted to call, not that he actually *couldn't*. The war was hard for the girls; every time he missed a call, they worried that he'd never call again. So an apology and a few quality hours on the phone with them was time well spent.

Though now *he* needed to drink away the reminder that he might not come back someday. Not that *Jimmy Carter* stood into danger often, but there was still a war on.

"Mostly staff work." Commander Tommy Sandifer grimaced. Tommy was another of Alex's classmates from the sub school, though he'd lost his command when USS *Georgia* (SSN 817) went down. Alex had the dubious honor of pulling his friend—literally—out of the water, and Tommy had been stuck on the beach ever since. "Still waiting to see what my fate is for losing my boat."

"You got suckered by that French asshole. You're in good company," Teresa said. "Last count, he'd gotten at least twelve of us, and that's just subs."

Tommy scraped hands over his dark-skinned face. "Glad I didn't make the baker's dozen, I guess?" He shook himself. "I never was properly grateful for you picking us up, Alex. Sorry about that. I think I was a little shell shocked."

"Better in shock than being all the asshole you can be." Alex chuckled. "My last rescue went swimmingly—minus me swimming, because only you got the Alex Coleman Rescue Swimmer Special—until I had to talk to our special guest. Michelle Wollstonecraft tried to pull *rank* on me on my own boat."

"After you pulled her ass out of the water? That's crass."

"Tell me about it." Alex downed the rest of his beer as he caught sight of a familiar face at the bar. Just what he needed in his life: double the assholery. "Rumor—otherwise known the lack of as jerkass tweets—says she got taken out by someone *not* Rochambeau. Michelle wasn't graceful about not getting nailed by the best in the business."

"Add two more for *Kansas!*" Commander Chris Kennedy boomed from his seat at the bar, toasting with the lieutenant commander at his right. She grinned.

"Coming right up." The bartender grinned and walked back to the old-fashioned blackboard behind the bar.

Once, that blackboard had been covered in pictures of ships and subs that came to visit. Now, it was labeled "Sinking Scorecard" and was a list of all Alliance subs that sailed out of Perth and their kills.

Looking at the list always made Alex swallow, because some of the names on the list were boats that were on the bottom...with crews on eternal patrol.

Each boat was represented by a magnet shaped like whatever class submarine they were, with the name of the boat written inside it. Next to that was another magnet, this one with the CO's name written on it. Then the kills were listed by total, submarine, and surface—military only, since no one tracked civilian ships sunk by anything other than tonnage.

It was like the Wall of Honor back at the sub school, only this list scorecard didn't remove the dead.

Alex waved the waiter over for another drink as the bartender moved *Kansas* up into the number eight spot, just under the late and legendary Jane Phelps.

Name – Boat – Total – Sub – Surface
#1 – North – HMS GALLANT – *18-8-10*
#2 – Kins* – USS DARTER – *16-4-12*
#3 – Sivers – USS GUAM – *16-2-14*
#4 – Walker – USS IDAHO – *15-8-7*
#5 – Santiago – USS SKATE – *14-7-7*
#6 – Dalton – USS RAZORBACK – *13-5-8*
#7 – Phelps – USS MORAY – *10-4-6*
#8 – Kennedy – USS KANSAS – *10-4-6*
#9 – Preston – HMAS OBERON – *9-4-5*
#10 – Brown – HMAS DUMARESQ – 9-2-7

Teresa followed his gaze. "I'm on the part of the list on the other wall." She pointed, chuckling, but there she was, at number twelve. *O'Canas* – USS DOUGLASS – *5-2-3*. Even Tommy was on the list, grouped with six or seven other COs who had two kills each.

Hell, even *dead* captains ranked above Alex, retaining their positions on the list until someone overtook them. Three out of the top four Americans on the scorecard were all dead, with a Medal of Honor winner right behind the British terror Ursula North. Kenji Walker at number four was now the best America had left, followed by Alex's best friend, John Dalton.

Karla Phelps, next on the list, was dead. Alex swallowed. His was not a business where success bred survival, was it?

"Look, we found our anchor!" Kennedy's laugh made Alex's head snap around so quickly his neck cracked.

Teresa's hand closed on his arm. "He's not worth it," she whispered.

"*Jimmy Carter*...from spy sub to ambulance. What a letdown." Kennedy's sneer was so sharp you could've used it to shave. "But then again, no one ever expected you to have the guts to shoot, did they, Alex?"

"Oh, fuck you." Alex's chest was tight, remembering that day, remembering how what it cost to stop this asshole from killing innocents. It didn't help that half the crowd was watching them, because the O-Club had become a submariner hang out, and he *knew* these people.

Unfortunately, so did Kennedy.

"That's 'fuck you, *sir*' to you, Alex."

"Last I checked, we're wearing the same rank." Fury eased the pain of a ruined career, of the hopes and dreams Kennedy trashed when he decided to pin the blame for his actions on his XO.

"Have it your way. You want to talk about how you disobeyed orders and went to Admiral's Mast?"

"Sure. Let's add in how you tried to kill a sub full of civilians and start the damned war a year early."

Kennedy leaned forward, grinning wolfishly. "It was a war that needed starting."

"Not at that cost it didn't, you glory-minded fuck."

"Oh, look who's found some courage!" Kennedy threw his head back and laughed. "Took a year of war for you to find your balls—or does your wife keep them in a jar? Probably the best she gets out of you."

Alex snorted and leaned back in his chair, sipping his third beer. "Yeah, I know you've got nothing when you try insulting my wife. Good try, but she's got two Navy Crosses and can take care of herself."

The bar, previously hushed so people could listen to their exchange, broke out in titters. Kennedy flushed.

"You want to come prove how tough you are now? You want to finish what we started that day?"

"*We* didn't start anything. You went off on a power trip, and I stopped you. End of story." Alex shrugged, feeling strangely buoyed by Teresa's gaping expression. "And sure, yeah, I paid the price. But how many sub COs get to say they went to Admiral's Mast and survived?"

"Begging your pardon for interrupting, Captain, but we've got a call from the SUBRON to be ready to get underway first thing in the morning." Master Chief Chindeu Casey stepped in between them without even a glance at Alex, his expression professionally bland.

But Alex hadn't forgotten *Kansas'* chief of the boat, the one person ballsy enough to try to testify on his behalf in that rigged disaster of an Admiral's Mast. Alex told him not to, of course. Someone had to stay on *Kansas* and protect the crew from Kennedy.

"Tomorrow?" Kennedy blinked, shaking his head like Casey had hit him. "We're not scheduled for patrol for another week."

Casey shrugged. "Deck got shuffled and our card got pulled. We got tagged with Convoy 238."

"Great." Kennedy groaned. "Escorting convoys like we're the dregs." His eyes turned on Alex, narrowing.

Alex smiled and sipped his beer. "Happy sailing."

Kennedy lunged forward, only to be caught by the lieutenant commander at his side. "He's not worth it, Captain," she said quietly, her glare zeroing in on Alex like a sniper rifle's scope. "Let's go back to the boat."

Alex watched in silence as Kennedy, his XO, and Casey departed, feeling strangely buoyed. He hadn't seen Kennedy since he left *Kansas*—he hadn't wanted to—but it was strangely cathartic. Kennedy was still an ass, and Casey was still more decent than he deserved. The master chief snuck Alex a wink on his way by, hiding a smile behind Kennedy's back.

Damn, he felt bad for *Kansas'* crew, but there wasn't a damned thing he could do for them from across the pier.

Chapter 4

Who Needs Enemies?

1 May 2039, near the northern approaches to the Strait of Malacca

"Convoy clearing to port, Captain," her sonar watch reported.

"Very well." Patel waved a hand, sitting back. She was not interested in that convoy, nor the old submarine escorting it. Neither was a worthy target. They just happened to be near *Idaho*, which her sub crept ever closer to.

Maybe she'd sink them afterward. It would be good for morale.

"Predicted range in twenty minutes."

"Thank you." She smiled and returned to reading her book.

Projecting calm was important, and Avani Patel was one of the best at it. Her crew was a well-oiled machine after a year of war: quiet, efficient, and close in the way only people who had stared death in the eye could be. *Vela* was the best of India's submarines, the first *Requin-E* that India purchased from France. Although the export version of the famous *Requin*-class was slightly smaller than the second-generation Advanced *Requins*, they were still fast, silent, and deadly.

Someday, perhaps Avani's nation might build a submarine like this on their own. She hoped they would; knowing her pride and joy was built with French assistance—albeit in an Indian shipyard—irked her. Yet she was not one to turn down the advantages of captaining one of the most advanced attack submarines in the world.

Particularly when it let her become India's top submariner.

As a nation, India's customs remained a marriage of tradition and modernity. Women took rights for granted that they lacked in many nations and could rise high in politics and business. Yet the upper ranks of the military were still dominated by men.

Avani aimed to change that.

Having a patron like Khare helped. He was remarkably open-minded about her sex, which she appreciated, and full fanged in his own ambition. She liked that about him. She liked the missions he assigned her more.

She glanced up from her romance novel to study the plot. *Idaho* continued on her patrol pattern, undoubtedly hunting for Indian submarines attempting to keep American forces out of the SOM. Avani ghosted a finger over her lips and smiled.

The Americans were not as nearly good as they thought they were. Yes, their submarines were excellent, particularly the *Ceros*. Those boats were quiet and hard to kill. But the older *Virginias* weren't silent enough for these shallow waters, particularly when their captains liked to remain in communication with the outside world.

"They are due for a communications check in one minute, Captain," her first officer said.

"So predictable." She chuckled. "The Americans became creatures of habit because they were the best in the world."

"To be fair, we would not be able to hear them if not for our surface support," he said.

"Yes, but we have that. And they think we don't." The fact that said surface support was a Russian intelligence trawler disguised as a fishing boat irked her, but what could one do?

"They love to underestimate us."

"I would not say they *love* to." Avani grinned.

The first officer laughed. "Probably not."

"Captain, communication detected. Position report being broadcast by Alpha Seven November."

A7N was their Russian friend. *Vela's* own communications wire was out, trailing a quarter mile behind the submarine and set strictly to receive-only. That way, they could remain deep and still accept information when the trawler—whose true identification even Avani was unaware of—sent it.

She put her book down with a happy sigh. "Any communication

you put into the water *can* be heard, Samesh," she said. "Never forget that. It will get *Idaho* killed today."

"I will remember, Captain," her first officer promised.

"Range?" She turned to the weapons team.

"Six nautical miles."

Avani folded her hands in her lap. "Match bearings and fire, tubes one through four."

Pearl Harbor, Hawaii

The offices of Commander, Submarine Forces Pacific were old, plush, and paneled in actual mahogany. Fucking *mahogany*. Marco Rodriquez still couldn't believe it every time he walked into his shining turd of a palace.

Less than a month ago, he and all his not-so-precious worldly belongings had been crammed into a tiny stateroom on board a destroyer. Now most of those belongings—as well as some he'd left back in a storage unit in Groton—were in a seaside apartment that was *probably* outside the range of any missile attack. Assuming anyone got ballsy enough to lob munitions at Pearl Harbor. Marco sure wouldn't, not if he was an American enemy. Not after what happened last time.

"Sir?"

The lieutenant who stuck his head through the open office door was a foot taller than Marco, with a carrot top so bright his head might as well have been on fire, and with freckles that made him look twelve. He also stuttered if Marco so much as glared.

"Yeah...?" Marco tried not to sound like a grouch. Really, he did. The kid still flinched.

"There's, um, a message for you."

God damn this child of tomatoes and fire engines. Was his hand *shaking*? Marco lurched to his feet—that sinfully comfortable chair made it hard; he'd need to buy something ergonomic and not leather—and snatched the tablet.

"Fuck."

It was a SUBMISS/SUBSUNK message.

"*Idaho*, sir," Lieutenant Jones whispered.

"Double fuck." Marco felt like a thousand pounds landed on his shoulders. He stared blankly at the message tablet for a long moment, trying to find words. "Bring me a hard copy of this. I want to keep it."

"Sir?"

"Don't ask questions that I don't know the answers to, son. Just do it."

Jones gulped. "Aye, sir!"

Marco was too drained to watch him flee or even to swear again. He just dropped the tablet on the desk and stared out the window at the three subs nestled against the nearest pier.

He didn't even *know* Kenji Walker. Never met the guy. Even in America's small submarine community, their paths never crossed. But he knew Walker was a hotshot. He was probably the best they had with Jane Phelps gone.

Shaking himself, Marco strode out of the room on Jones' heels. It was time to figure out who they had in the vicinity to attempt a rescue. He'd watch the video data recording of *Idaho's* death after he sent someone to find the survivors.

2 May 2039, Red Tiger Station, the South China Sea

Ning was up on TRANSPLAT Six—nicknamed Suzy—showing her brand-new little sub racer off to Dr. Leifsson when everything went straight to pot.

One minute, she was coaxing her boss into maybe taking a ride in her DeepFlight Super Falcon IX—the sweetest, fastest, subracing submarine known to mankind—and the next, Ning Tang and Kim Leifsson were flat on their backs, staring at a steel gray sky. Their ears rang with the sounds of trumpets, too, but Ning was pretty sure those were explosions in the background.

She coughed, sitting up and discovering aches in parts of her body that a twenty-year-old shouldn't have. "What the *hell* was that?"

Kim scrambled into a crouch. "Looks like someone just blew up the security boat."

"Someone being the Chinese, Taiwan, terrorists, pirates, or *another* group that fell in love with Red Tiger Station and wants to make it their own?" Ning wiped sweat off her face.

She was starting to hate this place. For real. Once, she thought Red Tiger was a great place for the Fogborne team to finish their research without anyone noticing what they were up to had world-altering potential. Now it was a death trap smack in the middle of a wild-ass war zone.

"Great question. Stay down." Kim pushed Ning back to the hard concrete of the transportation platform and then pulled her over so they could hide behind a shipping container. "Whoever they are, they've got multiple patrol craft."

"Wow, look at you sounding all official like." Ning tried to keep her voice light and ignore the shouting coming from the east end of the platform, as well as the *ping-ping-ping* of gunfire.

"I grew up in Ukraine in the 2020s. You'd be amazed what you learn." Kim's smile was crooked.

"Really? I thought you were Swiss."

"My father is. But my mother was a diplomat, and they divorced when I was young." Kim shrugged. "I saw a lot."

"Damn." Ning licked her lips, trying to slow the way her heart wanted to race right out of her chest. Slowly, she eased herself to the side so she could see around the shipping container. "What's going on?"

The gunfire had stopped. One of the patrol boats was close to the platform now, and Ning watched several black-clad figures jump from the boat to the platform. They were all armed with some sort of automatic rifle, but she had no idea what. Her expertise was in nuclear reactors, not guns. Ning swallowed.

"Looks like they want something. No flags on their boats and they're not wearing uniforms. I think we have pirates on our hands."

"Sure they're not terrorists? They don't exactly dress up, either."

Kim shook her head. "Terrorists just blow things up and go home to brag about it."

"Point." Ning clasped her hands together to keep them from shaking. "Does that mean they won't care about us?"

"Depends on if they want hostages."

"Any luck on getting a taste of those new torps, Weps?" Alex asked over lunch the two days before *Jimmy Carter* was due to leave on yet another convoy escort.

"Base weapons officer told me I'd have better luck dating the president's daughter." Benji grinned. "I didn't tell him that I'd met her and she's nice, but she already has a girlfriend."

Alex almost snorted out his bug juice. Then he cocked his head innocently. "So...are we getting the torpedoes?"

Benji threw his head back and laughed. "I wish!"

"Damn shame."

Benji's radio crackled before he could say more. "Command Duty Officer, Officer of the Deck."

"CDO here, go," Benji said.

"Sir, the captain has a visitor on the quarterdeck. He doesn't seem to be carrying his radio."

"He's here with me. I'll pass the message." Benji threw Alex a look, and Alex shrugged.

"Oops. Guess I forgot it." He put his cup down. "I'll head up. Visitors are always fun."

Alex headed forward, pausing to greet a few sailors as he threaded his way through the passageways of his submarine. But the walk to the quarterdeck was barely long enough for him to wonder just who this mystery visitor could be. John and Nancy were both underway, with Nancy under a new boss who she already found lacking compared to the old one. John had been the first to get the new torpedoes and already sank a pair of *Akulas* and a *Scorpene*.

With Kenji Walker and Rico Sivers gone, that made John the best the U.S. had left.

Alex swallowed. The Union was picking off America's top submarines left and right. Was it on purpose, or was it just because they went where the fire was hottest?

Those musings brought him topside, where he caught side of a familiar, blond-haired and freckled explosion of a lieutenant commander standing near the brow. A smile split his face, and Alex found himself laughing like a loon.

"I'll be damned. Stephanie Gomez knows what a submarine looks like after all," he said.

Grinning, she saluted. "I admit it's hard to tell one end from the other when you're stopped, but I did figure out that the slanty walkway thing was the brow. We have those, too."

"How you been, Steph?" Alex shook her hand, leading her aft. "I didn't expect a visit, but you've made my day."

"Little old me?" She laughed. "I needed a change of scenery. *Dunham's* still up on the blocks after our collision with that Indian destroyer—it took forever for a drydock to open up for us—and I feel like the walls are closing in. So I figured I'd come find what trouble you're getting into these days."

"I could only be so luck as to cause trouble." Alex tried not to let his shoulders slump. "I'm afraid that the almost-oldest boat in the fleet is a pretty quiet place to be."

Steph squinted. "Almost oldest?"

"There're a couple of boomers older than us, but we're the oldest attack sub by far. And they're keeping those boomers even further from the action—their job is to hide."

"That sounds like a barrel of laughs. Here I thought that driving a nineteen-year-old destroyer was bad."

"Pfft. Your ship can't even drink yet."

Steph threw her head back and laughed. "Never change, boss. Never change," she said. "Damn, I wish we had some of your sense of humor over on *Dunham*. We seem to be the ship where Murphy lives."

"That bad?"

Alex could tell by the look on her face that Steph was drained, and he wished he could do more about it than commiserate. Long gone were the days when she was his second-in-command on Armistice Station; they'd made a good team, even in peacetime. Then they'd made a better one when guns came out and the French and Indians got frisky, even if Alex tried not to think about those wild and wooly days.

"Well, we've had a collision, a captain die when hit by shrapnel, and a helicopter crash all in the last eleven months. And let's not talk about morale. I've had two suicides just since we got that stupid hole and put her up on the blocks."

"Ouch." Alex grimaced. "Your captain on top of it?"

"Yeah. He's a good guy. Just about as personable as a brick wall." Steph shook her head. "Not that I said that to you, sir."

"You know your secrets are safe with me."

"Thanks." She sighed. "I'm not even sure why I came by, other than a great need to look at a ship that wasn't mine."

"Boat."

"Whatever." But she smiled. "Never thought I'd miss Armistice Station."

Alex shuddered. "I sure as hell don't miss the chaos at the end."

"Why not? We did pretty good, even with the odds against us." Steph snickered. "I never thought I'd put 'blew up some French marines and then hijacked a cruise ship on my fitness report,' but hey, it makes for a great sea story."

"Or some great nightmares."

She eyed him like he was a wild animal who needed special handling. "You're a weird man."

"My wife tells me that all the time."

Getting a meeting with the CNO was a lot more annoying now that she didn't work for him. This issue wasn't urgent enough to walk in on him or to kick someone else out, so Freddie took her chances with the appointment gods...and lost. Fortunately, Scrap, or Admiral David Chan, was kind enough to cancel three times instead of leaving her in the waiting room.

When she finally got squeezed in, Freddie had thirty minutes between lunch and a politician.

"Fucking Angler," Scrap said after they exchanged greetings, glaring at a half-eaten bagel still sitting on his desk. "Now he's after us for sub losses. Got the idea from that damned reporter at the *Post*, who's on about a 'captain problem.' But it's a good thing you're here, Freddie. Our Fairy-not-Godfather Senator wants to know why we're losing so many more *Virginia*-class boats than *Ceros*."

She grimaced and then opted for honesty. "They're older and don't get the cream of the crop for crews."

"Fuck, you know I can't tell the chairman of the Senate Committee on Armed Services that."

"The man was a naval officer. He can do the math and see that they're older." Freddie sighed. "Let me be blunt, sir. We have two problems. One, we built two generations of multi-purpose attack submarines while our enemies focused on sub killers. Two, we stopped chasing major torpedo innovation, instead allowing ourselves to get stuck with a super-stealthy but *slow* Mark 48. We assumed we were the best and had the best equipment...and then the French and the Russians blew past us."

The CNO frowned. "I thought the *Ceros* were supposed to solve that."

"No, the NSSN project Congress killed in favor of the *Ceros* was our sub superiority project," she replied.

"Cost?"

"Of course."

"Fucking A." Scrap slumped in his giant leather chair. "Okay, you're clearly here with a plan. Let's hear it."

"Restart the NSSN project. We already have a solid design. Update it with lessons learned from the war, lay the keel, and get that boat out fast," Freddie said. "We need it. Rumor says that the missile delays are going to get longer, and we *know* that the enemy is using satellite imagery to turn surface ships into targets."

"I thought that was a rumor."

"ONI confirmed it. This is going to be the war of the submarine, Scrap. They're the only stealth platform we've got." She smiled crookedly. "Oh, the surface ships and carriers will get another year or two. And they'll play sometimes, just like battleships got to shoot things every now and then in World War III. But the writing's on the wall."

"Okay, hit me where it hurts. How much is this idea going to cost?"

"Two billion for the first boat. That's three shifts at Electric Boat, not a cost-plus contract. It's a damned patriotic deal—cheaper than the *Seawolfs* were. They may lose money on it."

Scrap blanched. "No one's going to sign off on that when we're losing."

"We're going to lose by a lot more if we don't put something in the water better than the *Requins* and the *Yasens*. Never mind the *next* generation boats the French and Russians already have in the pipeline."

"Jesus, Freddie, you don't ask for much, do you?" The CNO crossed his arms and looked up at the ceiling as if for guidance.

"I'm going to recommission five *Los Angeles*-class boats, by the way. We need every hull we can get, and they've been in mothballs. We can use them close in to defend Alaska."

"How much will that cost?"

"It's within my budget." Freddie folded her hands, focusing herself with an effort. She could tell that Scrap was frustrated, but that was his fault for picking someone competent. He could've gone with another Admiral Trieu, who hid from problems until it was too late.

Not shaking the CNO was hard, but Freddie stopped herself. Discipline was remembering what he wanted, not yelling at small men.

If only Marco was here. He could do the yelling and swearing for her.

"Fine. I'll look at your NSSN project," Scrap said. "But on one condition."

"Name it, sir."

"A friend has a draft diesel design I'd like you to look at. Maybe share it with our new SubPac—what's his name, Rodriquez? Then tell me what you both think."

Freddie hid a grimace. Ah, this was the cost of getting her chosen candidate in for ComSubPac, wasn't it? But if looking at a design was all it took, she'd study the thing to pieces. After all, the United States hadn't fielded diesel submarines since the earliest days of the Cold War.

"I'd be happy, to, sir," she replied.

It was a pity she never asked who put the idea of American diesel submarines in the CNO's mind.

Ning and Kim watched, wide-eyed, as the pirates rounded up the three dozen people on the TRANSPLAT. Most were dockworkers, there to load and unload the ships that passed through. Before war engulfed the South China Sea, Red Tiger Station saw four times the traffic they did now, serving as an easy transfer station for ships who used to swap cargos out in nearby Taiwan. The water was deeper here, and there was no inconvenient channel to transit in, which cut the time for any cargo transfer down by several hours.

Time was money in the shipping business, so Red Tiger Station grew fast. Now, however, the number of cargo ships was cut by three-quarters due to the multi-faceted war...as were the other activities that usually transformed the platform into a hive of activity.

Subraces, once common, ended after it got too dangerous to take day trips to the station. Tourism ground to a halt once navies started shooting at one another. Cruise ships stopped coming before that; when China started making belligerent noises, those companies looked elsewhere. Even black marketeers were hesitant to use Red Tiger Station these days, unless they were in bed with the pirates or terrorists—or both.

"Hey, you! Ladies, don't think we don't see you. Up and at 'em." A pirate with an absurdly large gun gestured Ning and her boss out of where they were hiding, and both crept out.

He was dressed in black, just like the others, tall, brown haired, and heavyset. He looked like a mixture of four or five ethnicities; Ning couldn't place where he was from, only that he wasn't from Taiwan, and he probably wasn't American.

"C'mon, we won't bite," he said in annoyingly good English. "No one's here to kidnap anyone today, all right?"

Ning let out a breath she didn't know she was holding. "Pirates, I guess," she whispered.

"Maybe. Sometimes they hold people for ransom," Kim replied in an undertone.

She shuddered. "Hopefully stealing ships is easier today."

Ning ran her eyes over the ships moored on the nine piers that stuck out of TRANSPLAT Six like a weird spindle. Up front were the small ones, like her sub racer, which she devoutly hoped would go unnoticed. The Super Falcon sat low in the water on the surface and looked pretty ugly; you had to know what it was to want it.

Please not my million-dollar baby, she thought as loudly as she could. The sub racer had been delivered *yesterday,* and getting another one would take months!

"Hurry up, ladies, we haven't got all day." The pirate gestured with his gun, and they rushed over to join the knot of hostages.

She'd rather be stolen from than get shot, Ning decided, looking at that gun again. This was what insurance was for.

"Do you have kidnapping insurance?" she whispered to Kim.

"No, but Pulsar does." Kim looked pretty cool; Ning's appraisal of her boss increased. Damn it if the doc wasn't good under pressure. "We'll be okay."

"Just got to keep breathing, then." Ning's chest was tight like that *wasn't* necessarily a given.

"Just stay quiet and you'll be fine," the pirate said. "We want ships, not people. People are a pain. We've got to feed you and watch you and give you a decent place to sleep and such, or some navy'll hunt us down like we're from the seventeenth century." He scoffed. "Ain't nobody got time for that."

"Who are you people?" one of the men in the crowd asked.

The pirate turned to look at him. "If you have to ask, you probably don't need to know." He winked as several people drew back in fear and then laughed. "We're the Destroyers. Named for that there U-boat you see surfacing to send some more crew over to man those two cargo ships."

"You have a *U-boat?*" The same man's jaw dropped, and Ning couldn't help rolling her eyes.

"It's probably an export version sold by the original buyer. The Germans will sell them to almost any country with a flag and a bank account, but countries eventually sell them for scrap...or to less legitimate organizations."

"Right in one." The pirate grinned. "We bought *Destroyer* when South Korea was done with her. Not that the South Koreans are terribly happy about that little bit of advertising, but so long as we stay out of their yard, they don't complain too much.

"Besides, the South China Sea has *much* better pickings, if you know what I mean." He gestured at the crowd. "You fine people make excellent hosts."

Shivering, Ning watched with wary eyes as the other pirates swarmed the piers. They took the remaining security boat, a big green yacht, the two already-loaded cargo ship...and her Super Falcon.

Somehow, Ning wasn't surprised. Her sub wasn't the most expensive thing on the pier, but you could crane it up on the cargo ship—which the pirates did as she watched grimly, unable to intervene with a gun in her stupid face. And a Super Falcon was pricey, in addition to being the fastest type of sub racer in the world. They were all custom made, and Ning knew they sold high on the black market. She'd always been too curious for her own good.

So she said nothing. She just stewed in the feeling of sick emptiness, arms crossed and waiting for the other shoe to drop.

Strangely, it ended in a cheerful wave as the pirate guarding them skipped off to jump in their patrol boat. "You all have a good day now," he said. "Sorry about the inconvenience!"

Only after he was gone did Kim wrap an arm around Ning. "I'm sorry about your sub," her boss whispered.

"I hate this place." Ning sighed. "But I have insurance."

"I didn't think you were stupid enough not to." Kim shook her head. "Let's go below and call Pulsar. I'd like to know where the hell their security was for this."

Ning glanced right, at the bodies stacked nearly toward the north end of the TRANSPLAT. "I think we found them."

Kim grimaced. "Maybe. But as a shareowner of the station, Pulsar should've done better."

"But will they?" Ning snorted. "We both know the answer to that. Let's just count the days until they get us off this floating monstrosity."

"Deal."

Tahiti, French Polynesia

Video calls were a nuisance, even when in port. By and large, Captain Jules Rochambeau was successful enough to avoid anything he didn't like, but unfortunately, he could not avoid Admiral Jeramie Bernard, commander of all French submarine forces.

Nor did he want to, really. Admiral Bernard gave him the best presents. He just hated the pedestrian nature of sitting in front of a screen and talking to someone.

"*Amiral*, convoys are no challenge and offer little glory." Jules sniffed. "How am I to remain the deadliest submariner alive if I am sent after cargo ships?"

"Killing enemy morale is more important than sinking their warships." Bernard pursed his lips; Jules could see his displeasure even through the shoddy connection. "I wish to see if you can again use satellite imagery to savage Alliance ships."

Jules sat back, steepling his fingers. "I would prefer a task force, but an escorted convoy would work. If I must."

"Find one and kill it, *s'il vous plaît*. I am sure you can come up with something clever to tweet about it afterward."

Chuckling, Jules inclined his head. "Do you have a preference where I hunt, *mon amiral?*"

"The western Pacific seems to be thick with game," Bernard replied, smiling. "Our Russian friends have stopped to consolidate their advances around Japan, and the Indians are concentrating on their own front yard. Perhaps you can nip off a few choice contacts in the American supply chain between Hawaii and Guam or Australia."

"Convenient, as I am currently in Pape'ete." Jules smirked. His lovely submarine, *Barracuda*, was nestled against a pier meant for cruise ships in Tahiti's capital. Of course, cruise ships tended to avoid war-torn waters...so business wasn't what it used to be.

Pape'ete made a decent submarine base, however. There was even an international airport on the island, and supplies from French friends in South America were only a few hours away.

"*Oui*. It is almost as if I planned it that way." Bernard did not normally take interest in one mere submarine, but *Barracuda* was hardly just another submarine, was she?

Jules would not lie. He enjoyed the limelight, and being the best his country—nay, the world—had in command of a submarine filled him with joy. He knew there was competition, of course, from India's Avani Patel to his old friend Ursula North. The irascible Brit was probably the only Alliance submariner who could give him a *true* challenge, and he hoped she'd come hunting him.

It would certainly be less boring than sinking convoys.

Chapter 5

Woe Begotten Talents

6 May 2039, Red Tiger Station, the South China Sea

Everyone thought Ning was too young to notice how tensions were rising on Red Tiger Station. They forgot that while she wasn't *really* a hacker, she'd learned how to pick her way into any program for fun when she was twelve. That meant she was better than good at designing electronic crawlers to consolidate news reports, and everything happening in and around the station was...ugly.

Crime was up for the first time since the station incorporated their governing council five years ago. Piracy was rampant outside, and the ships that used to protect them—the Taiwanese Navy—were too busy fighting the Chinese to throw two farts in their direction, no matter how much Red Tiger's administrators bribed them. A few deserters somehow made their way onto the station last week, pursued by Chinese forces, and Ning had been unfortunate enough to be in the western café when they were found and bludgeoned into submission.

Then the Chinese departed without blinking, leaving Red Tiger Station on their own once more.

"Pulsar Power is going to pull us out of here next week," Doctor Kim Leifsson whispered, closing the door behind her and locking it.

Ning Tang cocked her head. Why was the doc whispering? And why did she double check the lock? The Fogborne lab was one of the best electronically shielded places on the planet, and not only because of the physical safeguards around them. She should know. She and Sam Yeung had coded the security themselves.

Sam was an okay coder. She usually told him that he was worse than he was, just to get a rise out of him, but lately Ning didn't feel like being so obnoxious. That stupid war between the many Chinas was raging like a madhouse, despite the thousand experts saying it would be "quick." And now piracy was at an all-time high in the South China Sea, too. Life was just grand.

"Can they do that?" Sam wrapped his arms around himself.

Ning scowled. "Like, will we go, or is it logistically possible?"

"Logistics. I'm obviously going. Aren't you?"

"Yeah. Pretty much anything to get off this place." Ning didn't like admitting fear, but after pirates stole her sub racer...well, no one needed to hit her in the face with reality twice. Ning was a nerd, not an idiot.

Sam shuddered. "It stopped being fun a couple months ago."

The members of their small team exchanged glances. No one needed to tell them that booking a civilian charter off Red Tiger Station was impossible; they all knew people who'd tried. Pulsar Security kept track of how many civilian ships and subs the pirates snapped up, and right now, it was sitting around seventy percent.

Those were *not* odds Ning was prepared to bet against.

She fidgeted, looking up at Kim. "Do you think they'll get a sub through?"

"I think they'll keep trying." Kim gestured at the completed reactor everyone could see through the window behind them. "We're sitting on the modern equivalent of a gold mine. *No one*, and I really mean no one, wants us to put those plans on the internet where some hacker can yoink them and sell them to the highest bidder. So they need us. And preferably the reactor model."

"We can change the world if we get out of this hole," Sam said.

Ning twisted in her seat to stare at him.

"What?" He shrugged. "We all know that fusion is the way of the future. Sustainable, safe power. I like being rich, but man, if we can make the world better while we're at it..."

Blinking, Ning stared at her friend and colleague while Doctor Kim beamed. She hadn't expected this from Sam—like her, he liked money, buying things, and getting rich while being super smart. She teased him about his crappy coding, but he really was brilliant. Just a little careless with his code.

But...making the world better? Sure, that was a nice bonus. Ning liked the idea of going down in history. But she really enjoyed her pile of money, too.

"I think Pulsar will license our design pretty quickly once we get it out of here." Kim's approving smile made Ning's stomach twist oddly. "Though that's going to be the trick."

"You guys aren't talking about giving it away for free, right?" Ning bit her lip.

"Oh, hell no." Sam grinned. "I'm not giving the money back, either. I just...I'm just kind of sick of all the shooting and want something that's *nice* for the world, you know? Instead of this endless war."

"It's been less than a year," Kim said.

"And it's a *world* war, Doc. The thing we as a world said we'd never do again."

Ning swallowed. "You know they're going to want to put our design on submarines."

She'd already started fooling around with ways to make that work, she didn't add.

Kim nodded. "Pulsar is a U.S.-based company."

"So we know where they're going." Ning smiled crookedly. "At least it's not to the Chinese?"

She wasn't ready to forgive them for beating those deserters half to death in front of her. Not in this lifetime.

"For sure. But we've got to get out here, first." Sam gestured upward, toward the chaos raging in the seas above and around them. "I'm still not sure those promised subs are going to even arrive to pull us off."

***

Near the northern approaches to the Strait of Malacca

The *Cero*-class submarine steamed through the water at a touch under her best silent speed, but she wasn't on the hunt for enemies. Today, catching any prey was just a bonus.

Still, the atmosphere on board USS *Douglass'* was upbeat. *Douglass* was, overall, a happy submarine. Her crew was a team, and the leadership treated them as such—including letting everyone indulge with a little ice cream when they made an unexpected kill. Commander Teresa O'Canas ate hers in her stateroom like a proper captain, of course; it was better to let the crew celebrate a little without her looking over their shoulders.

"Keep on like this, and people are going to start thinking we're making a difference," Lieutenant Commander Sally Weber, *Douglass'* XO, said twenty minutes after an Indian *Scorpene* who tried to hunt *Douglass* broke apart.

Hence the ice cream, which Teresa finished and placed the cup on her desk.

"Not going lie, turning the tables on her was pretty sweet. And these new torpedoes are a godsend." Teresa grinned. "They make life a *lot* easier out here. Particularly with that *Yasen* we sank on the way out here."

She wiggled in her chair, hating how small her stateroom was. But at least it was hers. *Douglass*, as a mid-run *Virginia*, had bigger staterooms than the newer *Ceros*. By pure accident, Teresa was sure. And while she sure would like a faster and newer boat, just like any sub commander, she really did like the extra space.

It wasn't that she was claustrophobic. It was more that she liked moving and hated staying in one place. Teresa knew she was a little scatter-brained and that her professors at the Academy had been kind when they called her hyper. It made her a great multi-tasker, but it had its drawbacks.

Thank goodness Sally was good at picking up the pieces she left sprinkled all over the boat like land mines when they weren't in the middle of a tactical problem. Those Teresa handled just fine. It was amazing how the possibility of death focused the mind.

"I'm still worried about how the Russians built all of them. We know the 2020s weren't exactly kind to Russia." Sally scratched behind her ear. "Their uneven torpedo distribution is exhibit A for Russian disorganization, but they have about twice as many submarines as they should."

"They probably built them underground."

"Do you have *any* idea how hard that would be, Captain? I know you magically avoided shipyard duty your entire career, but trust me, even the Russians would find that almost impossible."

Teresa shrugged. "Flog enough paroles and you can do it?"

"You're impossible. You know that, right?" Sally rolled her eyes fondly. "In fact, without Ukraine—"

The phone ringing cut her off, and Teresa snapped it up. "Captain."

"Ma'am, it's the officer of the deck. We're ten miles out from the SOM."

Teresa nodded, all good humor fleeing. "We're on the way." Her eyes found Sally as she hung up the phone. "Now the hard stuff begins."

"Hey, if it was easy, they wouldn't send us to do it, right?"

"You bet." Teresa managed another smile while worry gnawed at her guts.

Sneaking around the entrance to the Strait of Malacca while submerged and trying to find *Idaho's* survivors was no joke, and she knew it. Particularly six days after *Idaho* sank. There were thousands of ships out here, and any one of them could have picked up Kenji Walker's crew.

If a friendly had rescued them, *Douglass* would've been called off. But there hadn't been even the slightest whisper about *Idaho's* people, at least not as far as the Intel geeks could find. No one knew *anything*.

Douglass wasn't even the first boat sent after them. But the destroyer freed up from convoy duty to look for them was torpedoed three days ago—presumably by *Vela*, who they knew got *Idaho* from her attack center video—and the surface pukes refused to send another ship without a sub escort. *Douglass* had been way the hell out of the way in *Perth* but made best speed to the SOM when ordered to, and here they were.

Oh, and *if* they had free time, could *Douglass* look for *Gravely's* survivors, too? There were suspiciously few communications from the destroyer's crew, too.

Teresa shook her head. Alex made rescues sound easy in his stories, but he'd never had to do one in the insane traffic—not to mention enemy warships—surrounding the Strait of Malacca. It was like finding a needle in a haystack when there were several hundred haystacks around and you weren't even sure if the needle ever made it to the haystack. Or if the original haystack was still here.

Despite hours of searching, *Douglass* never found *Idaho's* survivors, but Teresa O'Canas was luckier than she thought. *Vela* departed two days earlier, and with her, the Russian trawler holding the survivors of USS *Gravely*. *Idaho* went down with all hands but proved excellent bait—and Colonel Nikolin gained a few interesting prisoners of war, after all.

No one reported their names to the International Red Cross. As far as the world knew, *Gravely* also went down with all hands.

Captain Avani Patel did not ask questions.

13 May 2039, Red Tiger Station, the South China Sea

"They had to try to evacuate us on Friday the Thirteenth, didn't they?" Sam Yeung kicked his suitcase, shaking his head. "Something is *bound* to go wrong."

"Shut your face," Ning said as casually as she could, trying to disguise the way her heart kept trying to skip a beat.

The crush of people was a dozen deep in the outbound lane in Red Tiger Station's Undersea Transfer Area, or UTA. Back when she was driving borrowed sub racers around—and dreaming of her own—Ning had visited this area often. The garage was just through the watertight door in front of them, and she'd already learned the hard way that parking a million-dollar sub racer on the surface was stupid. Her *next* Super Falcon was already on the way, but now it looked like she'd lose that one, too.

Ning was strangely okay with that. Insurance might not pay for this one, but Pulsar Power would. After all, they'd set up the transfer time *and* refused to wait a week until her sweet little sub racer arrived.

Grimacing, Ning glanced at *Valegro's* plans on her tablet. No way could a modified Migaloo M5 load a racer, anyway. Their sub-to-freedom had been the second M5 off the line, built way back in the mid-2020s as the Race to the Ocean Floor went wild. Lord only knew how many leaks they'd patched, but cargo room wasn't what passenger boats were known for.

She let her eyes play over the crowd. At least it was well-behaved, probably because of Gus' Shaved Ice sitting right next to the hangar door. Who would've thought shaved ice was a hit underwater? Not Ning. But Gus made almost any flavor you could imagine, and beef teriyaki shaved ice was pretty tasty after a long day working on the reactor. The line at Gus' was almost as long as the one in the UTA's outbound lane. She smiled.

Next down from Gus', you could buy scuba gear and rent the speed racers and their slower counterparts. Or there were the boats with glass bottoms you could barely see through, the ones tourists always bought tour tickets on because they were on Red Tiger Station to waste money. The water was too deep here to see much out of a glass bottom, but the pictures lining the four boat rental places certainly didn't show that.

Security was nestled between Bai's Racers and Diving With Galina, with two of the three guards napping and one pretending to watch the line while she played phone games.

Ning didn't blame her. There were a lot of people, sure, but everyone was well-behaved. Red Tiger Station just wasn't a place where people caused problems.

The problems *topside*, however...

"Third time's the charm, right?" Jake Lawrence was their one man security detail—something Pulsar sure as hell regretted shortchanging them on—and he looked as ready to leave as the rest of them. His formerly short hair was on the scraggly side these days, and his dark eyes had deep circles under them.

No wonder. Jake wouldn't get his bonus until they were all home safe.

"Here's hoping." Doctor Kim Leifsson looked about twenty years older than she had a few months ago, but things were really starting to suck out there around Red Tiger Station.

Even Ning couldn't keep her head in computers and ignore what was going on. The war overhead only made the waters around the station more lawless, and pirate attacks—or attempted ones—happened at least once a month. The Chinese stormed in last January, demanding RTS leadership's allegiance, only to be driven out by that same annoying pirate group, the Destroyers...who then demanded the station pay them for their services.

Ning wasn't aware of what deal the station council of managers struck with the Destroyers, but whatever it was, they went away. Another group came by and stole a shipment of electronics two weeks later, but at least it wasn't the Destroyers, who liked to steal entire groups of *ships*.

She was still smarting over their thieving of her Super Falcon, but Ning wasn't stupid enough to do anything overt. And she wasn't a good enough hacker to try to find them on the internet and ruin their lives, either.

"You all right, Ning?" Dieter Weber, their quality engineer, was an old man who generally left "the kids" to play their games. By kids, Dieter meant everyone who wasn't him and Jake, who although half Dieter's age, also enjoyed quiet entertainment like watching movies and playing chess.

"Sure. Just ready to get the hell out of here."

"I'm not sure how I feel about leaving via submarine garage rather than the TRANSPLAT." Dieter smiled tightly. "Connecting *two* underwater habitats together seems like doubling the opportunity for problems. Surface transfers have the advantage of being in an environment where oxygen wins."

"Not if you fall in the drink or a pirate catches you, Doc." Jake laughed. "The pirate threat level is too high for a surface transfer—there are two groups operating within ten miles of the station, and there was a surface skirmish between the Chinese and Taiwanese navies closer than that two days ago."

Dieter sighed. "Ten miles is a long way away."

"Not on the ocean, man. No stoplights."

The announcement system chimed. *"Ladies and gentlemen, the transfer submarine will arrive in ten minutes. Please have your boarding passes ready for inspection."*

"Sucks that Pulsar couldn't even charter a private sub," Ning muttered.

"I don't think they could get one willing to come out here." Sam toyed with his plastic boarding pass. "Took long enough for this one to pick up the schedule, y'know?"

"Just be happy that the managing council and Pulsar combined their bribing powers to get it here," Kim said.

"She's on approach," Sam said, pointing at the status screen to their right.

The screen didn't show raw sonar input—no one on the Fogborne team would've known what to do with that—but it did show the steady icon of a submarine approaching Red Tiger Station.

"About time," Jake muttered just as a second icon blinked to life on the screen.

"What's that?" Ning pointed.

The icon moved far faster than *Valegro*, blinking its speeding way toward the civilian submarine.

"I think that's a torpedo," Sam whispered.

No one contradicted him. No one said anything. They just stood in tense silence, watching and hoping Sam was wrong as second ticked by and the two icons grew closer.

The two icons merged, and then *Valegro* vanished.

No nation ever admitted to sinking the submarine.

Not even by accident.

"We're in the big leagues now," Nancy muttered, looking out at the majestic fleet surrounding them as *Fletcher* swung lightly at anchor.

Commander Ying Mai cocked her head. "Are you being sarcastic again, Captain?"

Nancy snorted. "Are you playing innocent?"

"Maybe."

They exchanged grins before sharing a moment of comfortable silence on *Fletcher's* port bridgewing. The sleek destroyer was at Christmas Island again, this time after a final training exercise before a secret-but-*big* upcoming operation that everyone knew was the United States' next attempt to retake the Strait of Malacca.

The Strait of Malacca was the world's biggest oceanographic highway and the shortest route between the Indian and Pacific Oceans. Stretching five hundred nautical miles between Indonesia and Malaysia, it was the longest strait in the world—and the busiest. More than a hundred thousand ships passed through the SOM annually before the war...a number now cut in half since Alliance-flagged or sympathizing ships were stopped—or sunk—by the Indian and French warships guarding the Strait.

They had to win the SOM back. Or *at least* force that key sea lane back to neutrality. No one would mind that; they all just wanted to stop having to drive the long way around by Australia.

"Admiral Anderson has grand plans, I think." Nancy shrugged. "But I'm not in her confidence."

"So much for being the flagship of the Little Beavers. It was nice while it lasted." Ying sighed wistfully. "Do we even still exist as a task force?"

"No one's told me yet." Nancy hadn't realized how used to playing fast and loose with rules and regulations she'd gotten under Admiral Rodriquez until he was gone. *She* would've called herself a lover of regs, but here she was, missing the renegade submarine admiral.

At least he didn't hang his flag on the carrier and never even visit the other ships under his command. Nancy only knew what Anderson looked like through video conferences.

"I suppose they'll tell us when we need to know," Ying said.

"I hope so."

Nancy managed not to make a face. She couldn't lie; she liked being at the tip of the spear. But she liked knowing what was going on even more. *Fletcher's* short stint as Admiral Rodriquez' flagship had been educational, and more importantly, it had let her be part of the planning for the task group. Her destiny had been in her own hands.

After the disastrous *First* Battle of the SOM—Nancy assumed they'd call the coming one the second—she never wanted to be left out in the cold by decision makers again. She still had nightmares of watching friends die that day, of fighting her destroyer her hardest and it not being enough.

She didn't want to say it, even though Ying's expression said she was thinking the same thing. Would going back to the SOM be the same this time? Would the demons they escaped a year before pull them under this time?

Nancy Coleman wasn't a coward, but she wasn't sure she trusted an admiral who shared none of her plans to lead them to victory.

23 May 2039, the western Pacific Ocean, in route to Guam

Word from intelligence warned Convoy 12098 that action against the enemy was imminent. No one was sure what the hell threat they were supposed to be facing, but all the convoy escorts closed up into full wartime steaming.

This was a larger convoy than *Jimmy Carter's* usual fare, and they even had another submarine in company. *Illinois*, a *Virginia*-class boat, was out running point for the convoy of twenty-seven merchants and six escorts, a few miles ahead of everyone, making sure they didn't steam into a trap. That left *Jimmy Carter* free to lurk on the most likely threat axis...until some idiot relegated them to the rear of the formation.

The captain's arguments against placing a submarine close to the convoy as a rear guard fell on deaf ears. Telling the convoy commander it was plain stupid made things worse—because senior officers, as a rule, hated it when someone was smarter than them *and* reminded them of the fact—but he wasn't wrong. The surface escorts would hear anything moving fast enough to overtake the convoy, and they made so much noise that no sub chained behind them could hear a damned thing.

Everyone in control heard the discussion between the various ships' COs. *Jimmy Carter's* tiny radio shack was barely big enough for the two required watchstanders if they cuddled, and Commander Coleman was too practical to kick one of them out when he could use the red phone in control. Even after the moronic convoy commander stuck his foot in, everyone listening expected *Illinois's* commanding officer to agree when Coleman had proposed that the two subs split up the forward sectors.

"Frankly, I'm surprised your boat can submerge," *Illinois'* captain said. Bud Wilson had no idea what the guy looked like, but the other CO sounded like a jackass. He imagined the dude was short, balding, and fat. Probably had a Napoleonic complex, too. Loads of them did.

Convoy 12098 had been assembled on the fly. No one from Smiley had even met the crew off *Illinois*, cause they hadn't set foot on shore between this one convoy and the last one. It was nothing new. *Jimmy Carter* bounced from one job to the next like an addict looking for a fix.

Good thing he liked beans. Bud figured they'd be eating a lot of them this cruise. Or pasta. It was always those two. Bud should've been paying attention to his sonar watchstanders, but Boxer and Spangler were good kids. His role as sonar supervisor only mattered when shit hit the fan. And it wouldn't. No idiot enemy was going to attack a convoy this well guarded. Escorting it was about as exciting as listening to one of Commander Peterson's inspiring speeches back on *Bluefish*.

Maybe it would be beans *and* pasta. The cooks on board Smiley were creative.

He sighed. Yeah, he could afford to spend his time pretending *not* to peek out the sonar room door and watch the captain deal with these morons. Knowing Commander Coleman, he wouldn't have left the conversation on speaker if he'd known it would turn out like this. Out of the corner of his eye, Wilson saw the captain grit his teeth.

"She might be old, but *Jimmy Carter* can do the job." Bud was impressed by how level his voice was.

Then again, surefire bet was that Coleman had *lots* of experience saying those words over the last year.

"Right. At any rate, I'd rather not have that old dea—submarine up here making noise so people can detect my boat."

"Asshole," Bud muttered under his breath, just as Coleman replied:

"I think it's safe to assume we won't be doing that back here."

Bud almost laughed. He caught the noise as a cough as Seaman Boxer twisted to look at him, her eyes bright.

"Keep your eyes on your console." Bud's grin robbed the order of any harshness. "Y'never know what might turn up."

"Back here, Sup? I can't even hear the shrimp fucking over the sound of those merchants." Boxer made a rude gesture at the console.

This time Bud let himself chuckle.

Boxer was a child after his own heart, an experienced sonar tech who'd made third class petty officer on *Texas* before being busted down to seaman. She blamed a particularly wild night involving four prostitutes, two kegs, and a stolen private airplane. Bud had checked up on that story, and damn it if Boxer wasn't already a legend in the service, even at twenty-one.

Boxer landed on Smiley because no other boat wanted her. Not that she was unique in that. Bud counted at least fifteen fellow idiots on the boat who'd made themselves too infamous for their former captains to keep. Still, after learning her new leading petty officer was as crazy as she was—and likely wise to her tricks—Boxer settled down nicely. Like Bud, she'd never had a problem standing a good watch. All of Boxer's lunacies came out on shore.

STS3 Spangler was another story. Tall and pale where Boxer was short and dark, Spangler was perpetually overweight and not a fan of good personal hygiene. Boxer, despite her disciplinary problems, was a neatnik. She kept her rack clean and her uniforms cleaner and never showed up late. Pity Spangler didn't want to pick that up from her. Wilson couldn't count how many times he'd reminded Spangler that *shaving* was part of being in the navy. He was also tempted to throw the big third class into the shower, or at least buy him deodorant.

Problem was, Spangler *was* talented. He knew his job and would probably make second class on the next exam. He'd done so well on *Utah* that he would've made the rank during the last promotion cycle if the boat hadn't been in the middle of sinking on exam day. Somehow Spangler and his fellow survivors slipped through the cracks and never been given the test. Knowing Spangler, he hadn't thought to complain, either.

Spangler was the quiet-nerd type, but him and Boxer being opposites made them an effective watch team. Wilson put them together on purpose, and not only because Boxer was the only one who could tease Spangler into taking a shower...or out of his infrequent funks.

Speaking of funks, Spangler was deep in one now, hunched over the console with his shoulders rolled up like a beetle. Under other circumstances, Wilson might've thought the other sonar tech was "in the zone" and concentrating, but there was double jack and nothing to listen to.

Boxer was right. At *Jimmy Carter's* station back here, they'd be lucky to hear a depth charge exploding over the ear-splitting rumble of the convoy. Not that they'd ever wind up in a situation where good old Smiley was depth charged. Oh, no. Not at Smiley's age. She was *fragile*.

Yeah, watching the drama in control was ten times more fun than listening to a whole lot of nothing.

"Conn, Sonar, torpedo in the water, bearing one-one-niner!"

The terror Spangler's voice jerked made Bud's head snap around so hard his neck cracked.

"Conn, Sonar, *second* torpedo in the water, bearing one-two-one!"

The speaker on the bulkhead was only two feet to Bud's right, and it was hooked into the same frequencies as Spangler's headset. His hand snaked out to twist the volume to "high" on its own, but Bud couldn't hear anything over the convoy's screws, not even the telltale high pitch of torpedo sonar.

"I got nothing!" Boxer sang out.

Bud threw himself into the third seat, grabbed a spare headset, and jammed it down over his ears.

"Sonar, Conn, talk to me!" That was the captain's voice from the internal net, and Bud stomped on his own foot pedal mike to answer it.

"Captain, I—"

"Screw noises! I've got two high-speed submerged contacts in-bound, bearing about one-three-zero at twenty thousand yards!" Spangler cut him off.

Bud forced himself to take a deep breath, ignoring the answer from control even as *Jimmy Carter* trembled under his feet, speeding up and rolling left into a turn. Raised voices drifted in from control, but he never heard them. Bud only slipped into his own zone, his unfocused eyes traveling over the sonar traces in front of him and his ears straining to hear...

Nothing.

Nothing but the sounds of the same merchant screws going roundy-round.

"What the *hell* are you listening to, Spangler?" He leaned across

Boxer to glare at the petty officer. "You got a training tape or something in there?"

It never occurred to Wilson that Spangler might just be playing a sick practical joke, even though he knew a sonar tech who'd done that back on an exercise in 2029.

They were at *war*. No one was that crazy.

"No!" Spangler's pale face was crunched up in terror, and now anger made his eyes wide. "Can't you hear it? There's—there's—*Conn, Sonar, third torpedo in the water, bearing one-niner-four!*" His voice rose into a screech. "*Fourth* torpedo in the water, bearing—"

"I've still got nothing!" Boxer said.

Bud couldn't hear a thing. "Spangler, I swear to God—"

"You're both deaf! You're going to get us killed!" Spangler was sweating profusely, his voice getting louder and louder—except, no, the increase in volume came in part from the fact that he still had his foot on the pedal. His mike was still keyed, and everyone in control could hear every word Spangler screeched. "Can't you hear that? We've been *boxed*, Wilson! There are torpedoes coming from everywhere and—"

Bud tore the headset off Spangler's head, pulling the microphone away before the other sailor could say more:

"—we're going to die!"

Tears were streaming down Spangler's face. He grasped wildly for the headset, but Bud tossed it down.

"Spangler, calm down!" Bud wrestled the larger man's arms aside to unplug the headset from the console.

"No! Can't you hear them? I can—"

"There's nothing out there!" Boxer said, but suddenly Spangler was on his feet and bolting toward the hatch.

"*Captain*! They aren't hearing the torpedoes!"

"Spangler!" Bud howled, jumping after his sailor, only to tangle his feet in his own headset's cord. He made it one step before pitching forward and face planting onto the deck. "Shit!"

"You want me to go after him?" Boxer twisted in her seat, eyeing Spangler's retreating form.

"No. Keep your damn headset on!"

Bud lurched to his feet and bolted after Spangler, who was lumbering drunkenly into control toward the captain. Bouncing off a console and resisting the urge to swear, Bud reached out for the younger sonar tech but missed as Spangler whirled away.

"They're not hearing the torpedoes, Captain!" Spangler flailed as a navigation technician dodged away. "I know they're coming. I *know* they are. You have to *do* something!"

Almost tripping over the bottom knife-edge of a hatch in his hurry, Bud finally caught up with Spangler, grabbing him by one flailing arm. "There aren't any torpedoes, Spangler—"

"*Shut up!*" The words were an ear-splitting wail. "I don't want to die, even if you do! There are torpedoes in the water, and *I heard them!* I can hear them *now!*"

Everyone in control stared at Spangler as he shook free of Bud, bolting forward again. Holding up his hands, Master Chief Morton stepped between Spangler and his intended destination—still the captain, whose eyes were as wide as hula-hoops—only to be caught full in the face by an arm as Spangler started thrashing.

"You have to do something!" Spangler stopped to howl the words like a toddler whose toys had been taken away.

"Goddamn it, Spangler!" Morton caught himself on a console and shook off the blow. "Get your ass back to your station!"

"*Not until someone* listens *to me!*"

When Morton tried to intervene again, another massive arm swept him aside; Spangler swung at everyone within reach, including Lieutenant Angler, who darted around from fire control to help. Another two fire-control techs tried to corral Spangler, only to suffer similar fates; one hit a console hard enough that sparks flew. People were shouting and Spangler was crying and—

Once upon a time, Bud Wilson had been a star hockey player in his hometown of Fergus Falls, Minnesota. He'd never enjoyed football, but getting in bar fights taught him how to use what mass he had. Now, he turned all those woe-begotten talents against Spangler, launching himself into a flying tackle. Bud hit the larger sailor's back, slamming them both into the metal deck with an audible *thunk*.

Chapter 6

Clash of Titans

Two hours later, Bud stood fidgeting in the captain's cabin with ant-like anxiety crawling up his spine. He sucked at standing at attention, but he was a pro at the good old thousand-yard stare. Usually, he used it when officers or chiefs yammered on about something he couldn't give two shits about, like liberty being a mission or living up to the navy standard. It was a damned useful skill when you were about to get reamed out, too.

And he knew he was really going to hear it this time. Bad enough that he hadn't noticed one of his own sailors going nutso, but Bud had *also* tackled said sailor to the ground, breaking Spangler's arm and sending them both crashing into the captain. Judging from the ice Baby Doc put on the captain's ribs and the way the corpsman glared at Bud, Coleman got one hell of a bruising from *his* impact with the chart table...which was Bud's fault.

Smashing your commanding officer into solid objects being a bad idea, Bud figured that the string of second chances he'd received was about to dry up as fast as the Sahara. Probably snapped in two right with those ribs on the boss.

Bud was still surprised Coleman hadn't kicked him to the curb last time. Getting sprung from the brig by the big boss twice was a record, even for him. Somehow, he managed not to grimace. Yeah, he was a troublemaker, but he loved the navy. He'd never considered retiring before spending twenty years in uniform. Going to war hadn't changed that.

Screwing up like this might.

"Relax, Wilson," the captain said after a moment. His voice wasn't inviting, but it wasn't as cold as Bud expected—it was almost whimsical.

Great. He'd already decided what to do with Bud, and he was going to *enjoy* it. No one on board knew what Commander Coleman was like when he was really mad, but Bud was about to find out, wasn't he?

Gulping, Bud relaxed and clasped his hands behind his back. After meeting the captain's gaze for a moment, he focused on the wall again. It was safer.

"What *am* I going to do with you?" Coleman asked.

"Pat me on the head and give me a milk bone?"

Shit. As usual, his mouth ran away with him. And he was already screwed, right? When he was a kid, someone told Bud he resembled the wrong character in a classic comic. Bud cheekily replied that his father was Mister Wilson and his middle name was Dennis. His first supervisor in the navy hadn't even tried to be clever and called him *The Menace*.

"I'm glad we're fresh out of dog treats." Coleman rolled his eyes. Was that a hint of amusement behind his scowl? Bud told himself not to hope. Coleman still held an ice pack against his midsection, and that was bad news. He was screwed. No reason to be a moron and start thinking he wasn't.

"Well, darn."

Then again, there was no reason not to keep going if he was going to get hammered. But the captain didn't drop an anvil on his head. Instead, he sighed.

"Are you *ever* serious, STS1?"

"When I'm working." Bud shrugged.

"Unless I missed something, you *are* at work." Coleman gestured around the stateroom, wincing as he moved too much.

Sure, he wouldn't want to decorate his apartment like this; Bud always rolled with his own idiot statements. Brash beat bending. "Doesn't count, sir. My job's sonar. The rest is just details."

"Some COs I know would rip your face off for that attitude."

"Well, it's a good thing that you aren't most COs, isn't it, sir?" Bud met the older man's eyes, grinning.

Coleman snorted and then grimaced. "For you, sure. For me, jury's still out." He shook his head. "Don't push *too* hard, Wilson. You did the right thing today, and that grants you a bit of leeway where I'm concerned. But try not to make a habit of tackling your shipmates."

"No, sir." Bud rubbed his jaw. Spangler had gone down, sure, but he hadn't wanted to *stay* down. It took Bud, the COB, and two others to pin to the deck until Baby Doc could stick him with a sedative, and Bud's face was turning an interesting shade of purple.

"How's Spangler doing?" Coleman asked. Despite his sins, Bud was still the petty officer in charge of the Sonar Division.

"Nuts." He winced. "I mean, I don't think it's his fault, sir. It's not like we could get his medical records off *Utah*, and Charlie—I mean Baby Doc—says someone should've diagnosed Spangler with PTSD before they decided to leave him here. An' he's useless, now, sir. Spangler keeps seesawing between whatever happened *there* and being here. Baby Doc says there's no way to tell when he's gonna be where. A real psychologist could help him, but we ain't exactly got one of those here on the boat.

"I've already adjusted the watchbill to make up for him, sir," Bud continued. "It'll mean some long watches, but I'll stand most of 'em. Spangler needs to go home first chance we got. Or at least to a carrier where they can treat him better."

"I agree."

The simple answer made Bud blink. *He* knew he was right, but he wasn't used to having superiors listen to him. "You don't want to talk to Mister Vincentelli, sir?"

He'd almost called him Ensign Unpronounceable, but the captain might not approve of the mostly affectionate moniker the enlisted guys and gals in sonar hooked on their division officer. Vincentelli couldn't help stuttering under pressure, and it was all in good fun. But Bud stopped himself. No reason to remind Coleman that he probably *should* be hammering a sarcastic sonar tech right about now.

"Do I need to?" Coleman cocked his head.

"Well, no. I mean, I just—"

"You're the leading petty officer in sonar, and we don't have a chief. That means I'll trust your expertise until you prove to me I can't. So far, you've done well."

Bud gaped.

Coleman speared him with a hard look. "When you're not drinking, anyway."

"Yes, sir." Bud's wasn't sure he'd *ever* had a CO take him at his word on anything other than a sonar contact, and even then, they usually looked for a second opinion. This feeling of being trusted was new and terrifying.

Bud hadn't cared what an officer thought of him since he'd been a lowly seaman whose buddies dragged him into binge-drinking in his first liberty port. If things kept on like this, he just might start to give a damn.

Just when Bobby really needed a drink, Commander Peterson's liberty policies grew more draconian. In a fit of paranoia only he understood, *Bluefish's* fretful CO put alcohol off-limits in the land of inexpensive beer and good food.

Peterson also decreed that even his officers had to go out in groups of three or more. And of course, that new rule put a cramp in Bobby's liberty plans. Worse yet, Peterson was a snob. *His* department heads were only expected to go out with other lieutenants, and there were only three lieutenants on board.

So Bobby resigned himself to being stuck on board the USS Blue-in-the-face.

After a miserable week of watching others have alcohol-free fun, the XO noticed they were ready to tear the walls down and took Lou's duty for the night. Bobby, Rose, and Lou didn't need to be told twice; they jetted off the boat before Vanderbilt could change his mind. Not that Peterson was there. The rules didn't apply to the CO when he could hang out with his wife.

"You look like you need a cold one," Lou said, munching on cheese sticks.

"Yeah, because my super sweet tea really is speeding me right along toward that drunken stupor I was aiming for." Bobby shrugged. "I mean, I *could* pretend I'm drunk. That might make me feel better for a while, and I could get all the embarrassment without the hangover. But in the end, I still wouldn't *be* drunk, so what's the point?"

"You could savor the tasty food instead." Lou gestured at the mostly empty appetizer platter. The department heads found the most out of the way, expensive, and overrated place in Perth, hoping that no one else from the boat would show up.

The place was way pricier than the quality deserved, too. Where the hell did the Mediterranean get all the customers when their food was so *not* awesome?

Bobby liked good food and was willing to spend money to get it. As a single lieutenant with no one to support, where else was he going to spend his money? Even the girl he just started seeing was a lieutenant commander, so she hardly needed Bobby's riches to keep her in house and home. *Though I'm not sure I'll forgive her for*

suggesting this place.
"I come bearing the solution to our problems." Rose plonked three beers onto the table as she returned from the ladies' room—and presumably—the bar. "You can thank me later."

Bobby fidgeted. "We really shouldn't..."

Lou held up a hand. "You, madam, are an officer and a lady. And my new hero. Don't let this childlike individual put you off."

But Lou hesitated, too. Rose crossed her arms.

"Screw it. We're not getting drunk and we're not getting caught. If we can't have a damn beer like responsible adults, I'm going to forget why I joined the damn navy in the first place. I'm a sailor, not a nun. Bottoms up, boys."

Rose was usually the rule follower. If she wanted to flout Peterson's ridiculous restrictions, who were they to say no? Bobby glanced at Lou, and they hefted their beers as one.

"To *Bluefish*." Bobby sneered. "May she continue to rot pier side while our friends go out and do the job for us."

"No." Rose's voice was surprisingly soft. "I'm not wasting a toast on that."

Lou cocked his head. "Then what do you want to toast to? The beer's getting warm, Weps."

"To absent comrades," she replied, lifting her glass. "To our brothers and sisters on eternal patrol."

A shiver ran down Bobby's spine. "Absent comrades," he and Lou echoed together.

The beer felt damn good going down, but Rose's words made Bobby swallow more than the drink. The world didn't begin and end at their broken submarine and miserable crew.

"You're thinking of Austin Heeter?" he asked.

"Yeah."

At Lou's confused look, Bobby explained:

"One of our classmates—well, mine more than Rose's, technically, since she graduated a semester late—was on *Guam*. With Commander Sivers."

"Oh."

What else could they say? Empty platitudes like *at least they went down fighting* were meaningless. Word in the fleet said Rico Sivers was about to become the submarine community's second posthumous Medal of Honor winner. Submariners didn't win the nation's highest award for valor often; before the war, there'd been a grand total of eight winners, spanning all the way back to 1923. Sivers would make ten. Although he and his crew deserved the honor—they'd almost single-handedly stopped an invasion of the Mariana Islands by Russia before falling victim to dozens of depth charges—Bobby wished for more living heroes instead of increasing the pool of inspiring-but-dead martyrs.

Austin Heeter had been near the top of their class, too. Everyone liked him, Bobby included. They'd even toyed with the idea of rooming together their junior year, until Austin opted to room with his lab partner and Bobby grabbed one of the other guys from the football team. But they'd stayed in touch after graduation. Bobby attended Austin's wedding two years ago and wondered who the navy sent to tell Deb the news.

"Screw what I said about not getting drunk." Rose lifted her beer with a purpose.

Lou put a hand on her arm, his southern drawl gentle. "It's not worth it. You know the captain'll find out, and then you'll be done for."

"Lou's right," Bobby said, swallowing his memories. "You'd be caught for sure, and the crew deserves better even if we don't agree with Peterson."

Glaring mutinously, Rose put her beer down. Bobby knew how she felt: angry, bitter, and guilty all at once. Their friends were fighting and dying as *Bluefish* sat next to the pier, fat, dumb, broken, and happy. Bobby didn't want to die, but he wanted to do his part.

"There are times I wonder..." Rose shook her head.

"Don't say it," Lou got in before Bobby could reply. "It won't help."

Yeah, they all suspected Peterson was extending their time in Perth, suddenly "remembering" repairs he should have put in weeks earlier just when the boat was almost ready to get underway. Bobby didn't think his CO was a coward, but Peterson was the type to blame his failures on anyone other than himself.

And his oldest brother wondered why he was getting out. Bobby couldn't change what his CO did. All he could do was his best, no matter what the circumstances.

24 May 2039, two hundred nautical miles east of Diego Garcia

"Conn, Sonar, hydrophone effects at long range!" Wilson's voice burst out of the speaking with no warning. "Torpedoes in the water, bearing two-nine-zero, range about thirty thousand yards, not inbound own ship!"

"Battle Stations. Right standard rudder, steady course three-one-zero. Ahead full for twenty knots," Alex ordered. He knew the opening moves of this game. Too bad *Jimmy Carter* never got to stick around for the finale.

"Battle Stations, aye," the chief of the watch replied, hitting the general alarm before she'd even finished talking. The screeching klaxon was enough to drown out the diving officer's repeat back:

"Right standard rudder, steady course three-one-zero, aye. My rudder is right fifteen degrees, coming to course three-one-zero. Engines are ahead full for twenty knots."

"Very well." Alex's sub vibrated and picked up speed, heading for his best guess of where the enemy might be.

Steer toward the sound of the guns. It was as ingrained in Alex as it had been in any World War II battleship skipper. *Jimmy Carter* was still with Convoy 12098, and it was just one day after Spangler's epic melt down. Alex's two broken ribs still ached like mad, and he hadn't slept well, courtesy of the injury. As someone who kept himself in decent shape and avoided pain like the plague, Alex found the experience of his first two broken bones nauseating.

Pills helped a little. Chewing on peppermints distracted him more.

Illinois remained on point while Alex's submarine brought up the rear. Leaving *Jimmy Carter* back there meant Commander Devon's submarine was the only warship positioned between the convoy and this new threat. Sitting almost ten nautical miles behind *Illinois* meant *Jimmy Carter* was too far away to provide meaningful support *and* unable to hear *Illinois'* attacker through the churning water kicked up by the merchants.

A few strides took him back to the open door to sonar. Wilson and Boxer were hunched over their consoles, listening intently. "I hope this isn't another false alarm," Alex said.

Wilson didn't even look up. "No fucking way, sir. I got these torps all dialed in, an' they're French-built F27 Rafale. Not the export version, either. If I had to guess, I'd say we've got us a *Requin* on our hands, 'cause I can't catch a whiff of the shooter."

"All right, then." Stuffing his hands in his pockets and heading back to control, Alex fought back the impulse to say something useless or cradle his arm against his chest.

Wilson wasn't an idiot, and Alex wouldn't treat him like one. Yeah, the kid could be trouble, but he'd handled Spangler as well as anyone could. If only Alex could say that for all of his hand-me-down sailors. The two Marty caught snorting crack back in engineering were another problem.

"Conn, Sonar, *Illinois* is at flank and is dropping noisemakers," Wilson said. "It's hard to tell at this range, but I think the French torps are in final acquisition."

Control was very quiet.

Jimmy Carter was still eight miles away from the *Requin* and had no track on the attacker. Neither did the *Virginia*-class boat. Alex could see the other American submarine's Link track dancing away from the tiny icons of inbound torpedoes on his display. Under other circumstances, Alex might have pickled off a few torpedoes of his own in the likely direction of the enemy, but hitting *Illinois* or a merchant from here would be easier than getting the French boat. The angles were all wrong.

"Very well," he said around the lump in his throat.

Suddenly, two more icons blinked to life on his display, less than six thousand yards ahead of *Illinois*.

"Conn, Sonar, I've got two more torps—"

"I see them, Sonar," Alex cut Wilson off hoarsely.

His boat was closing *Illinois*' original position at twenty knots, or 667 yards per minute. It was the fastest *Jimmy Carter* could go without being heard. At this rate, they'd arrive in twelve minutes.

It wouldn't be soon enough.

Alex had two choices: sprint and be heard, and maybe distract the attacker long enough to save *Illinois*, or stay silent and have a good chance of killing the enemy sub. He could feel the eyes on him. Everyone was waiting for Alex to make up his mind. They knew the odds as well as he did. Knew the potential price for what might be their first kill. Alex's eyes strayed back to the plot, calculating torpedo trajectories and doing the math one more time...only to come up with the same answer.

The navy wasn't paying Alex to put the survival of another submarine above the convoy he was supposed to protect. Alex's stomach heaved, and not from the pain.

He'd wait for the perfect shot and...make the enemy pay for *Illinois*.

Alex wasn't the only one waiting. Unbeknownst to USS *Illinois*—or for that matter, to FNS *Barracuda*—there was a fourth submarine in the area. And this one was perfectly placed to fire on *Barracuda* in minutes.

They were already in range, if barely, and only needed to wait for the legendary French attack submarine to wander a little closer. So far, Rochambeau's boat had obliged the unseen hunter in almost every way, and Ursula North's blood was cold enough to wait. Even if she *was* in position to help the closer American submarine, she might not have acted; she'd been chasing Rochambeau for almost a month, and this was the closest she'd gotten to the French superstar.

"Frankly, I would sacrificed one of our own boats to get him," she muttered, making the head of her principle warfare officer turn.

"Beg pardon, ma'am?" The younger officer turned to face her. In contrast to North's pale and haggard features, he was fresh-faced and fit. Where the captain was blond haired and green eyed with a sharp northern accent, he was dark skinned, bald as an egg, and sounded classically British. But looks didn't matter. Dedication and single-mindedness were what they had in common, and Lieutenant James Harrison was nearly as pig-headed as his commanding officer.

"Never you mind," Captain North waved him off. She looked years older than she had when he'd reported aboard four months earlier, but it had been a *long* four months. HMS *Gallant* had sailed three different oceans and faced off against multiple foes. Captain North beat them all...except Jules Rochambeau.

That explained why they'd been sent out after *Barracuda* and told to hunt Rochambeau until he was dead. James knew that Captain North had been given an unusual amount of latitude, and the Admiralty expected her to prove worthy of their trust.

"Yes, ma'am," he said. He'd was the newest of her PWOs, but James was the only one on North's wavelength. That was why he had the watch at action stations.

North snorted, and James suppressed a smile. Technically she was *Lady* North, but no one would guess that from talking to the captain. She was rough around the edges and abrasive. Oh, she was capable of acting like an officer and a lady, but usually she didn't bother.

When you were the best, you didn't have to behave. James shot her another quick glance. If he could become half the submariner North was, James would have no regrets. Not one.

"Come left to course two-nine-nine." Captain North's buzz saw of an accent rolled across the attack center.

Gallant swung quietly to the new course, and James returned his attention to the plot. *Barracuda* remained exactly where *Gallant* wanted her: tracking slowly east, certain no one could hear her.

The wildly maneuvering American submarine obviously couldn't find their attacker. The *Virginia* raced her way into a wild corkscrew turn, changing depth rapidly and dodging the first two torpedoes. Whoever was driving over there was a gifted ship handler, but not good enough. James grimaced.

Rochambeau had placed his second set of torpedoes with unerring accuracy. He'd *predicted* where the American would run, and James bit his lip as those last two torpedoes smashed head on into the *Virginia*-class submarine.

"That had to hurt."

He grimaced, thankful *Gallant* was too far away to hear the explosion. The Americans were their allies. They deserved better than to be used as a distraction...but if *Gallant* could sink *Barracuda* today, many fewer Americans would die tomorrow.

Fewer of his people, too.

"Don't feel guilty, James." Suddenly, North was behind him. "We do what we must."

"Yes, ma'am," he said. "Yet...it does feel dirty."

She snorted. "You're bloody right it does. Now let's kill this bastard so we can go home."

"Aye, Captain." James nodded.

"Make ready your torpedo tubes," North ordered, serious again, and her watchkeepers raced to comply.

"Sonar, do you still have a track on the other American?" James asked.

"No, sir. The explosion muddled all traces of them," the supervisor answered. "She was further out to begin with. I believe it was a *Seawolf,* but there's only one of them out here."

"And the damn Yanks don't bother to tell us where their boats are operating," another one of the officers muttered.

We don't tell them, either. James didn't bother to correct the younger officer. She was nervous and trying not to show it. This was Sub-Lieutenant Arbuckle's first real war patrol, and the first one was always the hardest.

"Very good," he replied to sonar instead. For a moment, James wondered what the *Seawolf* thought of all of this. Could they see *Gallant*? Probably not. Their sensors were older, and *Gallant* couldn't see them. Still, with so many cooks in the kitchen...

"Don't fret too much, James," North said softly. He had forgotten she was still standing behind him. "We'll take the shot, and then we'll worry about the other American."

"Yes, ma'am."

"I've got something, Conn."

Now was not the time to care about how Wilson forgot the formalities of watch stander communications.

"Talk to me, Sonar," Alex said into the speaker.

"Got a sniff on the fifty-seven hertz line. It's faint...but if that's not a *Requin*, my mama's a horse's ass."

"*Wilson!*" The scandalized whisper had to be the newly promoted Lieutenant J.G. Vincentelli.

Alex coughed to cover his laugh and then regretted it immediately. Those broken ribs from getting sandwiched between a flailing Spangler and the corner of the chart table still hurt like a sonofabitch.

Besides, a CO shouldn't start snickering in the middle of an engagement, particularly after *Illinois* sank so fast. Thinking of the other submarine sobered him up in a hurry. He'd told himself that he had to take the chance of watching *Illinois* go down, but Alex *had* hoped that the other crew would make it to the surface before losing their boat.

Those hopes died when *Illinois* exploded with such ferocity that Wilson and the other sonar techs tore their headsets off. *Jimmy Carter* hadn't been close enough for the sound to do lasting damage, but the amplifiers made it painfully loud.

Because Alex had stupidly put the feed on speaker in control, most of his crew listened to the other boat's breakup noises. They knew no one could get off *Illinois* alive. There would be no saving that crew. Their brothers and sisters from *Illinois* were now on eternal patrol.

"Try to resist the urge to tell me about your mother and instead focus on the submarine," Alex said, forcing himself not to think about *Illinois*. This was the only way to make their sacrifice worth it.

"Sorry, Captain. The computer's still kicking it around, but lord only knows if this software knows that *Requins* exist, let alone what one sounds like. But this sure as hell ain't a Chinese diesel boat, and that leaves a *Requin*."

Now he did allow himself a laugh. "Conn, aye." Turning away from the speaker, Alex speared Angler with a look. "Tell me when it's good enough for a firing solution, Weps."

"We need at least another couple thousand yards, Captain," Angler replied.

Alex grimaced, wishing he wasn't so good at math. "We could pickle off a few torps, but..."

"But if we do that, they'll know we're here." The XO's voice was strangely high, and when Alex glanced at him, George refused to meet his eyes. "And if they know, they'll get shots off, too, and we all know what just— I mean, we can't afford to miss. So we should get closer. Right, Captain?"

"If only it was that easy," Alex muttered, looking at the plot. And if only George didn't sound so terrified.

The *Requin* was headed the wrong direction, her course a tangent to *Jimmy Carter's*. The two submarines would continue to close for a few minutes, but they'd almost reached their closest point of approach. After that, the distance would open...unless *Jimmy Carter* did something dramatic.

The urge to order up flank speed, to drive in and *shoot* the son of a bitch, was almost insurmountable. But Alex had been born in the wrong generation of submarine commanders. Stealth was the name of this game. He had to keep sneaking in, lest the other sub realize where he was and escape. Or sink *his* boat. Shaking his head to clear it, Alex turned to his officer of the deck.

"Okay, Maggie. Let's do this thing. Crank on another knot and come left to three-one-five. Let's see if we can't get this bastard before he even knows we're around and then send him down to meet *Illinois*."

He could still hear *Illinois'* break-up noises in every pregnant silence. But it was his job, damn it, and there was no time for guilt. That would come later.

"Captain, are you sure you want to—"

George never got the chance to finish before Wilson's interrupted:

"Conn, Sonar, *new* contact bearing zero-five-two, single screw, type unknown—I've got a blade rate but jack shit else. Computer can't classify, and she's damn quiet, but I *think* she's going after the

Requin."

"Sonar—"

"You think?" George cut Alex off before he could finish. "You'd better do more than guess, STS1. We can't afford guesses right now!"

Grabbing his XO's arm, Alex squeezed until Kirkland stopped. Then he turned back to the speaker, forcing himself to sound normal. "Tell me when you know more, Sonar."

"Sonar, aye," Seaman Boxer answered.

George started to speak again, but Alex jerked on his arm. "Think about what you're saying," Alex hissed. "Think about how you *sound*." It made George gulp and, after a moment, nod shakily.

The new track faded in and out at random. If the *Requin* was good, this newcomer was just about even with the French sub. He had only the vaguest idea where either boat was and had no way of knowing if the newcomer was an enemy or not. What happened if he shot at the second one and it proved to be an ally? Friendly fire incidents weren't unheard of during wartime, but Alex would be damned if he'd precipitate one.

With a start, he realized that everyone in control was still staring at him and George. It was too quiet in the space, and George's reaction to the new report put everyone on edge. They were all worried, and he had to do something. Even if it was unconventional.

Forcing himself to breathe, Alex smiled crookedly and stuffed his hands into his pockets. "Well, this is fantastic, isn't it, Maggie? Two targets, and no way to know who one of them is. Just what I wanted when *I* woke up this morning."

"Me, too, sir." Her laugh was hollow, but some tension eked out of the room.

"Come over to three-three-five," he said. "Let's split the difference between these two and keep our options open."

And then they'd see if Alex couldn't shoot both at once. He hadn't asked for this situation, but if the enemy was going to set themselves up so helpfully, Alex would be more than happy to oblige them by shooting both.

Chapter 7

The Good Idea Fairy

Alex had no idea he was facing off with the best of the French, but Ursula North knew who she was chasing.

Jules Rochambeau had cut a swath through Allied shipping and warships. He'd killed more of her friends and colleagues than Ursula could count, not to mention the thousands of merchant sailors he'd sent to the bottom. Everyone that the Brits, the Americans, and the Aussies sent after him had failed to sink him. He was the best in the business, plain and simple.

He also used to be her friend.

She'd waited patiently, which was against her nature. Ursula was the type to rush in, particularly once intelligence told her that Rochambeau was using satellites to track large Alliance convoys and task groups. That told her where to go, but previous experience told her that she could not keep trying the same old thing. He knew her tricks. He had even sent her an electronic *birthday card* to try to taunt her into attacking him. No. She had to be smart.

So she let him creep up on her, turning the tables and using Rochambeau's own tricks against him. Ursula had even correctly deduced the point along Convoy 12098's route he would pick to spring his ambush, and she had watched while he killed the American submarine. Biding her time was difficult, but her persistence was about to pay off.

"Captain, we have contact on the *Seawolf* again," her sonar watch announced. "She's tracking from left to right, closing our position and *Barracuda*."

Ursula frowned. *Gallant* wasn't the quietest submarine in the ocean. She needed every trick in the book to remain undetected, including nestling up right underneath the sonic layer and using the disruption caused by the sinking *Virginia* to disguise her boat's noise. Unless the Americans had significantly upgraded their sonar suite, there was virtually no chance of a *Seawolf* detecting them.

Theoretically. She hadn't worked with a *Seawolf*-class before, but judging from the sensor suite on a *Virginia*—which were a generation newer and undoubtedly more sensitive—Ursula had a good idea what she was dealing with.

"Range is five-point-five nautical miles," the sonar tech added, making Ursula's head whip around.

"What?"

How the bloody *hell* had a *Seawolf* crept up on her? Old submarines were as subtle as an elephant in a crystal shop!

"I hold the *Seawolf* at—"

"Never mind that!" she snapped. The American was far too close. "Range to *Barracuda*?"

"Eleven nautical miles." The watch keeper sounded relieved.

Ursula knew she should stop snapping at people, but she *hated* it when her plans fell apart. Eleven nautical miles was further than she wanted to fire from, just four miles less than her torpedoes' effective range. Rochambeau could outrun her torpedoes from there.

She swore viciously, feeling like she was holding the end of an unraveling spool as it rolled down hill. Her options were growing more limited by the moment.

"Bearing to the *Seawolf*?" If she didn't call the American boat by name, perhaps she wouldn't feel guilty about using it as bait, too.

"Two-four-six."

The bastard was on track to slip between her boat and Rochambeau. Did he know who she was hunting, or was this just blind luck? Stupid American!

"The bearings are growing rather close, Captain," James said from her left.

Ursula scowled, but making faces at the plot wouldn't change the facts. If the two tracks overlapped, she'd never get Rochambeau. "I know, damn it."

"It's almost as if he thinks we're the enemy…" James stroked his chin.

"He probably does."

The wheels started turning in her head. Would the American be foolish enough—or ballsy enough—to fire on two targets at once? That wasn't a normal American method of doing business. They weren't this good.

She couldn't afford to hope this fellow wasn't crazy. "Stand by your weapons. Compute a firing solution on *Barracuda*."

The response was immediate. "Firing solution computed. Ready to fire on your command."

Wait for it, she told herself, watching the plot carefully. Rochambeau would not give her more than one shot. There'd be torpedoes coming at her soon enough, even if Ursula's aim was perfect. A dead submarine could still kill its attacker because torpedoes didn't *need* human input once they were fired. "Standby—"

"Captain, we've lost contact," Sonar interjected. "No traces of *Barracuda*."

"I beg your pardon?"

Ursula watched, numb, as her chief of the sonar watch leaned over the console, furiously changing settings. After several agonizing seconds, he turned to her and shook his head.

"He's gone, Captain. We heard a slight fade to the right, and something that might have been an indication of increased blade count, but then everything became silent."

Ursula started swearing.

"What do you mean 'vanished?'" Alex asked.

"I mean jack shit and nada, Captain. The Frenchie's just freaking *gone*." Wilson sounded ready to spit nails.

He swallowed back a sudden need to swear. "And you're *certain* that the other one is a British *Gallant*?"

"Yes, sir. Dialed right in, got her on passive broadband and reading auxiliary noises. Want me to call her on gertrude to make sure?"

"Shit." Alex slumped against the open door to the sonar room. He'd slipped into a perfect position between two submarines that he *thought* were the enemy, prepared to fire on both. Then the real enemy disappeared right when they identified the other one as a friend. *Jimmy Carter* finally got her chance, and Alex boned it up.

Shoulders slumped around him as the tension in control drained away into glum defeat. First, they watched *Illinois* die, and then they accomplished nothing.

"All right, Maggie," Alex said, forcing his shoulders back and his voice to come out evenly. He would not growl out his frustration. His crew deserved better, even if he wanted to scream. "Let's turn to port and open up on the *Gallant*. There's no need to go shooting our British friends and certainly no reason to allow them to shoot us." Alex checked another sigh. "Besides, if the *Requin* headed west, that could help us pick her up."

"Aye, sir." Maggie's expression gave away none of her feelings. Did she blame Alex for *Jimmy Carter's* shortcomings? "Left standard rudder, steady course three-one-zero. All ahead two-thirds."

"Left standard rudder, steady course three-one-zero. All ahead two-thirds, aye, ma'am," the diving officer repeated immediately, also sounding normal. Was Alex the only one with doubts?

He couldn't afford to think like this. No matter how little *Jimmy Carter* had accomplished, he was still in command of a warship. His people were counting on him. Once, a lifetime ago, one of his cadre at Norwich liked to say *get up or go home.*

Today, that was damn harder than he'd ever expected.

Excusing himself from control, he headed back to his stateroom. George approached like he wanted to talk, but Alex waved him off. He didn't have the energy to deal another minute complaint from his XO. Alex didn't want to think about George's panic or George's concerns. He just wanted to be alone. And that meant going to the one place the captain might manage not to be the captain for a few minutes.

As he shut the door behind himself, Alex knew that hiding away wasn't the right answer. But if he was going to get his head on straight, he needed a bit of time.

The Northern Approaches to the Strait of Malacca

"What's the definition of insanity? Doing the same thing over and over again?" The words came out before Nancy could stop herself.

Lieutenant Commander Davud Attar twisted to look at her from the tactical action officer's seat in *Fletcher's* CIC, a smile dancing over his lips. "Do you want me to look up the actual definition, ma'am?"

"No, please don't." Nancy grimaced, staring at the large screen displays. Sure enough, they both still showed the SOM, the same northern approach that got the *Enterprise* Strike Group barbequed last time *Fletcher* sailed this way. And while she didn't think Admiral Anderson was the colossal idiot Admiral McNally had been...

"What do you think about using the bombers, Captain?" Attar asked.

Nancy took a deep breath. "It's an…interesting idea," she said. "It feels a little like cheating. Or makes me wonder why we're even here if the Air Force is going to do all the shooting." She gestured at the plot. "I guess we can pick up the pieces if it works."

"Or find the submarines?"

"Only if we properly identify them first." She grimaced. "Forget I said that, Davud."

"My lips are sealed." His smile was fleeting. "I remember that, too."

"I think we all do." Nancy forced herself to sit back in her chair and radiate confidence. "But today should at least be a first in naval history."

"Gee, Captain, I'm excited to be involved."

Nancy laughed. Rear Admiral Anderson, their new task force commander, had come up with what *she* thought was a brilliant new idea. Nancy felt like it was just a derivative of their previous shoot-ships-with-Tomahawks idea, but she was a lowly commander whose opinion Kristi Anderson had not asked for and did not want.

The grand plan was to use air force bombers—whose pilots were more at risk of dying of boredom than enemy action thus far in the war—to drop "bunker-busting" bombs on the combined Indian and French fleet guarding the SOM. Supposedly, the enemy wouldn't see the bombs coming in time to maneuver or shoot them out of the sky because they came from stealth aircraft. Personally, Nancy felt like they were depending on the enemy to die out of sheer complacency.

"Captain, Air, Reapers are two mikes out," her air warfare coordinator reported on the internal net.

"Captain, aye."

There was nothing left to do now but watch. So far a minor player in what was predominately a navy war, the air force was eager to jump into the gap caused by missile shortages. They volunteered six stealth bombers out of the 13th Bomb Squadron, nicknamed the "Reapers," each of which carried two bunker-busting GBU-57B bombs.

Those precision-guided, thirty-thousand-pound bombs—part of the "Big BLU" collection—were designed to break open reinforced bunkers on land. Air force logic said they'd work fine on ships, and Nancy agreed that a thirty-thousand-pound explosive would probably break any ship in two...if you hit it.

"I really wish these bombs had command detonators," she muttered. "Then they might still work if they have a close miss."

"You think their contact fuses won't impact striking the water, ma'am?" Davud asked.

Nancy shook her head. "Not if the specs I read are correct. They explode when they come to a stop. Big danger to sea life on the bottom of the SOM, I guess?"

"Assuming they don't shred on impact with the surface," Davud pulled up some figures, "an explosion on the floor of the SOM might still break someone's keel. The average depth is less than two hundred feet, and that's a big bomb."

"That's more assumptions than I like, particularly since it includes assuming the air force can hit moving targets with a bomb designed for stationary ones. These ships aren't at anchor. That's why our seat-of-the-pants Tomahawk plan worked. We had accurate, unchanging GPS coordinates. Land attack weapons *like* stationary targets."

"All stations, Air, Reaper One is one mike out," Air reported, and Nancy turned to the big screen displays.

She hated being a spectator. It was less terrifying than combat, sure, but Nancy wanted to control her destiny. Not sit a hundred and fifty miles away and watch what happened through Link tracks.

"Each bomber has two bombs," Davud said. "Looks like they're targeting one per ship."

"What?" Nancy twisted to face him. "That's it?"

"Each B-2 can only carry two." Her tactical action officer shrugged. "And there's twelve enemy ships."

"Has the chair force ever heard of *missing*?" Nancy asked.

"Apparently not."

The enemy was formed up in three groups. The first was two Indian aircraft carriers with their screen of four destroyers. A vicious and cold part of Nancy wanted those ships dead the most; they were the ones who killed her friends last time *Fletcher* was out here, just a year earlier. They were also the closest to the northern mouth of the strait and the biggest threat to Task Group 23.

South of them, right around the bend before Batam Island, a pair of French frigates patrolled, probably searching for submarines. Then east, a French task group of two destroyers and a helicopter carrier monitored ships entering and exiting from that end.

Twelve bombs. Twelve ships. That didn't leave *any* room for error.

Nancy bit back the urge to growl obscenities. "I sure as hell hope their precision targeting is up to the task."

"All stations, Air, Reapers on target and beginning drop."

The one thing Nancy had to say in the air force's favor was that their B-2s were stealthy; the enemy never knew they were far in the skies above them before the bombs started dropping. Seconds later, each GBU-57B blinked to life on *Fletcher's* powerful SPY Radar, descending from on high toward the ships steaming below.

The B-2s were split into two groups and targeted the first and last formations first; Admiral Anderson must have recommended the air force go after the higher-value targets before bothering with the two lone frigates. If they sank even one of the three carriers, this would be a *massive* win for Anderson. Nancy frowned. The Indian carriers were going twenty-five knots and the French helicopter carrier twenty. Was that too fast for these bombs? Did air force bomber pilots know how to lead a moving target?

Acid churned in her gut. God help them all, this was either the worst or best battle plan she'd ever encountered.

Closing her eyes, she said a quick prayer for no sudden course changes. Just because she thought the idea was crazy didn't mean she hoped it wouldn't work. Tactics like this could save a *lot* of lives, and there was plenty of room in the war for the air force to play, too.

"Wow, these things are slow," Davud muttered.

Nancy clicked the icon of one of the bombs. *122 knots.* She did quick math in her head and swore. "Gravity. They're in freefall."

Davud groaned. "And if we can track them, so can—"

"TAO, Air, enemy launching air defense missiles."

"TAO, aye." Davud shook his head. "Now the question is how many are going to get through."

"Not enough." Nancy shook her head. "Not nearly enough."

In the end, the answer was two. Five others were shot down, and the other four were clean misses. The LHD took one hit forward that UAV footage indicated took her flight deck out of commission, and one Indian destroyer took a hit. The Indian destroyer sank; the French helicopter carrier was on fire but looked like it would recover by the time *Fletcher* and the task group turned away from the SOM. None of the bombs that missed exploded on contact with the ocean floor; their fuses were not waterproof.

Nancy just hoped they'd stay as unexploded ordnance or the SOM was going to be an *interesting* place to be a submariner for the next couple of decades. She made a mental note to tell Alex about that and maybe shoot an email over to Admiral Rodriquez. He might not be her boss anymore, but he had a lot of juice as COMSUBPAC. Maybe he could put in a word and stop Admiral Anderson from doing something like this again.

The only silver lining was that none of the air force's stealth bombers were shot down and wasted alongside their twelve very expensive bombs.

James heard the captain swearing before he made it into *Gallant's* wardroom and braced himself.

"Everything all right, Captain?" he asked, opening the door cautiously. He didn't *think* Captain North would throw something at him. She usually demolished inanimate objects.

"That bloody Frenchman." She slammed her tablet down on the table. "Do come in. Nothing Rochambeau's tweeted is going to make me bite *your* head off. I'd just like to sink the bastard, and that *stupid* American got in the way."

"We'll get him next time, ma'am." James took his seat cautiously and poured himself some tea.

Gallant had come shallow for the first time since their encounter with *Barracuda* and *Jimmy Carter*, and everyone took advantage of the opportunity to download their personal email. Unfortunately, it looked like Captain North found something else as well.

"The bastard had the nerve to send me an email—a bloody email!—saying that he 'misses old times' and he can't wait to face me again like we used to." North snorted. "As if this was all some exercise and we'd go for drinks after."

"You knew him before the war?" he asked before he could stop himself.

"Oh, yes. Relations between us and France cooled very quickly, you know. We were quite close for years—witness the fact that *Charles De Gaulle* is the same design as our *Queen Elizabeth*–class carriers. We shared technology for ballistic missile submarines, as well as tactics and training methods. Jules and I...we were once friendly adversaries. Friends, even." Her wistful tone was ruined by a snarl. "Now the rat abuses that."

"Do I want to know, ma'am?"

"Not what he sent to my personal email, you damned well don't," North replied. "But feel free to look the fucking tweet that the twat

sent."
Captain Jules Rochambeau
```
@JulesRochambeau
It is a pity that we missed one another, Ursula.
Perhaps #HMSGallant and #Barracuda will meet another
day…and we shall see once and for all who is better
at this game of ours.
```
@RoyalNavy
```
#submarines #war
```

James winced. "He's…calling you out. Personally. In front of the entire world."

"Yes, I got that. Many thanks."

"Sorry." He felt his face heat.

"No bother." She waved a hand. "I could kill him, but you'd only be collateral damage." Ursula scowled. "And I *would* have had him, if not for that annoying American. What the *hell* did *Jimmy Carter* think they were doing?"

"It looked to me like they were trying to set up a shot on both of us," James replied. He knew Ursula was in a mood, but he was her sounding board for a reason—he told her what she *needed* to hear, not what she wanted to.

She scoffed. "In that rattling old boat? They'd to better to use themselves as bait than try to sneak around."

James refrained from mentioning that *Jimmy Carter* had done a fairly good job of sneaking around. "We'll find *Barracuda* again, Captain."

"Yes, but in what century? It took us months to catch up to the cunt this time *and* good intelligence. No one can afford for that to happen again—Rochambeau is killing our people almost as fast as we can replace them."

By *ours*, Ursula meant the Alliance, of course. There weren't that many British subs down here facing off against Rochambeau; two-thirds of their active boats were up north, guarding against the Russians opening up another front. Russia was much closer to Britain than her other enemies, after all—except Alaska, where the U.S. was also on guard. But the Australians were part of the family, and as annoying as Americans were, they'd fought and bled many times by Britain's side. Every loss burned.

"Hopefully after this next port visit. I just got an email from our contact in Perth. The navy's got a shipment of those lovely new torpedoes for us."

"The one AIB got in bed with Lazark to manufacture?"

"Yes, the Advanced Spearfish Variant. It's supposedly a marriage between our Spearfish and the American Mark 48, just much faster."

"Then plot me a course and take me there, Lieutenant. I want every advantage we can get when we go after him again."

"Moored."

The sun had set over Perth, and there was no commodore here to greet him today. John was all right with that; the heady feeling of winning a Navy Cross had faded after an underway where *Razorback* posted great a big goose egg for enemies sunk, so they turned around after a four-day rest for another two week patrol.

This time, they'd had more luck, finding and sinking two enemy submarines and a destroyer. It wasn't enough to tip the scales in the Alliance's favor, but it helped John sleep at night.

Most of the time, he enjoyed being the top submarine captain in the U.S. Navy who was still breathing. It meant *Razorback* was the go-to submarine for hard missions, and he knew his crew craved those as much as he did. But John didn't like how he'd gotten there, couldn't forget the long list of friends whose boats and graves sat on the ocean floor. Every enemy he sank was one less friend to lose.

His phone rang, making him jump and his XO laugh. John wagged a finger at her. "Don't you giggle at me, Madam Abercrombie. One of these days, you'll be old and easily startled, too."

Patricia just snickered harder and headed down the ladder to control, leaving John alone in the sail. He hit the talk button.

"Dalton."

"John! It's good to hear your voice," the familiar voice of Rear Admiral (Upper Half) Admiral McNally said cheerfully.

"Admiral!" John hadn't expected a call from his old boss, particularly not since the last he'd heard, McNally was living under whatever rock the navy put him under after the First Battle of the SOM.

Not that the second had been a rousing success, from what he'd heard, but at least no Americans died.

"It's just Jeff these days," McNally replied. "I retired last week."

"I, uh, congratulations, sir?" John wasn't usually at a loss for words; he knew McNally used to aspire to make it all the way to the top in the navy, but the First Battle of the SOM changed him. John walked away with a silver star, but McNally...

"Well, you know I wasn't going anywhere in the navy after that bullshit in the SOM," McNally said. "No one cares about the problems that brought us to that situation; they just wanted someone to blame, and I was the man in the chair. Fair's fair, I suppose. I was in command."

Well, that was a healthier attitude than John expected. "So what are you up to now that you've earned some freedom, sir?"

"I've moved back to my hometown in Florida, would you believe it?" McNally laughed. "I've got some friends down here, and they've talked me into running for the Senate."

"The *what*?"

"I've always wanted to make a difference. I suppose I'll just have to do it out of uniform."

John felt like someone had kicked him in the gut, but man, he was glad he was registered to vote in Pennsylvania and wouldn't have to explain why he would never in a million years vote for his old CO. Hell, he didn't care what party McNally was. He'd vote for the other one.

Watching McNally freeze up under pressure once was enough, thank you very much.

"Wow. The Senate's a huge step—you think you can jump straight there?" he asked.

"Might as well try. I've got a few friends in the Beltway from my time on the CNO's staff, so I'm not flying blind," McNally replied. "And you know, John, if you ever want a taste of something outside the navy life, just let me know. I could use someone like you."

"Thank you for thinking of me, sir, but the navy's working out pretty well for me right now. *Razorback* is a damn fine boat, and I couldn't ask for a better crew."

"You deserve it. I've never forgotten how you had my back in the SOM. But keep me in mind when you get out. I plan on being in politics for a good, long while!"

"I'll do that. Thank you." John wouldn't mention that he wanted more than the two stars McNally managed. His Navy Cross should grease the skids in that direction for him, too, unless he did something stupid along the way. Or got himself killed.

"Well, I'd better go. It's early and the wife is after me to cook breakfast. Great talking to you, and keep it together out there! I know you'll do great."

"Thank you, Admiral."

John hung up and stared at his phone in silence for a long time. Jeff McNally would never get elected to the Senate, right? Surely there was some sanity in the world.

Chapter 8

Who Needs Enemies?

6 June 2039, Perth, Australia

Three days after pulling back into port—three whole days this time, with just another three before *Jimmy Carter* was scheduled to pick up another convoy—Alex and John headed out to the Perth Officers' Club together. It said a sad thing about the war that Alex had an easier time getting together with his best friend than he did his wife, but submarine patrols—even those of fleet boats and convoy escorts—lined up better than subs and surface ships did.

Surface ships stayed underway longer than submarines these days; they could resupply underway more easily, and while subs *could* carry months' worth of food...they ran out of torpedoes pretty quickly. Or at least the fleet boats did. Subs escorting convoys inevitably found themselves resupplying in whatever port the convoy formed up in.

"No rest for the weary, huh?" John asked as they got out of Alex's ragged Jeep.

"Do I look that tired?"

"Like you've been run over by a hippopotamus."

Alex laughed. "It's not that bad. Just a shit ton of convoys and not a lot of chance to make a difference. Almost lined up on a French *Requin* last time, but I waited too long to take the shot and she vanished into thin air."

"Don't take it personally. Those bastards are slippery," said the man who'd sunk the second most famous one.

Alex just shook his head. "Nancy told me she'd trade places and take my boredom if I'd take *her* admiral with crazy ideas that don't work."

"I heard about that. Stealth bombers against warships?" John laughed. "Sounds like someone was trying to play submarine in reverse."

"Might've worked, except their ordnance was too slow. Gravity's a bitch when you're against ships used to shooting down missiles that break the sound barrier."

"Thank God they don't have torpedoes that can do that."

"No shit." Alex shuddered as they made their way through the crowd to the bar. "Every time I think about it, I wish Nancy'd gotten out of the navy before this furball started."

John laughed. "Seeing as how you're still wearing that wedding ring, I can bet you weren't dumb enough to say that to *her*."

"Do I *look* like someone with a brain the size of an amoeba?"

"You really want me to answer that, Alex?"

He grinned. "Speaking of getting out, how's Janet doing?"

"Stuck at home and angry. Wishing she stayed in the air force, though she won't say it. She's moved to a new division at Lazark, though. Top secret shit, actually making a difference in ways I can't say here." John turned to the bartender without missing a beat. "Jack and Diet Coke, please. And some crap beer for him."

Alex rolled his eyes. "Feral Golden Ace for me."

Their drinks arrived after a lengthy wait; the officer's club was bursting at the seams. Alex recognized dozens of faces, too, returning waves and greetings from both friends and casual acquaintances. After a while, a tall, red-headed commander wandered up.

John slapped the newcomer on the shoulder. "Ken! I'll be damned—I didn't think you were back yet. Have you met Alex Coleman?"

"Not that I can recall," the other man replied with a Southern drawl. A surreptitious glance at his uniform showed Alex that the other officer also wore a command-at-sea pin over the nametape on the right side of his working uniform, but there was no unit patch or other decoration that might hint at what boat he came from. His expression was aloof, almost as if he'd rather be anywhere other than swimming with the proletariat in the common sea of the O Club.

A nudge from John made Alex take the offered hand and smile. Something rubbed him wrong about the other officer, but if he was friends with John, Alex would ignore that. He craned his neck up to look the newcomer in the eyes. "Nice to meet you."

"Likewise." At least his tone wasn't as snobbish as the look he was giving everyone.

John put his drink down to finish the introductions. "Alex, Ken Partridge is in command of *Delaware*. Ken, Alex has *Jimmy Carter*."

Partridge's cool look warmed. "It's always nice to meet a fellow captain sentenced to a boat other than a *Cero*."

Alex chuckled. "It's like modern-day leprosy."

"And everyone avoids us because it might be catching, save for fools like this one here." Partridge gestured at John, who held his hands up.

"Hey, you don't hear those snide remarks out of *me*," their friend protested. "Besides, Ken, I hear they're about to slap the Navy Cross on you for that last patrol of yours. *Six* surface combatants, was it?"

Having red hair and an extremely fair complexion meant Partridge colored easily. "Seven, actually." Partridge fidgeted.

"And that means this overgrown teenager turned in one of the best patrols so far in the war." John grinned. "Of course, *I* know that he's always been an overachiever, but that's because Ken was my XO in a past life."

"Congratulations," Alex said. "That's a hell of a patrol."

He shoved a stab of envy down. His boat's failures weren't Partridge's fault, and what mattered was that someone, *anyone*, made a difference in the war. Too few did. No one wanted to say that the Alliance was losing...even if they were.

"I was lucky." Partridge shrugged again. "And it was only the once—the patrol before that was decent, but nothing to write stories about. Not like John or Ursula North, that's for sure."

"That's hardly a fair comparison." John snorted. "Lady North must have either an angel or the devil riding on her shoulder to keep on the way she has. Sometimes I think the woman's inhuman."

"Do you now, Captain Dalton?" an unfamiliar voice interjected, cutting into their conversation like a buzz saw. All three Americans jumped.

Ursula North stood right behind Partridge, arms crossed. She was a good-looking woman if you got past the glare, with emerald-green eyes and black hair highlighted by two streaks of white on the right side. She wore the standard Royal Navy working uniform, as did the four officers gathered at her back.

John's mouth dropped open. "Ah, well—"

"Don't worry about it, Captain Dalton," North cut him off with something that might charitably be called a smile. "I'm not here to sink you." Eyes blazing, she swung to face Alex. "You're in command of *Jimmy Carter?*"

Behind North's left shoulder, a tall and dark-skinned British officer winced.

"I am," Alex answered slowly, refusing to wither under her glare.

"You ruined my bloody shot."

"Come again?"

"You. Ruined. My. *Bloody*. Shot," North repeated, carefully enunciating every word. She held her hand up inches from his nose, her forefinger and thumb almost touching. "I was *this* close to bagging Rochambeau until you and your damned ancient submarine blundered straight into the middle of things! I realize they must have gifted you with that metal monstrosity for a reason, but do they teach you *nothing* at American submarine school?"

Alex reared back, reeling. "That was *Rochambeau?*"

"Of course it was bloody Rochambeau, you fool! Who do you think I was chasing, Horatio Nelson?"

"I—I didn't know." Alex forced himself to meet North's fiery gaze. "I'm not going to apologize for doing my job."

"For failing at your job, you mean?" She sneered. "Next time, leave the hard work to the professionals, Coleman, and stay out of my damned way."

North whirled away before Alex could respond. She stalked off, her officers following as she vanished into the suddenly quiet crowd. Everyone was staring. Whichever bits of Alex's nerves North's fury hadn't ruined, the dozens of eyes on him certainly did. He turned back to the bar with an effort, trying to pretend that he wasn't suddenly in the spotlight...or burning with shame from a tongue-lashing he wasn't sure he deserved.

Red Tiger Station

"Turn on the news!" Sam Yeung barged into the small compartment Ning Tang called her own on Red Tiger Station, interrupting her video game.

He had her key code—Sam was her best friend, and Ning hated

people knocking because it made her jump—and the door hadn't been locked, anyway. She didn't understand peoples' obsession with keeping secrets from their friends; who she was was who she was, and Ning wouldn't apologize. So her riot of posters and paintings were on full display for anyone who came in, along with her mismatched rainbow furniture.

"Really?" She rolled her eyes and paused gameplay.

"Yes, really. Just do it, okay?"

"Fine." Ning flopped back on her red couch and swapped out of her game to a news program. A moment later, the screen on the wall flicked to the station standard news, featuring an anchor with slicked-back hair in mid-sentence.

"...after a major fleet battle near Zhanjiang, it appears that the People's Liberation Army Navy's fleet has gone from bad luck to worse. Word has reached us that the battle—which took place three days ago—was a significant defeat for the PLAN and a victory for the Taiwanese, or Republic of China, Navy.

"Worse yet, the PLAN continues to be hampered by internal defections. Reports of as high as twenty-five percent of PLAN personnel defecting have surfaced. In some cases, entire ships or submarines have gone over to either Taiwan or the Chinese Democrats.

"Meanwhile, an official alliance has been announced between Taiwan and the Chinese Democratic Movement, the newest name of the coalition of groups pushing for democracy inside China. All these groups have been emboldened by governmental weakness in the face of mutinies and attacks. Now fighting under the banner of the Republic of China and with largely Taiwanese leadership, this alliance gives China a unified enemy but also a larger threat to face."

"Holy bejoles," Ning said as the news swapped to a local report about a station-wide shoplifter who'd been caught yesterday. "You think this might mean they'll stop fighting topside?"

"Maybe if we're lucky?" Sam shoved an empty fast-food container to the floor and slumped into her spare chair. This one was purple. "I'd really like to leave this place, but Pulsar says we're safe."

Ning grimaced. "I'd like to see them live out here. If it's not pirates, it's war, and if it's not war, it's pirates…"

"It's almost like they want to leave us here until they figure out what to do with our design," Sam said.

"I dunno, maybe change the world?"

He chuckled. "They sure paid us enough for that. Real fusion that you can fit on a submarine, but hey, who wants to put it on a submarine, anyway?"

"Part of me wants to buy some old Russian sub off the black market and install the reactor, but that'd be *really* hard." Ning chewed her lip. "Converting a diesel to nuclear, even fusion..."

"Halfway to impossible."

"That's why I want to do it, dummy." She stuck her tongue out.

"I bet the price of old Russian subs is up by a thousand percent with the war on. Even rust buckets are probably in the tens of millions."

"More like hundreds. I checked." She sighed. "And besides, the U.N. declared the Taiwan Strait and parts of the South China Sea a no-sail zone for warships. No one would deliver them."

Sam frowned. "No-sail zone? Is that like a no-fly zone?"

"Yeah, same thing. Except no one's enforcing it, so it's not doing jack to China, Taiwan, and everyone else's mother up there shooting." She shrugged. "They've probably got their hands full with one war. Why borrow another?"

"I just wish we weren't stuck *under* the second war. You know, the one that no one's paying attention to," Sam groaned.

---

7 June 2039, Perth, Australia

The sun was setting in Perth, but Alex wasn't topside to watch the gorgeous orange and blues war for supremacy in the sky. He was holed up in his stateroom for his evening phone call with Nancy—and for once, their evenings lined up. Diego Garcia was only three hours ahead of Perth; compared to some of their previous time-zone juggling, this was nothing.

"So, let me get this straight," Nancy said, chin resting in her hand. For once, they were both in port and could use a video call; the metal of both ship and submarine messed with their signals a little, but if neither of them moved much, it felt almost like they were at home. "You got bullied by a Brit for *doing your job*? What a bitch."

Alex laughed. A day had passed, and the sting had worn off a little, though he'd crawled into the nearest hole—his stateroom on *Jimmy Carter*—as soon as he could escape socializing at the Officers' Club. "She wasn't Princess Charming, that's for sure."

"Well, I got bad news for you, bucko, because your daughter is in line for that title, too. She's still on the Academy train, ready to report for Plebe Summer. Mom's going to take her up there on the twenty-ninth."

Alex leaned back in his rack and closed his eyes. "Well, I told her I was proud of her, and I still am. I couldn't get into the Academy, but Bobbie damned well did."

"That explains why she sounded less mad at you. Good job." Nancy laughed.

"Yeah, now *you're* the mean parent again. Things are back to normal."

"Glad to hear it." Nancy hesitated. "You hear anything about sabotage back home on the missile lines? The surface fleet is buzzing about it, but I can't tell if it's just rumors."

"Really?" Alex sat up. "Have they caught someone?"

"Hell if I know. Everyone's talking about that's why missiles are taking so long to get out to us, but I'm not sure we should blame sabotage when good old incompetence could be the reason."

"Or just lines can't be spun up fast enough to meet demand. You guys threw around a lot of metal in the early days," Alex replied. "Missed a lot, too."

"Hey, we're trained to shoot-shoot-look-shoot. No one ever talked about conserving ammo!"

He snickered. "Sucks to be you. Conservation of ammunition is *always* on a submariner's mind. It's harder for us to resupply down here, you know."

"Really? No, I needed your smartass to tell me that so I could figure it out."

Alex grinned, and for a moment, as Nancy grinned back, it almost felt like they were together instead of almost three thousand nautical miles apart. He tried not to think too much about why Nancy's ship was currently moored at Diego Garcia. She was at the tip of the spear, resupplying and rearming to prepare for the inevitable 3rd Battle of the SOM.

And *Jimmy Carter* was stuck in the Perth-to-Pearl or Perth-to-Bab-el-Mandeb Strait loop, dropping convoys off left and right. Sometimes they went exotic places like the Cape of Good Hope, but it wasn't like you could sightsee there.

But that was the job, and so was being separated. They lived with it.

The South China Sea, approximately 34 nautical miles off the coast of Taiwan

There were rich pirates, and there were dumb pirates.

The dumb ones dicked around with major navies and paid the price. The rich ones, however, found places to ply their trade while the navies shot at each other.

The idiots drove fancy submarines around, buying old Russian submarines like it was a fire sale. And what did that do? It pissed off Mother Russia, who remembered what it was like to be a world power and had few scruples with chasing down enemies and squashing them like bugs. Diego Reyes had heard rumors about the Russians' secret POW camps, and there was no Red Cross reporting for pirates. Nations viewed them as criminals, and with a war on...no one cared where they went. Thirty-seven of his colleagues had vanished into the great Russian maw. He had no desire to follow them.

Smart pirates—of which Diego was one—spent more money up front and bought U-boats. Secondhand, of course, because while the Germans would sell to any country with cash, they drew the line at pirates. And why buy new when German engineering remained the best in the world? Even drunk pirates couldn't break a U-boat, and God knew the Destroyers had tried to break *Destroyer*.

Not while drunk, though. Smart pirate crews did not drink on board. This was not the sixteen hundreds, and drinking on board was a great way to lose money.

One did not become a pirate because you enjoyed being poor.

"That *Atlantis* is still running toward Red Tiger Station, Cap," his navigator reported.

Diego sat back and crossed his ankles. "What's our CPA?"

"Closest point of approach to the station is six hundred meters on current course. CPA to *Atlantis* submarine is zero if they come right to avoid the station."

"Thank you." A wise pirate was polite to his crew. Keeping his people happy prevented mutiny. As did paying them *extremely* well.

Diego's Destroyers were professionals. Or as professional as a bunch of merry cutthroats could be, anyway. He didn't mind them stealing, but he required a certain amount of discipline. Operating submarines without it was a good way to sink and never surface again.

"Are they changing course?" he asked after another minute ticked by. The display in front of him said otherwise, but common sense said these morons *had* to change course soon. Maybe he wasn't seeing something.

A smart pirate welcomed viewpoints other than his own, particularly when he employed a smart and well-trained crew.

"No. They've slowed down to fifteen knots, but Red Tiger Station hasn't said they're opening the garage. And even if they do, Mush Morton couldn't dock at that speed."

"Your fascination with American naval heroes gets old, Jenny," he said. "Mush Morton wouldn't know what an underwater transfer station was if it dug him out of his underwater grave."

Jenny, his navigator, shuddered. "Way to be a macabre spoilsport, boss." She frowned. "Still not slowing. These cats *are* stupid."

"Range?"

"One nautical mile from us. One thousand meters from the station and closing fast."

Diego punched numbers into his console; he hated math and never did it in his head if he could avoid it. "They'll never stop in time. Come right and open the distance to the station."

Destroyer pivoted underneath him as Diego swore under his breath.

"You want to wait to pick up the pieces, Cap?" Jenny asked. "We'll know if they hit in...a minute twenty. Could be a good opportunity to snag some juicy prizes off Red Tiger."

Diego sighed. "No, we don't have boarding crews big enough for the station with us. Snapping up a pricey little luxury boat would've been easy, but Red Tiger is too big of a bite with the surface ships off delivering that Chinese frigate."

Jenny grinned. "Bet no one saw that coming."

"I'm sure they still haven't, what with the chaos happening around here."

The South China Sea remained a haven for smugglers, pirates, terrorists, and anyone with more ambition than morality. With China's three—or was it now two?—way civil war raging and the U.N.'s "no-sail" zone for warships in place, snapping up prey was easy.

It was simple for the U.N. to warn mariners to stay clear of the South China Sea. They'd even *mandated* that warships should stay out of the waters north of the Paracel Islands, lest their parent countries face U.N. sanctions. Those sanctions weren't as weighty as they might have been in time of peace—the belligerents fighting one another controlled the U.N. Security Council—but it scared most nations off.

Unfortunately, legitimate shipping *needed* that waterway. Seven countries bordered the South China Sea, and about twenty percent of global shipping had transited the area before the war. Diego imagined it was closer to ten or fifteen percent now, but that was still multiple trillions of dollars. Taiwan, Korea, and Vietnam remained major manufacturing hubs...particularly for those who wanted to avoid Chinese businesses.

Red Tiger Station's gross station product was about half a trillion dollars in a good year. That made it a target worth revisiting from time to time, particularly since its halfway decent defenses chased off smaller pirate organizations. Still, the moment Red Tiger Station became less profitable—or more dangerous—Diego would leave.

Captain Diego Reyes had two priorities: living and profit. And the second was worthless without the first.

He didn't bother watching the *Atlantis*-class luxury sub smash into the garage of Red Tiger Station. That mess wasn't his problem.

Chapter 9

SOS

19 June 2039, Norfolk, Virginia, Headquarters: Commander, U.S. Submarine Forces

The headquarters building for COMSUBFOR was one of the busiest places in the navy. You wouldn't know that from looking at the boring brown exterior; the bricks were old and worn, and the blue sign outside was straight out of the 1970s.

Inside, however, officers and enlisted sailors buzzed through activity, assigning missions to subs, juggling staffing, and filling gaps when boats went down. The casualty coordination officers were sadly busy, as were the chaplains...but under Admiral Hamilton's leadership, *changes* were happening. No longer did America's sub community sit still and wait to be hit. Now they were trying to take the fight to the enemy...a battle that started with every crew in every sub being properly staffed and supplied.

"Call for you on line three, Admiral," Freddie Hamilton's new aide said over the intercom. "And India invaded Nepal. You've got three messages in traffic about it. Admiral Rodriquez is in the 'to' line; you don't have to take action."

"Thanks, Joy." Freddie grimaced and took a moment to compose herself. Line three was her video line, and *of course* Lieutenant Commander Erickson hadn't told her who was on the other end.

Breaking in a new aide was always difficult, but Joy Erickson had been with her for two weeks. One would think that by now she'd realize that Vice Admiral Hamilton *always* wanted to know who she was talking to. That was one of the many reasons Joy was still on probation.

Most of all, Freddie hated getting bad news right before a potentially important phone call. This might be Marco calling about India invading Nepal. Or it could be her lunch delivery. With Joy, you never knew.

Freddie hit the answer button. "Vice Admiral Hamilton, COMSUBFOR."

"Admiral, it's a pleasure to meet you. I'm Rosanna Gambell, the chief operating officer at Pulsar Power Limited."

"The pleasure is mine, Ms. Gambell." It took all of Freddie's self-control not to let her eyebrows mate with her hairline. What the hell was Joy thinking, letting a direct call from one of the navy's biggest contractors through *without so much as a warning?*

Swearing like Marco Rodriquez felt very appropriate right now, but she couldn't do that with Pulsar's COO on the line.

The woman on the other side of the video line was impeccably well-groomed, with eyebrows sculpted so well that they probably cost more than the haircut Freddie got at the Exchange. Her makeup—a skill Freddie mastered but lacked the time to indulge in—was perfectly on point, too. And her suit probably cost a month of a lieutenant's pay.

Even *in* wartime.

"I'm sorry to call you direct, Admiral. I got your contact information from a mutual friend, Lily Garcia at Lazark," Gambell replied. Her smile was perfect, too. "And I promise that this request for assistance is working its way through official navy channels, but I wanted to talk to you face-to-face. Let's call this providing background, so to speak."

"Request for assistance?" Freddie echoed. She hoped to hell this wasn't about Nepal. Submarines couldn't do jack to stop an in-process invasion, particularly not when they were still losing boats left, right, and center.

But good lord, why was *Lazark* involved? They were manufacturing torpedoes as fast as they could—which wasn't fast enough—and Freddie couldn't afford to piss them off. No way was that name drop an accident.

"Yes. I'm not sure if you're familiar with Red Tiger Station. If you aren't, it's the fourth largest underwater station in the world, but it's in an unfortunate location—in the South China Sea, about thirty-three nautical miles off the coast of Taiwan. As I'm sure you can understand, that's a bit of a...hot area at the moment."

"It's also a little out of my area of responsibility," Freddie replied, mostly to buy time. "The U.N. recently enacted a 'no-sail' zone for warships in the South China Sea, *particularly* for the Taiwan Strait. That doesn't even take into consideration the fact that Red Tiger Station is within Taiwan's exclusive economic zone."

"It is. The station *is* majority-Taiwanese-owned, although Pulsar is a major shareholder as well." Gambell's smile turned strained. "But we're not asking for help for the station, Admiral. I understand you can't provide that." She looked away from the camera for a moment. "What we need is transportation for a small team of five. Just four scientists and one security escort."

"You haven't been able to transport them off?"

"No. The last two subs we sent were sunk, and air transportation in the area is, well, inadvisable."

"You can say that again," Freddie breathed. *She* wouldn't get on a helicopter around there, no matter how close Red Tiger Station was to the Taiwanese mainland. And getting on a ship might be even worse. Those thirty-three nautical miles between the station and Taiwan might as well have been a thousand miles when Chinese missiles started flying.

And *that* was assuming the Chinese hadn't mined that part of the South China Sea. Freddie shuddered. No, that was not an area she'd like driving in.

"The Taiwanese Navy is, obviously, unable to help at this time. And Pulsar *is* an American-owned company integral to the American war effort. So we have turned to the U.S. Navy for help."

"I'm sure you understand I can't give you any answer today," Freddie said, glad she had that shield to hide behind. No way would the CNO want to stick his neck out for five civilians stuck in the middle of a war zone. It was sad and dangerous for them, but sending a couple hundred sailors after five people was bad math. "I'll have to kick this upstairs."

"We understand that, of course. But I did want to add one piece of information that won't be in the official request—something that will matter to you as Commander, Submarine Forces," Gambell replied. "The Fogborne team has been working on a submarine-size nuclear fusion plant."

Them and five hundred other groups, Freddie didn't say. She managed not to lose her smile, too. The navy had at least three research teams on the project out at the Naval Undersea Warfare Center. None of them had accomplished jack.

"I hope it's gone well for them," she said as politely as she could, glancing at the clock. If she ended this call now, she could both remind Joy about proper call etiquette *and* catch lunch before her 1300 meeting with the CNO.

Gambell smiled. "It's gone better than we all hoped. They have a working prototype and are ready to go into production."

"Say again?" Freddie's jaw dropped, thoughts of annoying aides and french fries vanishing.

"We can deliver designs for fusion reactors to the navy within a month of the team being rescued from Red Tiger Station." Gambell folded her hands. "Does this sound like something worth fighting for, Admiral?"

SABOTAGE, INCOMPETENCE, OR CRIMINAL MISMANAGEMENT? *The Navy's Missile Shortage Comes to Light*

Mark Easley, Washington Post

June 21, 2039—The rumors started in January, but the navy refused to confirm them.

Ships sank, and sailors died. Stories sailed home about ships running out of missiles, but navy representatives claimed that was typical of war. Ships could only carry so many missiles, after all, and some were bound to run dry. But then the reports kept coming.

And they haven't stopped. Fourteen months into the war, we still regularly receive reports—not from official sources, mind; those are quiet when asked—about ships running out of missiles to defend themselves because they didn't have enough to begin with. This last part may be a surprise to readers who are unfamiliar with the navy's standard missile, or SM-6, which is both an offensive and a defensive weapon. What does this mean? The more a ship shoots enemy air targets, the less they can defend themselves.

This seems like a poor design, but it's the one we have.

The fact that supply lines can't keep up—as evidenced by the sole manufacturer of said missiles running shifts around the clock without making enough—seems like it should have been solved in the early days of the war. We are sending people out to fight, but what do they have? Beans and bullets are passé; they went out of vogue in the last century.

So why can't American manufacturers keep up with this demand? If Pulsar Power Limited—the designer and sole manufacturer of the *single* missile our ships need—won't expand their production lines, shouldn't they reach out to other companies? Don't we have the largest military-industrial complex in the world? Shouldn't this design be handed to another company to build for all they're worth? This stinks of a monopoly of the worst sort. The sort that kills Americans.

If a simple reporter can come up with the answer to this problem, it begs to ask why Pulsar—or the navy—hasn't already.

Is this dereliction of duty accidental, or is there something more sinister at play?

There are many questions that must be answered, and so far the navy has answered none of them.

***

FREEDOM UNION STILL ON TOP, GRAND ALLIANCE REMAINS UNDERWATER

Sofia Farley, New York Times

June 23, 2039—The U.S. Navy and Air Force have finally released the official casualty totals for the Second Battle of the Strait of Malacca. While the good news is that no American (or Grand Alliance) sailors or airmen died, the bad news is that desperately few of the enemy were destroyed. Twelve stealth bombers sank one ship and damaged one more, facts that the French and Indians are laughing about.

Russian media has made much of the American war effort, calling us unpatriotic, unwilling to make sacrifices, and all-around bumbling fools trading on a reputation built in the previous century. American military members are caricatures in their press, and the bad guys in a blazingly popular series of comics titled *Heroes of the Russian Federation.*

Are they right?

In the latest crushing defeat, Britain—the dogged and plucky hero of the last world war—has lost three undersea stations in the English Channel. *Three.* To France, the old enemy who England made a career out of either beating up on or carrying into this century. But now the French have taken three mid-Channel stations, bringing the war practically to Britain's doorstep. This is the first blow close to home turf for any of the Grand Alliance, barring Australia. Is the nature of the war changing?

And will that change bring about more disappointing losses for the Grand Alliance? The team that won the last world war was expected to win this one, hands down, yet the United States, Great Britain, Australia, Canada, and allies are struggling against France, Russia, India, and the assorted small nations that make up the Union for the Freedom and Prosperity of the Indian Ocean. Japan, once a valuable ally in the Indo-Pacific region, is even contemplating neutrality after their drubbing in the war's opening acts.

One year in, it is becoming increasingly obvious that this is *not* a repeat of the Second World War.

Just last week, Vice Admiral Jonas Kristensen, Seventh Fleet's Commander, said: "The navy of today is very different from the navy of the last century. We cannot build a ship a week—or even a month. Modern warships and weapons are too complicated. Sailors take longer to train. Every loss hurts more. We simply need time to regroup and reassess."

Regroup.

Reassess.

These are not positive words to hear when the Grand Alliance has its back against the wall. By now, the question is *how long* this reassessment takes. If the Grand Alliance hasn't figured it out fourteen months into the war, will they ever?

"Ugh, these articles are such trash." Lieutenant Commander Stephanie Gomez slammed her tablet down on the wardroom table with more force than necessary. On second thought, she was glad it had a hardened case. Damn thing was expensive.

"Then why do you read them, XO?" Lieutenant (junior grade) Angelina Darnell grinned. Like Steph, she was in *Jason Dunham's* wardroom to catch a late lunch, in her case after getting off watch as officer of the deck.

Darnell was *Dunham's* Assistant Operations Officer, and in Steph's opinion, the ship's top division officer. It was a shame that she was due to rotate off in just three weeks, but that was war for you—people left faster than peacetime and promoted quicker, too. Angie would put on lieutenant next month, a promotion some whispered was in exchange for the eye she lost in the Second Battle of Sunda Strait.

Steph knew that wasn't true. Angie was a brilliant young officer, and she hadn't let losing one eye slow her down one bit. She'd been the first of her class to qualify on every required *Dunham* watch station, as well as several optional ones, and Steph was proud to mentor her.

"Better to know what the enemy is thinking." Steph popped a cold fish finger in her mouth and grimaced. She hated cold food, but an XO's work was never done, particularly in the mad rush to get *Dunham* ready after getting out of the shipyards.

Dunham's wardroom walls were still stacked high with old-fashioned paper logs and qualification documents, all a testament to the hurry to get the destroyer back at sea. Steph would need to remind the department heads to put their crap away, but she figured she could give them a day.

Though if the supply officer didn't pony up something better for dinner, she might just make it an issue at their evening briefing, Steph decided, eyeing another cold fish finger. No, it wasn't worth the disgusting taste just to get some calories in. She'd buy a candy bar from the ship's store or something if she got desperate.

At least they'd gotten through workups with flying colors. None of the inspectors had anything bad to say, which almost worried Steph, who'd grown up in a day where inspections were feared, and *nothing* ever went right. Then again, back then, workups were longer than three days, too, and they didn't dump you right back out with a carrier strike group twenty-four hours later.

But at least they weren't going into battle today.

"The enemy? C'mon, ma'am, they're just reporters." Darnell scratched short brown hair above her eyepatch, cocking her head. "I'm sure they don't know jack about ships, but officers have complained about that since the days of John Paul Jones and—"

An almighty *jerk* threw both toward the forward bulkhead, throwing a plastic glass of juice right out of Steph's hand. It splattered against the forward bulkhead as a loud screeching noise filled the destroyer's wardroom and *Dunham* ground to a sudden halt. Plates flung themselves to the wardroom floor, crashing and shattering while Steph clung to the table for dear life. Seconds later, the shriek of the collision alarm sounded over the 1MC.

"Oh, shit."

Rocketing out of her chair, Steph sprinted for the bridge. Paperwork demons were fought in your cabin, but an XO's place was on the bridge when a collision happened.

A terrible, tiny part of her prayed it wasn't *Dunham's* fault. That was the last thing their bedraggled ship needed.

"Where do you want me, XO?" Angie asked, right on her heels.

"Head to the bo'sun locker and stay on your radio!" Steph took the steps of the ladder two at a time. "I'll call!"

"Aye, ma'am!"

Steph threw herself up the four decks to the bridge, sailors diving out of her path. She spotted broken gear and a few injuries out of the corner of her eye as she sprinted up one ladder after another, and Steph cringed. But her job wasn't to deal with medical emergencies; her job was to get to the damned bridge and help keep the ship afloat. They had corpsmen to help the wounded.

And once she got to the bridge, she could make sure they were properly deployed, too.

The fun stuff was over by the time Steph reached *Dunham's* bridge a minute after the collision. Commander Kellner, the captain, was already there, his face gray with shock as he stared out the forward window.

Steph dogged the aft door shut, hating the way the hinges squealed in the eerie silence. Eyes turned to track her, but still no one spoke. Kellner didn't move, still staring forward as Steph walked up to stand by his side. She opened her mouth, but no words came out.

Steph's stomach did a flip. She almost wished she'd stayed in the wardroom. Then she wouldn't have seen *Dunham's* bow buried in USS *Nitze's* side, with water pouring into the other destroyer's innards as sailors raced toward the gaping hole, desperate to stem the flooding.

"What happened?" she breathed.

"We lost rudder control when we were coming into planc guard," Kellner whispered. His shoulders slumped. "At twenty-five knots, it didn't take long to hit *Nitze* when the rudder slammed over to hit the hard stops."

Steph frowned. "I thought it was supposed to fail amidships."

Kellner just shrugged. "Might be a computer glitch. Ship's old enough."

"You contact *Nitze* to ask when they want us to back out of the hole?" Steph asked. *Dunham's* bow made a poor plug, but it was the only one the other destroyer had...and keeping them together like this *might* stem the flooding.
A little.
"Not yet."
"I've got it, Captain." Steph grabbed a radio and went to work.

Rihaakuru Station, owned by Maldives, occupied by India

The marines were done with the cleanup, which meant that Vice Admiral Aadil Khare was free to inspect his new domain. Six strong weeks of fighting around the Maldives—all properly pacified, for the moment—had given India the gift of three new underwater stations. The leadership on this one, Rihaakuru, had learned from the now-dead station managers at the Olhuveli Resort and Mining Company and the legendary Alderman's Station. Rihaakuru's leadership surrendered without a fight.

His marines still spent two days rooting out *unauthorized* resistance, mainly from American and Australian business owners who didn't know when to quit. But Khare was content to wait. He had conquered three rich stations for his homeland—at least two of which he suspected they were likely to keep at war's end.Khare was not an idiot. No one would let them keep the Sri Lanka, not with the history in the area. Perhaps the world might wink at the Maldives, if India fought and won enough battles. But the Maldives were known for little more than excellent beaches and vacation destinations. Their riches lay in the surrounding waters.

"Admiral, do you have a moment?" Captain Kiara Naidu, his chief of staff, jogged to catch up with him as he walked past storefronts whose sullen owners glared at him.

Or perhaps they glared at his armed escort. He cared not.

"Always for you, Captain." He smiled. Naidu remained one of his best officers and firmest supporters.

"I received word back from the people we hired to approach Red Tiger Station," she said in an undertone. "Or more precisely, I didn't."

"Remind me again why we care about a station in the South China Sea?" Khare scratched his chin. "Wait—I remember something about technology. Is it the fusion dream again?"

"Confirmed to be reality by Pulsar. They've reached out to the U.S. Navy, though we don't know what was said," Naidu whispered.

Khare's eyebrows rose. "It is good we are closer, then. What happened to your team?"

"They appear to have died in an accident involving explosives." Naidu scowled. "A civilian submarine fleeing a pirate crashed into the underwater garage at Red Tiger Station and everyone inside died."

"How...convenient."

"It appears to have been a complete accident. We can hire another team, but it will take time to get them in place."

"Do it." Khare shook his head. "We cannot afford to let the Americans achieve submarine-size fusion reactions before us. It could change the course of the war."

"I will pursue it immediately, Admiral."

Southern Indian Ocean, steaming toward Australia

Command conferences on the carrier were Nancy's *favorite* activity. She liked them so much that she even *narrowly* preferred them to carving her eyes out with tulips.

But command conferences meant hopping a helicopter to fly over to the carrier—which was a lot less fun than it sounded like when your helos were small things designed to hunt submarines, not carry passengers—and then fawning all over an admiral whose claim to fame was trying to bomb ships that could move out of the way. Nancy had no problem playing nice when her boss was competent, but her increasing suspicions that Admiral Anderson had more ambition than tactical sense were making it hard to behave herself.

At least Captain Julia Rosario was back in the fold, with good old *Belleau Wood* steaming off *Lexington's* flank. Nancy almost felt at home when she slipped into the briefing room, though the bad old days with the *Enterprise* Strike Group weren't exactly ones she remembered fondly.

"Fancy meeting you here." She plopped down into the seat next to Rosario. "I hear you got nominated as our air defense commander."

Rosario chuckled and then leaned in close. "A little birdie told me that I'm here to make sure Task Group Two-Three doesn't try any more hijinks with the air force."

"Really?" Nancy's eyebrows rose. "Admiral Anderson's going to love that one. But...you're ten feet tall and bulletproof, aren't you? I saw you on the last promotion list."

"I've got three months left commanding *Belleau Wood* before I move down to the flag cabin and form a surface action group. Want in?"

"Are you kidding?" A thrill ran up Nancy's spine. "If you can spring me from being chained to the carrier, *Fletcher* is all yours. I'd be honored to fight by your side again."

Everyone knew that Julia Rosario—soon to be Rear Admiral (Lower Half) Rosario—was a straight shooter with nerves of steel. She'd held things together when Admiral McNally went to pieces in the First Battle of the SOM, and then she again inherited command of a task force at the Battle of Cocos Islands. Despite being desperately wounded—Nancy heard Rosario needed major surgery afterward—Rosario held the islands after the Australian admiral in command died. *Belleau Wood* spent two months in the shipyard after that but came out fighting with Rosario back in the chair. She then survived the Battle of La Perouse Strait and scores of smaller engagements, carving out more of a legend for herself with every battle.

Rosario was *the* rising star in the surface fleet. Like Nancy, she exited the First Battle of the SOM with a prestigious medal—though she'd won the first Navy Cross of the war—and she'd continued her upward trajectory since then. Now it was about to earn her admiral's stars, and Nancy would be damned proud to serve under her.

Rosario shot her a grin but couldn't say more before Admiral Anderson stalked into the *Lexington's* (CVN 84) flag briefing room.

Kristi Anderson was a tall woman, with dark hair, eyes, and skin to match. She was fit, too, which Nancy respected; in fact, she was pretty sure Anderson could break most of the staff in half without breaking a sweat. Rumor said she had a couple of black belts, and Nancy believed it.

"Attention on deck!" the admiral's aide ordered.

They all popped to their feet, but Anderson's eyes bored in on one target: Commander Todd Kellner.

"Do you care to explain to me what the *hell* happened with *Jason Dunham*, Commander?" Anderson snapped. "*Nitze* is still fighting flooding nine hours later and barely under her own power! Worse yet, they have at least twelve sailors missing so far and *no* combat capability like this!"

Todd sucked in a shaky breath. His face was drawn and pale, nothing like the breezy confidence Nancy remembered from department head school. They hadn't been besties there, but they'd been in the same tactical group, and Todd was fun to hang out with when she wasn't wrestling her daughters' active sports schedules. "Ma'am, as I told you earlier, we lost steering control while coming into plane guard station behind the carrier. The rudder locked right thirty-five degrees, and by the time we could regain control manually, we were too close to avoid *Nitze*."

"Too close to avoid." Anderson's tone was mocking. "Why didn't you have after steering manned, Commander?"

"There's no requirement to—"

"Clearly there was a need," Anderson spat. "One you didn't foresee." She crossed her arms. "But that's typically been a problem with you, hasn't it? It seems that you're very fond of the shipyard. Do you *want* to go back? Perhaps avoid the war entirely with your broken destroyer?"

"Admiral, I resent the implication of that remark." Kellner squared his shoulders. "I am prepared to take responsibility for what happened. I am in command. However—"

"*Were* in command. You're relieved," Anderson cut him off for a second time. "Whether I press charges against you depends on how *Nitze* comes out of this." She wheeled around. "Commander Coleman, is *Fletcher* prepared to tow *Nitze?*"

"We are ready if so ordered, Admiral." Nancy didn't like Anderson's tone *or* her heavy-handed actions, but Anderson was her commanding officer. "However, if I might make a suggestion?"

Anderson's eyes narrowed. "If you must."

"*Nitze* is a flight IIA *Arleigh Burke* and outweighs *Fletcher* by about a thousand tons. We can tow her if we have to, but another *Burke* is better suited if you want to make good speed."

"Pity my other *Burke* looks like her nose is broken." Anderson shot another glare at Kellner. "However, you make a good point. Captain Rosario, can *Belleau Wood* tow a *Burke* with a purpose?"

"I'll let my XO know to make ready, ma'am."

Nodding, Anderson twisted back to Kellner. "You'd better not need a tow after causing all these problems, Commander. I'm of a mind to leave your ship to limp home without an escort."

Pointing out that *Jason Dunham* wasn't Kellner's ship now that Anderson had relieved him was such a bad idea, but Nancy might've done it had a chief petty officer not slipped into the room and handed Anderson's aide a message tablet.

"Admiral?" The aide swallowed. "There's...been another sinking."

"Crap on a cracker, can today get any worse?" Anderson wheeled on her aide, and the young lieutenant cringed. "What ship?"

"USNS *Cesar Chavez* was sunk right after conducting an underway replenishment with *Knox*."The aide gulped. "*Knox* dodged two torpedoes, but *Chavez* went down. *Knox* didn't dare linger to rescue her crew. Range to sinking site is approximately fifty nautical miles. *Knox* is inbound our formation at best speed."

"Are you fucking kidding me? What good are anti-submarine warfare frigates if they let the goddamned submarine sink the supply ship?" Anderson slapped her hand down on the lectern, making almost everyone jump. "Is there no one with guts and competence left in the surface navy?"

Nancy glanced at Julia. They both chose not to answer.

It was a good thing they didn't. Anderson's tirade continued for another five minutes, after which she detailed *Fletcher* and *Belleau Wood* to corral *Knox*, look for survivors, and hunt the mystery submarine. *Jason Dunham*, broken nose and all, wound up towing her collision victim...though not very quickly.

The good news was that they rescued 103 of the supply ship's crew of 135. But despite two days of searching, they never found the submarine who sank *Cesar Chavez*.

Two days later, it became clear that the submarine commander *wanted* to be found. At least in a metaphorical sense.

`Captain Jules Rochambeau`
`@JulesRochambeau`
`Please pass my compliments to the crew of @USSKnox.`
`  I did not know a Constellation-class frigate could`
`  sprint away from my torpedoes so quickly! I am sure`
`  their shipmates on the sinking @USNSCaesarChavez`
`  were happy knowing Knox got away.`
`#Barracuda #submarines #war`

Chapter 10

Tilting at Windmills

The United States Naval Academy, Annapolis, Maryland

June bled into July, and July into August. Plebe Summer ended somewhere in the maw of those months; later, Bobbie Coleman couldn't remember much more than endless marching, barked orders, and eating faster than she'd ever eaten in her life. Life at the Academy was hard but not crazy, and the physicality of it was challenging, but not impossible. Containing her individualism and shutting her trap...well, that was a challenge.

Normally a sarcastic, clever, and ruggedly independent young woman, Bobbie quickly learned that those traits weren't valued at the Academy, particularly not in a plebe. Her company officer counseled her three times before the academic year even started, usually for outbursts aimed at upperclassmen who thought picking on other freshmen was fun. It wasn't enough to get her in real trouble, but she knew she'd made herself the target of more than one senior midshipman.

Bobbie didn't much give a damn.

"One of these days, your stupid little crusades are going to get you in trouble," Mike Corbin told her as they sat in the library one afternoon, theoretically doing homework.

Mike was a typical navy plebe: fit, with hair short enough that you could barely tell it was brown, and with brown eyes that enjoyed laughing almost as much as Bobbie did. He had freckles for days and wore glasses that were probably the wrong prescription; Bobbie kept hinting that he should go see someone about that, but so far, Mike hadn't caught on to the fact that the navy would pay for new glasses.

He'd also somehow become her best friend in the months they'd been at the Academy. Bobbie wasn't attracted to him, but they had a lot in common. The Colemans moved too often for Bobbie to get close to a ton of kids her age growing up, but even those she kept in touch with were nothing like Mike.

Most of them couldn't take her going full-bore. Mike laughed her off or talked her off the ledge.

Now Bobbie paused in the middle of folding a paper airplane. "Zhang was being an asshole. He knew Scarborough needed to look at that website for class, and he yelled at her for looking at 'inappropriate material,' anyway."

"You still didn't have to be quite so…enthusiastic about telling him off," Mike said.

Bobbie rolled her eyes. "I mean, really? How is studying war crimes throughout history an inappropriate topic? Correct me if I'm wrong, but aren't we wearing naval uniforms?" She made a show of looking down at her own chest. "Yep. Still navy."

Mike groaned. "I give up. I won't try to stop you. Never again. Not even for your own health and welfare."

"Good." Her sister Emily always said that whiplashing from irritated to cheerful was Bobbie's best talent, so she grinned. "Now, if only Zhang the Asshole would catch on to that."

"Midshipman *First Class* Zhang, Bobbie. He's got a rank. Do you really want to get your face torn off *again*?"

"I thought you said you weren't going to try to fix me."

"Fine." He rolled his eyes. "You want me to ask what you think of this evening's reading, instead?"

She heaved a sigh and used that time to make sure she had her expression under control. "It's going to be as depressing as the others."

"That's harsh." Mike frowned.

"What? Don't tell me you find them inspirational. I'd know you're lying."

"It's not that… I mean, maybe they are a little. I think they remind us of what we're doing. And why we're doing it."

"I guess so." But Bobbie really didn't *need* reminding.

Evening readings were a tradition the Academy started last year. When she felt fair, Bobbie supposed they terrible. Three times a week, their squad leaders picked an award citation to read—usually from the current war, but sometimes great ones from past wars. The idea was to give the young midshipmen something to strive for, an ideal to live up to.

However, Bobbie didn't miss the fact that so many of the citations were posthumous...and most of those were submariners.

Kurt Kins. Jane Phelps. Kenji Walker. Anabella Santiago. The list went on, and almost all of those who won the Navy Cross (or the Medal of Honor, in Kins' case) were *dead*. Everyone but Uncle John, really. Bobbie would have known the names anyway, because she burned to be a submariner, but listening to her squad leader recite how they died just tore her heart up.

She shook her head. Bobbie overheard two of their upperclassmen talking earlier, and she knew the story behind today's reading. Commander Rico Sivers had been a friend of her uncle John's, and rumor said he'd be awarded the Medal of Honor after holding off half the damn Russian Navy when they tried to invade the Mariana Islands.

The award would be posthumous, of course.

Squaring her shoulders, Bobbie tried to push the thought out of her mind. If she thought about it, Mike would ask, and if she told him, sooner or later, everyone would know. Midshipmen with both parents in the service were rare. Every company officer on the Yard treated them with kid gloves. Everyone worried about what would happen to "some poor kid" who had both parents die, and Bobbie would be damned if she'd tell the bastards that they needed to watch over her like sick mother hens. She could take care of herself without their interference, and she didn't want to be treated like she was fragile.

She particularly didn't want them to know that her father commanded a submarine, no matter how old it was. Bobbie knew what could happen. She hated the evening readings because they reminded her of the dangers her father faced every day. Her mom wasn't much better; she commanded a surface ship, and somehow Nancy Coleman was always in the thick of the action. Between that and the death rate on subs...

"You okay?" Mike asked.

"Yeah. Why wouldn't I be?"

"I dunno. You just looked like you were on Mars."

No one could ever accuse Bobbie of being slow on her mental feet. Or of being a poor liar. "Thinking about war crimes. And the rumors coming out of Russia."

"Yuck. Why would you want that crap rolling around in your head?"

History would call August 2039 the worst month of the war for Alliance submariners, both for the sheer number of boats sunk and how the war spiraled out of control. What had been a lopsided conflict became a losing proposition in August; French, Russian, and Indian submarines ran amok while the Alliance struggled, unable to find anyone able to carry the fight to the enemy. The best of their best were on the bottom, and replacements the boats turned out to be easier than replacing their commanders.

There were isolated examples such as Captain Ursula North, still the best the Alliance had, but when the British Admiralty sent her up to the Java Sea, there were few left in the south who could hold a candle to the best of the enemy. North performed admirably, clearing out the multitude of smaller nations' sub forces that who allied with the Indians, but where she wasn't, Rochambeau *was*. He wasn't the only threat, just the most dangerous.

The first kill recorded for Rochambeau in August was *Flasher*, commanded by "Lucky" Joel Bennett. Bennett's crew pinned that nickname on him after they escaped Rochambeau three times. The name stuck; within two patrols, everyone in the sub community caught on.

Unfortunately, Bennett's luck ran out on his fourth round. Whether Rochambeau deliberately targeted *Flasher* was still a matter of rumor, but the French legend certainly knew about the nickname. Someone mentioned it to a reporter, and the nickname was plastered all over the war-followers' Twitter accounts in a flash. Less than two weeks after that revelation, *Flasher* went down with all hands. Rochambeau tweeted about it four hours later.

Later that same patrol, Rochambeau took down HMCS *Windsor*, commanded by the Royal Canadian Navy's rising star, Florence Bergeron. The brand-new *Sea Tiger*, who just arrived in the Indian Ocean, took half her crew to the bottom with her, including Bergeron. Rochambeau also received a little credit for causing one of the more bizarre sinkings of the war, despite being in port at the time, getting sun in the neutral Seychelles.

But everyone knew that Jason Shea's *Silversides* had encountered *Barracuda* on their previous patrol—Rochambeau even tweeted to mock their escape—and the miss left Commander Shea rattled. He said he was fine, but no one missed the way his hands shook or his features went pale at the thought of getting back underway.

Still, no one expected Shea to drive *Silversides* straight into the teeth of the enemy, barging into the midst of a well-defended Indian convoy. He barely fired a shot and certainly didn't sink a single ship. *Silversides* went to the bottom with 140 men and women aboard. A blogger started calling it "Suicide by Way of the Enemy," and the phrase stuck.

Rochambeau tweeted that he wished that more Allied sub commanders would do that and save his crew the bother that sinking them required.

The odd sinkings didn't end there. Rochambeau wasn't blamed for *California*, only because no one knew who to blame. Naturally, ire landed on the commanding officer, Commander Darrel Richardson. An acquaintance of Alex's from Prototype, Richardson was straightforward and reliable—not the type who was careless enough to run his submarine headfirst into a seamount, which was the usual explanation when a submarine straight up vanished.

Someone must have sunk *California*, but no enemy subs were detected in the empty stretches of ocean *California* had transited between Pearl Harbor and her assigned station in the Indian Ocean. Her SUBMISS/SUBSUNK buoy never activated, and no last-minute signals were detected. There wasn't even a place to start looking. And Rochambeau never tweeted, either.

The careless submariner award of August 2039 went to Commander Brenda Vicar, who took *Narwhal* too deep fleeing Indian torpedoes and somehow survived the experience…only to smash her boat smack into an underwater mountain an hour later. Vicar was as lucky as she was careless, however, and successfully babied her maimed submarine to the surface. She only got a third of her crew off before a lucky *Scorpene* stumbled upon *Narwhal* and torpedoed her, but at least there were sailors alive to tell the tale.

Rumors said more than a third of *Narwhal's* crew made it off, only to be sent by the Indians to a Russian POW camp, but both nations denied it. Civilized nations followed the Geneva Conventions and reported prisoners' identities, and there had been no problems of that sort in this war.

Then Rochambeau sank an entire convoy singlehandedly, complete with old-style periscope pictures of all five escort warships going down, and the Allied sub community took another body blow. The French news media went mad, and even Americans talked about this arrogant old-world submariner with something approaching awe.

Even Captain John Dalton struck out in August; assigned the task of finding Rochambeau and sinking *Barracuda*, he was in the wrong corner of the ocean when the Frenchman sank convoy 35433. The resulting tweet made his squadron commander, Commodore Banks, rescind the mission and assign *Razorback* to her first boring convoy escort of the war, which headed John directly away from his enemy.

Admiral Rodriquez rolled his eyes, cursed Banks under his breath, and let it slide. He couldn't counterman every order a squadron commander gave, even the dumb ones. Besides, he had bigger fish to fry and another battle for the Strait of Malacca to plan—assuming Admiral Anderson didn't bite off more than she could chew.

Bobby O'Kane and Rose Lange raised another illicit drink to classmates on eternal patrol, wondering if they'd ever get back in the fight. Bobby, who owned the submarine's schedule as navigator, didn't mention that *Bluefish* had been assigned to escort Convoy 35433 until they were "too broken" to get underway. Maybe Rochambeau would have killed them, too. But maybe the presence of a submarine would have scared him off.

Meanwhile, Commander Peterson discovered another critical repair *Bluefish* required. They'd lived with a broken bow thruster through three patrols, but now it absolutely had to be fixed.

Alex Coleman studied tactics and chased paper dragons. By now, he knew his boat wasn't going to be assigned any important task, but battles happened if you planned for them or not. He'd be ready, even if his chance never came.

Ursula North gnashed her teeth and prayed for another shot.

1 September 2039, Pearl Harbor, Hawaii

He still wasn't used to the office.

Replacing the sinfully comfortable leather chair had been step one. Now Marco had an expensive ergonomic chair—he was an admiral, after all—behind the shiny wooden desk big enough to host a Thanksgiving buffet. He'd also started papering the walls with hard copies of every SUBMISS/SUBSUNK message from submarines under his command, a questionable decorating choice to be certain, but one that never let him forget the depth of his responsibility.

Getting arrogant would be easy in this gorgeous office with the high-rise view. Pearl Harbor was everyone's favorite homeport, and COMSUBPAC had one of the best corner offices in the world. Marco was cocky by nature, irritating, bombastic, and somewhat rude. But he wasn't about to lose sight of his goddamned job. In the good old World War II vernacular, he needed his people to *shoot the sonsabitches*, and then Marco needed to bring them home.

His phone chirped, and Marco picked it up himself. He hated having his aide screen shit; they always got things wrong. The carrot-topped kid was out, unable to keep up with Marco's grinding work ethic. So was his replacement. Aide number three was Lieutenant Commander Caralyn Lo, and so far, she seemed sturdier than the last two. Problem was that she was pregnant and due to go out on maternity leave in two months.

Well, Marco would enjoy her competence while it lasted.

"What's up, Freddie?" he asked his boss and counterpart.

Theirs was a weird relationship. He reported to COMSUBFOR, or Commander, Submarine Forces. That was Vice Admiral Freddie Hamilton. But COMSUBLANT, who was his Atlantic Ocean counterpart, happened to live in the same body as COMSUBFOR. Freddie had both jobs, which was a stupid consolidation move he thought the navy could do without, but since they didn't have someone competent enough to make COMSUBLANT if they just left Freddie with the top job, Marco kept his mouth shut.

"I heard rumors that the submariners out west are calling you Uncle Marco," Freddie said.

Marco felt his face heat. He recognized the historical reference as quickly as she did, and if the sub force wanted to call him Uncle Marco the way they'd called Vice Admiral Lockwood "Uncle Charlie" during World War II...well, hell, he'd keel over and die of constipation before he admitted he was embarrassed.

"Don't pretend you don't find it funny," he said a little more gruffly than he intended.

"I think it's adorable."

"Shut it, Freddie."

"It's also an honor, you dummy. You've gotten the Mark 84s out to the fleet, and you've started untangling the mess of patrols so they make *sense*. You've also stepped on the idiot squadron commanders who are hamstringing their captains into shooting from the stratosphere. You've earned, it, Marco."

"I know you didn't call me to talk about this." Marco couldn't take compliments. Not from her.

His boss, counterpart, and friend chuckled. "You're right. I need you to send a sub on a mission of questionable sanity."

"Well, that's sounding right up my alley," he joked before the admiral inside him could get up in arms.

"Is this line secure?" she asked.

"As much as it can be with hackers in the employ of every government. Only thing better is for you to fly out here or send it in fucking Morse Code. No one knows Morse these days."

Freddie laughed. "*I* don't know Morse, Marco."

"Well, then I'm the only one with a good goddamn of a prayer of understanding it, so we're all safe. Do it in Spanish and double confuse the Russians. Or Spanglish, if you prefer."

The moment of levity was needed, particularly with all five August SUBMISS/SUBSUNK messages right there on Marcus' wall. However, it couldn't last, so he stopped laughing and cleared his throat.

"What's your flavor of questionable sanity, Freddie? I'm not into sending someone on a guts-flailing, fuck-all death ride if there's no good tactical reason," he said. "Contrary to what the small-minded amoebas think, I'm not really crazy."

"I know you aren't, but I need a boat to go rescue some people from a station in the South China Sea."

"The fucking what?"

"You ever hear of Red Tiger Station? The big one off the coast of Taiwan."

"Yeah, I went there when I was XO on *Illinois*." Marco didn't enjoy thinking about how his old boat got sunk by that French dick weasel, or how Ursula fucking North had stood by and let it happen. Even worse, her tactics had been goddamned sound, and he couldn't even *blame* the woman.

Illinois had been a good boat, and he'd had a damned good time on Red Tiger Station, renting a racing sub and pushing it so hard that he needed the insurance to cover the damage. Damn, that had been fun.

"Pulsar has a research team there they need to pull off, and they've asked for our help," Freddie replied.

"Ain't that smack dab in the middle of the U.N.'s nifty-ass 'no-sail' zone for warships?"

"The CNO and SecNav have approved the mission."

Marco snorted. "Well, that's fucking nice for them. Doesn't change how much the U.N.'s going to shit a brick all over one of my submarines if they get caught."

"This is important. You know I wouldn't ask if it wasn't."

"Then stop tap-dancing and tell me *how* important. Who am I going to tell? I'm not married any more than you are, and I sure don't have a girlfriend or boyfriend to pillow babble with. The only relationship I have time for is with my desk." Marco giggled. "At least she's pretty."

"Oh, for crying out loud, Marco, *must you?*"

"Why does the navy need to pick up these *particular* big-brained idiots who weren't bright enough to get out from under a brewing war before it started?" he asked.

He could hear Freddie slumping in her chair when she sighed. "I told them you wouldn't sign off without knowing. Fine. Pulsar's cracked submarine-sized fusion reactors, and that's the team that's on Red Tiger Station. You good with fetching them now?"

"Fuck yes I am. You should've said that in the first place." Marco sat back in his chair and grabbed his stapler, disassembling it without looking down. "It's not going to lessen the consequences if someone gets caught, though, and that's a long-ass way from any help."

"It might be better now that the Chinese Republican and Taiwanese Coalition are a hairsbreadth away from taking Hong Kong," Freddie said.

"Ha! You really think an invasion quieted anything down? They landed Taiwanese troops in mainland China last week. No way is that going to *calm* anyone down. China's going to go berserk trying to push them out."

"Fair point." She paused, and he heard rustling in the background. "I was thinking you could send *Jimmy Carter*."

"That old rust bucket?"

"They took the spy equipment off her, but she was still designed from the keel up as a spy submarine. *Jimmy Carter* is tailor made to go places where she isn't wanted," Freddie replied. "And...as much as I dislike her captain, he knows when not to shoot. He proved that on Armistice Station."

Marco cocked his head. "You know the man?"

"An unfortunately lengthy acquaintance." Freddie groaned. "He doesn't know how to keep his trap shut, but diplomacy isn't exactly required here, is it? What we need is someone who knows when *not* to shoot, because we can't afford to start *another* war. Little though

I like him, I have to admit that he tried damned hard not to start this one. He's not a trigger-happy idiot, and he's a creative S.O.B. He'll find a way to get the mission done."

"Huh. I might like this cat, assuming he survives."

Diego Garcia, British Indian Ocean Territory

"Intelligence suggests that Rochambeau and other French COs are using satellite imagery to track and target surface ships," Lieutenant Commander James Harrison said during *Gallant's* weekly intelligence brief.

Captain Ursula North sat back in her wardroom chair and rubbed her nose. "Is it working?"

Anything that mentioned that French peacock made her blood boil; stepping on her temper was hard. But she had to be smart—or *smarter*, since that American bumbled into the midst of her best and smartest tactic—so she would sit on her fury like a good girl.

"Apparently, Rochambeau sank an American strike group in the GOA."

"I bloody hate that man." She sighed. The Gulf of Aden was right inside Ursula's current operating area, but of course, Jules would not be there now. He was too slippery. Ursula shook herself. "Well, two can play at that game, can we not?"

"Assuming we can get the satellite imagery, I can't see why not." Harrison spread his hands. "The Yanks are, of course, slow to share such things, but I imagine that fleet will talk to them. Is it worth the effort, Captain?"

"Beats letting him have a propaganda victory."

Ursula knew her mission. She no longer had orders like an average submarine CO, who had a specific target to sink or protect. Then they went back to port after less than a month underway. A year-plus of war had taught everyone that short and sharp missions were the best way to hit the enemy and survive.

But not for Ursula.

No, Ursula had a broader mission: hunt and kill Rochambeau and *Barracuda*.

But that didn't mean she couldn't take out targets of opportunity along the way—or, better yet, intrude on his spotlight enough that he came looking for *her*. She knew her old friend couldn't take not being on top, which meant he would hate it if she stole his thunder.

If she could reduce Rochambeau's media impact, that would be a victory in itself. The bastard was too handsome and too popular. While he lived, France punched well above their prewar weight. Of course, they'd built a lot of good submarines—Ursula was forced to admit that the *Requins* were the best attack boats in the world—but Rochambeau alone accounted for twenty-five percent of their success. His presence in the Indian Ocean freed up other French subs to lurk in the Mediterranean and snatch up critical stations there. Not to mention those stolen in the Channel! Thinking of those made Ursula see red. What remained of the EU screamed and waved their collective arms in protest, but France ruled.

The first step in stopping them was sinking *Barracuda*...so that was what Ursula would do. Then her sisters and brothers in the Royal Navy would have to step up and rule the waves once again.

Ursula left the wardroom wearing the same scowl that felt etched into her features these days. But she did not care. She could be a happy woman once her duty was done. Until then, she would push and push and push.

Her officers knew that and accepted it. The intelligence briefing ended soon thereafter, with all eyes on their new mission: match Rochambeau's efforts, and then best him.

Getting satellite access approved took almost twelve hours and two arguments with an idiot American air force officer. After that, it was just a question of filtering through the images until Ursula found a nearby target. By then, she was fighting back yawns and downing tea, but Ursula didn't care.

"This process is a bleeding nuisance," she said to Harrison as they watched the imagery of FNS *Amiral Louzeau* departing Port Victoria. Ursula had hoped for more than one ship; taking out an entire task force, a la her enemy, would have been delightful. But beggars should not be choosing. A top-of-the-line frigate was a good first target.

Harrison sat back in his chair and rubbed his eyes. "I think I prefer sonar."

Ursula grunted, glancing around *Gallant's* wardroom. The space did seem very small after three hours' sorting through imagery on a small laptop screen, didn't it? "This is longer-ranged, but it's slower than fucking molasses."

"Aye, it is."

But they had a mission now, so Ursula got her submarine underway from Diego Garcia and maneuvered into a waiting position. How had Jules done this without going insane? She was wasting days on this one ship!

Two more agonizing days passed before *Amiral Louzeau* stumbled into their engagement envelope. By then, Ursula was pacing like an enraged tiger, swearing at the intelligence team, who provided the images at the speed of frozen amber.

Harrison continued conning the submarine like a consummate professional.

Finally, Ursula could order: "Match your bearings and shoot, Mister Harrison."

Her team, aching for action as badly as she was, jumped into motion. *Amiral Louzeau* did not stand a chance.

Damn Jules Rochambeau to hell, she thought as *Gallant's* torpedoes slammed into the frigate. *Amiral Louzeau* went down with barely a whimper.

Gallant never betrayed her location, either, having used nearly real-time data from satellites to maneuver into the frigate's path. However, Ursula's raging headache told her that this four-day-long track was not for her. It might be "less" work, but she was not interested in playing this game again. It was far too slow.

Chapter 11

Casanova

5 September 2039, Red Tiger Station, the South China Sea

Seventeen sub racers flirted through the water east of Red Tiger Station, corralled by lines of red-and-green underwater buoys. The buoys were barely visible at this depth, but they had an installed sonar transmitter and they showed up well on the integrated systems in the racers. Every racer was required to be up in the local "Loop," or underwater connection between submarines. It monitored approaches and departures from the station, as well as races like this one.

"We should head back," Sam Yeung said from the back of Ning's sub racer. He smacked a closed fist on the fiberglass partition for emphasis.

"C'mon, where's your sense of adventure? The race starts in ten minutes." Ning Tang grinned and flexed her hands on the controls.

This little two-seater sub was a relatively new purchase, made with that second million-dollar bonus they'd earned for finishing a usable, small-sized fusion reactor ahead of schedule. Pulsar Power LTD already promised them a *third* bonus for building a portable model, and the Fogborne Research Team was on track to earn that, too.

Ning could afford to spend a little time in her toy. She'd earned it. And so had Sam, even if he was a worrywart. This was the first race held at the station in months, and she was determined to participate now that her *replacement* sub racer had arrived after pirates stole the first one. Ning was still waiting for the insurance payment from that racer, but she knew it would come through.

Thankfully, the bonus was big enough to stretch to a second racer. What else was she going to spend her millions on, anyway?

"I don't like the reports of piracy around here." She could hear him fidgeting with his tablet. "Ever since that sub crashed into the hanger, they've been getting worse."

Ning rolled her eyes. "No one's going to bother with small subs underway. We'd be impossible to catch."

"You don't know that. Aren't these things so expensive they already stole one from you?"

Her cheeks burned. "Yes. But not while I was driving it."

"News says pirates completely took over Green Tour Market. That station's only a hundred miles from us."

"C'mon, pay attention. You're supposed to be my navigator, and the race is about to start," Ning said, not wanting to think about pirates. She wanted to have *fun*.

It wasn't like pirates could really put a dent in Red Tiger Station, anyway. Last time, they'd rushed off the TRANSPLAT before security could get there, and for good reason. Red Tiger was a superstation, and any stupid and uppity pirates would get eaten for breakfast if they stayed too long. Sure, things were nasty in the South China Sea, but the racecourse just went around the station. It was clearly marked on her heads-up display, and so were the icons of the seventeen other competitors' speed racers.

One challenge of underwater races was that visuals were for crap down here, even at only five hundred feet. Even with lights, you couldn't see very far, so navigation was instrument-only. That took two sets of eyes, particularly when one of them was driving. Ning had good reflexes—you had to, if you were going to pilot an underwater rocket at up to ninety knots—but no one was good enough to do this by themselves.

Her speed racer was a DeepFlight Super Falcon IX, the latest and greatest design by the best maker of racing submarines. More like an underwater fighter jet than a clunky submarine, it was fun to drive, maneuverable, and faster than anything else in this race.

A fifteen-second countdown flashed onto her screen, the numbers blinking in green.

"Get ready."

Sam sighed. "I'd say I was born ready, but you'd know I was lying."

"You need to get out more." Ning laughed. "Have a little fun."

"My idea of a good thing to spend one-point-three million dollars on is *not* this glorified torpedo."

"Hey, what's money for if not to spend?"

"I'd say change the world, but we've already done that." Sam tightened his harness. "Why did I agree to this again? If I puke on you, it's your fault."

Ning ignored him and focused on the controls. The numbers kept flashing downward:

3

2

1

GO

Ning slammed the throttles forward, and the little green sub racer burst into motion hard enough to slam her back into her seat. Bubbles erupted around the racer as it roared through the water; its shielded propulsor was meant to cut down on cavitation, but even technology could only compensate for so much. Sam made an *oof* noise behind her, a cross between a whimper and a gasp, but she tuned him out. Her eyes were riveted on the electronic track, flicking between that, the surrounding subs, and the depth and power meters to the right.

Maintaining depth at speed was the Super Falcon IX's one real flaw. If she didn't keep a firm hand on the controls, or spent too much time looking out the windows, they'd start drifting up or down, and then—

"Damn it!" There was one other Super Falcon in the race, owned by Hans Albino, and while the Falcon VIII was faster off the mark, its steering wasn't nearly as good. Albino's boat nearly veered into Ning, who had to plane up ever so slightly when its shadow crossed her path. "I think he did that on purpose."

"Hard to tell. Hans is an idiot," Sam panted.

Ning goosed the throttle a little more to open up a few extra meters between her boat and Hans's. She didn't like wasting battery power so early, but if it got away from him, it was worth it.

"First turn's coming up. Brace yourself," she said.

"I'll puke down and not forward. Promise."

"So nice." Grinning, Ning eased back on her inboard engine by twenty percent. That would let her turn tighter, leaving Hans—and everyone else—in her dust.

"Got something big on sonar. So big the auto sensors picked up at range," Sam said.

"What kind of range?" Ning whipped the boat into the turn, cutting as close to the line as she dared. Going out of bounds was a disqualification, and she wanted to *win*, not end up splattered against Red Tiger's anti-collision nets.

She gunned the inboard engine back to ninety percent power. Battery was still good; cavitation was within limits. Not bad.

The little boat vibrated like a massage chair as she hunkered into the seat, her hands light on the controls. Man, this was heaven.

"Right on a kilometer. Max range." She could hear Sam's frown. "It's almost big enough to be a warship. Coming in fast. Depth...about four hundred feet."

Ning chewed her lip, concentrating on keeping in front of two subs trying to gain on her. "Red Tiger Control will keep them outside the course."

Another turn roared up; Ning reduced the inboard engine again and cut it as tight as she dared, gaining a half dozen more precious meters. Her closest competitors still couldn't keep pace with her, and when she checked on Hans and his fast Falcon VIII, he was stuck behind two Triton Speedsters who couldn't get past each other.

Her lead was up to twenty meters. Ning held back a smile. A lot could go wrong before the end of the race.

And yeah, that bit shadow of a sonar contact kept closing with the race, but who cared what a non-competitor was up to? That was Red Tiger Station's problem.

"One lap down!" Ning's console *dinged* cheerfully, marking her as in the lead. She was going too fast to see out the windows now; everything outside was a mask of bubbles and cavitation. "Two to go."

"You know, I think—"

The underwater emergency channel, always dialed into the speaker on her left, crackled. "All underway submarines around Red Tiger Station, this is the independently owned U-Boat *Destroyer*. Surface immediately or we will fire on you."

"Say *what?*" Ning sat up so fast she almost let go of the throttles, and the sub racer's nose dropped. Their depth sank dizzyingly fast, sailing from five hundred feet deep to six hundred before she could blink.

Twitching her fingers, Ning leveled the sub off two hundred feet above the ocean floor, just shy of Red Tiger Station's various pipes, power lines, and other apparatuses. She was off track for the race, but even fun-loving Ning knew that no longer mattered. Icy terror crept up her spine.

"You're going to surface, right?"

"No. That's probably suicide. And they'll steal my sub. *Again*."

Ning kept her eyes glued to the screen, aware that the slightest twitch of her fingers could send her sub crashing into a pipe. That would mean a messy death, probably quicker than messing with pirates, but still sucky. "We're faster than any off-market torpedo they can buy, anyway. Probably."

"We are?"

"Sure." Ning wasn't positive about that, but her ninety-knot sub was quicker than any torpedo she'd read about, aside from those crazy ones rumor said the Russians had. And any super-cavitating underwater rocket thing had to have crap for accuracy. "They're pirates. They've been here before to steal ships."

Sam made a strangled noise somewhere between a cry and a scoff. "And this makes them *less* likely to shoot us *how?*"

"Um, if they want to make money, they can't leave all the expensive subs on the bottom. Torpedoes do bad things to little submarines." She smiled with more confidence than she felt, keying up the quickest route to the hanger. "That's assuming they can target us. We're small. Really small. So I'll just sprint to the garage, and we'll hide until someone meaner comes and chases these pirates away."

"What if they don't?"

Perth, Australia

The last thing Bud Wilson wanted was a chief. Chiefs stuck their noses in his business and decided that STS1 Wilson was a "project" they were going to fix. They assigned him *developmental* tasks to keep him out of trouble and "build his career," then patted themselves on the back like no one had ever done that before. But the joke was on them; overzealous chief petty officers couldn't handle him. Whatever fixing there was to be done, Bud intended to do himself.

He'd gone to a couple of AA meetings, at least when he could make them. *Jimmy Carter* usually wasn't in port long enough for him to find one. They'd been boring, though, and Bud found himself thinking about fingerpainting on the ceiling, so he quit. He signed up for an online course, too, but it wasn't like they got a lot of bandwidth underway or were near the surface often enough—so that was toast, too. Besides, it was boring and stupid and just talked about the costs of drinking too much, which *Bud already knew*. But he'd tried. For real.

Bud's problem was that he wasn't really an alcoholic; he was just the worst kind of drunk. He'd always known that, even back on *Bluefish*, when he got in trouble about half the time he wasn't stuck on the boat on liberty risk. Back then, he hadn't had a reason to stop himself, because why behave like an angel when the captain was going to treat you like a misbehaving child no matter what? He figured he might as well earn his punishments. But Bud didn't drink all the time. No submariner could, though it was easier back on *Bluefish*, who was hardly ever underway.

Yet...Bud felt different now. Weird as it was, he felt like he belonged on *Jimmy Carter*. He didn't want to disappoint his shipmates. Even Lieutenant Unpronounceable was kind of cool once he got over being embarrassed by his sailors.

That brought Bud around to why he didn't want a chief. Unfortunately, the XO hadn't asked his opinion when he'd badgered SUBRON 29 into giving them STSC Bradley, so Bud trudged out of sonar and into control to meet the man.

Control was pretty quiet; they were in port, and it wasn't like anyone was on watch. The only people around were Velasquez, who was busy jury-rigging a new monitor in to replace a broken one over in fire control, and whoever-the-new-guy-was with her. That kid was so new he squeaked, and he jumped every time Velasquez asked for a tool.

Bud rolled his eyes and stuffed his hands into his pockets. Damn being the divisional leading petty officer. Why was this his job? Sonar was doing just fine.

That had to be the new dude. He wore a chief's coveralls, had dark skin, and was looking around *Jimmy Carter's* control room like it was Mars. Bud dredged up a smile and stuck his hand out. "Bud Wilson."

"Gus Bradley."

Bud's eyebrows shot up. Most chiefs insisted their first name was "chief" and were generally a dick about it. There were a couple of awesome chiefs in the navy, but he figured that *Jimmy Carter* was already tapped out. They had Master Chief Morton, who filled their quota all by himself, and Chief Stevens wasn't half bad. Doc Chester was awesome, too, but corpsmen were a different breed.

Bud crossed his arms. "Lemme guess, you've been warned about me?"

"Only about twelve times." Bradley chuckled. "Your reputation precedes you. Master Chief Baker on *Bluefish* and I go way back."

"Figured." Bud shrugged. "Welcome aboard, anyway?"

"XO warned me about you, too," Bradley said. "But then Weps pulled me off to the side to, um, *gently* tell me that the XO worries a lot because he cares. You catch my drift?"

Nah, Bud couldn't call the XO a neurotic mother hen to his new chief's face. He needed to let the guy experience Lieutenant Commander Kirkland a bit more first. Not that he'd have to wait for that opportunity with *Jimmy Carter* getting underway again in the morning for some supposedly quick convoy escort to Diego Garcia. "I've experienced him, Chief."

Hey, maybe this meant *he* wouldn't have to shield his guys and girls from the XO. There could be a silver lining to this chief business after all.

"You stay sober, and we'll be fine, STS1," Bradley said. "I don't give a shit about where you've been or what you've done. They sent me here because I didn't suck up hard enough to Commodore Banks when I was too busy trying to help get new torpedoes out to boats in the squadron."

"Oh, so you're a fuck-up, too." Bud felt a weight lift off his chest. "In that case, you'll fit right in."

Bradley laughed. "Don't tell the XO. I don't think he's caught on yet."

"Cross my heart, Chief. Cross my heart."

Red Tiger Station

"Well, that was fun." Ning tried to smile after they were back on the station, but Sam's glare made it hard.

"Yeah. Pirates stealing submarines. *Fun.* That's my word for it."

"I got you back safe."

Sam sighed. "I know. It's just…how long are we going to stay out here like sitting ducks? Pulsar keeps saying they'll pull us out if things get dangerous, but that was a real submarine out there. A *U-boat.* Seriously. Is this World War II?"

"No, the Germans are neutral." Ning shrugged. "I bet they didn't have actual torpedoes, anyway. It's a lot easier to buy a thirty-year-old U-Boat on the black market than it is torpedoes, and they didn't seem to want to shoot people last time they were here."

"I'm sure that'll make my parents feel worlds better."

"Your funeral if you tell them," Ning said. "I'm sure not telling my family." She didn't want to admit that she was shaken, but yeah, that hadn't been much fun. Maybe she wouldn't race her new sub again soon.

They snuck back before the pirates' allies turned up. While the bad guys didn't have torpedoes, they did have nets, which were great at sweeping up smaller submarines. Ning and Sam watched it all from safely inside the hanger; Sam had a friend at security who let them see the live video.

Until now, the war hadn't seemed like much of a threat. No country was going to put torpedoes into a station full of civilians. The French got *so much* flack over the civilians who got hurt on Armistice Station that no one wanted to repeat that, and while things were a mess in China, everything was pretty civilized on the ocean. It was the twenty-first century. No one made war on innocent civilians.

Except the pirates, apparently.

"They have to get us out of here. Fast." Sam swallowed. "Maybe Doctor Kim can call someone?"

"I don't know." Ning bit her lip, wishing she could disagree.

"*I* don't want to know what's going to happen if we stay."

"Me, neither."

---

7 September 2039, The United States Naval Academy

The steady mist of rain over the Yard that afternoon drove midshipmen inside. The boggy ground canceled most athletic activities, leaving Bobbie Coleman cranky, stiff, and bored.

"Back in the bad old days, I hear they didn't let plebes on the internet in Bancroft," she said to her best friend, poking at yet another website on her computer.

Mike Corbin was sprawled in her roommate's chair, with one foot dangling over the arm and the other on the floor, a position that rumpled his khaki uniform more than their upperclassmen would approve of. Bobbie's roommate was out with a study group, which was great with Bobbie, since they tolerated one another at best, so they had some time to hang out without the annoying chirp of *homework, homework* making Bobbie crazy.

Mike shrugged. "Probably just rumors. You can't even start doing homework without the internet. Next you know, you'll say plebes weren't allowed to have computers."

Bobbie giggled. "Maybe in the dark ages."

They laughed until Bobbie stopped scrolling on a newly posted video when it appeared in her feed.

"Check this out," she said.

"Is that Rochambeau?"

"Yeah." Bobbie felt her expression harden. She followed Captain Rochambeau on Twitter, of course. Every war junkie did. It was often the fastest way to learn that he'd sunk another American warship, and she dreaded the day she'd see *Fletcher* or *Jimmy Carter's* names in an arrogant tweet.

"Let's see what the asshole has to say," Mike said.

Grimacing, Bobbie turned the volume up. The video was mid-interview, in English for some reason. Did he *want* to rub his successes in? The bastard spoke good English, too, if accented, and he looked far too comfortable sitting in a big leather chair across from a pretty reporter. Rochambeau wore his dress uniform lightly, and while Bobbie couldn't recognize specific French medals, he sure had a lot of them.

"It's all about innovation in tactics," Rochambeau said with a smug smile. "He who is able to continuously improve will always have the edge."

"And would you say you have that edge, Capitan?" the interviewer asked. She was also French, blond and bubbly. She was drooling over Rochambeau a little too much, though he seemed happy to encourage that.

"*Bien sûr.* Of course." He winked, eating up her attention. "I would think my record speaks for itself, *n'est-ce pas?* I have spent one and a half years dancing around every Alliance ship or submarine sent after me, and *Barracuda* is still here. Even Lady North and *Gallant* can't catch me."

"Has Captain North tried? I hear she is the best captain the 'Grand Alliance' has to offer."

Bobbie didn't like the sneer in the reporter's voice when she said *Grand Alliance*, but she supposed that was the French for you.

"Lady North is an old...acquaintance. And I'm sure she's on my tail. In fact, I hope she is." Rochambeau's eyes gleamed. "I've already invited her to come out and play."

The interviewer giggled. "I don't think I saw that tweet."

"Oh, you wouldn't, *ma chere*. I just sent her an email."

Bobbie's jaw dropped. "He just *what?*"

"I...I mean, I guess that goes back to when the French and Brits were allies? So were we, I guess." Mike cocked his head. "Maybe some of our sub COs actually know this guy."

"He seems like a real jerk."

They listened to the rest of the interview—it was mostly just egotistical drivel—but Bobbie couldn't get the idea out of her head. Maybe her *dad* knew Rochambeau. Why had it never occurred to her to ask?

But she could. She could ask him the next time they talked...though definitely not with Mike around. She might be able to trust *Mike* with the secret that both her parents were deployed and in command, but the more people who knew a secret, the more likely it was to be found out in the Yard. Someone else would hear.

Nope, Bobbie was going to keep her mouth shut where anyone and everyone could hear her. Even if the worry was eating up her inside.

Chapter 12

Rules of Engagement

13 September 2039, Perth, Australia

Spring in Perth was beautiful. Birds sang in the skies, and after a rough winter—made though by losses more than the weather—even the seagulls sweeping down to steal French fries were welcome. Boats staged barbeques and pizza nights on aft decks, and music warred from one side of the pier to the other in the afternoons once inspections and repairs were done.

Fleet boats not in the readiness phase turned over to caretaker crews so their actual crews could get genuine rest and relaxation. Most were put up in the "Q" or bachelor's quarters on base, but some ended up out in town. All enjoyed pools, beaches, and good food in the Perth springtime, away from their boats and the war—even if it was just for a week or two.

Fleet boats got full on briefings at the SUBRON headquarters and time to rest between patrols. Has-beens like *Jimmy Carter* received an hour-long visit from Commodore Banks' snooty chief of staff, Commander Rusty Hawkins, after a ten-day convoy escort to Diego Garcia and an immediate trip back that left everyone exhausted.

What Alex wanted was a good night's sleep. Maybe then he could banish the pounding headache that had pursued him ever since Diego Garcia, playing sambas behind his eyelids and making him want to snap at everyone. What he got was a man who couldn't look further down his nose at *Jimmy Carter* if he'd been Pinocchio on steroids.

"The mission is to infiltrate the South China Sea without being detected by China, Taiwan, or any of the other forces present," Hawkins said to Alex's assembled officers.

Hawkins stood in *Jimmy Carter's* wardroom like he'd rather be anywhere else, glaring at the PowerPoint presentation on the wall monitor like it had murdered his mother. For all Alex knew, maybe it had. *Death by PowerPoint* was a common sentence in the navy.

The wardroom was packed with *Jimmy Carter's* officers and senior enlisted, everyone who needed to be briefed in on this sudden and insane mission. But people lining the walls did little to hide the age of the wooden plaques and old school, printed pictures hanging there or the way the flatscreen monitor on the wall was probably as old as Alex's daughter Emily. Smiley's wardroom was comfortable, not shiny. The blue vinyl on the chairs was worn, its seams splitting here and there. The couch in the corner was no better, though the junior officers swore age improved its comfort when it came to taking naps.

"What if we're detected?" Benji asked. "Last I heard, the U.N. passed a resolution barring warships from the area. I assume that includes submarines."

"If you are so...*unfortunate* as to be detected, the politicians will deal with the fallout. I imagine it may happen in a boat this old." Hawkins' shrug and scowl said what he thought of *Jimmy Carter's* stealth capabilities. "However, you are ordered to do your utmost to avoid detection and engagement with any of the various powers in the South China Sea. You are certainly *not* free to fire upon any of the belligerents."

"And if fired upon?" Alex asked. He'd read the orders already and found them a contradictory mess. Some politician with no military mind had written those rules of engagement, ordering *Jimmy Carter*—in the middle of a war—to only fire if fired upon.

Subs died that way.

"Then you may respond with an appropriate level of force."

Alex folded his hands and reminded himself to play nicely. Antagonizing Commodore Madison's right hand was a great way to get even worse treatment whenever his boat was assigned to SUBRON 31. Or maybe he'd get really lucky and Madison would take a page out of his previous boss's playbook and decide to explore decommissioning *Jimmy Carter*. That'd be just great.

"Care to elaborate on what 'appropriate' means?" he asked.

"I'm sure you'll figure it out when you're in the moment, Captain." Hawkins narrowed his eyes. "However, you may not fire on any unit you have not properly identified. Taiwanese vessels are not to be fired upon, regardless of circumstances."

"And pirates?" Licking his lips, George wiped his hands on the legs of his coveralls, crossing his legs to the left before changing his mind and re-crossing them to the right. "The news says they're all over the area, and several groups have purchased old *Kilo*-class diesels and U-Boats."

Hawkins sneered. "If you can't outrun or out-sneak an antique diesel, you shouldn't be in this business."

"I'm not saying we can't." George's nose wrinkled. "I'm just trying to cover all possibilities, Commander."

"The newest *Kilos* sold on the secondhand market were commissioned in 2000. Surely you can overcome a thirty-nine-year-old diesel?" Hawkins coughed and looked around the wardroom. "Then again, that's not much younger than this boat, is it?"

"And what about the Chinese *Kilos*? They're much newer." George's voice rose several octaves.

Hawkins didn't quite roll his eyes, but the way his narrow shoulders twitched sung an epic dirge about how little he thought of George Kirkland and his concerns. "You should not expect to engage Chinese units. I already said that."

"I'm confident we can remain in stealth until it's time to dock with the station," Alex cut in, glaring at Hawkins until he stopped trying to bully George. God knew, he agreed that George was being a worrywart, but the XO wasn't exactly *wrong*, either. Just terrified of his own shadow. "Smiley may be old, but she was designed for this kind of mission. I *am* concerned about detection while we are loading, however. You said we should expect a team of five and their gear?"

"Yes. The gear should be limited, I imagine. Pulsar wasn't specific." Hawkins gestured vaguely. "Whatever it is, I'm sure you have room on this giant boat of yours."

"We'll manage."

"We'll also be sending a team of recon marines to provide security during the onload." Hawkins' face twitched. "They are reasonably familiar with submarine operations, and no SEALs were available."

"Reasonably familiar," Maggie muttered from Alex's left, rolling her eyes. "Does that mean they know the end with the torpedoes from the end with the screw, or just that they know not to walk outside when it's wet out?"

Benji snickered behind his hand.

"How many marines should we expect?" Alex wished his orders had specified.

Hawkins shrugged. "A squad or so. We're still working out the details."

"We're scheduled to get underway in two days. The details *would* be appreciated," George said, and for once, Alex agreed with every word out of his mouth.

"And you'll get them when we have them, XO," Hawkins replied. The false smile he wore didn't fit his narrow face; it made him look like a nerdy shark, all primed up to stab someone in the back.

For a moment, Alex considered letting Hawkins and George go at it. There could be entertainment value in it, and if George made a fool of himself, which he would—Hawkins was an ass, but far from stupid—maybe Hawkins would tell Commodore Madison that *Jimmy Carter* needed a new XO. That pipe dream let Alex fly high for several long seconds, until common sense, and his ever-present headache, brought him crashing back down.

Unfortunately, George picking fights with the chief of staff would just make the boat look bad, and Alex not stopping them would make *Jimmy Carter* get a double-long stay in the doghouse. If there'd been a better XO available, Alex would've gotten him or her in the beginning...assuming anyone was motivated to send such a person to his old boat in the first place.

"Is there anything else, Commander?" Alex resisted the urge to rub his face; damn, he was tired.

"No, Captain, that is all."

Hawkins left without a farewell, but Alex didn't call him on it. Nor did he walk the chief of staff to the brow; Hawkins was an adult and a naval officer. Presumably, he'd been in a submarine before; the man wore dolphins, but no command-at-sea pin. Hawkins could find his own way out. Besides, Alex had a mission to plan.

Was this mission insane? Maybe a little. Part of Alex was reeling, because he knew he was being asked to sneak in a place that no one in their right mind would go. Avoiding pirates was bad enough, but a three- or four-sided civil war where he wasn't allowed to shoot anyone? That just opened up opportunities for a *real* enemy to hide among the chaos and shoot *Jimmy Carter's* ass off.

These orders were made of absolute horseshit. But arguing with Hawkins would've been as productive as doing a high dive off Mount Everest and hoping to find water at the bottom. Hawkins didn't outrank him and had never held command, but what he *did* hold was the commodore's ear. And even if Alex called Commodore Madison, who seemed to be a logical type, even if she ignored *Jimmy Carter* like everyone else, she probably couldn't do a damned thing.

It was damned obvious that these orders came from so far above his head that Alex would get a nosebleed searching for the source. With his luck, it was Admiral Hamilton.

Why did every terrible moment in his career have to loop back to her?

Alex shivered. He'd done the right thing on *Kansas*, and damn it all, he'd do it again. He just wished that it hadn't made the sub force's ranking admiral hate him.

He turned to his officers. "All right, people. Our orders are as clear as mud, but we know a few things. One, we're heading into the nautical wild west where the United Nations has *specifically* prohibited warships—which includes us—so we have to be stealthy. Two, our primary mission is rescuing a group of scientists. Three, we can't fire on anyone until they fire on us. Questions?"

"Yeah, why are these scientists so important?" Benji grimaced. "Sorry, Captain, but we're all thinking it. If we're going to break international law, it'd be nice to know why."

"Ours is not to reason why, Weps." Alex chuckled. "Let's just get the job done. Good news is that your weapons room is going to get a complete changeover—your fairy torpedo godmother has declared that we get forty-two brand new Mark 84 ASVs."

Benji whistled. "Hot damn. Screw international law, Captain, I'll take it!"

"I'll start working on where to put the marines, Captain." George was already scribbling on his tablet. "I assume at least two officers. The rest should be fine in the torpedo room."

"Thanks, XO."

"I've already started the nav plan, sir," Maggie said. Her eyes were on the laptop she always carried into the wardroom. "It's going to be a shitshow once we get into the South China Sea, though. There's chaos everywhere, and rumors of minefields, too. We'll have to be careful."

"Sounds like fun." Alex grinned. "I'll approve it as soon as it's done."

"And that leaves me." Marty leaned back in his chair, stroking the new mustache he sported. He was the very image of the sleepy engineer, right down to a coffee stain on his coveralls. "I'll have my boys and girls go over the boat from bow to stern—we'll work with Benji's sonar operators to comb through everything and make sure there's nothing that squeaks, rattles, or even thinks about getting loose. You'll have a quiet boat, Captain, if I have to get out and replace the sound-absorbing tiles myself."

Damn, Alex had a good crew. It was a pity that when the navy finally gave them a challenging mission, it was the mission *no one* wanted and the navy thought likely to fail. Dread coiled in Alex's stomach. The subtext was so obvious that Commander Hawkins might as well have shouted it: *Jimmy Carter* was expendable.

"All right, we've got a plan. Let's get to it."

Mid-Indian Ocean, not far from Diego Garcia

The formation of warships steamed quietly—too quietly. Oh, it looked good and every ship was in position, but every officer and sailor in the task group knew they were no longer the best of the best. Task Force Twenty-Three, once the lean destroyers of Admiral Marco Rodriquez's hungry "Little Beavers," had grown into Strike Group Twenty-Three, built around a nuclear-powered aircraft carrier, two cruisers, and all the escorts that demanded. It was as close to a modern fleet as the navy had, but the navy didn't call mobile groups fleets these days.

"*Fletcher*, this is Strike Group Two-Three. You are released to proceed on duties assigned, over."

"This is *Fletcher* Actual, roger, thank you, out." Grinning, Nancy put down the handset and turned to the officer of the deck. "Let's exit the formation and form up on *Belleau Wood*."

"Exit the formation, aye!"

Everyone on *Fletcher's* bridge was excited to leave Task Force 23, now known as the *Lexington* Strike Group. What started as a great team had disintegrated when Admiral Anderson took over for Admiral Rodriquez. It wasn't just the hairbrained scheme to use air force bombers that lost the Second Battle of the SOM. It was her leadership. Anderson yelled and carped. Rodriquez *led*.

So did Julia Rosario, which was why Nancy was damned glad to be the first ship to join the *Belleau Wood* SAG. Their surface action group would get a nifty name at some point, but for now, it was just *Fletcher* and *Belleau Wood* heading for Diego Garcia.

Nancy felt like a giant weight had lifted off her shoulders. She could *breathe* for the first time in months, and she finally didn't feel like an angry teacher was looking over her shoulder with every move she made. Was it embarrassing that Admiral Anderson reminded her of her third-grade teacher? Ms. Wayne had been downright evil, from hating the way Nancy held her pencil to the way her hair looked. Every meeting with Admiral Anderson—of which there were far too many—felt like her third-grade classes.

Fletcher wheeled away from the formation at thirty knots, cutting across *Lexington's* stern and falling in behind *Belleau Wood*. The cruiser's own turn put her on a perpendicular course to the carrier. Eventually, they'd come further right and head back toward Diego Garcia as the strike group went out to sea, off to do one useless exercise after another, until Admiral Anderson got another "brilliant" idea.

Damn, Nancy was glad to be done with that bullshit.

"All right, Ying, I'm going to go to my cabin and call the other half. He's getting underway tomorrow, and I'd like to have a chat before he goes underwater and doesn't come up again for a while," Nancy said to her XO. "Call me if you need anything."

"You got it, Captain." Commander Ying Mai laughed. "Say hi to the other Commander Coleman for me."

"Will do." Nancy wagged her finger at her bridge crew as they snickered. "Laugh it up, children. Sometimes Mom *does* want to talk to Dad."

Laughing, Nancy left the bridge and headed down three decks to her cabin, pausing to speak to a few sailors on the way. Despite the war, her people were full of smiles and laughter, joking easily with one another. They were hard at work, too; a pair of engineers were working on a valve as she walked by, while another two checked the installed firefighting systems leading into CIC.

Keeping *Fletcher* in fighting shape was a full-time job for everyone on board, not just her captain. Nancy was glad to see her crew attacking their tasks with ease, however; a tense and unhappy crew quickly became morose and despondent. And a crew that thought they were going to lose battles generally found the fastest way to die.

Making a mental note to schedule a steel beach picnic when they reached port, Nancy entered her cabin, kicked her boots off, and flopped on her rack. She closed her eyes for a moment, putting most of "the captain" aside before checking the clock and then dialing *Jimmy Carter's* captain's cabin from memory.

Timing their calls was always hard. Command would've made

it bad enough, but with a war on, she and Alex missed as many calls as they connected. But they tried to schedule times when the underway person could call whoever was in port. Sometimes it even worked.

Today they got lucky.

"Hey, babe." Alex's voice sounded tired but clear from a thousand miles away and across a satellite line. "How's the destroyer life today?"

"Oh, you know. Heading toward Diego Garcia, finally free of being chained to the carrier." Nancy snickered. "I think Admiral Anderson is still pissed off that Captain—sorry, *Rear Admiral*—Rosario stole *Fletcher* away. She was just a tad short-tempered about it at our last staff meeting."

Alex laughed. "Don't join me in the Hated by Admirals Club, Nance. The food sucks and the service is slow."

"Hey, you know I don't mind being wherever you are."

"I'm starting to think whoever told me you were the smart one lied."

Nancy giggled in a way she never could when she had her *serious captain face* on. "I'm sure that was someone back at Norwich, probably Janet, maybe Paul. You know how everyone at the Wick is. We're all shady."

He snorted. "You can say that again."

"So are you finally getting a break after that last whirlwind convoy escort?" Nancy asked, hearing the tiredness in Alex's voice.

"We're underway again in two days." He grunted. "I can't say to where."

"At least that sounds more interesting than your usual fare?"

"Hah. Something like that."

A chill ran down Nancy's spine. *Interesting* for a submariner usually meant dangerous, and while she knew Alex was ready to chew bulkheads down with his impatience and boredom, she…kind of preferred it when he was bored.

Nancy knew she didn't have much right to fret. She was the one standing into danger most of the time, who'd been in the middle of the missiles flying and people dying. But at least her destroyer was *on* the surface; Alex's boat would have to make it *up* to the surface to escape death. Just thinking of him trapped in a slowly sinking submarine always left her cold.

Alex, of course, always laughed and told her he was way more likely to die a quick death by explosive decompression. It didn't help.

"Maybe we'll finally cross paths," she said instead of fretting. In the year and a half of war, it was shocking how their commands had never encountered one another underway. Nancy looked forward to the day that changed.

"I'm going to say that's unlikely this time, babe."

"A girl can dream, all right?"

Alex chuckled. "Just don't tell me if there are hot guys in those dreams, okay?"

Alex headed topside after getting off the phone with Nancy, his mood considerably improved. Yeah, his mission was a tough one—maybe a little insane—but at least he had a damned excellent wife to bitch to when it was over.

Donning a hard hat, he eyed the crane swinging torpedoes down the forward hatch. Torpedoes were bigger than non-submariners always thought; a Mark 84 was twenty-plus feet long, and the warshots were painted bright blue. Were they supposed to be camouflaged underwater, or was that just to tell them apart from the white practice torpedoes? Alex shook his head.

He'd tried damned hard to fire two of the old torpedoes a few months ago, but that had worked out about as well as a sandwich made out of dogshit on a shingle. And now he got all the shiny new torpedoes along with orders not to fire them. Great.

At least the onload team was operating in accordance with SOP. Safety observers were posted, and every crane operator had a spotter. No one was goofing off, either, and the Australian team seemed to know their business. Spotting Benji Angler just aft of the sail, Alex wandered over to join him.

"How's the onload going, Weps?"

"Good so far, Captain." Benji grinned. "We've got all the old torps off, and this is the third Mark 84 to swing over. Even better, base weapons says we can have fifty-two of them if we can fit them."

Alex chewed his lip. "You still got your eight Harpoons?" He really didn't want to give up his longest-ranged ship-killing weapon, even if he wasn't supposed to shoot anyone in the South China Sea.

It was a damned long trip to *get* to the South China Sea, and no one in their right mind would tell him not to shoot the enemy on the way there. Alex planned on taking the southernmost route and avoiding as much of the civil war-torn waters as he could, but that put him in places where *actual* bad guys just might shoot at him.

He didn't enjoy admitting how much a part of him relished that thought.

"Yep, got them all the way up forward and port. Easy to load if needed." Benji gestured at the new sonar chief petty officer. "Chief Bradley and I crunched the numbers and looked at the design, and the weapons room is rated to fifty, so we can fit the extra six in. Safely, too. We've already got the attachment points."

Alex resolved not to ask about *that* mystery. "I'm not going to lie. I like the idea of forty-eight torpedoes. You loading eight straight into the tubes?"

"Unless you want us to pop any Harpoons in there, yes, sir."

He shook his head. "I think Harpoons may be the last card we play on this mission. It's much harder to figure out where a torpedo came from."

Benji laughed. "Damn straight, sir."

"Did anyone over at the weapons depot tell you *why* they were suddenly so generous?" Alex asked. After months of requesting the new torpedo, getting a full weapons room of them—and two extra!—was almost surreal.

"Not a peep, but I thought it was better to take the torps and not ask too many questions," Benji replied.

"Good philosophy." Slapping Benji on the shoulder, Alex wandered around the edges of the onload for a few minutes, chatting with sailors. He kept half an eye on the new sonar chief, who wasn't *supposed* to be so heavily involved in torpedo loading, but he seemed to know his stuff, so Alex didn't ask.

Not far away, Wilson and Vasquez laughed together while they waited for another torpedo to swing over from the pier, but since both looked sober, Alex didn't dig into that, either.

Later, when he got down to his stateroom and checked his email on the secure network, he discovered a two-line email from none other than Commander, Submarine Forces Pacific himself. Reading it made his eyes go wide and a chill race down his spine.

If I have to send you into a death trap, the least I can do is send you in well-armed.

Try to bring back the torps so we can send you out to do something pretty with them.

- Uncle Marco

COMSUBLANT Headquarters, Norfolk, Virginia

Freddie Hamilton rubbed her eyes and sat back in her chair. The design on her computer screen was pleasing to any submariner's eye, with smooth lines, lots of room for weapons, modern sensors, and a decent amount of space for expansion. It looked...okay. A decent starting point. In peacetime, when they had the leisure hours to study a project to death, she might even feel good about the design's status. But not now.

Sighing, she turned to look at her "I love me wall" and shook her head. Freddie let her eyes linger the wood-mounted crests of the submarines she'd served on—five in total, from her division officer tour to her last command on board USS *Columbia*—to the pictures mounted beside them. The matting around each was signed by her fellow officers from each boat, by friends who had once been family.

She pinched her nose. Freddie had lost touch with some of those friends, and others—like Jay Michaels, who served as a division officer with her and Marco Rodriquez—had died in the early days of the war. None of them had been in submarines...but plenty of the officers they trained had.

No, this wouldn't do.

Fortunately, Freddie had this number on speed dial. Captain Andrea Jimenez picked up on the second ring, complete with the sizzle of something cooking in the background. "Good morning, Admiral."

"Hi, Andrea. Working from home, today?"

"Kiddo's sick, but the line's secure." She could hear the smile on the other end. "You calling about the NSSN?"

"Right in one." Freddie chewed her lip.

Andrea Jimenez was the navy's rising expert on submarine design. Like Freddie, she started in attack boats, but Andrea took an off-ramp toward two master's degrees and a PhD in naval architecture. Now, she worked as the navy's rep on the team designing the next generation nuclear attack submarine, knee deep in Electric Boat's plans. Andrea was the one naval officer who Freddie trusted to get the design right, because she was smart, capable, and took no bull from anyone.

"You have doubts," Andrea said.

"Well, it looks a lot like a *Seawolf*, Andrea."

"That's because we threw the *Cero* specs out with the bathwater and went back to our sub-killing roots. I know money killed the *Seawolf* program decades ago, but man, they were built to hunt other boats like nothing else we've ever made."

Freddie frowned at her rapidly cooling breakfast sandwich. "The spec-ops capabilities of the baseline *Ceros* and *Virginias* have proven very useful over the years."

"You're sounding like an admiral. About one in twenty boats use 'em. We did a survey of all active attack boat COs."

"That few?"

"For certain. War changes the rules, Freddo. What they need is more torpedo tubes, a larger weapons room, better fire control/sonar integration, more speed, and better stealth. Oh, and not that broke dick bow thruster from the early *Ceros*."

"That's the wish list of every sub captain to ever submerge." Freddie rolled her eyes, staring up at the ceiling and wondering if she was the only sane submariner left alive. She'd never sell a six-billion-dollar boat to Congress, and that was what a modern *Seawolf* would cost. She could do math.

"Boss, if we're not creating a warfighting boat, what the hell am I here for?" Andrea asked. "We stripped out the big SEAL locks and left the vehicle connections. Popped in a huge weapons room and expanded to eight tubes. We did keep the vertical launch system, but it's optimized for Harpoon II, the Long Ranged Strike Missile, Evolved Sea Sparrows, or even Standard Missiles. You can put a Tomahawk in there, too, but it's a waste."

"You're putting ESSM on a *submarine*?"

"Why not? A close-in missile that can target air or surface targets increases a commander's targets tenfold."

Sticking her elbows on her desk, Freddie rested her chin on her folded hands and let herself imagine. Missile warfare was relatively new for American submarines: they could shoot at land targets (with Tomahawks) or surface targets (with Harpoons). Lucky subs got LSRAM, which had a longer range than Harpoons and could shoot a surface target further out *if* a submarine could track it. But that was it.

Aircraft—either helicopters or fixed-wing aircraft—could air-drop torpedoes and ruin a submarine's day. Both types carried sonobuoys, and some helicopters carried dipping sonar or magnetic anomaly detectors, which let them find a submarine *without* being inside their element like another submarine. That meant a sub couldn't shoot back when a torpedo dropped out of the sky.

Unless Andrea had her way.

Her instinctive reaction was to defend the *Ceros*; Freddie had commanded one, and they were damned good boats. But it was a different world now. War needed submarines optimized for killing other submarines.

Spying and special operations were nice abilities to have...but they had *Ceros* for those missions, didn't they? *Parche* in particular.

"All right," she sighed. "If you're confident—and E.B. is, too—I'll push this."

"I'd go to sea in her, ma'am."

"That's good enough for me." Freddie paused. "You know, we might have a new reactor design for you... Can you make that section modular for construction?"

"Easy enough. That's how we've built boats for decades. Besides, we won't go to final design and keel laying for several months, even with the war to speed things up."

"More's the pity." Freddie might not paper a wall with SUBMISS/SUBSUNK messages, but that didn't mean she forgot them.

"There is one other thing. Some Department of Defense group keeps bothering Electric Boat with a design for a *diesel* boat, if you can believe it." Andrea chuckled.

"A *what*?" Halfway to finally taking a bite of that breakfast sandwich, Freddie almost choked on thin air. "The last diesel boat was laid down in 1957!"

"Undersecretary Fowler is really pushing it."

Freddie's stomach rolled, and she dropped her sandwich, remembering the coward she'd been stuck on Armistice Station with. "I know the man."

"He's very eager, man. Doesn't know when to shut up in meetings." Andrea coughed. "But seems to have friends in high places—or thinks he does, anyway."

"How...exciting."

It was time for Freddie to prepare for a different kind of war, wasn't it?

Chapter 13

That Rock and a Hard Place

14 September 2039, Perth, Australia

The next day—right at reveille, which came damned early after a torpedo onload that lasted past one in the morning—a knock came on his stateroom door.

Groaning, Alex squinted at the clock and wondered why in the world anyone in his crew was up when he'd put out the word that work wouldn't start before ten. "Yeah?"

George slipped in before Alex could even sit up.

"Captain, I don't know where to put all their gear." George was actually twisting his hands as he fidgeted.

Alex stared at him, blinking sleep out of his eyes and thinking longingly of sticking his head under the pillow. "Whose gear?"

"The marines, sir. They're here."

"Put it in the special forces locker. We still have one of those, don't we?" Alex thought hard about what gear had been stripped when the navy decided *Jimmy Carter* was no longer their super-secret spy submarine. "It should be plenty of room for what, twelve marines?"

"Thirteen. And there are *three* officers, sir. We expected two."

Biting off a groan was so hard Alex felt like he should win a medal for the effort. "Just stow it in the locker. And we have room for three extra officers if the senior one rooms with you."

"Oh. Of course, sir." George nodded convulsively. "I'll get on that."

He blinked, finally seeming to notice that Alex was still under a blanket. "Did I wake you, sir?"

"Yes, and I'm a damned ogre when I haven't had coffee, so if you'd see if there's a pot on in the wardroom on your way out, I'd appreciate it."

"I'll get right on that, Captain!"

George vanished, leaving Alex wishing he dared go back to sleep. But it was zero-six-thirty. Four hours was enough sleep, right? He'd certainly survived on worse.

Swearing under his breath, Alex heaved his legs out of bed and grabbed his uniform. It was time to greet some marines.

But coffee first.

Otherwise, they would *not* like who they met.

Mid-Indian Ocean

The transit had been quiet so far, allowing *Fletcher* to catch up on some much-needed training. Being chained to an aircraft carrier meant serving the carrier's needs, which usually left *Fletcher* in plane guard. That position was close behind the carrier, canted slightly off to one side in case an aircraft crashed on landing and dumped their pilot in the drink. It seemed like a simple job, but driving so close to an unpredictable and *large* ship took a lot of concentration on the part of the bridge team. Particularly when that carrier was *Lexington*, who was known for forgetting to call in her course changes and sudden speed changes.

There was a legendary story about how *Lexington*, during unannounced engineering drills, put on a full astern bell and almost slammed right into *Belleau Wood*. Her captain hadn't apologized, either; instead, he complained to Admiral Anderson when *Belleau Wood* left her assigned station to *avoid getting hit* by a hundred thousand-ton carrier.

Anderson, predictably, blamed *Belleau Wood*. Then-Captain Rosario took the tongue lashing like a professional, and her ship protected *Lexington* in a surprise skirmish the next day...by steaming so close to the carrier's starboard side that sailors could toss each other ballcaps. Which, sailors being sailors, they did. During the battle.

Anderson couldn't exactly complain about *Belleau Wood* shooting down a dozen missiles trying to eviscerate *Lexington*, but Nancy suspected that was one of the reasons she was so happy to see the last of Captain Rosario and her cruiser. Their prickly admiral didn't like being overshadowed, and she sure didn't like when someone did it with sass.

Now-Admiral Rosario wasn't so cantankerous, which was why *Belleau Wood* and *Fletcher* now steamed in a very loose formation, both catching up on training, morale activities, and sleep. Neither knew what awaited them after their upcoming stop for fuel and weapons in Diego Garcia, so now was the time to catch up.

Nancy's poison of choice was an amazing e-book titled *Around the Yellow Bend*, which she was three-quarters of the way through and eager to finish. Unfortunately, a call from CIC interrupted her when the heroine was *just* about to find out who the murderer was...so Nancy put her e-reader down and hurried to *Fletcher's* Combat Information Center.

The hum of activity in CIC was a little higher than usual; Nancy could almost taste the tension in the air when she walked in. But her crew was experienced, bloodied by too many battles. They were attentive, but no one was frazzled yet.

"What do you have, STO?" she asked as she walked past two rows of consoles to get to the front table. Chief Warrant Officer Anna Nagel was *Fletcher's* Systems Test Officer and had the watch. She was a hardened prior enlisted sailor who earned her stripes the hard way—by earning every rank from deck seaman to master chief petty officer and then into the officer ranks. She was *Fletcher's* resident expert on the Aegis Weapons System, and their second best tactical action officer.

"We've got something on the SHARK." Nagel fiddled with her glasses. "Not sure if I believe it or not. The passive systems on that thing are...well, not exactly something I'd trust my mother's life with."

Nancy resisted the urge to chuckle as she dropped into the seat at his right. "You say that about everything on the SHARK."

"No shame in telling the truth, ma'am. This so-called sub-*hunting* drone is more like a sub giant neon *attraction* blinking in the water. It's usually so loud that it leads them right to us."

SHARK was one of the newest systems the navy had saddled *Fletcher* with. One of the downsides of getting cut loose from the carrier was that their surface action group now became the testbed for every gem the good idea fairy dreamed up, and SHARK—which was nowhere near as dangerous as the creature it was named after—was the latest.

Theoretically, SHARK was an underwater sub-hunting drone. It had active and passive sonar and could use both away from the ship deploying it, both widening the search envelope and disguising the ship's location. Theoretically.

The idea was to build some sort of "wall" between surface ships and enemy subs, a defense that was sorely needed. Enemy boats sank surface ships like *Fletcher* without even blinking, and Nancy liked anything that helped protect *Fletcher*. Well. She liked anything that *worked*. The jury was still out on SHARK, but its verdict didn't seem like it was going to be positive.

She sighed. "I thought we were keeping the sucker at least ten nautical miles away because of that."

Nader scowled. "Eighteen today. That's why I can't tell you what the hell it's listening to. Stupid thing is on the fritz again. Might be a reciprocal bearing, might be a sub right up our ass."

Nancy dropped into her chair, eyes narrowing. "You think it's a real contact?"

"The problem is I don't know, ma'am. I hate kicking the can upstairs, but this one's your call. SHARK says there's a contact—though it can't decide where—and our organic sonar can't pick it up. Something's fishy."

"I guess this is why they pay me the big bucks, huh?" Nancy reached for the phone for the bridge. It was time to start sub hunting—

"TAO, Captain, OSS, I've got something here," the optical site operator reported. "Looks like a periscope, maybe? Could be a log?"

"Put it on the large screen!" Nancy ordered. The OSS, or optical site system, was a huge, high-res camera mounted near the top of *Fletcher's* mast. It gave the destroyer a set of electronic eyes that could zoom in better than any lookout with binoculars. And it was particularly useful in sub hunting. Any surface warfare officer could share the weird fact that most submarines were spotted visually, even in this technological age.

Granted, technology helped the good old mark one, mod zero eyeball here. That optical site system let an operator spy a periscope ten miles off the starboard side, even when only a few feet of it protruded above the waves.

The image blinked onto the large screen display in front of Nancy's console. It was a zoomed-in view of the ocean's surface in brilliant full color, shown on a hundred-inch vertical screen. The operator slewed the screen to starboard, skipping the view over the surface until it stopped on a vertical, black, pipe-like object sticking out of the water.

It might be a log. Or a telephone pole. Nancy had tracked both; there was no shame in prosecuting every contact. She squinted.

"TAO, OSS, periscope silhouette is a rough match to either a Russian *Yasen* or a *Virginia*-class," the optical site operator said over the internal net.

"Any *Virginias* in a patrol area around here?" Nagel asked.

"TAO, OSS, negative. No patrol areas around here at all."

Nancy grabbed a headset and stomped on the foot pedal to speak before Nagel could reply. "Bridge, Captain, set general quarters and launch the ready helo."

"Bridge, aye!" the officer of the deck replied.

A whirlwind of activity surrounded Nancy as her crew rushed to battle stations, but she ignored it. Her crew formed a well-oiled team now; they worked together seamlessly to ready *Fletcher* for battle. Even the newest members, brought on board during their last port visit, had survived one battle by now. They were all veterans. No one doubted one another, and everyone knew where they belonged on the watchbill.

No one complained about being woken up by the general alarm. The cooks cursed when their lunch preparations were interrupted, but they cooled and stowed hot pans quickly, changing over to cold cuts and paper plates. Everyone else on board donned their flash gear, special fire-retardant gloves and mask worn only at general quarters, and settled in for a good fight.

The likelihood of this submarine being an ally was small; friendly submarines advertised their presence to avoid friendly-fire incidents. Only enemies snuck up on you like this. Nancy's heart did a familiar pitter-patter, but her hands were rock steady. "TAO, Captain, put a datum on the periscope and spin up an ASROC."

"TAO, aye, break—the sonar bearing matches what SHARK holds," Nagel replied. "Merging tracks."

"Captain, aye."

Fletcher rolled into action, turning toward the threat and preparing to face off with an enemy submarine. Within minutes, her ready sub hunting helicopter was in the air, roaring across the waves to hover over the location of the enemy submarine. Meanwhile, *Fletcher's* CIC computers computed the solution and readied an Anti-Submarine Rocket Torpedo for launch.

The ASROC was just a precaution, of course. *Fletcher's* first line of defense was her MH-60 helicopter, which could detect, prosecute, and engage a submarine—all without the risk a surface ship faced when closing the distance to a submerged contact. Nancy's lip curled. Part of her disliked the fact that aircraft were better sub killers than ships...but she was a practical woman.

And she sure as shit wasn't going to trade her pride for her crew's lives. Not today.

"Longbow one-zero-eight closing on contact," the air controller reported. "Periscope sighted."

Every nerve in Nancy's body felt alive, like she was an arrow strung to a bow and ready to fire. This was both the best and the worst moment of a battle, when *Fletcher* hung, suspended in time, not knowing which way the enemy would twitch.

"Longbow one-zero-eight dropping MAD."

MAD was the helicopter's magnetic anomaly detector, which would feed track information to the aircraft and the destroyer. That way, if the helo didn't drop a torpedo on the sub's head and kill it, *Fletcher* could launch that ASROC and do the trick.

Nancy itched to give the order. *Fletcher* was close enough to this contact to give her the chills. Eighteen miles was a little farther than most subs like to shoot. Only conversations with Alex left her at *all* confident about that fact, but her husband wasn't an expert on Russian boats. Besides, a *Yasen*-class boat was faster than her destroyer.

Never mind the ramifications of a Russian boat being so damned close to Diego Garcia. Diego Garcia was the Alliance's last bastion in the mid-Indian Ocean and the only thing that kept the nearby underwater stations and small islands safe. Half the reason so many damned battles were fought over Christmas Island was because the Indians wanted to cut around behind Diego Garcia, and—

"Captain, ASTAC, Longbow one-zero-eight reports good track!" the air controller said. "Lining up for attack run now!"

Nancy opened her mouth to acknowledge the report when a voice blared out of the loudspeaker to her right. "*O'Bannon*-class destroyer, this is *Kansas* calling you on Navy Red, over."

"What the—" She jerked upright, reaching for the radio circuit's handset. But she never got a chance to speak.

"*O'Bannon*-class destroyer, this is *Kansas* Actual," another voice said. This one was clipped and angry, each syllable rolling out of the crackling crypto dance like an approaching freight train. "Call your fucking helo off before the entire neighborhood knows where I am and I sink you in retaliation, over."

"For fuck's sake, that man sounds like someone pissed in his Wheaties," Nagel muttered. She still stood behind the TAO console, having just turned over the watch to her relief, who just shook his head.

Lieutenant Commander Davud Attar was the combat systems officer and had heard far worse out of Nagel. Now he keyed the microphone on the internal net. "ASTAC, TAO, instruct Longbow to hold fire."

"ASTAC, aye."

No one questioned. Everyone heard that obnoxious, self-important voice booming out of the speaker. But only Nancy knew who it belonged to.

She'd never met Chris Kennedy. By the time the bastard took over *Kansas*, the boat was on deployment. Three-and-a-half months later, Kennedy threw Alex under the bus for *Kennedy's* arrogant mistakes. Part of Nancy really wanted to meet the prick in a dark alleyway. Or maybe just a bar where the music pounded loud enough to drown out violence.

Lips curling, Nancy bit back a swear. She couldn't have any of those things. She had to be professional, because she was the damned captain.

"You want me to answer that before he shoots us, ma'am?" Nagel asked.

She snatched the Navy Red handset. "I've got it." Nancy took a deep breath and put her best Captain Face on. Her eyes darted down to the tactical plot, and then Nancy's smile turned real. "*Kansas*, this is *Fletcher* Actual," she said. "I apologize for my helicopter, but I didn't see you come up in Link when you approached the surface, over."

"*Fletcher* Actual, this is *Kansas Actual*," Kennedy said, and Nancy didn't miss the stress he put on the last word. No, he hadn't missed her little insult, had he? She wasn't sorry. "Our purpose in this area is classified, as all submarine operations are. We do not come up in Link unless necessary. Clear your helo away from my position immediately."

His last request was the only reasonable part of that diatribe, so Nancy waved a hand at Attar, who passed the order along for Longbow to return home to *Fletcher's* deck. Then she lifted the handset again.

"*Kansas*, this is *Fletcher*, perhaps my understanding of submarine operations is incomplete, but I received a briefing of all sub stovepipes and operating areas along our course, and you are not inside one of them, over."

Kennedy either thought she was an idiot or that he could bamboozle her. Unfortunately for him, Nancy was both married to a submariner and liked to read tactical memos. She knew for a fact that subs weren't supposed to surface without coming up in Link outside of specific operating areas. There was a war on, and that meant a lot of people—her included—were inclined to shoot first and ask questions later.

No one really wanted friendly fire incidents, but a stupid sub took a lot more risks than a smart one. Coming up in Link meant sharing their track location with other Alliance ships in the vicinity, which in turn meant those ships wouldn't sink the submarines. Win, win, in Nancy's view.

"You have no idea what my orders are, over."

"I can wager a decent guess that they weren't to run tracking drills on American warships in route to Diego Garcia," Nancy replied. "Over."

Because she *was* married to a submariner, Nancy could guess what the idiot was doing. Why was he running tracking drills on her ship and then coming to periscope depth like it was the Second World War? Ego, maybe. Or boredom. Nancy didn't care.

A long silence followed, so she decided to fill it.

"*Kansas*, this is *Fletcher*. I've recalled my helo and will proceed on duties assigned once recovery operations are complete." There was no reason to tell him about SHARK if he hadn't noticed it; Nancy might be biased, but she wasn't counting on *smart* out of Chris Kennedy. "I recommend *not* running your tracking drills on the cruiser twenty miles astern of me. *Belleau Wood* is likely to drop an ASROC on you before you can blink, and that would suck for everyone, don't you think?"

Julia Rosario might be an admiral, now, but her replacement—her former executive officer—was no dummy. And he was just as quick off the mat as Julia.

Not that Nancy wouldn't warn *Belleau Wood*. But it was nice to jerk Kennedy's tail a little. The idiot deserved it. Who played stupid games like this during wartime? Did he *want* to get his ass shot off?

She'd only be too happy to oblige if there weren't another hundred and twenty-some-odd other unfortunate souls onboard *Kansas,* many of whom Alex still liked.

Plus *Kansas* was a goddamned national asset that the U.S. still needed. Damn this idiot.

The long pause finally ended with Kennedy's static-filled snarl: "This is *Kansas* Actual. Roger. Out."

"Captain, OSS, periscope's gone sinker," the optical site operator said.

"Captain, aye." Nancy turned to face an astonished Attar and Nagel. "Well, that was a productive afternoon, wasn't it?"

"Remind me to never get on your bad side, ma'am." Nagel grinned.

"Do you know that fellow, Captain?" Attar asked more quietly.

"Nope." Nancy sat back in her chair. "Never met him. Secure from general quarters."

Fletcher eased back into her normal underway routine within ten minutes, recovering her helicopter shortly thereafter. Meanwhile, Nancy picked up a different phone, called her admiral, and told her about stupid submarine captains.

She told Rosario the entire story, trusting her boss not to blame Nancy for being biased when Kennedy was so stupid. Rosario laughed and offered to track *Kansas* on active sonar until Kennedy bled from the nose.

Not that they'd give their positions away like that. Sonar that went out came back, and everyone around you could hear it. Still, it was a nice thought.

Red Tiger Station, Arrival Terminal

Her colleagues called her *Rani*, though that wasn't her name. She didn't use her own name professionally and never would; in her line of business, doing so risked everything. Still, a nickname referring to the legendary Rani Durgavati was the highest compliment. She was no sixteenth-century Indian queen and her enemies were not the Mughal, but Rani would indeed take her own life before she was captured.

Her handlers knew that, which was why they'd referred her to Captain Kiara Naidu. Naidu was a woman of many talents, but spy craft was not her area of expertise. She knew how to fight a ship and was learning to command a fleet at Admiral Khare's side, but Naidu needed someone like "Rani" to the dirtier jobs.

At least this one was interesting.

Rani had never been on an underwater station before, though she'd always meant to visit one. Her duties to India had taken her to most corners of the world...but not under them.

Stepping off of the ship at Transportation Platform Five, or TRANSPLAT Five—which had a ten-foot-high painting of a duck labeled "Duckworth" at its center—felt like being on shore. So far as Rani could tell, the platform was just a small, manmade island in the middle of the ocean. Yes, the tour guide on board her ship stressed that they were only thirty-seven miles off the coast of Taiwan, but Rani could not see the shore. Ergo, they were in the midst of the ocean.

The air was sharp with salt, but not nearly as heavy as she expected. Following the crowd and gaping like the tourist she pretended to be, Rani noticed the eyes watching her and the *long* line waiting to board SS *Farsea*, the tour boat she'd arrived on. Rani and twenty-seven fellow travelers were more visitors than Red Tiger Station received in months, and many people waiting to leave watched them with outright disbelief, muttering about why anyone would come out at all.

They didn't need to know that Rani's superiors had paid five times the going rate to get *Farsea* out here or that they bribed two pirate submarines to escort the boat instead of hijacking it. In fact, *Rani* wasn't supposed to know that; however, she'd slipped into a corner to overhear a conversation between a gregarious pirate captain and Captain Naidu, which was far more informative than she expected.

Information was her currency, and Rani intended to thrive.

Now, her outward curiosity hid the calculating mind categorizing details. The walk down the TRANSPLAT wasn't long, as *Farsea* got a good berth near the front with little traffic coming in and out. But walking on the metal mesh platform felt strange; she could see the water beneath her feet, and Rani was not sure she liked the sensation of waves moving the platform back and forth. Before long, they reached a bank of decorated elevators, again labeled *Duckworth* and covered in duck-themed décor. Rani guessed that was the name of the platform, though perhaps she was wrong and it was an entire wing of the station?

The elevator ride down was identical to those above water, right down to the same boring music. There was no way to tell they were underwater; her ears barely even popped. Rani knew that Red Tiger Station was on a plateau and they weren't too deep, but stepping out of the elevator and seeing *windows* still sent a shiver running down her spine.

Now she felt like she was underwater. The windows weren't numerous—thankfully, there weren't walls of them, as there were in her nightmares—but there were enough. The soft blue glow to the lights only served to further remind her that she wasn't on solid ground, though thankfully that faded as they approached the center hub of the station itself.

"Red Tiger Station has five working TRANSPLATS and one under service," the tour guide said. "Each sticks out of the center like spokes of a bicycle wheel. Here in the center are the oldest and most successful businesses."

"Sure, if the hub of your bicycle is shaped like a hotdog," someone near her muttered.

Rani smiled and tuned out most of the tour guide's words. She already had reservations at the Oyo Casino and knew where to go. Her room was midrange, nothing too nice, nor too shabby. Nothing to garner attention.

She would shop and gawk for the next few days, establishing herself as an innocent tourist caught here by circumstance. It helped that Rani looked younger than her thirty-three years; she could blend in with the revelers and pretend to be happy. No one would suspect her of spying on the Fogborne Team, once she found them.

Splitting off from the group, Rani headed down the main thoroughfare, past the museum, the build-your-own electronics emporium, and past the eager young people advertising their services out of a makeshift alley. She had just two suitcases with her, both of which looked completely innocent because they were. She could build her own electronic spying gear if needed. And whatever weapons she needed, Rani would find here. Wherever there were humans, there were weapons.

Past four restaurants and a designer cheese shop, Rani finally reached the casino. Its gaudy flashing lights left her vaguely nauseated, but she tuned them out. She would have to gamble later, the more to look like a carefree tourist. That was fine. Her orders were flexible, anyway.

Rani was to take her time and get close to the Fogborne Research Team. If she could befriend them, so much the better. If not, a knowledgeable spy was more than enough. And when the time came...

India would gain their secrets.

One way or another.

Freshly shaved and with a clean set of coveralls making him look mostly presentable, Alex headed straight to the wardroom for that precious coffee. A year in command hadn't made him hate mornings any less, but caffeine helped him pretend. The headache pounding behind his eyes warred with the desire to go back to bed; the hot shower had banished it for a few minutes, but nothing short of two cups of coffee would make him feel human.

Alex might've been the boat's biggest coffee drinker by a long shot. But it was navy coffee he loved. Nancy was into the frou-frou flavored stuff. She bought a fancy French press and did unspeakable things with coffee beans that made Alex cringe. Then she filled it up with loads of cream and sugar, enough to make both a dentist and a doctor cry. Give him black, normal, *strong* coffee any day.

Alex could almost *taste* it already. Navy coffee was the bitterest black, and despite his sweet tooth, he never put sugar in it. The chief cook in the wardroom took pride in never cleaning the coffee pot while on deployment, which meant each successive pot grew stronger and stronger until the stuff damned near grew its own legs. The pot was barely ever empty; between officers going on and off watch and everyone's general need for the only free energy booster the navy provided...well, it got a workout.

Unfortunately, when he wrenched open the door to *Jimmy Carter's* tiny wardroom, there were three marines inside, one of whom was so tall that his head almost brushed the overhead.

Alex stopped, craning his neck to look up at the giant. He was a muscled man with darker skin, with tattoos peeking out from under the tight-but-regulation rolled sleeves of his camouflage uniform, the collar of which bore a lieutenant colonel's silver oak leaves—an equal rank to Alex's own. His head was shaved, and his eyes were dark, and they narrowed when they spied Alex.

"I was wondering when you'd grace us with your presence, Almighty Captain," the giant rumbled.

George, to the lieutenant colonel's right, went so white Alex wondered if he might faint.

"Well, if you have the decency to show up after breakfast like a civilized human being, you might've got me sooner," Alex retorted. "Then again, what can someone expect out of a marine? Not brains or courtesy, that's for sure."

Now the two young officers next to the lieutenant colonel straightened angrily, not quite glaring at someone who outranked them by a good margin. But their eyes flicked to the colonel's back, as if waiting for direction—and hoping for violence.

"You're still salty before coffee, huh?" the marine asked.

"Damn straight I am."

"It's fucking great to see you, Alex!"

Before Alex could say a word, he was swept off his feet in a fierce bear hug that squashed the ribs he'd broken when Spangler tackled him. He squeaked, which wasn't a very dignified sound for a captain to make, but George was already having an aneurysm over there, so what did it matter?

"Put me down, you humongous excuse for a human being." He laughed. "Are you still eating barbells for breakfast?"

"I'll take eggs when they're not available." But at least he put Alex down.

"Good, because we're fresh out of free weights you can eat." Chuckling, Alex shook his head. "Man, it is good to see you, too, Paul. How did you swing this gig?"

"Word went around that they needed a volunteer to do something crazy with a submarine, and since I had a bit of experience with that, I figured I might as well pony up," Paul Swanson replied. "Didn't find out it was *your* boat until afterward. Then I might've said no."

His wicked grin took any sting out of those words, but George still looked offended on his captain's behalf, which meant it was time to explain.

"Paul, this is George Kirkland, my XO. George, this is Lieutenant Colonel Paul Swanson, my old college roommate, best man from my wedding, and partner in crime from previous nefarious adventures."

"Pleasure. Any friend of Alex's is a friend of mine." Paul grinned. "And that includes XOs."

George shook Paul's hand, looking vaguely queasy. "It's an honor, Colonel."

Paul turned to introduce his two squad leaders, both young captains: Leon Prosser and Jackie Lucas. George bustled the two junior officers out quickly, showing them to the stateroom they'd share with two of *Jimmy Carter's* division officers.

"You get a decent mission briefing?" Alex asked, finally pouring himself that cup of coffee. He didn't bother to offer one to Paul; he knew his friend only drank the stuff out of desperation.

"Something about some special engineers or scientists and sneaking into Chinese waters." Paul shrugged. "Seemed fun."

Alex snorted. "Close enough. Getting there's going to be dicey, and I've got no idea what we'll face on Red Tiger Station."

"Well, you leave the station shit to me and worry about the driving. As long as you don't smash *this* sub into a ship, I think we'll be okay."

"No promises." Alex winked.

"Don't you fucking dare!" Paul howled.

Chapter 14

Cold Reminders

14 September 2039, the Coral Sea

Teresa O'Canas never could sit still for long. Diagnosed with a form of ADHD as a child, she struggled until seventeen years in the navy molded that short attention span into an *excellent* ability to multi-task. She called it self-defense; her officers and crew laughed and said she changed topics fast enough to keep them dizzy.

Maybe Teresa was a tad eccentric, but *Douglass* was a happy boat. She knew her people trusted her. Most even liked her! That meant Teresa no longer worried about the stupid stuff. No, she wasn't gorgeous. True, some long-ago Mexican ancestor bequeathed uncontrollable hair to her, and her features were best described as flat. She had fits of self-conscious worry about both as a young division officer, but she no longer gave a damn what she looked like.

Looks didn't matter nearly as much as her combat record. *Douglass* had managed a pretty good war so far, sinking a trio of Russian submarines—and a French *Scorpene* that wandered too far away from its island base—over her first four patrols. Since then, things had gotten even better. Teresa's boat wasn't on the top of the sinking scorecard, not even with the top ranks thinning fast as subs crashed to the bottom, but *Douglass* owned a respectable record for military kills. With ten subs and six military surface ships confirmed, Teresa and *Douglass* had slid into the number five spot, right behind the late and great Rico Sivers.

Commander Sivers also had sixteen kills, but his predated hers...as did his Medal of Honor. Teresa wouldn't surpass him until she sank a seventeenth enemy combatant.

But the important metric, the one hanging in the forefront of everyone's mind, was that *Douglass* was actually America's second best *surviving* submarine. Everyone ahead of them was dead, except *Razorback*. Captain John Dalton was at that proverbial seventeenth kill, and while Teresa wasn't on a mission to best her fellows like Kurt Kins, knowing she was close did make things exciting.

Even the boring-as-watching-paint-dry convoy missions interspersed between the thrilling moments were just the price of doing business. Besides, the last convoy commander Teresa worked for had foolishly taken Convoy 151 into a known operating and refueling area for Indian diesel submarines, allowing *Douglass* to bag two further enemy kills three days ago. It could be worse.

Teresa knew that she'd been damn lucky to catch one of the *Scorpenes* snorkeling and recharging its batteries, and she'd been even *more* fortunate to spook the second one out of hiding before it was in effective range of *Douglass*. Still, she'd take what she could get. Teresa O'Canas wasn't sure how she'd come off the bench to get near the top of the list of Alliance submariners, but she was here to do a job. Even if being just under John Dalton and Ursula North terrified her.

Unfortunately, those two *Scorpenes* took seven torpedoes to kill—one of which was a dud, an unfortunate side effect of rushing the new Mark 84 into production. Even worse, *Douglass* hadn't been able to reload during her last port visit. That left her with only six torpedoes: four in the tubes and two waiting on the rails. She didn't have any Harpoon IIIs, either; her vertical launch tubes were full of Tomahawks, which everyone knew were useless against ships, particularly after that trick Uncle Marco pulled at Christmas Island. No way would the Indians fall for that again!

Oh, well. Escorting that last convoy hadn't been part of the plan, but another sub going down meant that she had to make a high-speed transfer down to the south Pacific. Teresa was used to the game.

On the bright side, the new convoy Teresa hooked up with at the end of that sprint was carrying more torpedoes from Pearl Harbor to Perth, so she supposed it was worthy of escort. Hopefully, keeping it alive would put her first in line for more torps.

Now they were only four days out of Perth and those promised torpedoes. Six fish should do until then, particularly when Teresa had no intention of looking for trouble. For now, she had twenty minutes before lunch, so she turned to personal messages, re-reading an email from her son.

Jonas still wasn't happy living in Michigan with his dad. *Teresa* wasn't delighted with that, either, but Jacob was a town councilor in the middle of freaking nowhere. That boring little town was as safe from the war as anyone could get, which was where she wanted her son. And it wasn't like she could leave a teenager alone at home in Groton while she waltzed off to war. Part of every single parent's pre-deployment checklist was family care planning. In her case, that meant turning over temporary custody to her ex-husband.

Jonas loved his dad, but Jacob Hernandez had remarried and moved far away when he was just eight. He spent some of each summer there, but usually, it wasn't this long. He was adjusting, but his emails showed he still wasn't comfortable. At least he seemed pleased that his mom was proving to be a true, old-fashioned warfighter.

Teresa grinned to herself. She was no Mush Morton, but damn it, she was holding her own.

A new email popped into her inbox, and Teresa grinned. She and Alex Coleman had been emailing back and forth since leaving the Submarine Commander's Course fourteen months ago. There were things that a CO simply couldn't discuss with her own crew, and it was nice to have someone else to bitch to. A captain *had* to appear competent and confident, and you just couldn't complain to the people you led.

Besides, Alex was always entertaining. He had an insipid XO and a low tolerance for stupidity, which meant his rants were energetic and expletive filled. His wife didn't understand the submarine-specific stuff, and John Dalton was up on a pedestal, probably too busy for pedestrian bitching like this. That was a friendship Teresa never had quite parsed—she found Dalton stuffy and arrogant—but she was happy to be the sounding board for her frustrated friend.

Teresa never doubted that the navy's decision to bury Alex Coleman in *Jimmy Carter* was stupid. Despite rumors about him going to Admiral's Mast a few years ago, there was a quiet brilliance about him. By the time their class had been halfway through the Submarine Commander's Course, everyone had known he was *good*. If they had to pick one of their classmates to follow into combat, Teresa knew they'd all pick Alex. But Big Navy had a long memory. Whoever he'd pissed off, he'd pissed them off good.

She was midway through her response to his latest email about his XO's inability to take a joke when *Douglass* rolled into an unexpectedly tight turn, vibrating, and picking up speed.

She grabbed the phone. "Conn, Captain, what's going on?"

Teresa typed a quick farewell on the email as she spoke, promising to finish the story of the two *Scorpenes* later. The last thing she needed was to get to control and discover that her OOD had been asleep at the wheel and let one of the lazy merchants get too close—

"Captain, we've got hydrophone effects bearing one-two-zero and one-two-five, at least two torps inbound at USNS *Lewis and Clark*," the officer of the deck replied in a rush, his young voice tight with tension.

"Man Battle Stations and I'll be right there." Teresa clicked send as she rose. She hated leaving things unfinished, even small matters like a personal email. It went out to the remote server immediately; *Douglass* had the latest connectivity upgrade and could send and receive data from as deep as a thousand feet.

After living a long life full of secrets and silence, being able to email someone right before she went into battle was damned liberating. Teresa felt lonely if she didn't have at least a dozen people to keep in touch with, so this lifeline kept her sane in a captain's lonely world.

But it was time to put her game face on, so she abandoned her computer and rushed out of her stateroom. It didn't do for the captain to hurry *too* much—after this long at war, that hinted that she couldn't trust her crew. She slipped past sailors as they raced to their battle stations, securing hatches, closing valves, and donning flash gear, smiling and nodding greetings. Most grinned in return; *Douglass's* crew was confident, strung like a bow ready to fire.

Heart beating firmly, Teresa reached control less than thirty seconds after giving the order for her boat to go to battle stations. The general alarm was still blaring, and she had to raise her voice to be heard. "What d'you have, Carson?"

By chance, her navigator was already on watch, so there was no delay required to allow a new officer of the deck to get situational awareness. The navigator always had the deck for battle stations—it was tradition, and besides, Carson was *Douglass's* best shiphandler.

Carson Burrows was a tall, lanky, and awkward African American, but there was no sign of discomfort now. He knew his business. "*Lewis and Clark* is dropping decoys and making best speed away from the torps, and the idiot destroyers have gone active on everything. The sonar picture looks like mud, ma'am. We're not picking up anything."

"Glorious."

"You want me to call *Murphy* and ask them to cease pinging?"

Teresa's XO asked from her right.

"Probably no use. They're feeling threatened and won't listen." Teresa shook her head. "Let's go a bit deeper and see if we can't use the surface guys as beaters, instead."

"You got it, Captain." In contrast to Carson, Lieutenant Commander Sally Weber was solidly built, sandy-haired, and shorter than pretty much everyone on board. However, she was also ferociously competent and was rapidly becoming one of the best friends Teresa ever had. Sally was unflappable in combat and far less prone to pacing or fingerpainting on the bulkheads than her captain.

Carson ordered the boat deeper, and Teresa fought the urge to fidget. Usually, she used exercise to banish her inner wiggling demon, but that wasn't an option now. Instead, she kept her eyes focused on the plot, watching the track of *Lewis and Clark* and the torpedoes following her. Modern Link technology gave sub commanders greater situational awareness than ever before, but even the unification of four warships' sensors—*Douglass, Michael P. Murphy,* and two Canadian frigates—couldn't detect the enemy sub's location. In fact, they couldn't tell how *many* enemies were out there; for all Teresa knew, there might have been a dozen French or Indian subs.

What a time to only have six torpedoes.

Teresa pursed her lips. This far south, at least the enemy probably wasn't Russian. In Teresa's experience, Russian submariners were either stellar or terrible, and the fact that they couldn't find this guy put him or her into the former category.

"Hydrophone effects have ceased, Captain," the sonar supervisor reported from his station to her right. Unlike earlier classes of submarines, *Virginias* like *Douglass* lacked a separate sonar room, which eliminated communications delays but made it harder for the sonar operators to concentrate. "The computer says there's a ninety-nine percent probability of them being F21 mod two."

The F21 mod 2 torpedo was the second-best submarine-launched weapon in the French arsenal. Although the French Navy had shared a lot of technology with the Indians, they hadn't shared these torpedoes. Only their newest nuclear attack subs and the *French*-manned *Scorpene*-IIIs carried them. The F21 could be fired at long range and had a speed over fifty knots. It wasn't as fast as its successor torpedo, the F27 Artemis, but…Teresa had to take this threat seriously.

"They did say that the French varsity were down here," she said to Sally, who smiled.

"Good thing the admirals decided to send ours, then."

Teresa met her XO's eyes and grinned, heat touching her cheeks.

"Damn straight," the chief of the boat said, and several other sailors laughed out loud. Teresa's smile grew. Her people were damn good, and they were *ready*. She passed a few orders to the OOD, and *Douglass* swung into the search with a vengeance.

Ten frustrating minutes ticked by while *Douglass* weaved slowly along the bearing correlating with the direction the torpedoes originated from. The initial parts of a search always tried Teresa's patience, and before long she started wandering around control, speaking quietly with her watchstanders as they waited. She liked the attitude she sensed: focused but ready. Not too eager, but not afraid, either. Perfect.

Finally, *Douglass* got her first sniff.

"Captain, there's a faint narrowband contact on the fifty-seven hertz line." The sonar supervisor squinted, cocking his head and staring at his waterfall display. "Bearing is about...zero-two-two. Range is hard to figure, but I'm thinking over twenty thousand yards."

Teresa blinked and then strode across control to look at the main plot again. But Sally, over with the fire control party, took the words right out of her mouth.

"Are you sure about that bearing, Chief?" the XO asked, her repeater showing the same data as the main plot did. "That's over 190 degrees off the estimated torpedo firing position. Could you have a reciprocal bearing?"

Chief Osborne paused to punch commands into the sonar computer before shaking his head. "I've got it on the tail and the starboard array, XO, and intermittently on the bow dome. There's no way the computer inverted it."

Huh. That was odd. "Do you have a class correlation?"

"That freq could make it a couple of French boats, Captain," Osborne replied, his eyes locked on the screens. "It could be one of their third-generation *Scorpenes*, or maybe a newer *Requin*. But the nucs usually aren't this quiet, ma'am—we're having a bitch of a time holding the track. I'd bet it's a brand-new diesel operating on battery, and that makes it a *Scorpene III*."

Teresa's eyes met Sally's again, but now neither of them was smiling. They both could do the math. Teresa's next stop on her seemingly aimless wander brought the captain to her XO's side.

"Two boats, you think?" she whispered.

Sally nodded. "A diesel couldn't have fired those torps and gotten over there so fast."

"This just got more complicated." Teresa heaved a sigh. "Those newer *Scorpenes* are quiet little bastards, aren't they?"

Sally scowled. "Too quiet."

"Sonar, keep your ears open. We're probably dealing with two enemy subs out here, maybe more." Teresa squared her shoulders. "Designate the new track hostile and put a datum in at our best guess where the torpedoes were fired from."

"Aye—" Chief Osborne cut himself off. "Captain, we've lost track. Got a slight hull popping noise first, but I can't tell if he's gone deep or shallow."

"Very well." It was all Teresa could do not to howl, but this was how the game was played.

"You want me to notify the convoy, Captain?" Sally asked as *Douglass* resumed her search.

Teresa chewed the inside of her lip. For a moment, she hesitated, her shoulders tense, almost paralyzed by indecision. Feeling like an ocean of calm in the midst of control's action was abnormal for her; Teresa was accustomed to being the center of attention. But something gnawed at her instincts.

Should she stay in stealth? Maybe. But it was better to risk the miniscule chance of detection and call the boss. Otherwise, her own allies might drop torpedoes on *Douglass's* head. Besides, the convoy commander's standing orders required expeditious reporting of all contacts. Weaseling out of that was hard when she wasn't actively tracking either of the enemy or closing for the kill. She had time to make the report.

"Yeah. Damn good idea, XO. Let them know we have two probable enemy sub contacts, ID unknown, but probably French *Scorpene IIIs*. Recommend new convoy course," she glanced at the plot again, "three-zero-zero to avoid."

Teresa had done nothing wrong up to that point, but she hadn't done everything right, either. A product of a peacetime navy, a year of war had taught her a lot of lessons—but not all the right ones. She'd done well so far, but those peacetime habits doomed her in the end.

The Naval Undersea Warfare Center estimated that the probability of another submarine detecting a *Virginia*-class during short voice transmissions was around seven percent. But their best guess was just that: a guess.

And it was wrong.

Michael P. Murphy acknowledged the contact report, and Teresa watched the plot as the auxiliary ships—a mixture of oilers, ammunition carriers, and civilian foodstuffs and parts carriers—turned to the course she recommended. Meanwhile, *Douglass* changed depth again, moving her towed sonar array beneath the thermal layer and slowly closing the range to the enemies' last known positions. Although older than the new *Cero*-class, *Douglass* and her sisters were still among the quietest submarines ever built.

Teresa, like her colleagues commanding other American subs, *knew* her sonar equipment was the very best in the world. That mentality was a holdover from the Cold War, a time when the U.S. Navy was unquestionably the finest in the world...but it didn't account for the new multi-power world.

The French Navy, or *Marine Nationale*, was one such force, and Jules Rochambeau remained their very best. Armed with a submarine that had been designed, built, and tested in under two years—instead of having been studied to death for over a decade or more—he wasn't constrained by things he "knew" to be true. While Teresa was busy searching for *him*, Rochambeau silently slipped *Barracuda* into a firing position just off *Douglass'* starboard bow, closing the range to under ten thousand yards.

Teresa's best guess had been wrong, too. *Barracuda* was the only enemy sub stalking her convoy, and the *Requin*-class subs really were unequaled. The U.S. Navy had lost a step, and Teresa O'Canas—the second best submariner America had—was a product of a system that couldn't cope with someone like Rochambeau.

"Anything, Chief?" Teresa asked Osborne after ten minutes of silent searching. Not fidgeting was harder than ever. Commanding officers weren't *supposed* to pace. Pushups would really have helped, but her crew would probably think she'd gone crazy if she started a workout in the middle of an engagement.

The sonar chief shook his head. "These guys are *good*, ma'am. I read the TACMEMO on the *Scorpene IIIs*, but I honestly didn't expect them to be so damn quiet. I'm searching the area they *ought* to be in, but I can't hear a damned thing."

"Hm."

Her instincts were twitching. She knew something was wrong, but there wasn't time for Teresa to dig her way to the truth. Sally met her gaze again. There was something hanging in the air, an answer just out of reach.

"Come right a little, Carson," she ordered. "Maybe closing the range with these guys will help a bit."

Douglass turned to split the difference between the two estimated positions. Diesel boats moved slowly on battery power, even the advanced ones like the *Scorpenes*, and by that logic, neither contact could go too far without *Douglass* hearing. *Douglass* had advantages in speed, endurance, and maneuverability over a smaller diesel submarine. A *Scorpene* might be quieter, but once *Douglass* found one, she could kill it.

Another minute ticked by, and then two. Finally, another sonar tech spoke up.

"Got something!" Petty Officer Fernandez shouted, her voice shrill and loud in the silent space. "Narrowband contact on the tail and starboard side array, closing our bow. Contact correlates to a...*Requin* class SSN?"

"Check that again!" Chief Osborne's hands flashed over the keyboard.

Teresa's head whipped around to stare at the sonar stations. *If that's—*

She almost got there in time.

"Track ID confirmed." Osborne twisted to look at Teresa, his eyes suddenly wide. "Unique characteristics match hull number 722, *Barracuda.*"

A chill ran through control. *Everyone* knew *Barracuda*'s reputation.

"What's the range?" she snapped.

Osborne grimaced. "Ma'am, best guess is something between ten and thirty thousand, but it's remaining steady, and we need a course change to—"

"Make tubes one and two ready in all respects, including opening the outer doors!"

"Make tubes one and two ready in all respects, including opening the outer doors, Weps, Aye!" her weapons officer replied, his voice high and tight.

Teresa had to hurry over to turn the firing key *Douglass* rolled onto her new course. It was one thing to use a pair of passive bearings to guess at another sub's range, but if Teresa was going to shoot at Jules Rochambeau, she'd need the best damn firing solution she could get.

"Key is green!" she said.

A few long seconds ticked by. Too long.

"Tubes one and two ready in all respects. Outer doors open. No firing solution," her weapons officer reported.

"Very well." Teresa held her voice steady, glancing at the plot. *Douglass* was still turning, not level enough for good fire control data.

They weren't fast enough. Her heart was in her throat. American

COs weren't trained to shoot from the hip. She'd read John Dalton's patrol reports and had taken them to heart; Teresa knew that getting in close was the way to go, even with their newer and faster torpedoes. But sixteen years of training was hard to overcome.

In a peacetime navy, each submarine was treated like the two-billion-dollar national asset it was. Every submariner was taught to triple check *everything*. Particularly firing solutions.

Abruptly, the icon representing the tentative position of *Barracuda* started blinking.

Fernandez swore. "Captain, we're losing contact!"

"Come back left," Teresa ordered Carson, wanting to kick herself. She turned to Sally and spoke in an undertone. "I should've shot when—"

"Torpedoes in the water!" Fernandez's screech split the stillness. "Torpedoes in the water, bearing one-zero-nine!"

God, that was right off her starboard bow, the textbook perfect shot. Teresa opened her mouth to order an evasion course, but Osborne got in first.

"Torpedoes are active and homing, fired from close aboard! *Range six thousand yards and closing fast!*"

Twenty minutes later, the automated message popped into the queue at COMSUBPAC headquarters in Pearl Harbor, Hawaii. Because of a quirk in navy organization, Commander, Submarine Forces Pacific was also responsible for all subs in the Indian Ocean, which made him the world's busiest submariner. Three minutes after that, an aide knocked on the open door to Vice Admiral Marco Rodriguez's office.

"We got another one, Admiral."

The man that the sub force affectionately called "Uncle Marco" sat back in his chair and sighed. "Well, shit."

"Yes, sir." There wasn't much else for the young lieutenant to say, so she just handed her boss the hard copy of the message.

Uncle Marco was old-fashioned and didn't like to receive traffic on an electronic tablet. Everyone knew that Rodriquez took a copy of the SUBMISS/SUBSUNK messages home (when he wasn't sleeping on his office couch), but no one knew exactly what he did with them. One copy papered the walls of his office, but what about the other? One of his former aides claimed that he burned them as kindling. A retired acquaintance from his OCS days said he slept with them under his pillow. Some people thought he buried them in the backyard like a weird-ass time capsule.

There were a lot of mysteries surrounding Marco Rodriguez. The one thing everyone could agree upon was that the Puerto Rican-born admiral was one of the toughest and least politically correct officers in the navy. He was loud, and he was foul, but a SUBMISS/SUBSUNK message always shut him up.

"Fuck," he whispered, scowling at the paper. "Get me Commodore Banks on the phone."

"Yes, sir." She turned to hurry out the door.

"Wait!"

The bark stopped her cold in the doorway. "Admiral?"

"Scratch that. Call Banks yourself and tell him that I'm poaching *Razorback* and Dalton for Operation Sandicast. I'll call Dalton myself, but I don't have the stomach to talk to that lazy-minded S.O.B. today."

"I'll get right on it, sir." What the aide thought of her admiral insulting another flag officer—and one of his subordinates, to boot—she kept to herself.

"Captain?"

Awareness wandered in slowly. When he opened his eyes, John Dalton was face down on the wardroom table, his right cheek stuck to the blue vinyl tablecloth. How had he gotten there? He blinked, straightening with an effort.

Oh, he ached. How long had he been asleep? Better yet, there was a napkin stuck to his forehead, adding to his humiliation. He slapped it off. A captain needed to preserve *some* sort of dignity. *Not much of that going on here if I've got floral print tattooed into my face*, he thought, glaring at the napkin.

Every bone felt heavy. How could he feel so exhausted after napping? And so ready to go back to sleep? Shaking off the cobwebs, John looked up at his communications officer.

The young lieutenant was suspiciously red in the face. Was he laughing or embarrassed to have found his captain—winner of the Navy Cross and top living submarine commander in the U.S. Navy—drooling on the tabletop like a toddler?

John didn't want to ask. He cleared his throat. "What's going on,

DJ? You decide I slept on the table long enough?"

D.J. shook his head so fast John feared for his glasses. "Ah, no, sir." Whatever he thought about his idiot CO's sleeping habits, D.J. Cunningham clearly intended to keep to himself. "Admiral Rodriquez is on the phone for you."

John jolted upright. "Admiral Rodriquez?"

"Yes, sir. He, uh, called the quarterdeck when you didn't answer your direct line."

"Well, I'll have to hide better next time, I guess." It was all John could think of saying, but his heart was in his throat. Why was the commander of *all* the subs in the Pacific calling *him*? As the child of a two-star general and a one-star admiral, John wasn't particularly afraid of flag officers, but he still hurried to his stateroom, wondering where the hell he'd stuffed the number to the direct line for COMSUBPAC's office.

Razorback was one of the newest boats in the fleet, but John's stateroom still wasn't much larger than a closet. It also was a short sprint from the wardroom, which meant he didn't have to pass a lot of staring sailors along the way.

Not that John was really worried about his reputation at this point. He commanded a happy and razor-sharp crew—pun intended—whose trust he knew he'd earned. His predecessor had looked like a movie star and frozen up in combat. John was a touch overweight, fighting baldness, and knew how to kill the enemy. He also knew who his people preferred to follow.

Still, the last time COMSUBPAC wanted to talk to him—the fired Admiral Brown, who didn't survive hoarding new torpedoes in a warehouse—a staffer called John. Having an admiral call him direct was...ominous.

Much to his surprise, the phone was still ringing when he scooted into his stateroom, slamming the door shut without looking. He grabbed it quickly.

"Captain Dalton."

"Where the hell have you been, Dalton?" the voice on the other end barked. "Is your crew so damned incompetent that they can't find their own CO on a three hundred and seventy-foot-long submarine, or were you hiding from your wife with a prostitute?"

John's jaw dropped.

"Don't answer that," Rodriquez snapped. "I don't want to know."

"Admiral, I—"

"I don't give a rat's ass what you get up to in your free time, Dalton," Rodriquez cut him off again. "What I *do* care about is if that boat of yours is ready to roll. I've got a job for you."

John knew Admiral Rodriquez had a reputation for cutting corners, but an admiral jumping the chain of command like made his jaw drop. "Sir, my boss—"

"Is Commodore Banks, I know. I'm poaching you." A beat. "Are you ready?"

"Yes, sir." John had no idea what he was ready for, to do, or even if his immediate superior knew he was volunteering *Razorback* for something, but he knew it would be interesting.

Commodore Banks would have kittens, but John didn't like him much, anyway. Besides, he had the Navy Cross. He was six feet tall and bulletproof. No mere commodore could sink him, not as long as John kept turning in results.

"Good. We just lost *Douglass*"—Rodriquez's gravelly voice caught—"so I need someone fast. You'll be running point for an operation named Sandicast, working *with* a surface action group but still directly under my command. Clear?"

John hesitated. "That's a pretty vague order, sir."

"No shit, Captain." Rodriquez snorted. "You'll get more detailed orders, but in short, we're reopening the Strait of Malacca, come hell or fucking high water, and you're going in first. Your job is to clear the path for the SAG."

"You do remember that my experience in the Strait of Malacca wasn't that great, right, sir?" John swallowed.

"Yeah. You want some revenge for that goddamned goat rope?"

A thrill ran through John, chasing away the old terror. He'd never forget the First Battle of the SOM, the sheer terror of being on a carrier as the ships around him were torn apart and then as *Enterprise* herself went down. He saw in his nightmares again and again, even over a year later. Sometimes, he woke up, expecting to be on that life raft, soaking wet and half-carrying an admiral whose brain and ambitious went to mush when the shooting started.

Sometimes, he woke up drowning under the pressure.

Yeah, he wanted revenge.

John also wanted to be an admiral someday, so he had to think like a strategist. The Strait of Malacca was one of the world's busiest waterways. Almost five hundred nautical miles long, the narrow waterway between Malaysia and Indonesia was a natural chokepoint between the Indian and Pacific Oceans. Over forty percent of the world's seaborne trade traveled through the SOM, with over 180 ships per day at the war's onset.

Avoiding the SOM by going all the way south doubled the distance a ship needed to travel. The first two battles in the SOM were disasters for the U.S. Navy; John, of course, remembered the first personally, including the swim afterward. Since then, the Indian Navy had owned the SOM lock, stock, and barrel.

He sucked in a deep breath.

"You can count on *Razorback*, Admiral."

Chapter 15

Letters from Beyond

14 September 2039, outbound from Perth, Australia

Alex stared at the screen, hoping the words were a fatigue-triggered hallucination.

He had reason to be tired. *Jimmy Carter* was submerged and outbound from Perth, with Paul's marine detachment on board. They were a motley crew, which was to be expected; special forces of any sort were usually a weird bunch, and Paul liked to recruit oddballs. Alex, who had worked with some of them before, wasn't surprised.

George, however, spent most of his time conspicuously *not* glaring at his new roommate, who anyone with eyes could tell he didn't like. That meant Alex was the ringmaster for a circus he didn't want but couldn't avoid, turning what should've been a pleasant time with one of his best friends into teeth-grating misery. Even exchanging funny stories with Paul resulted in George fretting in a corner, glaring at Paul like he was stealing his captain's attention away. Which he was.

Paul was trying to behave...mostly. But his sense of humor meant the division officers loved him, and he laughed uproariously at every prank they pulled on George. Which they'd started again now that the XO's roommate was willing to "forget" to lock the stateroom door.

It would've all been in good fun if George had a sense of humor, but his rigid despair left Alex nursing headaches and feeling like he should interfere. Any normal XO would've gotten over himself by now, but George...

Alex shook his head and looked back at the computer screen. Maybe the words would change. *Jimmy Carter* just finished downloading the mail one last time before submerging; they were going deep and quiet for the next eleven days, and Alex had no plans to pop the comms wire up until they hit the halfway point. Then he'd make one last check-in before staying silent until *Jimmy Carter* arrived at Red Tiger Station. The infinitesimal chance of detection in such contested waters was too much, which meant this was the last set of messages they'd get for almost two weeks.

Even this communications check took place in the dark, with *Jimmy Carter's* communications wire at its maximum depth. This mission was top secret—and that meant minimizing the number of people who even knew what direction they headed going out of Perth.

All those thoughts vanished out of Alex's mind the moment he re-read the words:

SUBMISS/SUBSUNK UPDATE ICO USS DOUGLASS SSN 811

"Fuck." The whisper slipped out before he could stop it, grief making his throat tight.

Every submarine in the U.S. Navy carried an emergency buoy, designed to float to the surface if the submarine went below a programmed depth or the timer wasn't reset on schedule...and the buoys almost *never* released by accident. Some COs even welded them down to eliminate noise, and sometimes they were destroyed by battle damage, but damn near every buoy that released signified a lost submarine. Alex could think of exactly *one* accidentally released SUBMISS/SUBSUNK buoy since the war started.

That statistic didn't bode well for Teresa's submarine.

Alex skipped past the message header.

SUBJ: SUBMISS/SUBSUNK UPDATE ICO USS DOUGLASS SSN 811

RMKS: 1. INITIAL SUBMISS/SUBSUNK BUOY SURFACED 141652Z SEP39 AT POSIT 13 13 02.9 S 156 01 24.9 E.

2. COMSUBPAC RECEIVED DATA/LOG UPLOAD VIA SATELLITE AT 141652Z SEP39. LAST LOG UPDATE AT 141652Z SEP39, SAME TIME AS SUBMISS/SUBSUNK BUOY RELEASE. DOUGLASS APPEARED TO BE IN EXTREMIS AT TIME OF UPDATE.

3. FORTY-EIGHT (48) EMERGENY ATTEMPTS TO CONTACT DOUGLASS FAILED. ALL SCHEDULED COMMUNICATION TIMES MISSED SINCE BUOY LAUNCH.
4. USS DOUGLASS SSN 811 OUT OF CONTACT FOR TWENTY-FOUR (24) HOURS.
5. STATUS: MISSING, PRESUMED LOST.

Twenty-four hours. Twenty-four hours was a lifetime for a submarine to be out of contact when the navy was doing everything short of raising the dead to find you. There was no way to miss the launch of your own emergency buoy, either. The alarm went off two minutes before a time-triggered launch and was loud enough to wake teenagers. Better yet, it didn't shut off until you reset the timer.

Sure, a submarine might accidentally dive beneath their own crush depth long enough to cause the buoy to release, but if that happened, one of the follow-on attempts to contact *Douglass* would've gotten through.

Nausea bubbled in his stomach; Alex clapped a hand over his mouth to stop from throwing up. He'd known Teresa for over ten years. Out of all their classmates from the Submarine Commander's Course, he would've bet on Teresa coming home. She was one of the sharpest of the bunch, solid and dependable. She was a good tactician, too. She was no Mush Morton—none of them were—but Teresa O'Canas had talent.

Had. The word swished around like acid in his mind, and Alex slumped in his old metal chair. His eyes burned. Could Teresa have survived? Much though he wanted to, he couldn't sprint *Jimmy Carter* across the Indian Ocean to *Douglass's* last known location and find out. For once, he was on a mission that mattered...while one of his best friends was either dead or—at best!—awaiting rescue that might never come.

When Alex wiped a hand over his face, he wasn't surprised to see it shaking. God, he hated this. He hated not knowing how Teresa's boat had been sunk or if she was still alive. He hated not being able to do anything.

But that was the name of the game, wasn't it?

No one ever promised him this job was easy. Grimacing, Alex closed the message and went back to work.

Some said war saved the newspaper business.

Others, more charitably, pointed out that most newspapers—chief among them the *Washington Post*—had done a good job of reinventing themselves for the digital age. Between interactive content and embracing the twenty-four-hour news cycle, the *Post* was a frontrunner in the news business once more, particularly since their journalism and in-depth reporting remained unparalleled.

"This is a ridiculous tip, boss."

Mark Easley sat back in his chair at the corner cubicle he'd fought for and arched an eyebrow at Dottie O'Brian. His editor, however, didn't twitch one perfectly manicured muscle.

Dottie was always the picture of a well-put-together manager. She had to be. Mark, on the other hand, could afford to wear jeans, untucked shirts, and scuffed shoes. He shaved his dark stubble regularly, only because he hated the way it felt, but he was two weeks into an ill-advised mustache he was too proud to shave off after growing it on a dare. His sister said it framed his gray eyes well, but Mark was pretty sure that was a lie.

He stuck the end of a pen in his mouth as Dottie looked down at him. Mark contemplated putting his feet up on the desk but decided that might be a little rude. Dottie was on her way up. Making an enemy of her was just dumb.

"Define ridiculous," she said.

"First off, I'm not a science guy." He held up his hands before she could interrupt. "I'm a *special interest* columnist—I like meaty people issues, sometimes interspersed with military idiocy. That means this is so far outside my swim lane that I can't even see the pool. Second, even a liberal-arts-loving guy like me knows that fusion is some whacko scientist's wet dream, not reality."

"You're an investigative journalist." Dottie crossed her arms. "I'm asking you to investigate."

"I'm the wrong guy. I'd have to spend two weeks teaching myself the subject—or finding some non-existent expert to teach me—before I could write something every Tom, Dick, and Sherry could understand. Give it to Hank."

Hank Carson twisted in his seat from the cubicle across the aisle. He was a heavyset, dark-skinned man with laughing eyes and glasses as thick as Mark's fingers. He was also the best poker player Mark knew. "What'd I do to you, Mark?"

"You'd a science and technology nerd. Dottie's got a scoop with your name all over it."

"I was *trying* to give this to you, Mark."

Mark waved a hand. "My mantlepiece is full enough. Give it to Hank. He can probably make it understandable, assuming this tip isn't absolute crap."

"It's from someone—well, I can't say who. But they're reliable." Dottie shifted on her three-inch heels to peer at Hank. "Do you know anything about nuclear fusion?"

"Some, sure. Enough to talk at parties, anyway."

"Way better than me!" Mark laughed.

"All right, fine. *Hank*, please come with me. Mark...go write something about human tragedy, will you?"

Dottie turned on those expensive heels and led Hank into a conference room, ignoring Mark—which was just what he preferred his editors doing, anyway.

---

20 September 2039, Diego Garcia, British Indian Ocean Territory

A storm brewed in the distance, its gray and dark clouds contrasting with the clear blue waters around the Chagos Archipelago. Mostly uninhabitable and unimpressive, the group of sixty tiny islands sat in the middle of the Indian Ocean, just south of the equator. Originally discovered by the Portuguese in the sixteenth century, the island was named Diego Garcia for the European explorers involved in the initial expeditions.

Originally settled by a muddle of French lepers, British shipwreck survivors, and a coconut plantation, the island became a British colony following the Napoleonic Wars. By 1942, RAF Station Diego Garcia was established, but that base was closed four years later. However, when the U.K. started withdrawing from the Indian Ocean in the 1960s, the United States stepped in, and a deal was made to maintain a mutual defense position. The United Kingdom purchased the Chagos Archipelago from Maritus for three million pounds, creating the British Indian Ocean Territory, or BIOT.

The U.S. promptly leased the BIOT, turning it into a forward naval base with the addition of two airstrips and military housing. Throughout the Cold War and the years that followed, the base was mostly used for military pre-positioning ships, which carried heavy equipment for invasions that never came. Once war broke out in the Indian Ocean, however, Diego Garcia quickly became home to many more ships.

"Rudder amidships. All engines ahead two-thirds," Commander Fletch Goddard ordered. He waited until *Parramatta*'s bow was clear of the slip before ordering: "All engines ahead full."

Diego Garcia was still a backwater port, but it had grown significantly since Fletch visited the place as a lieutenant. Then it was a sleepy base with nice beaches, two bars, and one tiny barracks. Now, it was a bustling hive of activity less than a thousand miles from the Indian mainland, bristling with defenses and busy with supplying nearby ships.

Even more importantly, Diego Garcia was only fifteen hundred miles from the Strait of Malacca. That put his frigate in a perfect place to join a new strike group headed towards everyone's favorite battleground.

Fletch had mixed feelings about the battle he knew was coming. The SOM was the world's trading lifeblood, but he'd lost too many friends in those waters already. Two bloody battles full of losses—mainly on the Alliance side—stained the waters in the Strait of Malacca, and he wasn't sure that the coming third one would be much different.

But this was why he'd given up that shiny new destroyer the admiralty wanted him to have and taken the aging frigate instead, wasn't it? Fletch needed to be *in* the fight, and so far, *Parramatta* had proved herself worthy. His crew had turned into top-notch submarine hunters...but the next battle would need something else.

His eyes flicked up as they passed an American destroyer, his crew rendering honors to their ally and receiving them in return. Fletch turned to his navigator. "Ah, it's my favorite American destroyer."

"May I ask why, sir?" the navigator asked.

"USS *Fletcher*. Such an excellent name." Fletch grinned.

"Do you know her captain?"

"Not at all, though perhaps I'll remedy that one of these days." Fletch shrugged. "We've sailed together, and she seems an excellent tactician."

Fletch raised his hand in a wave to the slender figure standing on *Fletcher*'s port bridge wing, and Nancy Coleman returned the gesture.

"Hopefully, they have better luck than we did with supplies." The navigator grunted. "I'm not looking forward to all those beans."

"Captain." Charlie's voice came at his elbow just as *Parramatta* entered open water. Fletch tucked his chin to look at diminutive XO's face. They'd called her *Wee Charlie* at the war college, and one look at Charlie Markey left no one wondering why. "The ops plan has just arrived."

"About damned time." He knew the battle group composition, but he didn't know the specifics of their mission. Fletch wasn't against improvising, but throwing an entire fleet around without a plan was asking for disaster.

"They're calling it *Sandicast*," Markey said as they headed below to Fletch's cabin.

"What the blazes does that mean? Is it even a word?" Fletch's degrees had been in language and diplomacy, and he was a stickler for proper grammar and spelling.

His XO giggled, sounding like a schoolgirl instead of the proper warfighter he knew she was. "Not that I could find, sir. Perhaps it's American."

Fletch punched the combination into the door of his quarters. The captain's cabin on *Parramatta* was nowhere near as grand as the one he'd given up with the destroyer, but there was a sense of history here that *Warrego* lacked. *Parramatta* had commissioned in 2003, *thirty-six* years earlier. A glance at the commanders' plaque on the wall reminded him that he was the twentieth captain to command his sleek but aged frigate. This might've been *Parramatta's* first war, but she had traveled the four corners of the world and made her mark, capturing pirates, saving lives, and showing the Australian flag in faraway lands.

No, Fletch didn't need a fancy ergonomic chair and a new daybed. The lumpy couch didn't bother him, either, even though it was patched in one corner with the wrong color vinyl. The wood paneling in the cabin was worn but *warm*, welcoming in a way that reminded everyone that *Parramatta* was an old and wise lady. The few mementos on display in the stateroom mostly belonged to the ship rather than her captain, too; Fletch wasn't silly enough to bring priceless memories to sea with him. Enough captains got their ships and belongings sunk out from under them. He left the knickknacks on shore.

Sinking into his perfectly aged leather chair, Fletch pulled the ops plan up on his computer. The electronics were all new, courtesy of

Parramatta's many upgrades, so angling one of his three monitors so Charlie could read it was easy. He had no secrets from his XO. If he dropped dead during the night, it would be her job to fight *Parramatta* in the coming battle. Knowledge was everything.

His eyes swept over the summary page, taking in the timeline. He could read the specific details later.

Time 0+00: U.S. SSN (1) enter SOM from North and sweep ahead of main body. Mission: destroy all enemy submarine forces within SOM. U.S. SSN (2) take station at southeast end of SOM. Maintain blocking position. Mission: Prevent entry of enemy submarine or surface forces into SOM.

3+00: Advance surface force enter SOM from North, SOA 30 knots. Advance surface force consists of Surface Action Group (SAG) Alpha. US DDG (2), AUS DDG (1), AUS FF (2), US LCS (1). Mission: Seek and destroy enemy CDCM batteries and surface assets.

3+30: Main body enter SOM. Main body consists of U.S. CVN (1), U.S. CG (2), UK DDG (1), U.S. DDG (2), AUS FF (1), U.S. LCS (1). Mission: Seek and destroy...

Odds favored *Parramatta* as part of the advance surface force. Fletch drummed his fingers against his desk. Even with a sub going in ahead of them, the first ships through would get hammered. That attack boat might take out the enemy subs in the narrow strait, but its CO would neither know nor care about the coastal cruise missile batteries. *That* would be the SAG's problem. And Fletch would be in the thick of it.

"Well," he finally said. "This will make for an eventful day."

"Yes, sir. It will." Charlie's eyes met Fletch's. *This* is what they had signed up to do. Not sit in a shipyard somewhere silently gathering dust.

It was nice to finally have an opportunity to make a difference.

Lunch time at Red Tiger Station was always a madhouse. There were four food courts, but in Ning's opinion, no one put much thought into the *location* of the stupid things. One was way the hell out on the east side of Red Tiger, near nothing but apartments. That was great at breakfast and dinner time, but when people were at work and wanted food, it was a real pain in the behind.

The other three were clumped way too close together, with nothing interesting out near Fogborne's corner at all. And she didn't really like the "street" vendors who'd taken to setting up stands nearby. Sam ate just about anything, and Doctor Kim said it was fine, but there were times when Ning wanted greasy, stupid American food.

Unfortunately, that meant she had to walk through the crowd at the Green Court in order to reach Blue Court, trying to ignore her stomach rumbling the whole way. Sam was off eating some hero or gyro or whatever, so he hadn't wanted to come with her, which made Ning stomp just a little more than she needed to.

At least she didn't have to go to Red Court. That was out by the garage and an even longer walk. Sighing, she added herself to the embarrassingly long line. Ning considered running equations in her head for a moment and then pulled her phone out to start playing her second favorite game.

"Excuse me, Ning?"

Ning Tang turned to face Audie Meyer, the deputy commander for the Pulsar Security detachment on Red Tiger Station. She was a tall and willowy woman who didn't look like she could tell one end of a gun from another—but what did Ning know? She'd never so much as touched a firearm. Ning didn't see Audie much, unless there were *real* problems on Red Tiger Station, but even then, those didn't usually touch the Fogborne team, so Ning didn't much have to care.

What she wanted to do was get her lunch in peace. Fast food french fries were her sin, the greasier the better. They helped her think her way through complex problems like containment fields and laser equations.

Maybe she *should've* gone to the other end of the station. Red Court always had shorter lines.

She turned and pasted a smile on. "Hi. What's up?"

"Can we talk for a moment? Nothing scary, but it's important." Audie seemed a little rattled, so Ning looked around.

No pirates.

"Sure." Swallowing, she followed Audie into a small security office just behind the taco place. "I'm not...in trouble or something, am I?"

"No, of course not." Audie smiled and gestured Ning into a red plastic chair that creaked and was even more uncomfortable than it looked. "I just needed to talk to you about the Fogborne Project."

Ning shrugged, glancing at the monitors to her left. They showed all parts of the station but focused on Blue Court—and the Fogborne research cell, which was way the hell two platforms over from here and in its own private corner. "That stuff should probably go through Doctor Kim."

"I hear you're the one who made the breakthrough," Audie replied. "Rumor at Pulsar says the design is yours—and believe me, the company is *very* happy with you."

"I have the best job." Ning was too off-kilter to grin; she didn't *like* this stark room. Red Tiger Station was famous for a riot of colors and art, which was why she loved it here despite the threats of piracy, flooding, and a war or three dropping on their heads.

The room was empty except for Audie. That was strange, too.

Audie leaned forward. "How would you like to make even more money for doing it?"

Ning laughed nervously. "I, uh, I'm doing pretty well. You probably know that since you keep people from kidnapping us or stealing our money. And that next bonus for getting the plans and prototype off station is pretty awesome, too."

"I can get you more."

"What?"

"I have some friends who would like a copy of your design. Just the plans. And they will pay you double what Pulsar is to get it." Audie glanced at the door and then looked back at Ning with a smile. "The only caveat is that you can't know where the design is going."

"That sounds kind of...ominous. Like, dark web and black-market kind of stuff I don't really want to get involved in," Ning said, babbling to buy herself a little time.

Ning was twenty-three. Why did so many people think finishing her PhD at seventeen left her with no common sense? Sure, Ning had been innocent at the start—she wasn't stupid and knew she lacked world experience—but she wasn't dumb enough to fall face first into this trap, thank you very much.

"It's just a way of doing business. All it means is that you'll sign a nondisclosure agreement." Audie held out a tablet. "I'm sure you've seen a hundred of those."

"I signed a noncompete agreement, too." Ning fidgeted and the chair squeaked, weird tingles running through her bones.

"This isn't competition. Just...giving yourself a bonus."

Ning frowned. "You work for Pulsar. I'm sure this is *totally* above-ground."

Now it was Audie's turn to squirm. "This is a good offer. You should look at it."

"I think I should leave." Ning stood, brushing the tablet aside. "I'll, uh, see you later."

Bolting out the door, she bypassed the french fry line and rushed to the Fogborne team area. Not looking over her shoulder was hard, but surely Audie wasn't a threat. She just wanted...

What *did* Audie want? Ning should've asked who those "friends" were, but now it was too late. Swallowing, she headed for Doctor Kim's office. This wasn't something she should stay quiet about.

Diego Garcia still didn't have a lot in the way of pier space. The heavy lift ships who used to call the base home were now anchored in the harbor; no one knew if a full-on tank invasion would ever be necessary in this war, but those ships—and the tanks, trucks, and other equipment on board—weren't what the navy needed right now. Nancy heard some talk of offloading the equipment and turning the ships into supply carriers, but so far, they'd just sat offshore, swinging at anchor.

Fortunately, there was enough space on the quay wall for *Fletcher* to moor just aft of *Belleau Wood* and forward of USS *Lionfish*, a fast-attack submarine. It was a tight squeeze and required the help of a tug to get the destroyer in, but onloading missiles required pier space, so they had little choice.

Aft of *Lionfish*, Nancy spied another Australian frigate getting ready to depart. HMAS *Bogan* was decades newer than *Parramatta*, sleeker and faster, but unproven. As far as Nancy knew, the coming battle would be *Bogan's* first. She wished them luck.

She met Rear Admiral Rosario on the pier just as *Bogan* cast off all lines.

"Strange, isn't it?" Rosario's smile was crooked. "Part of me wants to be there with them."

"And part of me could do with never seeing the SOM again." Nancy shuddered. "I *might* even take the long way around, even if we win it back."

Rosario chuckled. "I wouldn't go that far."

"So what's the mission, ma'am?" Nancy refused to be like her husband and stuff her hands in her pockets. Instead, she clasped them behind her back, glancing over her shoulder at her destroyer.

Fletcher was still beautiful, despite the battle scars. Sure, she could use a fresh coat of paint, but they were at war. Keeping equipment up and *Fletcher* armed were far more important than worrying about spit and polish.

Her eyes flicked to *Bogan*, whose unmarred sides gleamed. Yeah. They were new at this. The poor Aussies on board probably didn't even know which equipment liked to glitch yet.

"Seek and destroy," Rosario replied. "After we leave here, we'll hook up with an oiler, top off the gas tanks, and then meet HMS *Diamond* as she comes out of the Red Sea. Then the three of us will go on the offensive and hunt Indian and French surface assets—including their supply ships."

Nancy nodded. "So, like Admiral Rodriquez wanted to do before Task Force Twenty-Three got poached for Christmas Island and everything else."

"Exactly. Three ships should be a small enough force that they leave us alone." Rosario's gaze shifted east. "And we both know there's about to be a hell of a fireworks show to make the enemy look everywhere but at us. I aim to use that."

"*Fletcher's* got your back, Admiral." Nancy grinned. She'd only been in one fight under Julia Rosario, but she knew who she'd follow into the storm.

Rosario clapped her on the shoulder. "Then let's load those missiles and get out of town."

Rani watched the girl flee the security office, cocking her head.

It was a pity that the simple option—offering money—had not worked. A few days' spying on the Fogborne Team had identified the youngest member as the weakest link: Ning Tang often wandered off by herself, and she rarely paid attention to her surroundings. Audie Meyer—a long-term investment on the part of Indian intelligence—knew Ning well enough to confirm Rani's assessment, which was why she'd put the security officer up to making that monetary offer.

Sadly, it would not be that easy.

Shrugging, Rani continued to shadow Ning as she fled toward the Fogborne Research Team's secure area. She was confident that Audie would not betray her Indian paymasters, at least not if she wanted to keep her boyfriend out of prison. That thought made a thin smile cross Rani's face as she passed a falafel stand, the scents of which filled the wide "tube"-like street connecting two of the station's main platforms.

She had been in the intelligence business long enough not to be surprised by how corruptible security types were. Audie Meyer might have accepted a mere bribe, but the addition of a small amount of blackmail—such as the evidence that her longtime boyfriend was embezzling money from WAAS, where *he* worked in security—guaranteed her loyalty. Even if Pulsar pressed her, Audie would hold firm.

After all, WAAS, otherwise known as the Worldwide Acquisition and Services Group, was a far nastier customer than Indian Intelligence. The intelligence community had rules that sovereign nations followed. WAAS, an underwater conglomeration that came to power with the Rush to the Ocean Floor, was a cross between an old-fashioned mafia and a hungry capitalistic behemoth, with the morals to match.

Indian Intelligence was no danger to Audie. But if they slipped WAAS evidence that her boyfriend was embezzling...well, Audie knew the risks.

Rani turned her attention back to Ning Tang as the Fogborne's youngest member turned a corner, slipping past a surf shop—why was a surf shop underwater?—and a bakery. The girl paused to look over her shoulder, but by the time her eyes found Rani, Rani was absorbed in a display of chocolate cupcakes.

She would let her flee today. Rani was not in a hurry. She would wait until Ning regained her confidence. Then she would act.

India needed the information inside Ning Tang's head, and if Ning would not provide it willingly, Rani would provide Ning Tang to India.

Alex hadn't expected an email from beyond the grave.

Jimmy Carter slowed again, her Type 2 periscope barely breaking past the waves. This was the midpoint of her run to Red Tiger Station, which was quiet so far. But they were about to enter much more contested waters as they crept closer to the South China Sea, so Alex deemed it wise to check the mail one last time before going in.

He'd opted for a southern approach instead of the typical western one, avoiding the Strait of Malacca and slipping through the various seas around the Indonesian Archipelago. That eventually let *Jimmy Carter* transit north through the Sulu Sea and hug the Philippines, which were far calmer waters than the middle of the South China Sea. There was still nasty fighting near the Spratly Islands between a couple of the Chinas, both on the surface and under it. Alex was happy to skip around north of that. Hopefully, they'd nip into Red Tiger Station from the south, and no one would be the wiser.

Emails crept in slowly along the comms wire once the boat went shallow; there was a lot of data to unpack, and it all came rolled up in one mess of information that the server doled out a bit at a time. Alex wasn't in a hurry to check his email after the last shock he received, so he waited until the download was almost complete before heading to his stateroom.

Then he caught the sender's name on his screen.

This time, he bolted for the head he shared with George, barely making it to the toilet in time to leave his lunch in the bowl. Alex vomited again and again, until there was nothing but bile. Then he cleaned his face and washed his mouth out with shaking hands.

Part of him wanted to return to control, to ignore the email. But he didn't have that in him, so Alex slid back into his chair, his eyes landing on the reply to the last email he'd sent Teresa.

His stomach lurched. It had a time stamp matching the launch of the SUBMISS/SUBSUNK buoy. Alex knew what that meant. The release of the buoy triggered an emergency upload of all messages waiting in the queue. He'd heard of personal emails that went out at the same time a friend or family member died. He'd just never received one.

Sucking in a deep breath, Alex forced his hands to stop shaking and opened the email. He owed Teresa that much.

Teresa's last words were strangely upbeat, promising a story about two *Scorpenes* he would never read. Should he offer this up to her ex-husband? Alex didn't know the man, but he was sure the navy could get the email to him. It was classified, but these days that mattered less and less. Too much information about the war was on the internet already. A few lines about submarines Teresa had already sunk really didn't matter, not when the navy was announcing losses and ships sunk on a weekly basis.

Teresa's son, Jonas, would probably want to read this someday. Alex pushed the email to saved items and decided he'd fight that battle when his current mission ended.

On a whim, he googled *USS Douglass*. Unsurprisingly, the navy already released an official statement, including a summary of the patrols *Douglass* had completed and the ships Teresa had sunk. There was even an official U.S. Navy tweet about *Douglass'* loss:

FIRE WHEN READY: A MILITARY THRILLER

United States Navy
@USNavy
We mourn the loss of **@USSDouglass** and her crew today. Douglass went down fighting to protect a convoy of civilians in the Western Pacific. Our hearts go out to the family and friends of her crew.
#navy #submarines

There was no mention of survivors.

There were hundreds of retweets, ranging from people yelling at the navy for the loss to grief for the families. One, however, made Alex's blood boil:

Captain Jules Rochambeau
@JulesRochambeau
C'est dommage. Be faster next time.
#barracuda

Alex wanted to chuck his computer across the room. Rochambeau's bragging was nothing new, but it had never hit so close to home. He remembered looking that French bastard in the eye on Armistice Station, listening to his false words of friendship and knowing they were lies even then. Now...now Rochambeau was the worst—the best—the enemy had.

And Alex had *almost* been close enough to shoot *Barracuda* right out from under the smug weasel. One torpedo, or two, and he could've closed the loop that started before the war even began, when Rochambeau snuck up underneath USS *Kansas* and shot a submarine full of civilians...leaving *Kansas* with the blame.

The upward trajectory of Alex's career ended that day, but that wasn't even why he hated the man. He hated Rochambeau because he laid the groundwork for World War III and then later lit the fuse with gleeful abandon on Armistice Station. Without those two events, perhaps the world might have stepped back after the U.S. and India started shooting in the Strait of Malacca that first time.

And that damned braggart was at the center of both. Now here he was, tweeting how it was "such a shame" that he'd killed over a hundred people. *Be faster next time.*

"You all right, Alex?"

Rage or grief made him slow to look up, but that was Paul standing in the doorway to the shared head, his dark face pinched with concern. Paul called him "captain" in front of the crew—George would throw a fit if anyone didn't—but now he dropped the formalities, crossing the small stateroom to crouch by Alex's side.

"I will be," Alex whispered, wiping at his mouth. "You ever get an email from a dead friend?"

"Can't say I have. Death comes pretty fast in my business. There usually isn't time."

He coughed out a laugh. "She wrote this one right before her sub got shot out from under her."

"Fuck." An enormous hand landed on his shoulder and squeezed; Alex tried not to shudder in relief or grief. "I'm sorry, brother."

"Thanks, Paul." Alex scraped his hands over his face, thinking about Rochambeau's tweet.

Be faster next time.

On second thought, he'd leave the email from Teresa right where it was. Her family had suffered enough already.

And then he'd find a way to be faster.

Chapter 16

Not a Moment Too Soon

25 September 2039, Red Tiger Station

"You guys all packed?" Doctor Kim Leifsson had gathered the Fogborne team together in their break room, and while her expression was calm, Ning could tell from the way she picked at her nails that she was nervous.

The room felt eerily empty without papers and coffee cups strewn across every available surface. Even though their designs were electronic, everyone but Ning was old fashioned and liked to draft on paper. Even *Sam*, who was just a bit older than her and should've known better. But Ning hadn't realized how she'd gotten used to being surrounded by paper, how comfortable it felt. Homey, even. Now it was gone, and the room felt bigger. She shivered.

"You think this is actually going to happen?" Dieter Weber, their quality engineer, yawned, curling up on a couch Ning hadn't realized was decorated with a faint pattern of roses. They usually weren't visible under the spare parts bin. "The last, what, four attempts were all canceled. Why not this one?"

"This is the first time they've sent the navy." Sam Yeung sat to Ning's right, folded neatly into a big armchair. "I'm going to bet pirates won't scare *them* away."

"There's something other than pirates going on here." The words blurted out of Ning before she could stop herself, and four heads swiveled to stare at her. She flushed. "Couple days ago—I dunno, five?—Audie Meyer from Pulsar Security offered me a 'bonus' for giving some so-called friends of hers copies of the reactor plans."

"She *what?*" three voices echoed.

Kim's eyes narrowed. "Why didn't you mention this earlier, Ning?"

"I don't know. It was weird, okay?" Ning flung her hands up. "You weren't in your office when I came by, and then I kept hoping she'd say it was all a joke."

"You're going to have to report that, Jake," Kim said to their dedicated security guard.

Jake Lawrence nodded and pulled out his tablet. "On it." He glanced up at Ning. "I'll need the details, but it's probably just corporate espionage. Some other company bribed Meyer and now Pulsar's going to have to deal with her. Shame. I always thought she was one of the good ones."

"She seemed nice enough until she tried to get me to break my nondisclosure agreement, sure." Ning scowled.

"Point taken. I'll fill out the forms," Jake replied.

"Back to our evacuation. Are we going to be able to bring the prototype? It's disassembled and inert and should fit through a normal hatch," Sam said.

"Then there shouldn't be a problem," Kim replied. "No one said there was a limit on what we could bring, so long as it fits through a hatch." She smiled. "We're looking at an early morning departure, so we need to be ready tonight."

Ning's heart fluttered. Were they really going to leave? After so many *months* of trying, she was eager to walk on dry land again...and to get their design into safe hands and finally end this project. She had other things she wanted to do. Losing her life to fusion was *not* on her to-do list.

"I've got all the project files downloaded and on three devices. They're uploaded to the cloud, too, but that requires triple authentication to get at." Ning grinned. "That way, Audie's *friends* can't just creep off with it."

"Good work." Kim smiled. "So now we sit tight until the navy arrives tomorrow and we take our luxurious ride out of town."

"Could be cool." Ning shrugged. "I bet navy subs have all kinds of awesome tech."

She'd been on every interesting type of civilian submarine known to man—except the luxury yachts, which were just giant party busses—but never a navy boat. Ning was looking forward to that experience almost as much as she wanted to get out of this spring-loaded tin can.

"Uh, guys, we've got a problem." Sam held his tablet up, and Ning caught the headline:

FUSION IS THE FUTURE

Hank Carson, Washington Post

September 26, 2039

Ever since the Experimental Reactor Team in Provence, France, made a breakthrough with a usable, power-producing fusion reactor—albeit on a small *power* scale—the race has been on. Who can create a working fusion reactor and provide clean, safe, and renewable power? And now that there's a war on, who can put that reactor in a small enough package to be used on a warship?

Rumor says there may be an answer to both.

As most know, nuclear fission is still the commonly used form of nuclear reactions, both in civilian and military applications. Fusion, however, provides three to four times more energy without the same radioactive waste or a danger of a meltdown or runaway reaction. The only problem is that *deploying* fusion has been hard.

"Fusion is the dream of every scientist," Profession Jennifer Abel of Georgetown University says. "However, it's been the unreachable holy grail for so long. Every time we *think* we've achieved it, we discover we have to pour more power into it than we get out, which doesn't exactly achieve that goal of clean world power, does it?"

Ever since the war started, the Experimental Reactor Team at ITER—formerly a multi-national effort, but now utterly controlled by France and her allies—has pushed forward to replicate the self-fueling fusion reaction created by Christophe Girard. The Girard Reactor in Marseilles has powered half the French power grid for eight years, but it is the size of a football field.

No one has shoehorned a self-sustaining reaction into a smaller shell…until now.

Multiple sources indicate that Pulsar Power Ltd—a giant among global defense contractors—has finally hit a home run. With at least five separate research groups working on fusion power, Pulsar has often been called desperate to make this breakthrough, but now that work has paid off. A source within the organization hints that one isolated team has achieved not only a self-sustaining fusion reaction but has also created a portable—and usable—design.

Only time will tell how small this reactor is, but if these reports are true, it could change the world.

26 September, one mile south of Red Tiger Station

"You expecting trouble?" Paul murmured from Alex's right. He fit better in *Jimmy Carter's* control room than anywhere else; if Alex kept his old friend right by the periscopes, Paul was less likely to hit his head as they approached Red Tiger Station.

Alex shook his head. "No, but the reports of pirate activity are a little concerning. I'd rather not get shish kabobbed if we can help it."

"Well, if there are any on the station, my boys and girls are more than willing to help with that."

"I bet you are."

Alex had worked with Paul before, back in his days as *Kansas'* executive officer. Together, they'd taken down some pirates and exposed Alex to an unfortunate number of guns and pirates willing to use them—neither of which were experiences he cared to repeat. Having a gun waved in his face was *not* his kind of warfare, thank you very much.

"Damn, that feels like a lifetime ago, doesn't it?" Paul asked, clearly seeing Alex's expression. "Peacetime was so simple. Find the pirates. Stop the assnuggets from stealing shit. Rinse, repeat, and try not to hit my head on your goddamned tiny submarine hatches."

Alex snorted. "It's not my fault you're half gorilla."

"I keep telling you that it's *full* gorilla, Captain, sir." Paul stuck his tongue out at him, and half the watchstanders in control snickered.

"All right, children, enough fun time," Alex chided them with a smile. "Let's focus on the game. Navigator, you got the station location dialed in?"

"Yes, sir."

"Weps, how are we looking for security teams to back up Colonel Swanson's marines?"

"Armed and ready, sir. None of them are on the maneuvering detail watchbill and everyone's set," Benji replied.

"Excellent, thank you." Alex turned back to Maggie. "All right, let's go shallow enough to pop the wire up and talk to these people."

"Going shallow, aye, sir."

Alex watched with half an eye as Maggie conned the big submarine upward, but she knew her business and didn't need her captain leaning over her shoulder. Instead, he skimmed through the last intelligence update—now six days old—on his tablet.

"Anything I missed?" Paul asked quietly.

"Nothing new. Pirates, China, Taiwan, two other Chinas, and unknown forces. Do not fire until fired upon—and that goes for you and your peeps, too." He glanced up at Paul. "That going to be a problem? I know the war's got some folks on a hair trigger."

Paul shook his head. "We know who the enemy is, and until these cracker jacks prove they are, there's no reason to pop 'em."

"It's so reassuring when you talk like a teenager," Alex said dryly.

"Ain't it just?" Paul grinned.

"Level at two hundred feet, Captain," Maggie reported. "Comms wire streamed."

"Thank you, Nav." Butterflies started doing laps in Alex's stomach, and he squirmed. Damn it all if his old fear of public speaking didn't want to rear its ugly head again *now*.

And, oh, George was watching him with wide eyes, just looking for a reason to be afraid. Alex cleared his throat and forced himself to pick up the handset and get on with it.

Damn it all if he didn't need to clear his throat a *second* time before he could make himself speak, though.

"Red Tiger Station, this is Killer Rabbit, calling you on underwater standard, over," Alex said.

Silence responded. Not even a crackle of acknowledgment. Alex tried not to fidget, wondering if he'd spoken clearly or if he'd said something stupid.

"You think they're asleep?" Paul muttered.

Alex glared at him.

"What?" Paul snickered. "Who the hell saddled you with that moniker, anyway? *Killer Rabbit?* You've got to be kidding me."

"No one. It's our callsign." Alex waggled his eyebrows.

"You're kidding."

"Nope. Read your history. President Carter had a, um, *encounter* with a swamp rabbit that attacked his boat, and the press at the time called it a 'killer rabbit attack.'" Alex grinned. "We love to dip into history when picking callsigns."

"Oh, fuck, that's awesome. *Killer Rabbit* on a goddamned submarine. It's like something out of a terrible movie." Paul's shoulders shook with suppressed laughter until George lunged over to the pair, hissing:

"Colonel, if you would *please* not mock our boat's call sign, I would appreciate it greatly."

Paul blinked. "XO, I might be a meat-headed marine...but if I was mocking you, you'd know it."

"Gentlemen—" Alex started, only to be cut off by the radio.

"Killer Rabbit, this is Red Tiger Control. Welcome. You are on today's docket for underwater docking station three."

Alex almost dropped the microphone. *"What?"*

Ning found the walk from her apartment to the Fogborne area strangely long that morning. It was early enough that the station should've been quiet—or relatively so, because Red Tiger *never* slept; they just changed what was on the entertainment menu—but there were a lot of people about.

Including one twenty-something-year-old Indian woman who seemed to be watching her every time Ning *wasn't* looking.

She was sure she was paranoid, but the feeling didn't ease when she arrived in the break room again the next morning. Ning was the last to arrive, and Sam grabbed her arm immediately.

"He was here when I got here," Sam muttered, pointing at the stranger inside their private area.

Well, he wasn't quite a stranger. Ning knew who Jin Wu was, even if she didn't think he had any clue what her name was. Red Tiger Station's superintendent was a small but bombastic man who'd always been one of their better allies, making sure other businesses and research groups didn't impede on the prime territory Pulsar leased. Ning had said hi to him a grand total of once, though. A strange feeling crept up her spine, one that was cold and stiff all at once.

"Maybe he's here to close out the lease?" she whispered, shuffling closer to Sam, just in case. She was tired of roadblocks. Ning just wanted *out.*

"Mr. Wu, it's very kind of you to come see us off," Doctor Kim said, wearing a smile Ning knew was strained. She looked like she hadn't slept all night, with her hair in the messiest ponytail this side of a bee's nest.

"I'm afraid I've come for more than that, Doctor." Wu crossed his arms. "I understand you're all leaving today. I want in."

Kim stopped. "I beg your pardon?"

"I want off this station and into whatever gig you have with Pulsar. I'll make it worth their while." Wu grinned. "I know where every body is buried out here."

"I'm not sure I want to know about that, Mr. Wu." Kim glanced at Jake, who frowned.

"You might not, but your superiors will." Wu waved a hand. "I'll wait while you ask them."

"Why do you want out?" Jake asked. "You've got a good gig here. Like you said, you know all the dirt—so why back out?"

"This area is dangerous, and I'm a practical man," Wu said.

"It's seven in the evening back home. All the decision makers are in bed." Kim pursed her lips. "I can ask on the transport they've sent for us, but I don't know what the answer will be."

"You do that. I'll contact you again after they arrive." Wu nodded jerkily. "They'll be coming to underwater docking station number three."

"Thank you." Kim smiled politely until Wu was gone, after which her face crumbled into exhaustion.

"We'll be out of here soon," Ning said, moving over to wrap an arm around her mentor. "Right?"

"I sure hope so."

Ning swallowed and didn't say anything. Between that creepy woman watching her and Wu wanting to leave, she wasn't sure what to make of today. And now a new thought occurred to her: what if getting *off* Red Tiger Station was just as bad as staying?

She shook her head and tried to chase that question away. It would be hard to find a worse situation than being surrounded by pirates, greedy station superintendents, and corporate espionage...wouldn't it?

Alex needed a moment to catch his mental balance. Unfortunately, George was faster. His XO grabbed his arm in claw-like fingers, clinging to Alex like a drowning man.

"Sir, we can't use an underwater docking station. They're meant for submarines a tenth of our size!"

"Yeah, I know, XO. Let me tell these people that." Shaking George off was impossible; although he let go of Alex's arm, the XO stuck by his side like a bad smell. Alex shook himself and lifted the microphone. "Red Tiger Control, this is Killer Rabbit. I think you might've been misinformed on our size. We require at least a docking cradle, but best option is a TRANSPLAT docking, over."

"Killer Rabbit, Red Tiger, you've been assigned docking station three. Don't you worry; we can accommodate subs of *all* lengths, over."

Alex grimaced. "My length is four hundred and fifty-two feet—one hundred thirty-eight meters—and my displacement is over twelve thousand tons, over."

He hadn't wanted to put that information out there; it screamed that *Jimmy Carter*—disguised by her callsign or not—was a military vessel. And a big one.

"Sir, do you think we should've given them that much information?" George whispered.

Not rolling his eyes was so hard. "If we get lucky, they'll think we're a boomer." Alex dredged up a smile. "That should provide some anonymity."

"*Sir.*"

"Don't have kittens, George." Alex patted him on the shoulder and waited for Red Tiger Station to get over their surprise. Apparently, the navy hadn't sent word ahead.

How shocking.

After a long silence on the other end, a different voice asked: "Can you hover, Killer Rabbit?"

"That's affirmative, over."

"Then please proceed to docking station three. It should be marked on your electronic charts, over."

Feeling like he'd been slapped, Alex looked at Maggie. She spread her hands. "It's here, Captain. And the specs *say* we can fit."

"Do they?"

Alex didn't normally mind how his sub was almost a hundred feet longer than her younger sisters. Only the late model *Virginias* were around her length, and those boats were half missile boat, not pure attack submarine. To be fair, *Jimmy Carter* hadn't spent her entire career solely as an attack submarine, either. Alex's submarine spent over two decades as America's secret spy submarine, and she'd been good at it, too. She'd been built from the keel up for that role, with an extra hundred foot "multi-mission platform" added to her design that her two decommissioned sisters of the *Seawolf*-class didn't have.

The now-defunct MMP had been an underwater hanger, holding remote-operated vehicles, a cargo area, and a lockout area for special forces teams like Paul's. Unfortunately, most of those toys were gone, and the MMP was welded shut. But it wasn't like the navy could remove the MMP before pushing *Jimmy Carter* into the war...which meant all that extra length was Alex's problem.

"For some definition of fitting." Maggie grimaced. "With about twenty-five feet to spare, forward and aft."

"Joy."

George staggered close again. "Captain, you can't possibly be thinking of—"

Alex held up a hand, then walked over to the electronic chart to study it. "Weps, are our UUVs up to spec?"

"Um, they passed self-test last week." Beni blinked, looking over at Chief Bradley.

"They'll go where they're told, sir," the new sonar chief said. "But you know that UUVs like to dive to the bottom of their own accord, right?"

"Oh, yeah. I know." Alex scratched his chin. "But I don't think anyone really gives a good goddamn what a few UUVs cost right now."

UUVs, or Underwater Unmanned Vehicles—pronounced "You-Vees" by sailors—used to be one of the best or worst inventions the navy had ever bought. They were high-tech, unmanned vehicles that could expand a visual or sonar search pattern. Most captains stopped using them once the war started because they took so much maintenance, not to mention how they required a full sonar team to monitor the things.

If you didn't watch one, even for a moment, they loved to plunge to the ocean floor like a dive bomber and never come up again. In shallow waters, divers could retrieve them...but who wanted to send divers out in contested waters? Besides, the damned things were heavy, and risking injury to divers for optional equipment was part of a much different equation when you were at war.

Still, *Jimmy Carter* carried eight of the little monsters. Alex might as well use them.

"*Can* you slide up to an underwater docking station in this beast?" Paul asked quietly.

"Sure." Alex shrugged. "It's like a cat trying to mate with an elephant in the dark. You can do it, but it's not very fun."

"You want to spin up the UUVs as eyes, sir?" Benji asked, leaning forward eagerly.

"Bingo." Alex grinned. "They're already paid for, right?"

George went so white, Alex thought he might keel over.

Alex grinned. "Let's launch the UUVs, Weps, and I'll conn us in."

Paul leaned in, whispering: "Tell me you have thrusters on this super-size sausage of yours."

"Fore and aft. Spy sub gifts."

"Huh. Maybe then we won't die. Try not to fuck it up, Rook Buddy."

"Colonel!" Finally, George found his voice, and his whine was—of course—aimed at Paul's humor.

Paul held up his hands. "Sorry, XO, it's a Norwich thing. You do know your captain and I were roommates when we were wee fucking babes, right?"

"UUVs ready for launch in ten minutes, sir," Chief Bradley reported before George could find his voice.

Now all Alex had to do was ringmaster this bickering circus until he could drive his cat over to mate with an elephant.

The atmosphere was tense in the now-empty Fogborne center of operations. The reactor next door continued to run, but its trained crew was independent of the design team now. With their prototype stowed and their belongings packed, there was nothing to do...except worry.

Even a whisper sounded like a scream, so when Doctor Kim Leifsson spoke in a normal tone, everyone jumped.

"They're here."

Ning's head snapped up, the game she was playing on her phone forgotten. All of her interesting equipment was packed, and all she had was *Sharks and Ladders*, which was fun, but level 238 was getting annoying. Still, it kept her attention away from the echoing emptiness in their break room. "For real?"

"For real." Kim brushed hair away from her glasses as she smiled, her movements dragging. "Jake says they're docking now."

"You're supposing all of Pulsar Security is on the down low." Ning heaved a sigh. "With what happened to me, are you sure about that?"

"Hey, at least it was a bribe and not a threat." Sam never looked up from his phone, also playing *Sharks and Ladders*. Annoyingly, he was twenty levels ahead of her.

"So far."

"Jake also says that there's a *lot* of people near the underwater docking stations," Kim said as she tucked her phone away. "Apparently, word got out that a sub braved the pirates to get here."

Ning stuck her tongue out at Sam. "Told you there was something threatening going on. Betcha someone at Pulsar Security leaked it."

"You don't know that."

"And we don't know it wasn't. Pulsar arranged our ride out, so *they're* the ones who know about the sub, right?" she asked. Kim nodded, and Sam's eyes narrowed. "We didn't even know when the sub was going to be here, just that it'd come sometime this week if it came. But people are already all stacked up down there, probably trying to buy their way on board."

"I can't blame them," Kim said softly. "Red Tiger isn't a safe place to be these days. The garage getting destroyed...didn't help."

"Neither has all the pirate activity nearby." Dieter Weber, silent until now, pulled a file up on his phone. "I've been tracking it from news reports and Pulsar Security files. We're averaging three attacks per week over the last four months, and at least one of them causes deaths."

"That bad?" Sam asked.

Dieter nodded. "Worse this month. It's up to four attacks per week if I look at a radius of one mile around the station."

Ning shuddered. "Can we just leave this place?"

"That's exactly what we're doing." Kim squeezed her shoulder. "In fact, we should go join that crowd now, shouldn't we? We wouldn't want to miss our ride."

"Is Jake meeting us there?" Ning asked, thinking about the crowd and their disassembled prototype. They didn't *need* the prototype fusion reactor...but it was nice to have a working model. Building a new one would take time.

"He's there and so is the bulk of our luggage," Kim replied. "I helped him bring everything down before dawn."

"Here's hoping no one steals it," Dieter said.

"Dieter." Kim turned a disapproving eye on the quality engineer.

Dieter shrugged. "I am just saying what you're all thinking."

Kim sighed. "Let's get to the docks. Maybe we can get on the boat before we're scheduled to at noon."

Ning rolled her eyes. "Only if something suddenly starts going right in our lives for the first time in about a year."

Chapter 17

Good Old-Fashioned Greed

Jimmy Carter slid into Red Tiger Station's underwater docking station with an undignified *thud* that shook the submarine from bow to stern. But nothing broke and no one screamed; Alex considered that a victory.

"All stop."

"All stop, aye, sir. My engines are all stop."

"See? Like a cat mating with an elephant in the dark." Alex grinned.

Unlike most modern underwater stations, Red Tiger didn't even have a cradle for the gigantic submarine to rest on; instead, this station expected *Jimmy Carter* to sit on a trio of gigantic struts constructed parallel to the ocean floor. Sliding onto them was a copperplated bitch, despite Alex's serene smile. Coming in too high meant he'd ram the docking station with the side of his submarine. Too low, and he'd impale his boat on the struts. While he was fairly sure that the HY100 steel of *Jimmy Carter's* hull could withstand the impact, particularly at low speeds, what the hell kind of idiot captain wanted to find out?

Instead, he had to aim *Jimmy Carter* for the perfect sweet spot in the middle, crabbing the boat sideways so that she floated above the slats by just a few inches until ballasted down to rest on them. Then

Red Tiger Station could swing out the end of the docking arm to maneuver it over *Jimmy Carter's* spine, where it would connect to her midships hatch.

That arm extended and met the hull with a second *thump* as Alex fought back the urge to scowl. That was sloppy.

The idea of all of Red Tiger Station's personnel being so cavalier with procedures made worry gnaw at his gut. People who ignored procedures usually forgot *maintenance*, and Alex's boat sat perched on three metal struts that sure as hell required upkeep.

But he'd split before the damn things could break, he reminded himself. Even if they'd never encountered a twelve thousand–ton submarine before.

"You still haven't convinced me why any sane cat would want to fuck an elephant," Paul rumbled.

"That's because there's no reason. This design is stupid, even for a luxury boat worth millions with hull-mounted cameras." Alex shook his head. "I've driven one of those, if you recall. They aren't maneuverable enough to get in this hole without being scratched, either."

"When did you drive a million-dollar luxury sub, Captain?" Maggie leaned forward, her eyes gleaming with curiosity.

Paul's booming laugh droned out Alex's attempt at a response. "Oh, a couple years back. Last time your captain and I got together, he had a splendid plan to bait some pirates in with a Migaloo while me and my Marines trapped 'em." Paul grinned. "Ask him how well that shiny-ass Migaloo came out of the encounter."

"Better you don't ask me how I trashed it." Alex laughed. "It's a long story."

"Sounds like a fun one, sir," Maggie replied.

"It wasn't for the sub." Paul chortled, his great shoulders shaking with mirth.

Alex rolled his eyes, but he didn't get a chance to answer before George's voice blared out of the speaker to his right. "Conn, XO, I have the station security manager at the midships hatch. He wants to talk to the captain."

"On my way." Alex turned to Maggie. "Nav, you have the deck. We'll man the quarterdeck inside the docking tube, but I have no intention of staying here long enough to shift the watch. Keep the reactor hot and be ready to roll."

"You got it, Captain."

"You're with me, Paul." Alex gestured for his friend to follow, noting Paul taking quietly into his radio as he did.

By the time they reached the midships hatch—a short walk from control and on the same deck—half of Paul's team was on their heels. Wearing body armor made it a challenge for the marines to squeeze through the narrow passageways, and Alex heard them cursing and mumbling, though no one dropped behind. The rest were waiting with George at the bottom of the hatch.

Normally, Alex didn't find being surrounded by heavily armed marines comforting, but today... Today, instinct crawled around his spine like a fire worm, sparking with worry every few minutes. This mission had been too easy so far.

For once, he and George were on the same page. One look at George's sweaty forehead told Alex how unhappy his XO was, and the way George's fingers were clenched into fists told a story about how hard he was working to keep his hands from shaking. Alex hadn't realized anyone could look so scared when surrounded by friendly marines.

"Sir, I took a peek at the station topside. It looks...*busy* out there," George whispered.

"That's why we brought our heavily armed friends, XO." Alex clapped George on the shoulder. "Where's this security manager?"

"Their side of the hatch. I'm not letting someone like *him* on board." George squared his shoulders. "He talks like a snake, and the security risks alone make me shudder."

"Not a bad plan." Alex thought it a poor way to play host, but hey, they weren't really here to make friends, were they? Maybe George was right. Better to keep the snakes outside the barrel.

"Colonel, you mind being my battle buddy?" Alex glanced at Paul, only to find his friend suddenly armed up and ready. How did wearing Kevlar make Paul look two times bigger? The MP-4 semi-automatic rifle slung across his chest looked like a toy against Paul's frame.

"I've got your back, little brother." Paul grinned.

"You keep calling me shit like that and I'll leave your ass here." Alex chuckled as he climbed the ladder.

He shot up the up the two levels in a blink; cramped and vertical submarine ladders were nothing to someone who'd spent their career climbing them. Paul needed twice as long to squeeze his wide shoulders through the small hatch covers, muttering obscenities about sneaky submariners the entire way.

Alex reached the outer hull of his sub and took in his surroundings with a quick glance. The docking station attachment was little more than a yellow-and-red tube made of super-thick composite.

Part of it lay flush with *Jimmy Carter's* hull and formed an airlock against their hatch, surrounded with valves and caution labels. That segment was open, with the tube itself pressurized and sealed, but Alex still had to climb through another level before he landed on the flat section. From there, it was rather like an airplane's boarding ramp, just less flexible and made of much sturdier material.

It was also prettier, a riot of colors and artwork that attacked Alex's senses like a forest fire. After the regimented and muted colors of a navy submarine, it was almost too much. Pausing to wait for Paul, Alex let himself stare at the interior of the docking tube, wondering who approved decorations including palm trees, planets, kid's toys, and wild horses.

"This is a fucking eyeful, isn't it?" Paul said in an undertone, moving silently to Alex's side.

Damn, he hated the way the big man moved like a panther. Alex would never be half so athletic, not even back when he *tried* at Norwich. He shook his head, ears buzzing with worry. "Let's move."

"Your lead."

Stuffing his hands in his pockets, Alex walked down the rainbow-infused tube. He was sure he looked ridiculous: a skinny submariner followed by a lurking marine. But it didn't matter. He was here to get a job done.

One man waited for Alex and Paul in the tiny atrium off the ramp, smiling cheerfully while they completed the climb. He was short but well-muscled, with dark hair, eyes, and vaguely Hispanic features. Predictably, he was dressed in the same black ninja suit private security contractors adored, an outfit that mirrored the marines' battle dress uniform, just in all black. He wore two radios and a sidearm, as well as a utility belt full of phones, a taser, and other items.

Alex managed not to grimace. Rent-a-cops were annoying customers on their best days. He'd dealt with hundreds of them back on Armistice Station, each one thinking they were more important than the last. That getup looked cool to a civilian, but it screamed *amateur* to a professional.

"Captain! It's a pleasure to meet you. I'm Saul Miller, the Red Tiger Station Chief of Security."

"Commander Alex Coleman, USS *Jimmy Carter*." Alex shook the offered hand because it would've been rude not to but made a mental note to use hand sanitizer later. "This is Lieutenant Colonel Paul Swanson, Commanding Officer, Second Reconnaissance Battalion."

"Mr. Miller." Paul did not offer a hand, and Miller just twitched a little when Paul's giant paws landed on his MP-4.

"My XO tells me you had an urgent need to speak to me before we pick up our passengers," Alex said. He didn't like the way Miller kept trying to drift down the docking ramp toward his boat. Pretty much everything on a navy submarine was classified, even when the boat was thirty-five years old.

"I did." Miller's shifty smile made Alex's skin crawl. "I could see on sensors that your submarine is very...large."

"*Jimmy Carter* is unique." Now was not the time to get into how Alex's boat had a hundred-foot midsection she couldn't use. The latest *Virginia*-class boats were actually a touch longer than Alex's grumpy old lady, but they were mostly designed to be missile boats. Aside from the spec-ops stuff she no longer had, *Jimmy Carter* was a pure attack sub.

But nope, he was not here to give this dude a history lesson.

"She's one of the largest submarines we've ever hosted." Miller's smile grew, and his eyes flicked toward the hatch again.

Paul shifted, his right hand landing, ever so gently, on his sidearm. Miller just grinned.

"I'm always glad to help someone set a record," Alex replied.

Miller laughed. "I hope you're glad to help with something else, Captain. There are several influential people on this station who would like to leave...and they'll pay well for the privilege."

Alex blinked. "You've got to have other ways to leave than on a U.S. *Navy* submarine."

"Unfortunately, you're the only one to make it here in the last four months that has a snowball's chance of getting away."

"Well." Alex pursed his lips. "You've got my condolences, but my mission is plain. I'm only here to pick up one team—and Colonel Swanson is here to make sure those five people get off the station safely, if you catch my meaning."

Miller twitched again, his hand fluttering in the air *anywhere* but near the pistol at his side. "We don't want any trouble with the marines," he said. "But you're missing out on a great opportunity if you ignore the people who want to leave."

"Great opportunity being boatloads of cash." Alex figured he should just put it in the open.

Miller grimaced. "We prefer bank transfers."

"And I assume you're the suave and well-traveled gentlemen who's going to set all this up?" Paul rumbled from behind Alex's shoulder. His glare pinned Miller to the spot.

"Well, yes. I have a little experience."

"Experience in bribery. Hm." Paul shrugged. "I suppose that's common enough out here, though we do frown upon anyone offering to corrupt *marines*, Mr. Miller. And the navy."

"It's just payment for services—"

"Yeah, we get the picture, thanks," Alex cut him off. "Those services won't be rendered. Clear?"

"I won't be held responsible for people trying to get on your sub." Miller crossed his arms. "There's a crush in the docking area already. You need my people to control it."

Paul's laugh was deep enough to rattle Alex's bones. "Oh, I think three bored squads of recon marines will do fine. You just keep your people with weapons out of the way so they're safe, all right, cupcake?"

"You can't bring weapons on the station. There are regulations—"

"Sure there are, butterfly." Paul reached out and patted him on the shoulder. "We'll take our weapons away after we do the job. Don't worry your corrupt little heart."

"You might want to run along and tell your eager would-be passengers that their train is arriving at another station," Alex added.

"Good luck accomplishing your *mission* without my help." Glaring, Miller turned and trudged out of the atrium, glancing worriedly back at Paul every few steps.

Alex waited for him to vanish before he said anything else. "I think you'd better get some folks up there to establish a beachhead before that conniving asshole can make things ugly."

"I'll get Gunny Kochera in gear. She'll eat the idiots for breakfast. Lieutenant Montero will lead the team going to find our dear scientists," Paul replied. Then he cringed. "Please tell me your XO is staying on the boat."

"He'll go no further than this end of the tube. That help?"

Paul heaved a sigh. "I'd rather deal with French snipers, but sure."

Red Tiger Station

Rani watched the crowd, smiling. A few words in a few ears—Audie Meyer was not the Indians' only agent on Red Tiger Station, just the best-placed one—and crowds started to build. She had not predicted the near-riot brewing on its own, but it was useful. So useful that Rani didn't have to do the expected twisting of Audie's arm to precipitate a security incident so she could *create* a bit of unrest. A natural-born riot was so much better.

Cocking her head, Rani watched people gather belongings and press into a larger and larger crowd. She had underestimated how frightened these people were. It was, however, understandable.

Rani was no stranger to dangerous situations, but even she felt the shiver of fear here on Red Tiger Station. The Chinese Civil War was all too close, and if her employers did not have a comfortable arrangement with most of the pirate groups threatening the station...well, Rani would have been a lot more worried. Every intelligence officer was expendable, even the best in the business. She would be a fool to think that her nation would not forget about her in a moment if it suited India's interests.

But not yet. For now, she remained valuable. And so did her mission.

So Rani picked her way through the angry crowd, eating a burrito and blending in like she was just another denizen of Red Tiger Station, eager to leave. She even had a bag slung over one shoulder, like almost everyone else in sight. Did these fools really think the American military would pull them off? She supposed that it might have happened in peacetime; America loved their humanitarian missions. But in war, every nation looked out for their interests first.

That was why she had a spot reserved on a skiff owned by Eastern Enterprises, an imaginative pirate group starting to specialize in "insured" transport to and from dangerous areas in the South China Sea. They brokered agreements with other pirate groups not to have their ships stolen or passengers taken as hostages, trading safety for one of their ships for one of their fellows. Every seat on an Eastern skiff cost a fortune...but it would be worth it if Rani could steal one of the Fogborne scientists.

Ning Tang remained her primary target, but she was beginning to contemplate going for the gold and trying to nab the senior doctor. Kimberly Leifsson undoubtedly knew the most about the design, and last Rani spied her, the older woman looked so exhausted she could barely think. Separating her from the group might be easier.

And Rani could only imagine her superiors' glee if she brought Leifsson home. Whether Leifsson was willing or not, India *would* get the information they needed to get ahead in the newest nuclear race.

Rani was many things, but she loved her country. And she would give what India what was needed to win the war…no matter what.

COMSUBPAC Headquarters, Pearl Harbor, Hawaii

"Any news from *Jimmy Carter*?" Freddie Hamilton asked with little preamble. She hadn't even bothered to say hello when Marco answered her call.

"Jesus fuck, Freddie, is your mother on Red Tiger Station?" Marco asked as he disassembled a pair of scissors, leaving the phone on speaker.

"No, just people who might be able to *build us fusion reactors.*"

"Fine. Point." Marco huffed and moved onto his computer mouse. Scissors were too easy to reassemble, and he needed to keep his hands busy. "*Jimmy Carter* popped up their comms wire and let me know they'd arrived, but that's it. What's crawled up your ass about this? I mean, sure, fusion is cool if they're not lying, but odds are they're fucking lying. Or they're ten years from deploying a working reactor. And oh, by the way, Pulsar normally makes missiles, nothing subs carry. Why are you in love with them all of a sudden?"

"They've got their friends at Lazark calling in favors, and we *can't* afford to piss off Lazark," the other admiral replied.

"Oh. Shit." Marco heaved a sigh and looked out his office window at the gorgeous day outside. Was there ever bad weather in Hawaii? He'd never been stationed here before, but right now, Marco could use a good, old-fashioned Mayport, Florida, hurricane to match his moods.

"Yep. Pulsar's not shy about calling in markers. They *know* I need as many torpedoes as we can get, so they're using the big guns." Freddie's voice was grim. "I wish they'd called a politician."

"Don't say that. I've got Senator Angler and his Submarine Loss Committee crawling up my nether regions all day and twice on Sundays." Marco had never met a politician he liked, but he wouldn't piss on Senator Benjamin Angler III if he was on fire.

Angler was a smart operator. Marco had to give him that. He'd angled himself right into leadership if the new bipartisan senate committee on submarine losses and set out to investigate why America lost so many damn boats with gusto. Under other circumstances, Marco might *like* a fresh set of eyes on the problem, but not when he was busy trying to fight a damned war. Angler's fact finders were busy crawling all over Pearl Harbor. Keeping them away from Perth was a full-time job.

At least it gave his aide something to do. Marco didn't much like the kid. He got too nervous when admirals started thinking.

"I know. I tried to convince the CNO that offering our 'full cooperation' while trying to bring the fight to the enemy was a bad idea, but Scrap rolled right over me." Freddie's eye roll was audible. "He does that a lot. When he's not ignoring me."

"Hey, I'm not sure PAC Fleet knows my name." Marco sat back in his chair. "Actually, no, I've talked to him once. I'm not sure he knows I've got the sub job, though."

"Is he getting in your way?"

"Wouldn't care. I report to you." He bared his teeth. "And he's a shit-licking surface head who doesn't know jack about submarines. Couldn't find one with an electronic chart and active sonar."

Freddie laughed. "You shouldn't say things like that about four-star admirals."

"Fuck 'em and the destroyer he rode in on."

"You are incorrigible."

"Ha! You're lucky I'm educated enough to know the meaning of that word."

"Says the man with two masters' degrees, one of which is in mechanical engineering," Freddie replied.

"Me engineer. Me words no fucking word."

This time, it took Freddie almost thirty seconds to stop giggling. Marco smirked; mission accomplished.

Shit, the war sucked enough. If he couldn't make one of his oldest friends laugh, who the hell was he?

Still, he made a mental note to check on *Jimmy Carter*. He didn't normally give a good goddamn about the navy's oldest attack submarine—which she'd remain unless Freddie really *was* serious about recommissioning a few mothballed 688I boats that passed their prime when Marco was a lieutenant. Did anyone below his rank even know how to drive those things?

He shuddered. *Jimmy Carter* was newer than those *Los An-*

geles-class boats, but she'd been in continuous use. Hard use, too. Marco'd never served on her, because flamboyant, loud, and foul-mouthed idiots like him were not handpicked for spy submarines, but he knew her reputation.

Jimmy Carter bounced from mission to mission right until the new *Parche*—unironically named for the very old one—stepped into her shoes. The navy meant to decommission *Jimmy Carter*, but then the war wandered on in, so now a thirty-four-year-old former spy sub was out fetching special people from a really special place.

He sure as shit hoped the old girl was up to the task. Same with those *forty*-plus-year-old boats Freddie wanted to push back into service. At least they'd been modernized before being shoved into mothballs, but most of them had been on metaphorical ice for ten years.

Marco shuddered. There was a *reason* subs used to be decommissioned at thirty years. Pressure hulls couldn't be replaced without building a whole new boat, and once you let the water into the people space...

Yeah, he felt bad for the fool who pissed off Freddie enough to get sentenced to *Jimmy Carter*. No way was Marco going to war in a boat old enough for a man his age to date.

Red Tiger Station

One look at that growing crowd and Paul decided to lead the "go find the Fogborne scientists" team himself. There was an ugly undercurrent in the crowd's muttering, one borne of glares and shuffling feet that left his teeth on edge. No one had started pushing yet, but the group around the hatch leading to the boat was twenty to thirty deep and four times that many across, many of them carrying bags, boxes, and ridiculous shit like scuba gear, a dartboard, and even a desk chair.

Where did they think they were going? Worry churned in Paul's gut.

Riots really weren't his speed. Even in peacetime, no one wanted to send highly trained recon marines to face off with angry civilians; there were too many opportunities for that kind of situation to go right up a creek. Paul was old enough to remember the nasty days of civil unrest the early 2020s and young enough to understand its causes, and *he* found the idea of any boneheaded politician turning the military against civilians gut-churning.

The feeling was only marginally better when it was someone else's civilians. Paul didn't like the ragged feeling of desperation in the air. He wasn't trained for this. He was trained for war, trained to put bullets in the brain pan and turn to the next threat. Half these people looked at him like an enemy and the other half like a savior. What the hell was he supposed to make out of that?

He caught snippets of conversations when people weren't shouting, and they made his blood run cold.

"They're here to take us home," one man said.

"They'll kill us all and take the station," another woman said to her identical sister.

"I need to lock my store before they start looting," someone else added.

"Can they make the Chinese stop fighting?"

It was the child's voice that tugged at his heart; Paul wasn't married and hadn't found the right guy, but someday he'd sure like little ones. And this little boy wasn't more than four years old when he said: "I want to go home."

Goddamn this war. Paul wanted to go home, too.

He shook himself and put his colonel face back on, striding over to a quartet of marines surrounded a mean-looking gunnery sergeant. She was blond, tattooed, and tougher than Paul ever dreamed of being, and she was the best damned marine he'd ever served with.

Paul was a highly trained, decorated recon marine. He was a lieutenant colonel, and he knew his business. That meant he knew Gunny Kochera was better at this shit than he could be with another twenty years in the service. Kochera *breathed* the corps. She was one of the special ones, the kind every commanding officer worth a damn knew to value.

"Gunny and your team, you hold this down as an entry control point," he ordered. "Me, Lieutenant Montero, Boomer, and Frankie will go find these super nerds. Everyone else stays on the boat or in the boarding tunnel as our reserve."

Master Gunnery Sergeant Kochera grinned. "You got it, sir," she said. "I'll try not to shoot anyone."

"How you loaded?" Paul leaned into whisper.

"Rubber bullets, just like last time on that Migaloo. No fucking way am I poking holes in this creepy-ass underwater place."

"You read my mind."

So-called "rubber" bullets were usually used for police and riot control; marines trained with them—and used them when they went after people like the charming pirates he and Alex encountered a couple years back—but Paul didn't usually have much reason to load up with the things. There was a big damned war on, and he preferred to poke holes in his opponent when the chance presented itself. There was something annoying about the idea of letting enemies get back up again. So far, he'd had a boring war with lots of surrendering enemies...but they made recon marines for the wild jobs.

"Let's move." Paul gestured to his impromptu fire team and led them through the crowd. One nice part about being a six-foot-nine, broad-shouldered tower of humanity dressed in marine fatigues was that people dove out of his path. Anyone who didn't was generally willing to shoot him, and Paul knew how to deal with them.

Wary, tired, and eager eyes tracked his every step, but no one hefted a weapon. Paul grimaced. Would these people escalate to a full-blown riot when told they couldn't leave, or had the security manager already covered that? Unlikely. He seemed the type to rile them up, instead. Paul couldn't forget that threat.

Usually, the sight of marines did wonders to quell anyone's desire to riot, particularly marines carrying weapons, but the security manager was an ambitious dumbass with more money than brains. Great. He resembled all the non-recon commanding officers Paul had during his career.

His marines trucked through the station in a loose formation, trying to look less threatening. Maybe even casual? Paul wasn't great at that, not until he got a couple of drinks into a good night, anyway. But scaring civilians wasn't the way to go.

This wasn't his first underwater station, but it was the biggest by far he'd visited, and Paul had to push away the thoughts of what a nightmare storming the place would be. He could think of a couple ways to get in, but all these nooks, crannies, and tubes—he refused to call them streets, which Red Tiger Station seemed to—were a goddamned maze.

They crossed through the entertainment section, passing an adult "bookstore" where Paul couldn't spot any books, a video arcade covered in triple XXXs, two escort parlors, and a strip casino.

"Is that really a thing?" First Lieutenant Montero stared at the strip casino until they were around a corner.

"Looks like somewhere I'd have gone in my wild college days." Paul grinned when his young lieutenant blanched. Teasing the young'uns was so much fun.

"Sir, I didn't need that image."

Paul snorted. "Hell, I didn't, either." He shook his head. "You got the contact info for these people?"

Juan Montero was skinny compared to Paul, and he'd look depressingly normal if you came across him in a library. It probably helped that he was balding and wore reading glasses, despite two navy surgeons trying to fix his eyes over the years. Paul knew for a fact that Juan had been mistaken for a librarian more than once, an advantage Paul was sure he could use someday.

"Calling them now, sir," Montero replied. "Just had to tap into the local network."

"You're saying our comms shit isn't compatible?"

Montero shrugged. "Better than in some places. Everything here is made in Taiwan, and so's most of our stuff."

"Then call our wayward children up and let them know their taxi has arrived." Paul glanced around and then looked down at the schematic on his tablet. Thank goodness the crowds were thinner around here; everyone wandering in this area seemed to be about business, not ready to throw cans and rotten fruit. "This place is a maze and doesn't remotely resemble the fucking map."

"You know what they say about these stations, Colonel," Sergeant Fernandez spoke up, peeking around a corner. "They're like spiders with a thousand legs." He shuddered. "And too many eyes."

"Try not to get too high on conspiracy theories, will you, Fernandez?" Paul rolled his eyes.

"I just don't like being underwater, sir."

Paul grimaced. Maybe he should've drawn someone else out of the battalion for this mission, but he'd yanked almost the entire team from his *last* underwater mission for this one, figuring experience would serve them well. But Fernandez wasn't responding like a seasoned pro; he was acting like a man who'd gone overboard off a surfaced submarine, gotten a concussion in the progress, and nearly drowned.

"Then try not to look out the windows, Frankie." Paul elbowed him gently.

"They are creepy as fuck," Boomer—otherwise known as Sergeant Barbara Lin—said. She was a lanky woman with dark green eyes and even darker skin, and Paul had never seen her twitch away from anything in fear...except maybe the floor-to-ceiling glass windows in this underwater station.

Who the *fuck* did that where the water could crash in and kill you?

Paul shivered. Whatever engineer designed this place had to have been smoking something good.

"Got 'em," Montero said not a moment too soon. "They'll meet us near...compartment one-seven-seven?"

Paul squinted at his station schematic. "That's not on the fucking map."

"This is two-five-niner." Boomer pointed at a sign above a trash collecting station. "Two-five-seven is to the right, so I guess we go that way."

"They say they have a bunch of stuff." Lieutenant Montero still had his ear to the phone. "Something about a prototype they can't leave behind?"

"Well, this is another fine Marine Corps Day." Paul grinned. "Let's move out. Nothing we can't handle."

Marines could survive anything the world threw at them, after all. Especially *his* marines.

Leaving his twelve-thousand-pound submarine supported by three skinny struts made Alex vaguely nauseous. Not gluing himself to the UUV camera screens took everything iota of self-control he could muster, but Alex was a goddamned captain, and he had people to do that for him.

It didn't stop him from flinching every time his aging submarine creaked or twitched. Using three little pylons and one robotic arm to hold *Jimmy Carter* in place was like holding onto a cliff's edge by your fingertips. It could work for a while, but then...

"Excuse me, Captain. You've got an outside line phone call." Maggie still had the watch in control, and she found Alex over by the chart table, his eyes tracing their navigation plan for the outbound transit.

He definitely *wasn't* thinking about the fun of walking *Jimmy Carter* off those struts. No, sir, he definitely wasn't.

Alex frowned. "Come again?"

"Comms wire's still out." Maggie shrugged. "You want me to route it to your stateroom?"

"Please."

Shaking his head, Alex headed aft to his stateroom. Getting outside line phone calls while on a mission was something he wasn't used to. In fact, it was weird enough that he hadn't even thought to ask Maggie who it was. And now he couldn't go back and ask her without looking like a moron. Should she have volunteered that information? Probably. But he was an idiot for not asking.

Oh, joy. That cramp in his midsection was his stomach tying itself in a knot. Hatred of the unknown always did that to him. Blowing out a breath, Alex picked up the phone. "Commander Coleman, how may I help you?"

"Please hold for Admiral Hamilton," a voice on the other end said, and Alex's stomach did a backflip.

His least favorite admiral was kind enough not to leave him waiting long, but every second made the flipping butterflies in his stomach multiply. Alex bit a knuckle hard. He was not going down this road, damn it.

"Commander Coleman? Admiral Hamilton here."

"Yes, ma'am." Mouth dry, Alex wished his stateroom phone wasn't connected to a cord. He didn't have a drink in reach.

Stupid 1990s technology.

"Thank you for taking my call. This should more properly be Admiral Rodriquez's bailiwick, but he's a little occupied right now, so I volunteered to speak to you about the criticality of your mission."

How many words did she need for *don't fuck it up?* Alex tried not to grit his teeth. "I'm all ears, Admiral."

"We attempted to reach you three days ago, but you were apparently deep without your comms wire out."

"Ma'am, as stealthy as the wire is, it seemed foolish to remain in constant communication when I was taking my boat somewhere we're explicitly banned from being," Alex replied. "My orders were to remain undetected."

"Hm." An ominous silence from the other end stretched out so long that Alex started to wonder if he lost Hamilton. Unfortunately, his luck was never that good. Finally, she continued: "Very well. It is not an unsound decision, and I am glad you appreciate the necessity for stealth. It will be imperative that you continue to do so for the rest of your journey through the South China Sea—no matter what you face. Understood?"

"I understand my ROE, ma'am." Alex hated it, but he understood it—and the reasons for those orders. "We are not to fire unless fired upon and are to make every effort *not* to engage and remain in stealth, instead. You know, act like it's the 2020s and no one has heard of World War III."

"I see you're as droll as ever, Commander, but yes."

Alex wished he couldn't feel his stomach twisting into a hangman's knot. "*Jimmy Carter* was built for this kind of mission. We won't let you down."

"You had best not, Commander. That team you're bringing back could change the very future of submarine warfare."

Chapter 18

Chaos

100 nautical miles east of the Seychelles

"Change of navigation plan, Mister O'Kane."

The nasal voice made Lieutenant Bobby O'Kane jump. He had the watch in the control center of USS *Bluefish* (SSN 843), usually a boring stretch of eight hours that was sometimes—but rarely—punctuated with a few moments of wartime terror. As navigator, control was Bobby's home away from home, which meant he could always keep himself busy looking at navigation plans or cracking jokes full of pop culture references.

The crew enjoyed his jokes and games, but that wasn't why Bobby did them. Sure, he wanted the crew to be happy, or at least as happy as anyone could be with Commander Peterson always within five hundred feet. But they kept him sane. Or as sane as he could be on board USS *Blueballs*, which was the crew's latest nickname for their boat.

Bobby jumped because Peterson didn't usually sneak up on him. This captain was the call-from-his-stateroom sort. Anytime he showed up in control, it was like having the motivation sucked out of the space until they were left in a miserable vacuum. Five seconds earlier, Bobby *had* been in a good mood. He enjoyed being officer of the deck, loved driving the submarine and being underway. On *Bluefish*, the latter was hard; they spent more time in port broken than they did trying to take the fight to the enemy.

Bobby knew every restaurant, bookstore, and comic shop in

Perth. There were seven of the later, a depressingly small number for a city the size of Perth. There were more bookstores, which had been nice places to get lost in until he realized *Mrs.* Peterson, whose first name they were not encouraged to speculate upon, was a bibliophile. Bobby abandoned those for eateries and running more miles to avoid his captain, a choice that would've been ludicrous for a department head on any other submarine.

On *Bluefish*, it was situation normal. The sub was a like a dark pit of misery formed of liquid magnets, pulling you in like an inescapable whirlpool. There was a dizzy feeling of helpless misery that Bobby was all too used to. Even worse, it wasn't just that *he* couldn't change things on the boat. *Bluefish* didn't accomplish much, either. Aside from shooting two frigates a couple of months ago, *Bluefish* spent the war batting a bit fat zero. It made him ready to climb bulkheads backward and tear his admittedly short hair out. His friends were *dying* out here while Bobby ordered and reordered parts.

Commander Wade Peterson, on the other hand, was happiest when *Bluefish* was in port. Oh, he pretended otherwise, talking the talk of a great warfighter who hated being chained to the pier. He even complained to the squadron about the sorry condition of the six-year-old submarine he commanded.

Constantly.

Bobby pasted on a smile. "Where to, Captain?"

Bluefish had only been underway for fifteen days, but somehow Peterson swung a port visit for them in the Seychelles between patrols. The crew—whose morale was already in the dumps after contributing jack to the war effort, unless you counted feeding Perth's pigeons—was so excited Bobby could feel the electricity in the air.

He should've known that would never last.

Not on *Bluefish*.

"We've been reassigned." Peterson scrunched up his nose like there was a foul smell in control, and maybe there was. Maybe it was him.

Bobby batted the traitorous thought aside. "Where to, sir?" he repeated.

Finally, a smile blossomed on his captain's face. "We're going to the end of the Singapore Strait."

Red Tiger Station

"Wow, they *look* like marines," Ning leaned over to whisper to Sam as the five uniformed figures approached the Fogborne team.

They all wore camouflage-colored uniforms, something Ning had never seen in person, though she was a little disappointed that their faces weren't painted. Then again, what should she expect them to blend into here? She supposed they could wear blue and walk in front of the big windows, not that there were any of them right here.

Stomach rumbling, Ning glanced at the nearby donut shop and wished she'd eaten a bigger breakfast. It was too late now. Those marines looked like they didn't know the meaning of a snack break, even if she said please. Ning sighed and turned her attention to the empty tax prep store their prototype boxes sat in front of.

Jake, their security representative, had chosen this quiet corner for the team and their gear. From here, it was a quick walk to any of the docking stations. That wouldn't have been necessary if anyone had bothered to tell them *which* one their ride would arrive at, but Ning wasn't exactly admiring the planning going on here. Nor did she love the fact that they were hanging out in the shell of a bankrupt fast-food joint. At least there were tables?

"Have you ever seen a marine before?" Sam asked.

"No, but I watch movies." They looked cooler in the movies. Everyone but the big giant was disappointingly normal, particularly the short bald dude with glasses.

"Behave yourselves, children." Dr. Kim Liefsson's wan smile held warmth even when it wavered. They were all jittery with relief; the moment was finally here.

Months and *months* of trying to leave this place and there was finally a submarine willing to take them. Ning felt like she could freaking fly.

"You Doc Leifsson?" The biggest man in the group stopped a dozen feet away, and wow, was he huge. Ning was pretty sure he weighed as much as four of her, if not five.

"I am, and this is my research team." Kim gestured, and they all introduced themselves.

"Lieutenant Colonel Paul Swanson," the giant replied. He was bald or had a shaved head—Ning couldn't tell—and looked like a Pacific Islander, with darker skin and dark eyes. A hint of a tattoo peeked out from under one uniform sleeve, but she was definitely not going to ask about that. "Me and my peeps here are going to escort you to the boat, and then we're all going to sail away."

"Just like that?" Ning asked before she could stop herself. "Even with the pirates?"

"Pirates?" Swanson cocked his head. "On the station?"

"No, outside it. They're usually nearby, and they have at least one submarine." She grimaced, thinking of the amazing little sub racer she'd had to sell at a rock bottom price. Andrea Vargas was still bragging about the deal she got, and she'd already commissioned a new paint job she wouldn't quit talking about. Ning could afford a new racer, but the principle stung.

Swanson blinked. "I hadn't heard much about them, but I'm not the one driving the boat. Worst comes to worst, me and mine have done a little pirate hunting before." His sudden grin was a wicked thing, eager and hungry. "We're not exactly what I'd call averse to doing it again."

"We'd just like to get out of here." Kim grimaced. "We've had one too many false alarms on that front to feel confident about anything."

"Ma'am, I'm not sure who was jerking you around in the past, but marines don't just appear out of thin air. We're here and we've got a ride to get you out of here, so why don't we grab your gear and get a move on?"

Could it really be that easy? Swallowing, Ning glanced at Sam, who shrugged. What did they know about marines? They were in their twenties.

"We need to move these five boxes," Jake said, gesturing at the big plastic crates containing the prototype, hard copies of all their work, and some of their belongings. "They're all—" His phone buzzed, and their security guard dug it out of his pocket. "Lawrence here."

Several long seconds ticked by as Ning watched the color drain out of Jake's face. She inched closer to him but couldn't catch what was said on the other end before he hung up.

"The outer sonar net just picked up an incoming submarine that matches the pirates' signature." Jake cringed. "Sounds like they're twenty miles away and inbound."

"Well, that sounds entertaining. Boomer, Frankie, help them with their boxes and let's roll," Swanson ordered.

Sam, Jake, and Dieter each pushed a box—they were on wheels, but Ning was too tiny to see over them. Instead, she grabbed Sam's rolling suitcase. The walk to docking station three wasn't long, even lugging Sam's heavy crap, but the marines moved faster than she was used to, and Ning was out of breath by the time they arrived.

"Where are you going?" a shopkeeper asked her. Ning knew the woman a little; she liked the gummy bears from her shop and got them special ordered from home when she could.

Ning chewed the inside of her cheek. "Big bosses are being big bosses. You know how it is."

"Are you *leaving*?"

Ning glanced at Kim, eyes wide, trying to hide the sudden tightening of her shoulders. Desperate, she mouthed, *What do I say?*

Kim stepped forward. "Pulsar's decided we're needed somewhere else, that's all."

"But there's a ship here to get you? Or a sub?" The shopkeeper pushed forward until she was almost face-to-face with Kim. "You can actually get out?"

"It's a private charter." Kim glanced at Swanson and grimaced. "Sorry."

"But someone got through? *How?*"

"Excuse us, ma'am." Swanson finally stepped forward just when Ning wanted to sink into the ground and disappear. "We have a schedule to keep."

The shopkeeper took one look at the hulking marine and backed up two steps. "I'm—I'm just—"

"A private charter?" someone else asked. Ning didn't know him, but she felt her face go red. This was the worst. She *knew* everyone wanted to leave, but it wasn't their fault that Pulsar pulled whatever strings they did to get the freaking *navy* out here to get them. "In the middle of a war zone?"

Another person laughed. "Escorted by U.S. Marines? Private. Sure."

The crowd pressed in, and Ning backed up until her back hit Sam's chest. "Sorry," she whispered, cringing.

"S'okay." He swallowed hard enough that she felt it.

"Let's keep moving, people." Swanson's voice filled the sullen silence, and his presence seemed huge when he moved into the crowd.

Ning wasn't sure they'd part for him as more people pressed in, frowning and muttering, but Swanson never broke stride. The grumbles became louder, with every eye in the growing crowd glaring at the Fogborne team, but no one dared argue as they followed the colonel. The other marines brought up the rear, looking less threatening as they pushed comically large plastic containers, but the crowd didn't bother them, either.

Could it be this easy? Someone bumped into her, jostling Ning as she rolled the suitcase along, trailing the group. She liked having everyone where she could see them; it made everything feel real, even as the crowd objected.

The whispers didn't bother her, anyway. She knew Red Tiger crowds. They were all shout and no substance, like the time that everyone protested the governing council implementing additional safety measures on the TRANSPLATs after some idiots went overboard. Nothing changed and no one got hurt. Ning's neighbors were loud and annoying but generally harmless.

Then hands grabbed her and yanked her into the crowd so quickly Ning didn't even have a chance to scream.

At least a thirty seconds passed before Sam turned, saw his suitcase sitting there alone, and asked: "Where's Ning?"

Perdue Station 120 Nautical Miles northeast of the Cocos Islands

It was amazing how much harm nineteen months could do.

Two years ago, USS *Kansas* (SSN 810) was a happy boat. They'd taken down pirates and saved lives. Kansas had been the best boat in the fleet, hands down. Until the arrival of one Commander Christopher Atticus Kennedy.

Some boats blamed the war for their drop in morale. Others, Master Chief Chindeu Casey knew, found the war a great motivator. On Kansas, it was just situation normal, all fucked up. All because of their captain, whose ego outpaced his—sadly considerable—competence and whose temper was as volatile as a summer storm in Florida.

Take today. Today started with a tongue-lashing for Kennedy's least favorite member of the crew, the navigator. Lieutenant Grippo was regrettably competent and didn't deserve Kennedy's ire, but the gorgon who wore their captain's face that morning blamed her for two sailors goofing off on watch. Then the same two sailors went to

Captain's Mast for a silly joke, a fact that curled rage up in Casey's soul like a black tornado of doom. Pushing it down took a gargantuan effort, but twenty-five years in navy blue taught Casey to pick his battles.

Then Kennedy decided in the late afternoon that he was going to do a swim call. A goddamned swim call during a mother-loving navy war. And they weren't really in friendly waters! Sure, the Cocos Islands were two hours sprint away, but that piddly little archipelago was just a couple hops, skips, and jumps away from Indonesia. Like, twelve hundred nautical miles. Not far for a nuclear submarine, or even a conventionally powered surface ship. Indonesia didn't have many of them, but that didn't matter since they'd been run over by India. And last Casey checked, India was the fucking enemy.

"Smile, COB. You're having fun." Kennedy's grin would've been infectious if he didn't know the man, but since he did, it felt like poison.

"You bet I am, sir." Being the chief of the boat, or the senior enlisted sailor on board the submarine, gave Casey latitude to be sarcastic. And not to smile.

Kennedy ignored him, standing in the sail—the highest part of the jet-black attack submarine, which sat peacefully on the surface, with waves gently lapping against both her port and starboard sides—like a goddamned conquering hero. His hands were on his hips and his chin was up, like he was the best submarine CO in the entire navy.

He wasn't even that good looking, at least not to a critical eye. Kennedy was only about forty, like most commanding officers, but he was balding in the back of his head, and no amount of combing blond hair around could cover that up. His blue eyes were surrounded by wrinkles caused by his ever-present scowl, and Casey liked to think the lines on his face were from frowning. But no. The man was a freaking coin flip. Sometimes he was a charismatic bastard. Others, he was just a bastard.

Their sailors were happy right now, though, splashing through the waves and laughing. The poor sods needed it with Kennedy as the boss, though Casey noticed that the one member of the crew who could most use a break wasn't there. Lieutenant Grippo, bless her broken soul, was nowhere to be found.

Maybe the poor navigator was taking a nap. God knew she deserved one.

"Shit, COB, we did good yesterday." Kennedy's grin remained. "Perdue Station is back in the hands of its rightful Australian owners, and the Alliance might just put a base there. And we did the first submerged insertion of marines for an underwater assault. Pretty fucking cool if you ask me."

Times like this, Casey hated Kennedy. The bastard was right, and Casey sighed. "Yes, sir, it was. Lieutenant Colonel Signore's team was shit hot on that assault."

"So we were, Master Chief." Kennedy's eyes narrowed. "Don't you start selling Kansas short. There's plenty of other people who will do that for us."

"Never, Captain." That was a promise Casey could make in good conscience.

"You going to go for a swim?"

"Not today." Casey shook his head. "I'm feeling my age. Creaky and achy."

Kennedy laughed. "I'm going for a dip. You hold down the shop until the XO gets done with heads and beds."

"Aye, sir."

Casey returned his attention to the swimming sailors, his eyes tracking the pair on shark watch. They were attentive and practicing good weapons safety, which wasn't always a given, even with a war on. Submariners weren't experts with rifles, even easy to fire ones like the MP-4. The thing was almost as old as Casey—or Kennedy, who was just three years younger than Casey—which meant it was older than the sailors carrying it.

War made funny marriages like that, didn't it? *Kansas* herself was nine years old. That wasn't old for a submarine, but it wasn't new, either, not with Electric Boat rolling six new submarines off the line like clockwork every year. Casey's stomach clenched as he watched the young sailors of their crew relaxing in the waves or sunbathing. The new boats weren't enough. Kennedy's posturing and antics, his crossing out of their patrol areas and trying to find any target he could, weren't enough.

No one wanted to say they were losing the war. First off, because it would be shit for morale. Second off, because by now history wrote in blood that world wars were a hard and long slog.

Casey hadn't believed it at first. Not even when *Kansas* was there for the first shots of the war, fired six months before what people back home called the New D-Day. Disaster Day. The so-called experts said that the sinking of that civilian Neyk Four submarine was the tipping point that inflamed international relations so much that war was unavoidable. So when America's dumbest admiral got trigger-happy six months later and sank the wrong country's submarine on Disaster Day, resulting in a fleet engagement...well, certain countries were just too happy to go to war.

There was a reason Casey had enlisted in the navy. He didn't want to be a decision maker; he liked to get his hands dirty, digging into the guts of sonar computers or leading sailors on the deckplates. He was an operator and a leader, not a big thinker. So he didn't put a lot of thought into trying to figure out why France, India, and Russia hated the United States and her allies.

Not that anyone had to think hard about Russia. Russia and the U.S. hadn't been friends since the last world war, and Casey didn't have to love history to know how dependent on self-interest that friendship had been.

France and India, though, well, he'd been surprised by that. Growing up in the navy, both had seemed cordial enough. Nice places to visit, too. But he hadn't been living under a rock and missing the proliferation of underwater resources. Discovering oil, gems, scarce metals, and all kinds of other things under the ocean floor changed the landscape—and not just because of the way underwater stations popped up like mushrooms, either. Nah. It made countries greedy.

Not that nations weren't greedy before. It was kind of how countries worked. Casey didn't count his own nation out of that. He just knew it was true.

Perdue Station was a great example of greediness. Co-owned by three Australian corporations, the damn place was technically independent. Course, its founders lived down under, but that didn't mean the station flew the Australian flag. Having visited there before the action started, Casey could attest that Perdue Station was a multicultural rainbow of lawlessness. One of the main hubs for WAAS, or the Worldwide Acquisition and Services Group, Perdue was the kind of place you could buy and sell almost anything. Australia spent their minimal influence making sure that their subs could dock there every now and then, instead of trying to regulate a station that was in international waters where few laws applied.

Then shooting started and India got greedy, snatching up Perdue Station. Casey wasn't sure if the Indians wanted it for strategic reasons or for the precious gems Perdue mined off the ocean floor. Either way, they sent in marines back in January, trying to sneakily nab the station right out from under Australia's nose.

Unfortunately for India, Australia had allies. Allies with big navies, who were willing to send *Kansas* and a bunch of marines over to steal Perdue Station back. That was the good part. The bad part was that this was a big navy war, where submarines were going to the bottom like rocks because America's technology and captains weren't good enough.

Casey spared a glare for the hatch Kennedy disappeared through a few minutes earlier. Yeah. That one was tactically competent, but he still fell in the category of the damned.

Meanwhile, Master Chief Chindeu Casey had to figure out how to protect the crew from the asshole.

***

Rani half-carried the girl around two corners with her hand over her mouth, easily overcoming her wiggling. Then she set her down, holding her by the shoulders and looking her dead in the eye.

"Your name is Ning Tang. You work for Pulsar Power, Limited on the Fogborne Project's fusion reactor. You have two choices today: I can either make you *very* rich or I will inject you with a sedative and you'll come with me, anyway."

Rani was taking a calculated risk. Kidnapping was not her normal forte in intelligence operations; she'd assassinated a few people, but pulling someone out of a crowd was not something she'd done before. She needed the girl to cooperate so she could get her off the station. Chemicals were a last resort but one she was willing to stoop to if she had to.

Brown eyes met blue. Ning stared at her, chest heaving, terror making the whites of her eyes glow in the weird electronic-meets-sea-life lighting on the station. Rani preferred to work in dark alleyways, but there were none of those here; the best she could manage on Red Tiger Station was an alcove between a fish market and a trophy shop. Across the way, a busy toy store kept parents and children distracted. No one was looking at them.

If they did, Rani would kiss Ning and everyone would look away. Even modern, open-minded people didn't like public displays of affection.

"What do you want with me?" Ning asked. It was sadly predictable, even if Rani didn't kidnap people for a living.

"Like I said, I can give you a huge payday, or you can leave leaning on me like you're a drug addict who's had too much."

Ning's brows furrowed. "I already have a huge payday coming."

"Trust me. This will be better." Rani would have to lie if Ning asked for specific numbers; she was making this up on the fly. But she was certain her superiors would back her. They wanted this technology too badly.

Ning scoffed. "Sorry if I don't trust *kidnappers* to pay me."
Rani shrugged and didn't let the girl go. "Consider this aggressive negotiation."
"Like hell."
On cue, Ning sucked in a deep breath, and Rani clapped a hand over her mouth before she could call for help. Why were people always stupid? Ning was supposed to be some sort of genius. Rani had hoped for better.

She snuck a glance at the flow of people around the toy store, grimacing as yet another pungent whiff from the fish market hit her. Did they sell *only* day-old fish, or was there something rotten in the back? Rani hated fish. But the passersby were uninterested, probably because of the disgusting smell.

Ning tried to bite her, and Rani twisted her wrist away from the teeth, shoving Ning back with her spare hand. "Don't even start."

Ning glared daggers at her, and Rani smiled. *This* was more normal for her. When she wasn't skulking in shadows, Rani enjoyed infuriating people. It was one of the perks of her job.

Fun though this was, she was running out of time. Being exposed in this little alcove grew riskier by the moment.

"Make up your mind or I'm going to do it for you," Rani hissed. "Try screaming and I'll inject you faster than you can blink."

When she felt Ning tremble under her fingers, Rani knew she had her. She eased her hand off of Ning's mouth as the girl's face turned ashen wide with fear instead of anger.

"Don't be stupid," she said before Ning could speak.

Ning flinched. "I—" She cut off, eyes as wide as saucers.

"You're going to want to let the girl go, sweetheart," a voice crooned in Rani's ear.

A large hand landed on her left shoulder, and metal slid along her right shoulder until Rani saw the dull glint off a blackened knife blade. U.S. Marine Corps issue, her mind reported. KA-BAR.

"We're just having a friendly disagreement." Rani let her face transform into a smile, counting on Ning's terror to keep her silent.

"Sure you are, buttercup." The meaty hand shot out, grabbing her left wrist and twisting her arm behind her before Rani could react. She whistled softly in pain, trying to wiggle away from the marine, but he jerked her arm upward, trapping her. "You all right, Ms. Tang?"

Ning didn't answer until the giant frog marched Rani a step backward. Then she nodded, her movements choppy as her eyes snapped right and left in terror. "Yeah. Mostly. Sure." Ning gulped. "She said she has some drug to knock me out. Might want to watch out for that."

"Pretty sure anything dosed for you won't even get me high, but I'll be careful." The marine's laugh was a rolling rumble. Rani flinched away, or tried to, but he held her still. The bastard wasn't even using both hands; his free one tucked the KA-BAR away like Rani wasn't even a threat.

She finally managed to turn enough to glare at him, taking in a man over a foot taller than herself, with shoulders as wide as a doorway and muscles for days. Rani scowled.

"Now, I don't have much time to deal with you, sunshine, and I'm sure as hell not taking you with us. So why don't you tell me who you work for, and we'll all go home like nice little enemies?" His smile was cocky, and Rani wished she could fault him for it.

"The Seven-Sevens." The lie came easily; Rani had it in her pocket already. She never expected failure, but it paid to prepare.

"Who?" Ning slid along the wall until she was closer to the marine than Rani, chewing her lip. "The pirate group?"

Rani shrugged. "Word gets out. Everyone wants a piece of your work."

"Pirates are into kidnapping now?" The marine frowned.

"Pirates are into money."

"Hm."

She never saw the blow coming.

Hours later, Rani woke up in a pile of trash in the tube behind the fish market, decorated in fish guts and lying with her face on half a salmon. The smell came from here, she was sure.

It took two showers to wash the stench away, and by then, her skiff was waiting. Her superiors would not like her failure, but war had its ups and downs.

Approaching Perdue Station

India's troubles that day were not limited to Red Tiger Station.

INS *Vagli* had not been close enough to prevent the American takeover of Perdue Station. Captain Ranjeet Joshi and his submarine arrived just in time to see what little remained of the Indian forces fleeing the station, and he was starting to wish he had not rescued some of them from their mini submarines.

General Vinay Kapadia in particular.

"General, a submarine cannot retake the station alone," Ranjeet said for the fifth time. Not rolling his eyes was almost impossible, but Kapadia was his superior, albeit in a different service.

How little the Indian Army knew about their navy grew obvious with every hour General Kapadia spent on board. They had to teach him to use a navy *toilet*, for crying out loud. And the man somehow managed to get seasick on a submarine, which Ranjeet had thought impossible while submerged. He had been merely intolerable for the first four days, nitpicking at sailors' uniforms, conduct, and demanding the crew trade in their sneakers for uniform shoes—a battle Ranjeet won by teaching him about sonar through gritted teeth—but once the nausea passed, the general became a man on a mission.

Unfortunately for Ranjeet, that mission included his submarine. And it was far too late to throw General Kapadia and his men back like the ungrateful fish they were. Their minisubs were on the bottom and *Vagli* far away from that position, lurking near Perdue Station to spy on the enemy.

The general crossed his arms, highlighting, "An American submarine did."

Ranjeet wiggled from one foot to the other, struggling not to swear. "Intelligence indicates American marines were air-dropped in to attack the station, sir." He bit his tongue instead of mentioning that Kapadia received that same information. "We do not have that ability."

"You have my men on your submarine!"

A mere twenty-seven soldiers were not going to take that sprawling station back, Ranjeet didn't say. Instead, he smiled as gently as he could. "Unfortunately, we have no way to covertly insert your men onto the station. If *Vagli* attempts to offload your marines, they will flood the airlocks and kill everyone."

Ranjeet's sailors would not die, of course. Ranjeet would order his end of any boarding tube closed were he given such suicidal orders.

He was not prepare for the fire in General Kapadia's eyes when the man swung to face him. "Then we should destroy Perdue Station and deny its use to the enemy."

Chapter 19

Punching Bags

"Not swimming, COB?" Lieutenant Sue Grippo was *Kansas'* navigator and Commander Kennedy's favorite punching bag. It was a pity, because she was smart, competent, and had been a damned good leader before Kennedy got a hold of her. Now shadows framed her grim eyes, and she jumped when someone slammed a hatch shut.

Casey shrugged. "Someone has to be the adult supervision, Nav."

Grippo had found Casey reviewing watchbills in the control room while everyone else enjoyed the sun and water topside; it was quiet in here with most of the watch topside in the sail, and there was enough room for Casey to sanity check who stood on watch with who. *Kansas* was a small boat. It wouldn't do for sailors to be paired with their worst enemies. That bred even more drama than *Kansas* regularly carried around with her.

"I thought that was the XO's job," Grippo said.

"Ha."

Neither said more; they just exchanged a look and wry grins. Lieutenant Commander Mei Song was an odd duck, with dead eyes that screamed ambition and not much else. She stalked around the boat like a serial killer, leaving sailors increasingly uncomfortable after every berthing inspection.

Berthing inspections were normal. They were the XO's job, and one of the best ways to keep the boat clean. But Song conducted them with *way* more enthusiasm than any XO Casey had ever met, digging into the trash to find contraband, peeking in sailors' racks, and grumbling about "unauthorized bedding" like every boat in the fleet didn't have a collection of *Star Wars* sheets and Batman comforters. She even threw the kids' *comics* away when she was in a mood.

Never mind the tornado she turned into when she found porn.

Of course, Song got on with the captain like a house on fire. When Kennedy convinced their squadron commander to reassign the old XO, Casey had hoped for someone more like Commander Coleman, with the guts to standup to the madman in command. Unfortunately, they got his co-conspirator...who spotted him and Nav talking and stalked their way.

"Master Chief, pass the word to recover the crew," Song snapped. "The enemy is closing on Perdue Station."

Casey snapped his fingers, and the chief of the watch—who'd been talking quietly with the helmsmen not far away—straightened immediately. "On it, COB."

"What enemy, XO?" Casey asked as the word blared out through speakers all over the boat.

Topside, sailors scrambled for the nets laid against *Kansas'* sides, grabbing their towels, rushing for the hatches, and throwing themselves down the ladders. Commander Kennedy, who had swum further out than most, screamed for the shark watch boat to come pick him up, waving his arms wildly until the sailors on board obeyed. Control, however, remained quiet. Those soaking wet sailors would need a few minutes to grab their uniforms and get to their stations.

Meanwhile, Casey stood riveted, half terrified by the ferocious light in his XO's eyes and half hypnotized by it.

Song's eyes flashed. "Perdue Station reports an Indian sub closing their position. Says they've been given an hour to evacuate before the bastards put torpedoes in every structure." Her lips curled into a snarl. "We'll meet them before they do. Set battle stations torpedo."

"Are you all right?" Colonel Swanson—if she remembered his name right—asked.

Ning swallowed. Breathing was so hard, and her heart raced at a thousand beats a minute. She couldn't believe that just happened. What *had* happened? Why? She barely understood why someone would try to kidnap *her.* Her vision wanted to go black at the edges, and part of Ning wanted to run away screaming.

She could go back to her apartment here. That was safe. It was familiar. There was no one there to try to *choke* her or gag her or kidnap her. Her hands were shaking so hard she felt the tremors all the way up her arms. Gasping for air, Ning tried to focus on the toy store across the way. There were red trains out front going round and round on a track. She could hear a little electronic *toot-toot*.

Someone had tried to kidnap her. A horrible person who looked like a young woman not far from her own age. Why would she want to kidnap *her*?

Wait.

Of course they would. It was the design. The stupid, brilliant design. *Her* design, or at least mostly. Somehow, that thought brought her back to earth. Ning let out a shuddering breath that shook her entire chest.

"Maybe bruised. Probably fine." She bit her lip until it bled. "How'd you know I was gone?"

"Your friend Sam noticed, and a few people in the crowd were happy to help. You're popular here." Swanson's smile made him look gentler, Ning decided.

She still wouldn't forget he'd knocked that woman out with one hand. Then his words sank in, and Ning blushed. "I've been here awhile. It's easy to make friends."

"A few of the shopkeepers didn't like the idea of you being dragged away and pointed me in the right direction. One of the ladies at the fish market was particularly irate," Swanson replied.

"I buy sushi there," Ning said without thinking. Her throat closed up again. If she'd been kidnapped, would she ever have tasted sushi again? Sam loved to tease her because a Taiwanese-American girl wasn't supposed to love bad Japanese food so much. Ning swallowed.

"Hey." Swanson touched her arm with just his fingertips. How *could* a big man be so gentle? "You want to catch up with the others?"

"God, yes."

Ning wasn't a particular believer, but maybe she was...today. She kept herself from clinging to Swanson as he guided her back into the crowded tubes, steeling herself for the shouting as they got closer to the docking station. Ning didn't mean to flinch, but she still did.

She could feel that woman's hands on her shoulders. On her face, tightening like a vice. Ning knew her back would be bruised after being slammed into the wall like that, but right now, she just wanted to catch up with her friends.

Ning wasn't sure she resumed breathing until they were in the boarding tube for docking station three and past the quartet of marines standing guard there. One nodded at the colonel, and *she* had an even bigger gun in her hands, but it wasn't pointing at anyone.

Ning shivered and then thought twice about it. Maybe she liked that gun. It was pointed at people like her kidnapper.

"Are you okay?" Sam asked, pushing past two marines to get at her. "What happened?"

"Pirate got a little frisky," Swanson said. "You all need to stick together from here on out. Someone else might try something stupid."

"Something stupid like *kidnapping*?" Kim's jaw dropped.

Swanson didn't twitch. "Next one gets a bullet."

Kim opened her arms, and Ning flew into them like a child. She was an adult, a genius, and she didn't *need* comfort, but...it was nice. She gulped in a noisy breath, trying to feel normal and failing.

"Are you all right?" Kim whispered.

"I'll be fine." Ning willed the world to stop shaking. "I think."

"I'm sorry I didn't notice faster." Sam closed in to stand within an arm's reach, his hands fluttering like he didn't know what to do with them. "If I'd just...I don't know, been *talking* to you..."

"It's not your fault." Ning shook her head. "Don't be stupid."

"I don't—"

A sharp *thunk* cut him off, and everyone except the marines jumped. Their weapons came up.

"What the hell was that?" Sam yelped.

"It's getting ugly out there," one of the marines said. "Everyone wants to leave, and we're only here for you."

"It's not our fault they can't leave." Ning shuddered. "Don't they know that?"

"I don't think they care." Dieter looked grim. "Can we go?"

The voices behind them, outside the tube, were getting louder. Ning could make out people shouting obscenities, along with a chant of *let us out of here*, and someone else yelling about having a million dollars.

She rubbed her arms and leaned closer to Kim. Was her kidnapper awake now? Was she still out there? A dark part of Ning wished Swanson had just killed the woman. Did that make Ning a terrible person? She swallowed.

She wasn't built for this, Ning decided. She was going to find a nice and *safe* research lab to work out the war in after this. Maybe somewhere in the States. Pulsar would like that. She could move her parents from Taiwan, too. She could afford it. Besides, no way would Pulsar not pay her a bonus for that attempted kidnapping. They were the kind of company that thought they could solve everything with money.

That was a somewhat happy thought, because Ning was the kind of girl for whom money solved problems. She took a deep breath and looked at the shiny white boxes holding their prototype.

Yeah, Ning could focus on her accomplishments. She was so damned brilliant that some asshole pirates wanted to bribe her or kidnap her. It was a backhanded compliment, but Ning was pretty sure the rest of the scientific community would consider this a badge of honor in the future.

Swanson appeared to follow her gaze. "Let me call the boat about these god-awful big boxes. No one told me they'd be so big, and I don't think they'll fit through the hatch," he said.

Ning twitched. "We need our prototype model."

"Assuming we want to get our bonus." Sam crossed his arms.

"This is Pulsar property," Kim said. "We can't leave it here." She glanced back over her shoulder. "The submarine is...big enough, right?"

Swanson laughed. "Oh, that's not the problem. It's just the hatch size. The navy's weird about making them small so that guys like me have a hard time wiggling through."

Kim's eyes flicked from the boxes to Swanson and back again. "Are you serious?"

"Sure, when I'm geared up. Give me a sec, ma'am, and I'm sure it'll be fine. Captain Coleman's creative. He'll get your stuff on board." Swanson's grin was infectious, but Kim still frowned.

Ning just watched with a growing sense of horror. "Is our getaway going to get canceled *again*?" she whispered to Sam, reaching out to grab his arm like a lifeline.

She couldn't stay here. She couldn't.

"No way," he whispered back. "We'll go without the prototype. The important information is in our heads."

It wasn't like the "prototype" was a working reactor, anyway. It was just a scale model that *should* work, if fueled. But they hadn't.

Carrying a fueled nuclear reactor around—even with how stable fusion was—seemed pretty dumb. Ning was glad Pulsar wasn't big on that. The *actual* prototype was still running here on Red Tiger Station, manned by another Pulsar team whose job was to work reactors, not build them. Ning heard rumors that Pulsar was offering the reactor up to station management as a power source, but she didn't care.

Not as long as they got the hell off this sinking rock.

Swanson's radio crackled. "Colonel, Gunny, it's getting toasty out here." There was shouting in the background. "Some of these locals have started throwing stuff."

"Swanson frowned. "Anything deadly?"

"Nah. Charlie got hit by a tomato. Said it was tasty, and we're fine."

Ning didn't think they sounded fine as a full-throated *screech* of, "Let's see how brave you are *without the guns!*" rang out in the background of the radio call, but Swanson didn't seem worried.

"Keep me posted. Swanson out."

"Are your people going to be okay out there, Colonel?" Kim looked over her shoulder. "Without shooting anyone?"

"They've seen worse, Doc." Swanson shrugged. "And they're loaded with rubber bullets, anyway."

The sharp *thunk* of a body hitting metal punctuated his sentence, and Ning jumped.

The Mid-Indian Ocean, in route to the Singapore Strait

For the life of him, Bobby couldn't figure out why Commander Peterson was so damned smug about this mission. Now a part of Operation Sandicast, *Bluefish's* orders were to keep enemy shipping from entering the SOM and to assist against the Indian and French submarines already in the confined waters of the strait. On the surface, their job appeared simple, but Bobby knew it would be anything but.

Get to the bottom of the strait undetected, sure. They might as well do the Kessel Run in less than twelve parsecs while they were at it. What genius had decided that one submarine was enough for this job? Similar tricks hadn't worked the last *two* times the Alliance had tried to break into the Strait of Malacca. Apparently, the planners wanted to continue throwing crap at the wall until an idea stuck.

Someone should've told them that war wasn't spaghetti, but Bobby couldn't find the planners to throw marinara at them.

"Intelligence indicates the Indians might know we're coming," the XO said as he clicked on the slide labeled "overview." Bobby enjoyed *Death By PowerPoint* most days. Really, he did, but this brief was a generalized piece of trash. It looked like ninety percent of the pre-battle briefs he'd been subjected to over the years, with just more words on each slide. Rumor said Rear Admiral Marci loved words more than they loved her, and one look at this bloated slide deck told Bobby that someone on her staff had been busy.

Yes, retaking the Strait of Malacca was important. Bobby knew that. Everyone in the navy knew that. They didn't need four slides to tell them about prewar shipping patterns or how much tonnage—billons of dollars' worth, maybe trillions—sailed through the SOM every day before the Indians closed it to the Alliance. Everyone in the navy knew how much *longer*—almost six days—it took ships to transit from Europe to China, Taiwan, or other major producers in the east without the SOM.

We can't sail the SOM, and it makes us sad, was practically the title of the navy's favorite bedtime story. Maybe Bobby should make it into a song. After he survived this PowerPoint presentation, which he wasn't guaranteed to do. It might jump off the screen and eat him alive, or he could pass out from dehydration. Was it possible to die of boredom?

Bobby was having so much fun that he wouldn't trade this for an all-expenses paid trip to Disney World.

Oh.

Wait.

"However," Lieutenant Commander Vanderbilt continued, "Admiral Anderson has decided the risk is worth taking. Our job is to man the back door, keeping the enemy from coming through after our forces." Vanderbilt sighed almost imperceptivity, but somehow, the man kept a straight face. "Right now, we're the only sub assigned to that role, although the brief indicates that they might send someone else to assist us."

Bobby loved the Good Idea fairy. Who came up with this brilliant plan?

Rose Lange, *Bluefish's* weapons officer, crossed her arms and sat back in her chair, speaking in a flat voice: "We're supposed to hold off the entire Indian Navy all by ourselves. Ignoring the questionable intelligence of that tactic, what happens when we run out of torpedoes?"

"That's enough, Weps." Commander Peterson shot her a sour look, and Rose visibly bit her tongue. Bobby knew her well enough to know she had a lot more objections, but what the captain wanted, the captain got.

Was this a good time to mention that *Bluefish* only had twenty-one torpedoes? Rose, as the weapons officer, had tried multiple times to get them a reload while they were in Perth. Unfortunately, the base weapons folks didn't like submarines that didn't do jack. Bobby opened his mouth, but Commander Peterson's narrowed eyes swept over the rest of the officers and shut him down.

Wade Peterson was a short, olive-skinned man with hardly a hair left on his head. He looked like a go-getter, a trendsetter, like someone with the drive and the energy to get the job done and leave others gasping for air in his wake. But that didn't account for his perpetual frown or his cautious nature. His voice was deep and not well-fitted to turning high and nagging with annoyance, but Peterson hadn't read that memo.

His crew quickly learned to fear his heavy footsteps. Peterson wasn't hard enough to be respected and wasn't nice enough to be liked. He probably would've been all right in peacetime; he knew every policy and procedure cold, and he was great at making his boss happy. It probably helped that he and Commodore Banks went way back; they even were freaking *neighbors* back in Groton. Bobby had heard their wives were besties, too.

Bobby hated this boat.

An uncomfortable moment passed. *Bluefish's* sixteen officers glanced at one another, knowing that there were problems worth discussing but unwilling to brave their captain's wrath. An unhappy captain inevitably led to an unhappy crew...and *Bluefish's* crew had been beaten down enough. Pissing Peterson off just didn't seem worth the trouble. It wouldn't change their assignment.

"Anyway," Vanderbilt continued after he was the recipient of another patented peeved Peterson look. "We're not the key player in this game. The main force will be composed of the *Lexington* Strike Group: the carrier and her escorts. The advance force ahead of them will be more surface combatants with *Razorback* running point. We'll have to keep our ears open for *Razorback*; she'll be coming through the Strait a few hours ahead of the advance force, and she might have the enemy right on her heels."

Somebody whistled; Bobby wasn't sure who. But he certainly heard when one of the division officers, Ensign Tanya Chin, muttered: "Wonder who *they* pissed off to be assigned as the target?"

"You never know. They just *might've* volunteered for a chance to kill the enemy." Rene Shorn, Bobby's assistant navigator, scowled. "Last I checked, that's what we're out here for."

"Your enthusiasm is noted, Mister Shorn, but I'd appreciate you keeping it under control," Commander Peterson snapped. Rene jerked back as if he'd been slapped, but Peterson wasn't done. "I will not tolerate loose cannons or wild improvising. When *Bluefish* is called into combat, our actions will be measured, well-considered, and proportionate to the threat we face."

Their captain glared at each officer. Bobby's eyes found Rose, whose frustration oozed out of every pore in her body as she sat perfectly still, and he tried not to fidget. Sighing, Bobby chorused with the others:

"Yes, sir."

No, you couldn't *quite* call Commander Peterson a coward, but he wasn't a steely eyed missile man, either.

"Continue your briefing, XO," Peterson ordered, eyes narrowed.

Bobby envied the sailors and officers on *Razorback*. He bet Captain Dalton didn't spend his time squashing his officers' enthusiasm. Or maybe Peterson felt intimidated by it. Who knew?

Vanderbilt covered a few more specifics, mainly the capabilities of the enemy ships and submarines they expected to face, and then he turned to Peterson. "Do you have anything you'd like to add, Captain?"

Bobby tensed like a jackrabbit in a wolf's sights. Great. *Fantastic.* Peterson hadn't bothered to go over his plan for *Bluefish* with the XO before the briefing, had he? Vanderbilt was too conscientious *not* to cover tactics with the CO ahead of time. Which meant Peterson hadn't wanted to.

Yet Peterson had never struck Bobby as incompetent, just...fussy.

God help them if he turned out to be one of those captains who cracked like an egg under pressure. Bobby bit his tongue, trying to banish the thought. Peterson had sunk two frigates just fine. There was nothing to worry about.

Yet it might be better for *Bluefish* if Peterson cracked. That would leave Vanderbilt in command. The XO could fight the ship. But could the captain?

"We'll take position here, one thousand yards west of the entrance, and begin a standard patrol pattern," Peterson said. "Since the *Lexington* Strike Group is scheduled to commence their run at dawn, we will be on station two hours before that. We will remain covert at *all* costs and stand by to destroy anyone trying to get past us."

Peterson sounded confident, gesturing with a laser pointer at the electronic chart display on the wardroom wall, but the rolling feeling of fear sloshed from one side of Bobby's stomach to the other without slowing.

Bobby frowned. "Captain, looking at the time-distance, we could be on station eight or ten hours before dawn if we sprint and drift—"

"I said that we are going to remain *covert*, Nav." Peterson scowled. "There is no need to accept a greater risk than is required for the operation."

"I agree, sir, but what if someone slips in before we get there?" Bobby licked his lips as storm clouds colored Peterson's expression. "If our job is to—"

"Your opinion is noted, Mister O'Kane. Work up the navigation plan with a silent speed of advance," Peterson cut him off again.

"Yes, sir."

No, *Bluefish* wasn't the kind of boat where intelligent contributions to the captain's tactics were welcome.

Chapter 20

Shots Fired

Perdue Station

Kansas was ready for battle, with the customary hum of action in her control room as quiet as ever; no one joked about combat except the captain. Those were the rules.

His stomach rolling, Master Chief Chindeu Casey tried to smile when the helmsman looked over her shoulder, her eyes wide in concern. A good chief of the boat didn't fret, but damn, he wanted to.

Kansas had closed the distance with Perdue Station at forty-plus knots, letting the world know that America was on the scene. The aggressive approach was contrary to every prewar tactic Casey knew, and ninety-nine percent of the wartime ones...but it made Commander Kennedy happy.

And God help them all, their new XO seemed to be cut from the same cloth. Song and Kennedy were huddled together by the chart table, their heads bent together like a couple out of some soppy romance movie. Except they weren't planning dates, not those two. They had death and destruction on their minds.

Not that Casey minded killing the enemy. He even liked being good at it. That was the way people in uniform survived in war: they did their best to kill the other guy first and hoped the politicians sent them after the right people. And in his case, as an enlisted sailor, he had to hope like hell his leaders did the right thing.

Of course, as a chief of the boat, Casey had the ability to nudge those leaders more than a little. Or at least he was *supposed* to.

On *Kansas*, his twenty-five years of experience didn't count for nearly as much as COBs expected them to. Kennedy made a sport of pretending to listen while ignoring his advice, and Casey could do jack shit to change him. The captain was the captain, and right now, the guy was driving toward Perdue Station like his ass was on fire.

Every sailor on *Kansas* was tense. Casey could smell it in the air, could see it in the white knuckles gripping every control. The sailor on the helm clutched the wheel in hands so pale they could've belonged on a three-day-old corpse, and the planes operator next to her stared at the planes console like it might bite him. Only Kennedy and Song were happy, still plotting by the chart table like a pair of stupid little lovebirds.

The silence stretched on too long. Casey glanced left at the crew in the weapons corner. Weps didn't meet his eyes; the poor bastard was just trying to keep his head down and not become the captain's next least favorite person. His people pretended to be engrossed by the trio of stacked screens at each console, but Casey knew there was nothing to track a firing solution on. Not yet. Wherever the enemy sub was, he'd taken care to keep the bulk of the station between himself and a likely Alliance approach.

Smart.

Casey scowled.

"Captain, are you ready to slow?" Lieutenant Sue Grippo spoke up. As the navigator, she was the officer of the deck at battle stations. Kennedy's hatred hadn't changed that, though Casey could never tell if Kennedy wanted a punching bag or if he, somewhere deep down inside, recognized her competence.

He tried not to snort. It was probably the former.

Kennedy spun to glare at Sue. "What's our range to the station?"

"Six nautical miles and closing."

"Very well," he sneered. "Reduce speed to ten knots."

"Officer of the Deck, aye." Sue obviously had a lot of practice ignoring the vitriol, so she just relayed the orders and made it happen.

But the dark circles under her brown eyes were impossible to miss, as was the rigid set of her shoulders. Casey wanted to reach out to her, to tell her it would be okay, but he knew it wouldn't. So why lie? Lying just made things worse. Still, it hurt to watch her hold her breath and wait for the inevitable yelling to start. Master chiefs were supposed to help with problems like this.

Kansas slowed, the slight vibration in her decks vanishing. Casey shook himself. He had to put his head in the game and stop this mental bellyaching.

He walked over to the sonar operators, where their new-ish sonar chief, Chief Escalante was. Senior Chief Sali had finally gotten a much-deserved promotion and moved off the boat, and while Casey missed her, he was glad she was gone. Things were getting to the point where he wouldn't wish *Kansas* on anyone.

"How're things looking?" he asked in an undertone.

"Like there's a big station, a bigger ridge, and a bunch of blind darkness behind it," Escalante replied. "Even the best sonar can't hear through solid objects. We're going to have to pop our heads up or go round."

Casey grimaced; Escalante shook his head ruefully.

"I know better than to say that to the boss," he muttered. "This isn't *Jimmy Carter*."

"Stop making me jealous, Vic." Casey slapped Escalante on the shoulder gently.

"We can cry over a beer together later," Escalante said and then thumbed his nose at the waterfall displays, which showed nothing of interest except the big station sitting there, making tons of noise. "Assuming we ever see a port."

"You know we will. Captain loves a good party." That was safe to say out loud. No captain Casey had ever worked for loved a bar more than Kennedy. It should've been endearing, a way for him to bond with the crew.

Kennedy was just a worse bully when he was drunk.

"You bet I do, COB." On cue, Kennedy entered the conversation, striding to stand in the center of control. Not that he had to go more than two impressive steps; the attack center of any submarine was a cramped space, full of equipment, sailors, and sweat. But you couldn't tell that from the way Kennedy grinned and posed.

"How you want to find these guys, Captain?" Casey figured that if he asked the question, poor Sue might not get the full volcanic outburst.

"Fast and dirty." Kennedy's eyes gleamed. "I want to kill these fuckers before they can even think about—"

"Torpedo in the water! Two torpedoes in the water bearing zero-six-seven!" Chief Escalante didn't look bored now; his hands flew over the sonar console as he homed in on the tracks. "Torpedoes not inbound own ship!"

"What the hell?" Kennedy's head snapped around. "They wouldn't dare!"

"Find that sub, Sonar!" Song snarled.

"Sonar, aye. Torpedoes in acquisition," Escalante said. Then he swallowed, his gaze flicking to Casey. "Projected target...Perdue Station."

"No one would torp a station full of civilians," Kennedy said. His face was white.

"Captain, we've got action on underwater standard," the radio watch reported.

Kennedy slammed a fist into an angle iron. "Put it on speaker."

A buzz filled the room as the radio watch transferred the network over. "Underwater Standard" was shorthand for a specific frequency of underwater communications. By their very nature, any underwater communications were slow and short ranged. The only decent way to talk to someone was to stick an antenna above water and have it talk to another surfaced antenna that was attached to a submarine. Sending wireless signals through water was just unreliable.

Sometimes, however, subs were close enough to use the old-style "Gertrudes" to communicate via voice. For that, they used Underwater Standard.

"*—submarine threatening to shoot—oh, God, they've shot at us!*" a panicked voice filled the air. "*Mayday, mayday, mayday, this is Perdue Station! An Indian submarine threatened to destroy the station if we didn't evacuate, but we don't have enough escape craft, and they've fired on us! Someone please help!*"

"Captain, I've put a datum in the system to represent an estimated position for the enemy," Escalante said. "He's behind the station and out of our sonar envelope."

Kennedy scowled. "Very well. Officer of the Deck, come left and increase speed to fifteen knots."

Kansas' best silent speed was well beneath that; if things went right, the attacker would never know they were there. A cold hand gripped Casey's heart. But that wouldn't help Perdue Station.

His eyes locked onto the sonar display. Casey couldn't hear the torpedoes without a headset—and didn't want to—but he could see their tracks burning through the water. Two TEST 83 torpedoes had five hundred–pound warheads, and at that range, they'd hit the station in less than twenty seconds.

"Get me that bastard, Sonar. I've got two torpedoes with his name on them," Kennedy snarled.

Casey squeezed Escalante's shoulder. He knew the sonar chief wanted to stare at the tracks bearing down on the station instead of searching for the bad guy, but for once, Kennedy was right.

There was nothing anyone could do about those torpedoes. The idea of intercept torpedoes had been around for decades, and a dozen companies *tried* creating them. Unfortunately, no one pulled it off. That meant the only way to make a torpedo go away was outrun it or outfox it, both of which usually required noisemakers to distract the torpedoes...while the target made a course change so the torpedo lost lock.

Yeah. Perdue Station wasn't going to change course any time soon. At least not until the torpedo hit.

Casey cringed. He hated this sick feeling, and he really hated how familiar it was. Not being able to save innocent lives was the worst damn part of this war. How many convoys had *Kansas* failed to save so far because they were in the wrong place at the wrong time and Kennedy wasn't willing to risk detection to get at an enemy who had the drop on them? Kennedy was the kind of captain who waited for merchant ships to get sunk to give him bearings to the enemy. So...Casey was used to pushing this feeling of helpless fury and horror down. This wasn't a skill the recruiter told him he'd need when he joined the navy, but here he was.

"Take a look north." Casey leaned forward and pointed at a slight imperfection on the waterfall display. "What's that?"

Escalante frowned. "Whatever it is, it's outbound."

"Might be our new friend."

"Impact in five seconds," a sonar petty officer reported.

"*Mayday, mayday, mayday. This is Perdue Station, and an Indian submarine has fired on us. We have hundreds of people here,*" the voice on the radio said again. "*Someone please help!*"

"Do you want to answer that, sir?" Sue whispered.

Kennedy shook his head. "What the fuck good would it do?"

"Might let them know they aren't alone." Sue shrugged, looking away, her features ashen.

"Find me the assholes, Sonar," Kennedy snapped.

The underwater circuit crackled one last time. "*Is there anyone out there?*"

"Impact," Escalante said instead of replying to Kennedy, who just snarled silently and clenched his fists.

Casey shuddered. *Kansas* wasn't close enough to Perdue Station to feel the blast, but he could picture the blast in his mind's eye. Those TEST 83 torpedoes' five hundred–pound warheads would tear into a civilian station like it was made of paper. Perdue Station sat at seven hundred feet, and it was made of sturdy steels and some titanium...but one or two holes would be enough. Once water got in, people would start dying.

And an explosion would create more than one or two holes. Casey could imagine the water rushing into formerly watertight spaces, could imagine people drowning and fighting to get to safety that no longer existed. The lucky people would die in the explosions or in the resulting *implosions*. The unlucky bastards would drown or be aware of it when they were sucked into the sea.

"Fuckers," someone said in the back of control.

Casey couldn't disagree.

"I got a little something," Escalante whispered before Casey could try to intervene on Sue's behalf. "Not enough for a track yet, but got something moving from left to right, rough bearing around zero-five-two."

"Keep on it. Pop a datum down."

"You got it, COB."

"Get your head in the game, Nav," Song said, moving to stand next to a still-subdued Sue. "We need to get these guys."

Sue turned dead eyes on the XO. "What will it matter? Those people will still be dead."

"We can still avenge them."

"Yeah, but we couldn't save them." Sue slumped against the chart table. "We never do."

"Don't be dramatic, Nav." Kennedy rolled his eyes. "We're doing good work out here. And if we're late sometimes, well, that's just bad luck. The fortunes of war." He held his hands out, palms up. "Shit happens. We have to keep fighting."

Damn the man, Casey couldn't disagree with him.

"Can we at least send in a drone to see how bad the station got hit?" Sue asked. Her eyes darted around control. "We should be thinking about search and rescue if there's anyone alive, sir."

"We have to kill the bastard who took them out before we can think of any of that. Otherwise, he'll shoot us right in the back." Kennedy's jaw jutted out. "So get to work *finding* him or I will replace you with someone who will."

Sue flinched. "Aye, sir."

Kansas swung into her search, heading for the sonar ghost Chief Escalante held near the bearings the torpedoes had been shot from. The torpedoes fired told them that the attacker was Indian, as did the threats that were issued. Everyone knew that Indian AIP boats were quiet but slow, whereas their nukes were fast but noisy. There was no reason why *Kansas* shouldn't detect a nuclear attack boat in short order...but a good twenty minutes of searching turned up squat.

During that time, sonar picked up several escaping craft from the ruins of Perdue Station, some of which struggled to the surface and others that circled aimlessly. They also detected a pod of whales off to the north…but no enemy submarines.

"At least pygmy blue whales are rare," Chief Escalante muttered. "Their mating calls are pretty distinct. Back in peacetime, there'd be a lot of excited scientists rushing out here."

Casey patted him on the shoulder. "Probably not happening today."

"What was that, COB?" Kennedy whirled, his voice sharp and eyes zeroing in on Casey for the kill.

"Just wanking about whales, Captain." Casey kept his smile easy, even though he could feel everyone in control trying not to freeze. Acting normal was hard when Kennedy started pacing like a caged animal.

"What the fuck do whales have to do with anything?"

"They're all that's out here, sir." Chief Escalante was brave. Casey had to give him that. But he wasn't sure if Escalante was also stupid, because the man added: "Except the boats escaping Perdue. You want to go help them and salvage something out of this goat rope?"

Christ, Casey almost whispered. Chiefs were supposed to be honest in the face of power, but that was taking things a bit far.

"And what exactly do you think is a *goat rope* here, Chief?" Kennedy crossed his arms, his voice dangerously calm.

"Well—"

"It's obvious the Indian boat ran away immediately after torpedoing the station," Lieutenant Commander Song interjected before Escalante could put his foot in. "The cowards used the sounds of the explosion as cover and fled, probably in hopes that no credible witnesses would survive."

Kennedy's eyes narrowed. "What are you thinking, XO?"

"I'm thinking that if we rescue people from Perdue who heard the Indian transmission threatening to torpedo them, we can prove an Indian sub captain guilty of war crimes." Song's eyes gleamed.

"Not a bad thought." Kennedy nodded slowly. "Nav, change course toward the station."

"Navigator, aye." Relief was plain on Sue's face as she grinned and relayed the orders, but she deflated when Kennedy snarled:

"If *someone* had pointed that out earlier, we might've saved more of them."

His glare was on Lieutenant Sue Grippo, of course. As if it was her fault. Casey shook his head. There'd be no deflecting Kennedy short of giving him a job that made him feel important—which Song had just done—so it was better to go along with things and hope he changed target quickly.

Unfortunately, there was no way to know if *Kansas* heading for the station twenty minutes earlier might've saved more lives. By the time they arrived, ninety percent of those on Perdue Station were dead or dying in small pockets of air *Kansas* would never reach. Even in peacetime, *Virginia*-class boats were not optimized for underwater search and rescue, which was admittedly a very new art. In wartime...

Casey just did his job, helped survivors on board after the boat surfaced, and endured Kennedy's rage when he learned that none of them could provide a recording of whatever threats the Indian captain had made. The best *Kansas* had was the transmission they'd received...which was hardly enough to identify the Indian by name, let alone prove anyone guilty of war crimes.

Ambitions thwarted, Kennedy screamed at Sue some more and retreated to his stateroom. Meanwhile, Song scheduled an unplanned inspection of the weapons room maintenance plan and dug into Weps's playground to work out her anger. And Casey? He took a goddamned nap and wondered if he could convince his conscience into writing up a transfer.

Paul came back around the corner of the boarding tube and was greeted by a brewing riot. His small team of marines stood in the opening, braced against a crowd that wasn't *quite* ready to start pushing them. They were all over the station's security people, though, some of whom were down and getting kicked and pelted with trash. Paul felt sorry for them but didn't order anyone to help; that wasn't his problem, and it certainly wasn't his fight.

The crowd, however, was likely to be his problem if they couldn't push those stupid crates into the submarine. Paul grimaced. Submarines weren't his area of expertise—he'd stormed one from the inside before the war and captured another alongside a TRANSPLAT since the fighting started—but he didn't think shoving was going to solve this problem.

Nor was it going to make these people any happier.

"Get out of the way!"

"Let us leave!"

"You have no right to trap us here!"

He sided up to Gunny Kochera. "Getting bad?"

"I've seen worse." She shrugged. "Went to a rough high school."

Paul barked out a laugh. "You got any riot control experience?"

"Jack shit and nada." Kochera jerked her head toward the crowd, which was twice as big as it had been when Paul shepherded the scientists through. "They're getting angry, but no one's done anything dumb yet. Worst was when Pulsar Security tried to boss some old lady around. Her son took offense and threw the asshole into a bulkhead."

"Must've been the thump we heard."

"Yep. Never seen a more deserving jackass bounce off metal in my life." She pointed. "That fucktard by the red pillar. He tried to hit that tiny old lady, and if her kid hadn't taken care of him, I might've felt the need to do humanity a favor and remove him from the gene pool."

"Now, Gunny, you know we're not supposed to play those games."

"Play stupid games, get stupid prizes, sir."

Paul's eyes drifted over the shouting mass of humanity. "Someone out to tell these people that."

Chapter 21

Necessary Risks

26 September 2039, The Mid-Indian Ocean, in route to the Strait of Malacca—USS Lexington *(CVN-84) Strike Group*

John hid in the shadow of the aircraft carrier for the obligatory pre-operation teleconference, hoping that would keep the enemy task force from noticing an extra set of emissions coming from the *Lexington* Strike Group. The plan depended on *Razorback* getting into the Strait unnoticed; if the enemy knew there was a sub to hunt for, the chances of them finding *Razorback* increased exponentially. Getting to the Strait covertly gave John's boat a fighting chance.

After all, no one in their right mind thought their attack on the Strait of Malacca would come as a surprise to the enemy. As much as they *wanted* to catch the Indians with their pants around their ankles, there was no way the Indians would miss a fleet of surface ships heading their way. Sure, they *might* attack somewhere else...but the SOM was the grand prize, and John knew how much everyone wanted it.

That was probably why Admiral Anderson started the heavy pre-op planning so far out. The strike group was just under a thousand miles from the north entrance to the SOM, steaming through the gunky kind of weather that signified the end of monsoon season. Seas were rough, sailors on *Razorback* were puking as she kicked and rolled, and the sky was an orange-gray that promised retribution upon stupid submarine sailors who lurked near the surface.

Not that Anderson cared. She also a surface officer who considered *Razorback* just one more asset whose every move she should dictate...and who should remain in constant communication with the flagship at all times. John could feel his hair graying every minute he talked to her. Trying to explain how submarines worked to the ambitious and snarky admiral was like trying to teach nuclear power to a toddler.

Thank goodness for Uncle Marco. *His* operational orders allowed *Razorback*—and John in particular—a shocking degree of tactical latitude. All he was required to do was be in the Strait on time and stay ahead of the strike group; they left the rest up to him. John had never received a set of orders like this, but there they were, in black and white, staring up at him from the tablet that his radio watch had delivered to him in control.

Anderson got a copy, too, which shut her up. Mostly.

John had heard about Uncle Marco's one-man battle against the rest of the navy's employment of submarines, but he never expected to see it succeed.

"Well, if you need evidence that admin is still God in the navy, here it is." He passed the tablet to Lieutenant Commander Patricia Abercrombie, his XO. "If you don't write it down, it never happened."

Messages didn't often come along with headers longer than the text of the message itself, but John sure had a hot one.

TO: USS RAZORBACK SSN 857//
FROM: COMSUBPAC//
INFO: COMBATGRU 12
COMSTRKGRU 84
COMDESRON 26
USS LEXINGTON CVN 84
USS ANZIO CG 88
USS BULL RUN CG 74
HMAS SYDNEY DDG 42
HMS TERMAGANT D39
HMS TYRIAN D43
USS MORTON DDG 159
USS ERNEST E EVANS DDG 139
USS ARLEIGH BURKE DDG 142
USS JASON DUNHAM DDG 109
USS SAM NUUN DDG 133
HMS NORTHUMBERLAND FFG 301
HMAS PARRAMATTA FFH 154

HMAS PERTH FFH 157
HMAS BOGAN FFG 167
USS OAKLAND LCS 24
USS BILLINGS LCS 15
USS BLUEFISH SSN 843//
SUBJ: OP ORDER 3284//
RMKS/1. ENTER SOM ON OR ABOUT 03 OCT 2039 AHEAD OF MAIN FORCE.
2. SEEK AND DESTROY THE ENEMY. RAZORBACK ACTUAL TO USE BEST JUDGMENT ON EMPLOYMENT OF SUBMARINE.
3. GOOD LUCK AND GOOD HUNTING.
VADM RODRIQUEZ SENDS.//

"That's a lot of metal to throw at one battle, sir." Pat's eyes gleamed. "We're serious about getting the SOM back this time, aren't we?"

"And we're the only one out front." John made himself grin like a proper submariner. He couldn't think about the last time he'd been to the SOM, or the friends he'd lost. They'd never found Ernest Evans' body... Had he been ripped up as *Enterprise* exploded, or was the SOM his grave? John shook himself. "I guess that means we're masters of our own fate."

Pat laughed. "Better than being a SWO's puppet, Captain. Or being *Bluefish*, stuck at the back door."

"Damn straight. Let's hope no one changes their minds before the shoe drops."

Red Tiger Station

Jimmy Carter's midships hatch *was* big enough for those godawful white containers to fit through, but opening it while nestled up against Red Tiger Station was a great way to flood the entire submarine and die.

Alex sized the boxes up in a glance after joining Paul, the scientists, and a squad of marines in the docking area. "We're going to need a TRANSPLAT and a crane," he said. "No way can we load those things here."

Distant shouts from the crowd reminded *all* of them why they really didn't want to send the containers back through the station, but Alex couldn't think of another way.

He shivered, thinking about the last time he'd been on an underwater station and everything started falling apart. But Jules Rochambeau wasn't here, and the only marines around were under Paul's command.

Paul, newly returned from eyeballing the now-chanting crowd, grimaced. "You can't just, I don't know, jimmy them down the ladder?"

"They're too big." Alex looked over at the head of the Fogborne team. "I don't suppose they disassemble?"

Doctor Leifsson shook her head. "No, I'm afraid not."

"Well, then let's tell the station manager that they've got to make room for us topside." Alex shoved his hands in his pockets. "This is going to be cute."

"What, you think that'll somehow make the crowd worse?" Paul asked.

"Might. Or we'll entice some pirates. Reports say there's a lot of activity in this area."

"Yeah, they told me. Apparently, there's a submarine within twenty miles or so." Paul grinned. "Could be fun, assuming they're dumb enough to come after an obvious warship."

"Could be not fun, depending upon what ships they have. We're pretty vulnerable on the surface." Alex didn't want to think about having an old-fashioned gun battle on the surface; today's submarines weren't armed with deck guns, and small arms would do jack against a pirate.

A pirate submarine was less of a worry. Worst case, he could just outrun them.

"Eh, you're creative."

Alex laughed. "I'm glad I've got your vote of confidence."

Two hours later—and three arguments with the station manager, two of which concluded with *yes*, Alex *would* use force, aka the marines, to keep him from sneaking on board the submarine to escape Red Tiger Station—*Jimmy Carter* eased away from the underwater docking station and headed for the surface.

Maggie had the conn, but she played with a lock of her hair as the giant attack boat cleared the station and started her surfacing procedures, chewing her lip and staring into the middle distance.

"You all right, Nav?" Alex slipped up to her side, his voice low.

Maggie blinked. "Yes, sir. Just thinking about how much it must *suck* to get stuck in a place like this." She shuddered. "Makes me think about the future and how mine's standing still."

"Is it?"

"War kind of pauses everything, doesn't it?" she asked. "We're out here, doing what we have to, but our lives are put on hold. Careers, too, sometimes."

Alex cocked his head. "You're still thinking about how you wanted to transfer to intel?"

"Sometimes." Maggie shrugged. "I like making a difference, but..."

"But escorting convoys in the great dark deep isn't exactly scratching that itch?"

Maggie blushed. "I didn't mean it that way, sir."

"It's all right. I did." Alex chuckled and tried to ignore the way every eye in control drifted his way. He knew his crew felt the same way as Maggie, like they'd been left out in the cold while others fought and died. "I know. It's hard to keep your head up and keep pushing when we always draw the dreary convoy escorts where nothing happens."

"At least the drive here was suitably scary," Maggie replied. "And this little maneuver is a ton of fun."

"Hey, you did great. Didn't even scrape the paint."

"Gee, thanks, Captain."

"Anytime." Alex patted her on the shoulder. "We should get some good leave when we get back from this one, so you can try to get a little of your life back on track. That goes for all of you eavesdroppers, too."

"You really think we'll get some decent time off, Captain?" ET2 Vasquez asked from the weapons corner.

Alex watched the depth gauge as Maggie expertly brought *Jimmy Carter* to periscope depth. "I can't promise it, but I think so. This is the hairiest mission we've pulled, and that's got to count for something."

"From your mouth to Uncle Marco's ears, sir." Vasquez grinned. "My girlfriend would really like seeing me for more than five seconds."

"Girlfriend?" another petty officer asked. "I thought you had a boyfriend."

Vasquez laughed. "I'm equal opportunity, shipmate."

"Oh, fuck you," the other sailor replied.

"Petty Officer Cox!" George Kirkland's voice cut through the air like a bird screeching, and Alex fought not to cringe. "That is quite enough!"

Of *course* his XO re-entered control just in time to hear sailors joking. And predictably, he objected to sailors being sailors.

"Sorry, XO." Cox didn't sound particularly sorry, and Alex caught sight of Velasquez smirking before George turned his glare on her.

"Up scope," Maggie ordered before George could warm up for a rant, and Alex could've hugged her. "Surface appears clear visually, Captain."

"Clear by radar," a junior officer reported.

"Very well. Surface the ship."

"Surface the ship, aye." Maggie's crisp nod was all professionalism with no trace of her earlier uncertainty. "Diving Officer, surface the ship."

By peacetime rules, Alex should've been all over the surfacing operation. They should've taken at least fifteen minutes searching via the periscope, sonar, *and* radar, just to make sure they didn't do something stupid like surface underneath a fishing boat. It had happened before—more than once—humiliating the U.S. Navy.

But who was Alex going to surface under out here, a pirate? It would be a novel way of sinking one, that was for sure. *Jimmy Carter* would survive that easily. Her HY100 hull was tougher than any other American submarine in the water.

God help me if that's how I make it onto the sinking scorecard of this war, Alex thought behind a passive face. Still, he stepped up to the scope when Maggie moved clear, because he *was* a child of a peacetime navy, and looking around was a good idea.

One quick, sidestepping rotation told him the surface was indeed clear, at least within five miles of *Jimmy Carter*. The six TRANSPLATS of Red Tiger Station loomed off to port, little mechanical islands sticking out of an otherwise calm ocean. One of them was half burned and looked melted, but there were a few ships and submarines at all the others: merchants, trawlers, and fishing boats. He thought he even saw one whaler—was that legal in this part of the world?

"It's not as busy as I expected," Maggie said in an undertone as Alex stepped away from the periscope.

"There's a civil war on, and not everyone wants to play." He grimaced, making room for George to check as well. Why did George have to be so damned good at following some procedures and such a stick in the mud about everything else?

"Civil war seems like the only war where everyone gets a seat at the table." Maggie made a face. "Particularly out here."

"Yeah, but would you want to be an innocent merchantman—excuse me, merchant *woman*—stuck in the middle of this mess?"

"Captain, I don't even want to be on a submarine surfacing in the middle of it," she replied. "This seems dangerous as all hell."

"I agree with the navigator, Captain." George pulled away from the scope, scowling. "Exposing ourselves on the surface is a risk of the *highest* magnitude."

"Risks are part of doing business." Alex wished his head wasn't pounding so hard, but now wasn't the time to retreat to his stateroom and grab some painkillers. "We've got a mission to complete, and we need to be surfaced to do it. So how 'bout we stop complaining and get on with the show?"

"Sir, are we certain their 'equipment' is that important?" George asked. "We were ordered to remove the team, not whatever they're bringing with them. The danger to the ship outweighs whatever importance their cargo has—"

"You really want to explain that to Uncle Marco?" *Or Admiral Hamilton?* Alex didn't add.

"Opening the cargo door under wartime conditions just invites *trouble*." George crossed his arms. "Will these people even get a crane up there in time? How can we trust the station staff when their loyalty is unknown?"

"I assume we can trust the money Pulsar Power's put down." Alex held up a hand when George opened his mouth to argue further. "You have good points, XO, but we're here to take the Fogborne team—and their gear—back to Alliance territory. A little danger doesn't excuse us from that duty. We're at war."

George's nose wrinkled. "I still think the risks are unnecessary."

"I'm heading up to the bridge," Maggie said. "Do you care to join me, Captain?"

Oh, lord, did Alex want to get away from George's fearmongering. But he couldn't leave George here to fret and infect the watch in control. How did he counter this? George had good points, but damn, the man lacked courage.

A lurking form filled the hatch to his left, and Alex almost smiled. "XO, would you take Colonel Swanson midships to show him where the hatch is? He's going to have to form up a team to cover it when we're alongside."

Stiffening, George shot him a look that could almost be called a glare. "Aye, Captain."

If there was anyone he could trust to sit on George, it was Paul. Paul had no patience for cowardice, and he outranked the XO. He also out-massed him by at least a hundred pounds, so if he had to *actually* sit on him, Paul would win that contest, too.

Alex threw Paul a grateful look and then scurried up the ladder on Maggie's heels.

Diego Garcia, the British Indian Ocean Territory (BIOT)

"You ready to go off and try your hand at being the designated bad guy, Davud?"

Nancy found her combat systems officer—and battle stations tactical actions officer—standing on *Fletcher's* aft missile deck, watching the sun set over Diego Garcia. He must have heard her coming, however, because Lieutenant Commander Davud Attar just smiled.

"I think finding the weird places sailors hide contraband could be a fun challenge, ma'am. Just last week, the XO and I found porn stashed under—"

She held up a hand. "I really don't want to know. I've seen enough."

Davud grinned. "Sorry, Captain."

"Oh, no need to apologize. You'll see plenty when you head over to *Evans*. An XO's job is rarely fun, but it's always full of surprises." Nancy chuckled. "There will be plenty of shit-stained porn coming your way, I'm sure."

"Isn't that what you've got a chief engineer for?"

"Depends on how much you like Cheng."

They laughed together before Nancy sobered. "You ready for one last ride with us before you go? I won't lie. I'll be sorry to see you go."

"I'm proud to be on *Fletcher*, ma'am. Always am."

"Even if it means missing the next battle for the SOM?" she asked.

Davud shuddered. "The first one was enough for me." He didn't need to mention the unmitigated disaster of the second battle; they all tried not to. Or think of the friends they lost in the first.

"Same here. I think I've had enough glory hunting." Nancy wasn't sure she could say the same for Admiral Anderson, which was why she was relieved to be out from under the ambitious admiral's command.

Anderson was hunting for the *perfect victory*, the one that would launch her career toward a third star and beyond. Nancy had her fill of that with Admiral McNally, who froze up in the First Battle of the SOM and got three ships sunk.

He also might've started the entire war, but no one on the American side admitted that.

"I think there's probably *some* glory to be found in the surface action group that Admiral Rosario is forming up, Captain," Davud replied. "Or at least some good to be done."

"That's the key," Nancy replied. "We've got to do the job. Kill the enemy before they can sink our merchant ships. Find their submarines before they can wreck our economy. If there's glory to be found, it'll follow."

It was easy to say that as a woman who already wore the silver star, of course. Nancy knew her career was moving in the right direction; she didn't need another "great battle" to seal the deal. But she hoped she would've felt that way, anyway, even if she hadn't already been there, with her back against the wall, watching missiles fly, friends die, and ships burn.

No, she didn't envy the ships of the *Lexington* Strike Group going in for another shot at the Strait of Malacca. Nancy hoped they'd succeed. She hoped the overwhelming force Admiral Anderson put together would do the job.

She had no desire to be there in the event it failed.

The Mid-Indian Ocean, in route to the Strait of Malacca

"If that sub isn't on their toes, it's going to get very hairy for the advance group," Charlie Markey said quietly.

Commander Fletch Goddard and his executive officer sat in his day cabin, looking over the battle plan one more time. They still had seven days to plan, but Fletch knew the history of battles in this area: everything that could go wrong would go wrong. He sighed, staring at the wall over Charlie's head.

His day cabin remained sparsely furnished. Fletch didn't believe in bringing priceless mementos or nice decorations to sea; he'd seen too many friends have their favorite pictures sunk out from under them. No, he kept a copy of a picture of his son on one wall, and a poster of his favorite football team on the other, and that was enough. Well, and a couple of really good pillows. He'd be sorry to lose those if *Parramatta* went down, but one could not sleep on shit pillows.

"You're not bloody wrong." Fletch grimaced. "I don't like the last-minute swap, either. *Douglass* was part of the planning from the beginning."

"Hard to argue with it when *Douglass* is on the bottom." Charlie shrugged. "Still, it does feel a little like COMSUBPAC is covering his arse with the orders he gave *Razorback*, doesn't it?"

"Or like he doesn't trust Admiral Anderson," Fletch replied. "Toxic combination."

Charlie grimaced. "I really didn't want to get in the middle of an American admiral pissing contest this week. Particularly when one of them is doing it by damned proxy."

Fletch shook himself. Wool gathering over which admiral distrusted another most wasn't going to help his ship in the coming battle, and he had a thirty-six-year-old frigate to get through this fight. Particularly now that *Parramatta* was confirmed as part of the advance group, christened SAG (Surface Action Group) Alpha.

"That's not our fight. Let's get ready for the one that is," he said. "First assumption: *Razorback* is sunk before Dalton can take out the bulk of the forces in the strait. What then?"

"Then we're in the hot seat, and it's going to hurt." Charlie sat back. "Intelligence says the Indians placed Brahmos NG missiles in portable launchers on Penang Island when they took it from Malaysia."

Fletch grimaced. Malaysia and Thailand, both of which bordered the northeastern entrance to the Strait of Malacca, were part of the Alliance. Unfortunately, Indonesia, which bordered the north*western* side, was allied with the Freedom Union. Singapore hung on to neutrality by a thread, trying to play the modern-day equivalent of Switzerland and so far managing.

But Singapore's lack of belligerence couldn't help them here. Indonesia's wretchedly long coastline would be to the strike group's starboard side during their entire transit, and while reaching Singapore meant they could make a port turn toward neutral—if not friendly—waters, it would be a long five hundred miles before they reached that point.

Leaning back in his chair, Fletch wondered if Admiral Anderson had considered how that turn northward sent ships straight into the

South China Sea. That haven of piracy wouldn't be won back with a smart battle, which meant a lot of merchant traffic traveled through the Java Sea...straight through Indonesian waters.

Life was full of great choices, wasn't it?

"There are also missiles at Belwan on mainland Indonesia, and reports of CDCM sites on Rupat, Bengkalis, and Rangsang islands," Charlie continued.

"Any news on if they've taken the Andaman and Nicobar Islands? I know there was fear they'd move in on them."

"None yet. I sent an inquiry to Admiral Anderson's staff yesterday, but intel has nothing."

"Lovely. So cruise missile sites full of Brahmos missiles on at least four islands, plus Belwan. Plus potential fighter jets at Malikus Saleh Airport." Fletch glanced at the briefing again. "And intel indicates at least four submarines in the strait, as well as...six Indian destroyers, one French destroyer, one frigate, and assorted patrol craft."

"Theoretically, we outnumber them." Charlie rolled her eyes. "But it would be nice if the advance force wasn't being sent out like so much bait."

"Be nice. The admiral's promised us air cover."

"I'm getting sick of Yank promises, sir."

"We're all in this together, Charlie," Fletch replied. "We've fought and bled enough side by side to give them a little benefit of the doubt."

"Forgive me, Captain." She shook her head. "It's not Yanks in general I'm fed up with. More this admiral."

"Aye. That I can get behind." Fletch cracked a smile. "But you didn't hear that."

"Hear what, sir?"

The South China Sea, Location Unspecified

"Cap, we've got an interesting report." Jenny poked her head into Diego Reyes' luxurious stateroom aboard *Destroyer*. "*Siren* says she saw what looks like a navy submarine surfacing near Red Tiger Station."

"Really?" Diego sat up straight, the movie he was watching forgotten.

Siren was ex-*Passat*, a Russian-built *Nanuchka*-class corvette that he'd snapped up when she decommissioned in the mid-2020s. In fact, *Siren* had been the first ship in Diego's little fleet, and it was the prizes he took with her that enabled him to purchase his current flagship. *Destroyer* was far better suited to a pirate's life—submarines were made for stealth, and no one built them like Germany—but he kept his fleet of surface ships. They were useful for escorting prizes to port.

They also looked impressive.

"She sent pictures if you're interested," Jenny replied. "I forwarded them to your account."

Diego grabbed his tablet, pulling them up right away. Sure enough, there was a sleek, black submarine heading toward one of Red Tiger's TRANSPLATs, Suzy, if he wasn't mistaken. Only navies painted their submarines that boring black color. Even he'd had *Destroyer* painted a neutral gray with blue stripes; it wouldn't do to be mistaken for a belligerent and have someone kill his submarine while on the surface. Wartime was the one time that looking like a warship *would not do.*

He whistled. "This is an American boat."

"Is it?" Jenny shrugged. "I've never been great at telling them apart visually. Give me a sonar signature any day."

Diego chuckled. Jenny was an excellent navigator, but a little shortsighted on the intelligence side. But that was fine; he didn't pay her to cover intel. He had other people for that, like Cynthia Patterson over on *Siren*. She was damned smart and knew what to report.

"See the slope at the bottom of the sail? She's an American fast attack. Big bitch, though." He frowned. "Probably a late-model *Virginia*."

Diego started doing math. How much would the Russians or Indians pay for a *Virginia*? Would they double it if he could get the boat with her intelligence intact? Talk about the mother lode. The very thought sent a shiver down his spine.

"Cynthia also sent along another report," Jenny interrupted his daydreaming. "Something about a Pulsar Power research team creating a miniaturized fusion reactor."

"What's that have to do with this?"

"Apparently they're on Red Tiger Station."

"Oh, my." Diego looked at the pictures again, wondering how long it took to get an enormous beast like that underway again once they were pier side. Nuclear reactors took forever to start up, didn't they? Maybe he'd get lucky, and they'd stay for days. "Contact *Valiant* and *Pearl*. Tell them to head for our position as fast as they can. We've got a new target."

Jenny turned to go but then paused. "The team or the submarine?"

"Both, if my guess is right." Diego bared his teeth. "And if we get these two, we may never have to ply the pirates' trade again."

Chapter 22

Battle Plans

"*Moored, shift colors.*"
 Alex didn't like admitting he sighed in relief when *Jimmy Carter* was made fast to Red Tiger Station's number four TRANSPLAT. Maybe he'd been listening to George natter for too long.

Still, things appeared to be trucking along on schedule. Alex leaned against the edge of the sail and glanced around, taking in the five-spoked TRANSPLAT that lay against the water like a giant, mechanized starfish. Piers jutted off each spoke like smaller barnacles, and about half the berths were occupied. The ones around *Jimmy Carter* were not; they were at the last pier along the second spoke, closest to open water and—hopefully—away from any trouble.

Much to his surprise, the crane was ready and waiting for them. Apparently, that last spirited talk with the station manager worked. It was a little after noon, and a few hours loading wouldn't put them much behind schedule. All Alex had to do was get this done and then get the hell out of here.

He picked up his radio. "Swanson, Coleman, your team ready in the hangar?"

"Ready to rock and roll," Paul's scratchy voice replied.

"Captain, XO, we need a team on the pier before we open the side door!" George was tasked with supervising that evolution, but did he have to sound so panicked?

"Captain, aye. Break, Swanson, your other team ready?"

"Taking them to the pier myself."

"Aye."

Alex took a deep breath as Paul's team of eight marines jogged down the brow to the pier, weapons in hand. The other five were still guarding the Fogborne boxes, but Alex could see those coming down the pier on a flatbed pallet mover.

An alarm sounded, and Maggie's voice spoke over the 1MC: "*All hands stand clear as side cargo door opens. I say again, all hands stand clear as side cargo door opens.*"

He turned to look at Maggie as the giant door on *Jimmy Carter's* port side started opening. It was almost flush with the water line, and Alex *really* didn't like the idea of opening it way out here, where open ocean–size waves could get them, but what choice did he have? "Well, this should be fun," he said. "What's going to go wrong next?"

"Did you have to go and say that out loud, Captain?" Maggie shook her head like he was a misbehaving child. "You *have* heard of Murphy's Law, haven't you?"

"Yeah, but—"

"Coleman, Swanson, we got a bunch of civilians coming down the pier behind the gear." Paul's voice was level, but Alex could hear the tension beneath the professional cadence. "Gunny tells me the crowd followed them from below."

"See?" Maggie snorted. "This is what you get for asking what's going wrong next."

"Captain, aye. Break, Weps—how long does your team need to open that door?"

Benji's voice sounded strained. "At least ten mikes, Captain. The hydraulics are old and cranky. Not sure what'll happen if we push them."

If Alex squinted, he could see the crowd marching down the pier. How long would it take them to reach *Jimmy Carter*? Shouts traveled well across open water when the wind was right, and he could hear people screaming obscenities already over the door's hydraulic squeals.

Fucking joy.

Washington, D.C.

Freddie Hamilton cleaned her glasses on a cloth and tried not to look annoyed. Toying with them bought her time to get her temper under control...and lord did she need it.

Not for the first time, she wished Marco Rodriquez was here. Marco would've called this political pimple something foul, like a shit-eating wank hammer, and then the conversation would've ended with Martin Fowler being kicked out like the weasel he was. Marco would've died before he let this self-important politician lecture him.

Freddie did not have that luxury.

Undersecretary of State Martin Fowler was a worm who she had far too much experience with. Like many government flunkies, he thought he knew more about the navy than he did and was frequently found at bars within the Beltway bragging about how *his* tactics would've won the war already. Most people ignored him like the windbag he was once he started drinking.

Pity more didn't ignore him when he was sober. In the office, Fowler had the secretary of state's ear. A self-proclaimed "Man of Peace," Fowler was nonetheless willing to stick *other* people's necks out...provided he was never in danger. His bland wrapper of curly, dark-blond hair, cheap sweaters, and glasses hid a malicious center that couldn't handle danger, fear, or any of the other "shallow" emotions warfighters dealt with every day. Somehow, even after a handful of those warfighters saved him on Armistice Station, Fowler still managed to look down his crooked nose at every uniformed service member he encountered.

"I'm afraid the State Department simply can't support that position." Fowler folded his hands, affecting a smile Freddie knew was anything but apologetic. "Our study of weapons and submarine proliferation indicates that diesel submarine production outnumbers nuclear submarine production by a factor of two to three."

Maisie McClean, the Secretary of Defense, narrowed her eyes. "I do not see why that means you cannot support the proposal, Mister Undersecretary."

Fowler ignored her, despite the fact McClean was on par with his absent boss, turning to the chief of naval operations. Admiral David Chan knew less about submarines than McClean and Fowler put together, but it was nice to see that Fowler's misogyny survived the fight on Armistice Station.

"Admiral, certainly you can see that faster built diesel-electric submarines are the answer. Your navy is bleeding badly. Our analysis is that other nations have successfully filled the gap with diesels, specifically those with Advanced Independent Propulsion. I see no reason why we can't do the same."

Admiral Chan, callsign "Scrap," hesitated. Freddie could see the argument—and the endless facts and figures Fowler's staff called up earlier to support it—were swaying him. She cleared her throat.

"Admiral, if I may?"

"Of course." Scrap turned a blinding smile toward her. "Mister Secretary, you know Admiral Hamilton, of course. She is the navy's senior submariner, and our top expert on this subject."

"I'm sure the navy has studied the new design exhaustively, Admiral." Fowler wrinkled his nose. "However, the world has changed since the new SSN design began. We must change with it."

Freddie had shed *blood* with this man. It would be nice to have him acknowledge her existence. If not her expertise.

She sucked in a deep breath. Now was not the time to think like Marco and dream about throwing Fowler out a window, or what might've happened if they left him back on Armistice Station. It was a pity the man had a top-secret clearance. Otherwise, abandoning him might've been justified. It was the one thing she and Commander Coleman agreed on.

"Diesel submarines—even AIP—are well-suited for navies who expect to fight battles in their own front yards, Mister Secretary," Freddie said once she was certain she had her temper under control. "Our submarines undertake long deployments and spend extended amounts of time underwater. Even the most advanced diesel cannot meet U.S. Navy requirements."

"And yet..." Fowler made a show of checking his notes. "The average submerged period during the war has just been three weeks. An AIP boat can do that, can't they, Admiral?"

Freddie gritted her teeth hard enough to give herself a migraine. "They can, but you're already talking about a theater of war that is ten thousand miles from home."

"So we put them on a heavy lift ship and deliver them." Fowler's eyes gleamed; the man always liked to think of himself as an expert.

"Let's not talk about how good of a target that would make for our enemies." Freddie tried not to smile. She failed.

Fowler sniffed. "I dislike your tone, Admiral."

I dislike your cowardice, she didn't say. But it was hard. Instead,

Freddie shrugged. "Mister Secretary, I apologize if dislike for the enemy has colored my tone." She smiled sweetly. "But the fact remains the navy needs boats that can operate in any and all environments—including long-distance deployments. I would also personally hesitate to put a diesel under the ice, which is a requirement when operating in our northern theater against Russia."

"Russia has not yet made aggressive moves against Alaska."

"Respectfully, Martin, you know that won't last," Secretary McClean spoke up again. "*We* haven't initiated hostilities in the north because we're short on ships and submarines. Russia probably hasn't for the same reason. But eventually, someone's shipbuilding programs will catch up, and whoever moves first will have the advantage."

"Then we should certainly build diesel submarines." Fowler flashed Freddie a victorious grin before refocusing on the secretary of defense. "They're faster *and* cheaper to build. All our enemies have them. Besides, I'm not proposing we replace *all* of our nuclear submarines with them. Just your 'New SSN' design. In the interest of speed, of course."

"It would require an entirely new design." McClean shook her head. "That requires years of study and work."

Fowler cocked his head. "I'm sorry, did you not know that Pulsar already has a design for a *Pegasus*-class AIP diesel boat? One they're ready to start production on next week, if funded?"

McClean's eyes narrowed. "Why is this the first I've heard of that?"

"That's a good question, Madam Secretary." Fowler beamed. "Vice Admiral Hamilton here has already reviewed the design and made a few useful suggestions."

"Admiral?" McClean twisted to look at her, and Freddie did not like the way the Secretary of Defense's eyes narrowed. Maise McClean didn't like getting caught off guard, particularly not by an officious worm like Fowler. "Care to explain?"

"I was given an informal look at a *potential* design," Freddie replied, her shoulders tensing. "I looked at it as a professional courtesy. Nothing more."

To her right, Scrap fidgeted. Would the CNO admit he strongarmed her into looking at the proposal? It hadn't been a terrible design, heavily based off the old Australian *Collins*-class, but Freddie sure hadn't signed off on it. Had Scrap?

McClean turned her laser gaze back on the State Department weenies. "Mr. Fowler?"

"Surely that level of review provides an excellent leg up. We could enter production quickly. Pulsar is already securing yard space."

"How fast?" Scrap leaned forward in his chair. "Fast enough to help mitigate some of our current losses?"

"Sir, one diesel boat—no matter how advanced—cannot match a nuclear attack sub," Freddie said.

Scrap waved a hand. "The optics will help us, though. NSSN can't get into production for at least six months, and then it'll be more than a year until she's in the water. Can your *Pegasus* beat that?"

Fowler grinned. "Admiral, Pulsar's timeline says we could have the first boat in the water by this time next year."

Freddie opened her mouth to argue and then snapped it shut once she caught sight of Scrap's grin. That thousand-megawatt thing could've powered Chicago for a month with electricity leftover. Even Secretary McClean looked cautious but eager, which meant Freddie's objections were going to be overruled no matter *how* smartly she made them.

Better to save her ammunition—and her credibility—for another day.

Somehow, thirteen marines kept a full-on riot from rushing the submarine.

Alex didn't think it was the dozen sailors he sent to help. Even armed with nine-millimeter handguns, sailors didn't look nearly as threatening as Paul's team. Nor was it Red Tiger Station security, who just kind of folded when the crowd pushed them, wandering off and watching from the sidelines instead of trying to hold a perimeter. The marines, however, looked like business. Paul pulled them in as close to the boat as he dared, too, just far enough out to cover both the side door, which was finally open, and the brow leading up to the midships quarterdeck.

It helped that it was hard to rush a tiny brow less than four feet wide. An angry marine with a rifle at one end and annoyed sailor at the other deterred most people. That set the crowd to throwing things, from vegetables to tennis balls to trash. Supposedly safe up on the sail, Alex dodged a beer can and swore.

"That fucker was full," he said as it bounced off the hull and into the water with a splash. "What a waste."

"Nice to be loved by the locals, huh, Captain?" Master Chief Morton took the riot with a typical COB's aplomb, shrugging.

Alex scowled. "You know, I've played this game before, and it wasn't much fun last time, either."

"Was that on Armistice Station *with* or without *Kansas*?"

He turned a narrow-eyed look on his senior enlisted advisor. "You've got too many friends, Master Chief. That's not a story I like sharing."

"Your nasty secrets are safe with me, sir. But I know Master Chief Casey." Morton winked. "You might even say I trained him."

"Admitting you're old as dirt isn't a good look."

"Eh, everyone knows I pulled my retirement papers and signed up for one more tour on Smiley when shit went down and the world chose violence." Morton shrugged. "Ain't no surprise to anyone who knows me. I'm an old asshole, but I'm your asshole, sir." He nodded at the crowd. "And I've seen an angry mob or two in my time. No reflection on your leadership or your actions. Sure as shit ain't your fault that we're here to pull five lucky fuckers off this station while the rest rot."

"I wouldn't want to be here, either," Alex whispered.

"That's why we joined the navy, sir. So that at least when we're at the mercy of someone else's piss-ass choices, we're mobile."

Alex surprised himself by laughing. "I guess so."

"If it's any consolation, Chin told me about what went down on *Kansas*. You got the raw end of the deal…but I'm glad it meant we got you here on *Jimmy Carter*. Old girl's got some life left in her yet, and if anyone's worthy of her, it's you."

"Thanks." Alex swallowed, his stomach full of eels. "You tell anyone else on the crew?"

"Not my story to share." Morton grinned. "But I should probably get down and put some spine in the XO. He's down there trying to 'help' Weps, and we all know how that's going to go, don't we?"

Alex groaned and turned his attention back to the chanting crowd. *Take us with you!* was the main cry. More colorful ones—in several languages—were largely drowned out, but Alex could make out some of them. He was better at math and computer languages than he'd ever been at anything other than English, though, so he only understood a little. Paul had taught him enough Spanish that he recognized some of the twisted suggestions his sailors and marines received. He imagined the Chinese shouts were much the same.

People were people. Particularly when they were frightened.

USS Lexington *(CVN-84) Strike Group*

"I don't like this," John muttered to his XO as yet *another* request for information came from the strike group.

Lieutenant Commander Patricia Abercrombie grimaced. "Makes those independent orders feel a little constricting, yeah."

"Not that." He crossed his arms. "Oh, I don't like them asking for information every forty-five seconds, either, but I don't like the way it ups our chance of detection. I read the last data dump from *Douglass* again, and they were up in full comms when they went down. Voice and data."

They stood in a quiet corner of *Razorback's* efficient attack center. They were between exercises and the normal underway watch was manned, so the hum of activity was minimal, just officers and petty officers doing their jobs well. John never could hide a shiver of pride every time he looked at them. This was *his* crew. He hadn't trained them, but they were his. Was it wrong to be grateful that Dave Harney had lost his cookies when faced with two plum targets? Poor Pat had to push that bad news upstairs, but it ended with John in command of *Razorback*.

John had inherited an uncertain crew, but damn had they come together in the year he'd been on board. Once, he'd thought nothing could compare to his command ride on *Cero*. Now...

"NUWC"—Pat pronounced the acronym for the Naval Undersea Warfare Center as *new-ick*—"says there's like a seven percent chance of detection in full comms."

"NUWC also said we had the best torpedo in the world with the Mark 48 CBASS and we'd never need to close to under ten nautical miles to fire." John's smile held no humor. "And that our boats are the quietest in the world."

She sighed. "Anyone who's ever tried hunting a *Requin* knows better than that."

"Exactly. I'm a big believer in American ingenuity and brilliance, but we've gotten spanked pretty good so far this war. If we've learned *some* of our assumptions are wrong, why aren't we questioning the others?"

"Sir, you keep saying stuff like that, and I'm going to wonder why you're not a flag officer."

John laughed. "I've only been a captain a couple years, and I don't have enough gray hair."

Before Pat could answer, the radio watch approached. "Sorry for interrupting, Captain, but you've got an outside line call."

"A what?" John twisted to stare at the unfortunate petty officer, who shrugged. She knew her captain's bark was way worse than his bite.

"Admiral Rodriquez said you wouldn't mind taking his call in your stateroom, sir."

"When you put it that way, I sure won't." Shaking his head, John slapped Patricia on the shoulder. "Hold down the fort and try to minimize how much we send to the carrier, will you? I'll see if I can finagle us some better orders for the runup to the battle."

"I'm on it, sir."

John cast a quick look around the attack center before ducking out. Everything was in place for the battle. His people were sharp and ready. Why was he so worried?

Right. He was going back the Strait of Malacca.

Shaking himself free of the memories before he reached his stateroom was hard, but *not* being at his mental best when talking to Uncle Marco was like asking a hungry bear not to eat him.

"How can I help you, Admiral?" John asked as he picked up the phone, glad that his boat was at least not receiving yet *another* video call. He didn't want to think about how much data that left swirling around the atmosphere for detection.

"You can fucking live through this battle, that's what," Rodriquez's accented voice replied. "Your next set of orders won't come in writing for a bit—I'm still ironing the dates out—but I thought I'd do you the goddamned courtesy of telling you myself."

"Orders?" A lump formed in John's throat. "Sir, I've only been on *Razorback* thirteen months."

"And you're still alive, by some fucking miracle. Need I remind you how many of your peers aren't?"

"That would be more of an argument to leave me where I am."

"In a perfect world, sure. But not in this fucktastic universe." Rodriquez snorted. "Sooner or later, your dance card is gonna get pulled. That means I need to yoink you out of that boat before it happens and, in payment for your many sins, move you on to bigger and better—well, bigger things, anyway."

John needed a long moment to make his mouth move. "Bigger,

sir?"

"We need admirals like you," Rodriquez continued. "But you're too damned junior. The CNO'll have kittens if we try to pin stars on you without giving you another command first, so I'm giving you the sub tender *Nereus*. Don't fuck it up, and you'll be commanding a squadron this time next year."

That would make him a commodore with less than twenty-five years in the navy. Making flag had always been John's goal, but he'd never imagined stars would come so fast. And yet—

"How soon do I have to leave *Razorback*?" he asked as his chest grew tight. Would this battle be his last patrol? Was this his last chance to make a difference, and if so, did it *have* to be in the goddamned SOM?

"Your orders'll be along in a couple weeks. Probably detach you a little before Thanksgiving, let you go home, spend six weeks or so with the wife and decompress—assuming you like her enough to do that."

"Of course I do!"

"Then you'll take command of *Nereus* in mid-January after having shaken some of this shit off your boots."

"Sir, I don't need—"

"The fuck you don't. You all do, you just don't know it," Rodriquez said. "You'll need to slow down from the fast attack life, learn about your new surface ship, and be a human being before you have to think about being a warfighter again. Consider it a fucking Christmas present."

"It's September, Admiral."

"Like I said, don't die, all right, John? We need more people like you to pass on what you've learned, to teach others to *think* like you. You can't do that if you're dead on the bottom."

John swallowed. No pressure, there. All he had to do was drive his submarine into the Strait of Malacca against an unknown number of enemy forces, sink as many of them as possible, and survive. All in a place that tried its damnedest to kill him once. But there was only one thing to say.

"Aye, aye, sir."

Twenty minutes did nothing to change the atmosphere on Red Tiger Station's TRANSPLAT for the better. If anything, the long process of loading the first cargo container through *Jimmy Carter's* side door only made the crowd antsier. And louder.

Alex's cell phone rang. Jumping—he'd forgotten it was even in his pocket, but he always grabbed it before surfacing—he pulled it out and answered it. "Coleman."

"Captain, I'm a person with interest in the boxes you are loading on board your submarine," an unfamiliar voice said. "And I understand the crowd is making it dangerous for you to remain on Red Tiger Station. I can make it well worth your while for you to depart now, without loading that material on board."

His jaw dropped. "Excuse me?"

"Name the account, and you'll receive ten million dollars—American, of course—for leaving those boxes behind."

Alex glanced around wildly, but there were at least a dozen people on the pier on the phone, and he couldn't tell if there was shouting coming from both ends or just his. And the rioters wanted to leave with *Jimmy Carter*, not get him to leave Fogborne's research behind.

"What the hell is going on here?"

"We can up the offer to fifteen million."

Alex had faced attempted bribery a few times when he was on Armistice Station, but that'd been peanuts. Small change. People wanting to know ship and sub arrival and departure dates—classified information, to be sure, but nothing worth *millions*. He'd always reported it, because his career had been in the crapper, not his common sense. Selling classified information was a federal offense.

This...he wasn't sure what this was. Sure, he could probably pull chocks, play the safety card, and cry that the riots chased *Jimmy Carter* away. Paul was a good enough friend to back him up if he *really* felt that way, but Alex didn't, and Paul shouldn't. And holy shit, he'd read the article on a Pulsar team cracking fusion and put two and two together, but fusion was a pipe dream...

"That team you're bringing back could change the very future of submarine warfare," Admiral Hamilton had said.

"Who the hell is this?" he demanded.

"That's not your concern. You don't even need to tell us if you'll take the deal. Just leave the containers, and you'll find the money in your bank account," the unknown voice said. "But if you prefer an alternate account, you will have to tell me now."

"You know what?" Alex Coleman said. "You can fuck right off."

He hung up the phone.

"What's our range, Jenny?"

"Twenty nautical miles and closing, Cap. Two hours at current speed, could make it a bit faster if you want to push it."

Diego shook his head, sitting back in the comfortable chair he'd had installed in *Destroyer's* control room. It paid to be a pirate and not a naval captain; there was nothing like personalizing his submarine. "Are *Siren* and *Weirwood* on time to play catchers?"

"*Weirwood* is five minutes behind us. *Siren*'s already on station." Jenny grinned. "The Americans have no idea she's nasty; she's just sitting there, flying a Filipino flag, all innocent like."

"Good." Diego grinned. "We'll wait for them to pull away from the station and take them before they submerge. We'll be the threat, and then the surface ships can snap her right up."

"There's going to be a lot of American sailors on that submarine." Jenny's face twitched. "You thinking about ransom?"

"During a war? Hell no. Nobody'll pay up in the time worth feeding them. We'll put them on rafts and send them back to Red Tiger Station. It'll probably take months for their navy to pull them off." Diego smirked. "By then, we'll be *long* gone."

She shrugged. "We could sell them to the Russians. I hear they have a bounty for Alliance submariners."

Diego scowled. "A stupid pirate makes a *really* deadly enemy of the U.S. Navy. They won't forgive us in a hurry for stealing one of their submarines, but how bad do you think they'll want us dead if we sell a hundred or so of their people?" he asked. "Submarines are just metal. People breathe."

"Good point." Jenny shuddered. "I like breathing, too."

"And I like *rich* breathing, which is why we're smart pirates, Jenny. Now let's take this prize."

The shouting echoed through the hull, even into the wardroom. Alex could ignore it—even if every *thump* of something hitting the boat reminded him of the sound of explosions back on Armistice Station—but it made Doctor Leifsson twitch.

"Thank you for taking the time to load our gear," she said, grimacing as another something *splatted* against the hull. "And I'm really sorry about, well, *that*."

"Don't worry. *Jimmy Carter* is made of HY100 steel. It'll take worse than some trash and tomatoes to hurt her," Alex replied, ignoring the way George muttered about the sound-absorbing tiles coming loose.

The youngest scientist on Leifsson's team seemed to hear him, though. She looked Taiwanese and impossibly close to the age of Alex's oldest daughter. Her head jerked up, eyes wide. "They won't come off, will they? That would be a problem. People could hear us."

"Of course that would be a problem." George was almost vibrating with anxiety. "Anything that increases our sonar signature is a problem, Miss...?"

"*Doctor* Ning Tang." The girl smiled. "I have a PhD."

George's eyes nearly bugged out of his head. Alex held up a hand. "XO, will you go get on the horn with Red Tiger Station and see what's holding up our departure?"

"I'm on it, sir." Happy to have a task, George bustled out.

Alex felt another sand of exhaustion trickle in. How many more times would he have to come up with something useful for George to do?

"We're glad to help, Doctor," he said to Leifsson. "Now, Weps—Lieutenant Angler—is getting your gear stowed, and we'll be underway as soon as the station lets us. But first, I have a question. What the hell do you have in those boxes that's so important that someone just tried to bribe me to leave it behind?"

"Bribe?" Leifsson stared.

"It's probably the same assholes who keep trying to bribe *us*," Tang said. "They never say who they are, but they're always flashing money around in the millions."

"Sounds about fifteen million shades of right." Alex's eyes narrowed.

"But what are they trying to pay for?" Maggie asked. She'd already reported the attempt—intelligence was one of her collateral duties, and Alex told her right away—which meant she had almost as much time to think it over as Alex did. And unlike George, she didn't freak out. "Fusion's the future of the nuclear world, sure, but no one's made a real breakthrough in years. Workable fusion isn't going to be portable for a decade."

"Um." Tang raised her hand. "You just loaded the prototype on your submarine."

"I just *what?*" Alex asked.

"Technically, it's a model. But it would work if fueled." Leifsson's smile was apologetic. "The real reactor is powering Red Tiger Station, though that's the larger version."

"C'mon, you have to understand how amazing fusion is. No runaway reactions, no meltdowns, no radioactive waste," Tang said. "You get three to four more times energy than *fission* reactions, with none of the dirty stuff and like...two percent the risk. If that. Controlling a fission reaction is an engineering nightmare."

"You do know there's a fission reaction being controlled just aft of you," Marty drawled.

"And do you *enjoy* that?" Tang asked.

"Ning!" Leifsson said.

"I do," Marty replied.

Tang crossed her arms. "You're weird."

"Doctor Tang, every officer in this room is a trained nuclear engineer," Alex said. "We all appreciate the benefits of fusion. It's just been the holy grail for so long that hearing you've achieved it in a submarine-size reactor is like having a thousand birthdays come early."

"More like a million." Tang smirked. "You should see how Pulsar reacted."

"Hey, Cap? I just got an interesting message." Jenny twisted in her chair to beckon him over, and Captain Diego Reyes reluctantly rose to join her.

"What do you have? I hope it's nothing to chase us off our prey."

"No, it's a better offer for the scientists and hardware on board that American submarine. It just went out to all pirate groups in the area...someone—and by someone, I mean a contact I know works with the Indian Navy—is willing to pay ten million big bucks to get their hands on them."

"Well, now," Diego purred. "That changes my mind about grabbing people, doesn't it?"

Chapter 23

Hide and Seek

Paul's radio crackled, barely loud enough to be heard over the shrieking crowd. "Swanson, Coleman, five mikes."

"Aye." He didn't like admitting that his sweaty fingers almost slipped on the *talk* button, but riots were really not Paul's area of expertise. Holding one back with just thirteen marines—himself included—was a pretty picnic he hoped never to feast from again.

The pier was full to bursting, from where the marines guarded *Jimmy Carter's* slowly raised side door and brow to the other—fortunately empty—side. Shouting people filled the space all the way back to where the pier met the TRANSPLAT proper, spilling over onto the next pier over.

"I could really do with some riot shields right now, Colonel," Gunny Kochera panted. Her right eye was black, courtesy of a thrown bean can, but she was better off than Frankie. His broken right arm was bundled up against his chest while his rifle was nestled against his left shoulder. No one in the crowd knew Frankie couldn't shoot worth a shit left-handed.

Paul didn't mean for them to find out.

The crowd had grown exponentially in the hour it took to swing those five damned white crates on board. Paul didn't know or care why it took submariners so long to crane anything over; it looked easy, but hell, nothing was simple on a submarine. It was his job to hold the line and keep the angry locals away, which so far threats and a few shots in the air had done.

Unfortunately, there were a few assholes in the group who understood the concept of strength in numbers. They were the ones pushing from the back, yelling for others to do the same, shoving against the marines like they were goddamned Greek hoplites.

"All right!" Paul bellowed over the din of the crowd. "Time to carve out a little space! Fire team one, take aim at fatty and nonlethal parts. Fire team two, take out those trash cans to the left. Fire team three, we're in reserve. Nonlethal aimed shots only. *Open fire!*"

The sharp *crack* of automatic rifles split the air as his people obeyed. Until now, Paul had avoided shooting into the crowd, and he *still* didn't want to hit anyone with a rubber bullet. The 2020s had shown the world how much damage a "nonlethal" bullet could do, and Paul was not about to put his team on anyone's nightly news.

But he needed to win back some space, and there was nothing like coordinated fire from eight marines to intimidate a crowd. Shooting the big honking trash bins toward the end of the pier made for a great big *bang*, too; people shied back, some running for the safety of the TRANSPLAT hub.

Others went down as if cut by a giant scythe, screaming as rubber bullets hit thighs, shoulders, and stomachs. Paul didn't have time to cringe. At least it hurt less than the real bullet he might've put in these people for threatening his team during a time of war.

Paul snuck a look at the side door. The damn thing was almost shut, its thirty-something-year-old hydraulics squeaking like a dying pig. He cocked his head, judging angles. No way could someone jump up and grab that thing now, not even if they qualified for the NBA. "Cease fire! Targets of opportunity only! Fire team three, fall back to the brow!"

His smallest fire team scooted through the space their shooting made, sprinting for where Boomer and a quartet of nervous sailors guarded the ramp onto the ship. They made it there without incident; most of the crowd was still running or cowering.

"Fire team two, move out!"

The second group, led by Gunny Kochera, thundered up the brow, taking up station on the slippery deck of the submarine for over watch.

"Hey, you can't leave!" someone in the crowd shouted.

Just watch me, Paul didn't reply. Poking the beast really wouldn't help. "Fire team one, move!"

Paul was the last man on board, gesturing the sailors ahead of him. One idiot from the crowd grabbed for him, but Paul swept him aside with a bear-like arm, and the fool flew backward, yelping. Only once he reached *Jimmy Carter's* quarterdeck did he turn back, his heart pounding in his ears.

He grimaced. No, that was the sound of a man slamming what was left of a metal trashcan into the pier over and over again.

"Take us with you!" someone else shouted.

"Sir, there's no one there to man the crane and take the brow!" Lieutenant (J.G.) Alvaro, shouted from the quarterdeck up to Alex, still up in the sail.

Paul glanced at Kochera. She gestured rudely toward the empty crane. "None of us shot him, sir. I think he ran away."

"Fuck it, cut the thing loose and we'll drop it in the water!" Alex cut a hand through the air like he was slicing someone's neck.

Paul half expected the young officer to hesitate, but she grinned. "Sullivan, Barnes, go grab axes and go to town on that brow. Just try not to let it scrape the tiles on the way down."

Glancing up, Paul caught his old roommate's eye as Alex grinned. Damn, Alex's crew was as crazy as he was.

A gaudily painted corvette watched *Jimmy Carter* pull away from the TRANSPLAT from less than a mile away. At first glance, the corvette's military lines were lost in the riot of colors; it was easy to forget she was Russian-built and armed. That was the idea, of course. Most of her victims thought she was just a rich man's yacht.

No one on *Jimmy Carter* took much notice of the corvette, either. They were too focused on leaving Red Tiger Station in a hurry. Spray from the submarine's propulsor hit the floating pier in her wake, rocking it back and forth like a cheap raft. The pirates on board the corvette couldn't hear the crowd screaming, but they laughed as people struggled for balance.

No one fell overboard, which was something of a pity. It was still fun to watch, entertaining enough that no one studied their target's lines long enough to realize she was not the *Virginia*-class submarine they believed her to be. Instead, they shrugged and talked about how they didn't have time to earn money with rescue-and-kidnapping operations, so no one minded much.

What they did mind was the way the American submarine tripled the five-knot speed limit and submerged before they were even a thousand yards away from the station.

"Shit!" *Siren's* captain threw her plastic coffee mug and didn't watch it hit the floor.

"*Destroyer, Siren*, they just submerged. Quick bastards, you'll have to track them with sonar."

Diego Reyes came out of his chair before he could stop himself when the report came through the speakers in his submarine's attack center. They were ten miles out, and the American was *already* submerged? He knew their procedures took longer than that; they should be on the surface—and a sitting duck—for at least another hour.

"Jenny, tell *Siren* to get on top of them and stay there. They have to be staying shallow." His lip curled. If the American wanted to play hardball, Diego could play along. He'd enjoy this more than they would.

"On it, Cap. Want to increase speed?"

"Yes, come up to fifteen knots." They could remain silent, traveling on batteries, at that speed. *Destroyer* wasn't just any old diesel-powered submarine. She was an advanced U-boat, made with air-independent propulsion that allowed her to recharge her batteries without snorkeling. That gave her much longer legs...and much greater speed.

Of course, the attack submarine ahead of them could outrun them. They had a *nuclear reactor's* worth of power and a much bigger propeller. But they had to know to run.

Diego would make sure they didn't.

"Oh, and Jenny? Make sure *Weirwood* is ready with depth charges. We might have to scare these bastards a little."

Diego bared his teeth. *Weirwood* was a Chinese type 054 frigate, likewise bought on the black market after she decommissioned. She was barely thirty years old and bristled with every weapon Diego could buy—which, given his successes, were quite numerous. He didn't *like* wasting weapons, but on a prize like a *Virginia*-class submarine...he'd do whatever it took to scare them into surrendering.

Even if it had gotten harder now that they'd submerged.

"Freddie, if you keep calling me like this, people are going to think you like me," Marco said.

Today, he'd answered the phone himself. The call had come in while he was reading one last intelligence update before bed, snuggled up with a tablet in his apartment and pretending not to care about anyone while he drank a hot chocolate laced with whisky. Not too much whisky, of course—Marco couldn't afford to be a drunk—but a little took the edge off and helped him sleep.

"It's three a.m. here, you idiot. I'm not calling you to read you love poetry," she replied, her voice scratchy.

"Then fucking tell me what you want so we can both go to sleep."

"I just got confirmation that there's a leak about *Jimmy Carter's* mission. It's going to go out in the *Post* tomorrow," she said.

Marco sat up fast and downed his cocoa, feeling the fiery burn of whisky in his throat. "Fucking what?"

"I need you to reroute them to Diego Garcia. We don't dare send them back to Perth now."

"That could've waited until morning, Freddie." Marco shook his head, trying to clear it. "The leak's more important—right?"

"Maybe. I got a tip from a friend who works at the paper, but they can't tell me the source. I'm worried it's on the boat."

"You think it's that CO you don't like? That Coleman creature?"

"No. He's so honest he might hurt himself trying to lie." Freddie's growl came through loud and clear on the secure line. "He's a pain in the ass, but not a security risk. Not that one."

"Roger that. Someone else on the boat, then. Leaves us about a hundred and thirty other options. About one-fifty if you count the marines." Marco groaned. "No way we'll figure that out from here."

"No, but we have to keep this team safe, Marco. If we lose them...we lose the future."

Marco swung his legs out of bed and grabbed for his uniform. "Let me see what I can do. I'll get back to you."

"Just don't send any more assets into the South China Sea," she said. "The CNO told me he'd rather *Jimmy Carter* sink than admit we're there."

"Someone ought to tell that asshole we're at war," Marco growled.

"I try to every day," Freddie replied. No wonder why she sounded so exhausted.

"Remind me to never try for more than three stars, okay? I've got your back when you aim higher, but fuck all for those political jobs," he said. "Now let me get to work and see if I can't pull a miracle out of my Puerto Rican ass."

Jimmy Carter had just turned north when the radio watch tapped Alex on the shoulder. "Sir, we got orders to redirect to Diego Garcia."

Alex twisted around. "Really?"

"Yes, sir." The sailor handed him the message tablet.

A quick scan of the message didn't tell Alex anything useful; he scowled. "Looks like we're going through the SOM."

"Are you serious?" Maggie's jaw dropped. "That's the worst piece of water in the world to sneak around in. Even worse than *here*."

"It's either that or the Sunda Strait, and that sucker gets as shallow as sixty-six feet. Surfacing to go through there violates the stealth requirements in our orders." Alex shrugged. "Either way, it's a copperplated bitch."

"Yes, sir, it is."

George fluttered up to his side. "Sir, there's no way those orders are correct—"

Alex just handed him the tablet and ignored the inevitable explosion of nerves. He was so tired of George's mini breakdowns that he rode right over the inevitable sputtering. "Let's get the nav plan together, Maggie. Hopefully, common sense will break out before we get there, but if it doesn't, let's figure out a way to creep under half the freaking Indian Navy without them noticing us." He shrugged. "At least it might make a fun trifecta of avoidance: China, Taiwan, and India. Maybe we'll get some French ships, too, and then we can go for the superfecta?"

"I didn't know you were into horse racing, sir." Benji grinned as he took the watch over for Maggie.

"I'm not, but my youngest daughter's obsessed with everything that's got four legs. You can see how that goes."

"Sir, we can't—" George started.

Alex held up a hand. "XO, there's a war on, and we've got orders. Someone"—he didn't mention that it was likely to be Admiral Hamilton—"is concerned that the Fogborne team's location was leaked, so we're taking them to Diego Garcia instead of Perth. We might think our orders are *stupid*, but unless they're illegal or immoral, we don't have a lot of a leg to stand on."

"Captain, they're *unsafe*."

Alex sighed. "So's fighting a war, George."

It didn't feel like war on Diego Garcia.

Nancy found it strange. The little atoll was smack in the middle of the Indian Ocean, right dab in the center of the entire war. Yet it was the sleepiest place Nancy had been in *months*, right down to warm beaches and quiet shops.

Granted, it was a military base, with guards and crew-served weapons on every corner. Nancy wasn't sure why that reassured her; maybe it made her feel like she hadn't been fighting in vain.

"Is it just me, or does the lack of air defense weapons around here make you nervous?" she asked Julia Rosario as they sat on the beach together.

Fletcher and *Belleau Wood's* crews had some time off; the ship bringing their supply onload had been delayed until September 30th, three days away. After a day of crawling all over her destroyer, Nancy decided to let her hair down and head to the beach, only to find her admiral had the same idea. So she and Julia headed to the beach together, dipping their toes in the sand and watching their sailors run around like maniacs.

"I'm trying not to think about it." Julia brushed red hair out of her eyes. "You'd think that after the second battle of the war happened here, they'd be more careful, but..."

"But it's been over a year?" Nancy drew a stick figure in the sand with one toe. "It's the same old song. Priorities."

"Which is why Admiral Anderson got the nod and our original supply ship." Julia's smile was crooked. "Rank hath its privileges."

"I don't know. I'm good with sitting on a beach instead of going into the SOM a third time. I could do without a three-peat."

"I missed the second one, though I'm not sure you could say I *missed* it." Julia's laugh was a touch bitter. "I think we were still mending a hole in *Belleau's* side when you experienced that goat rope."

Nancy laughed. "I never envied someone for damage before, but now that you mention it..."

"For now, I'll take the beach." Julia leaned on her elbows back and looked up at the sky. "Missile onload tomorrow, and then hopefully a supply ship. Your sailors bitching about the lack of food on the base?"

"Not so far, but only because there's plenty of beer."

"Sounds about right." Her admiral sighed. "Well, I'm going to enjoy the sun for the one day we have. I recommend you do the same."

"That's probably the best idea I've heard all war," Nancy replied, smiling. If she was lucky, their supplies onload would be delayed, and they'd say in Diego Garcia another week. Maybe a touch longer.

Nancy wasn't one to avoid duty, but it would be nice to see Alex when he arrived.

"Conn, Sonar, submerged contact on the forty-seven hertz line. Likely bearing two-eight-five with the station behind us." Chief Bradley's voice broke through the easy murmur of voices in *Jimmy Carter's* control room, crackling slightly as it came through the speaker to Alex's right. They were barely three hours out from Red Tiger Station, and he'd been in the middle of explaining how to drive a submarine to Paul, who loomed over the helmsman like a clumsy demon, his head cocked curiously.

Benji had the watch, so he took the call. "Sonar, Conn, estimated range?"

"Too faint to tell, sir, but if I had to guess, I'd say a diesel operating on batteries under the layer. That'd mean close."

"Shit." Alex swore just as Benji turned toward him, eyes wide.

"Captain, do you want to go to battle stations? I know ROE says we can't fire unless fired upon…"

"But it would really suck to get shot at and not be ready." Alex nodded. "Do it."

"Where do you want me?" Paul asked.

"Whatever corner you can squeeze into is fine," Alex replied, then glanced up at his hulking friend and grimaced. "Try by the periscope."

Paul laughed. "I was going to say me and *squeezing* don't go real well together, but I'll try. Just shove me if I'm in the way."

Alex turned toward the speaker, nicknamed the *bitch box* by generations of sailors. "Sonar, Conn, can you get a class identification?"

"Negative." Bradley sounded annoyed. "This puppy's good, sir."

"Conn, aye."

Alex forced himself to breathe out, trying to look calm as organized chaos enveloped *Jimmy Carter's* attack center while the crew rushed to battle stations. How many times had they done this for real? Not nearly as many as they had in drills. A shiver ran down his spine.

"All right, people," Alex said as calmly as he could. "Let's find this guy and figure out who he is. He's probably the pirate sub the station said is incoming, but we *don't know that*, so let's not make assumptions. Let's also try not to get shot while we're at it. Maggie, make a course change in case they're tracking us."

"You got it, Captain." Maggie finished relieving Benji of the watch and ordered the course change, causing *Jimmy Carter* to roll slightly left.

Alex leaned back against the periscope stand and watched his team work. The efficient murmur of voices whipped around the room, and there was an undercurrent of excitement in the air that he wasn't used to. It almost reminded him of that day on *Kansas* when they face the Neyk—they weren't ready to shoot, because they *couldn't* shoot, but everyone was on edge.

"Sonar, Conn, anything?" he asked after several minutes.

An ominously long moment passed before Wilson answered: "Conn, Sonar, contact is still faint, sir, but I'm betting a German AIP U-Boat. None of the things I'm picking up passive line up with any of the boats owned by anyone out here."

"A *U-Boat?*" Paul leaned forward on Alex's right. "Are they serious? Are we in a World War II movie?"

Alex snorted. "Modern U-Boats are state of the art, and the Germans sell them to almost anyone with a country code and a bank account. It could belong to seventeen different nations out here."

"According to *Jane's*, there are several nations, sir." George frantically flipped through the electronic version of *Jane's Fighting Ships*. "Closest is Singapore. They have type two-one-eights."

"Conn, Sonar, I can hear the XO. This baby's not one of Singapore's. They're *quiet* fuckers. This dude has got something creaking back aft now that I've got a track on him," Wilson replied. "Computer can't decide between type two-one-two and two-one-four, but I'm betting on the latter. Probably bought on the secondary market from Indonesia or South Korea."

George leaned into the speaker. "Sonar, Conn, we did not ask for a history lesson." He turned to Alex. "Sir, this sub could be from five different nations who legitimately sail these waters. Indonesia, South Korea, Singapore, and the Philippines all have German-built submarines of various types." George gulped. "And India still has three."

"Yeah, that sucks." Alex shook his head. "Wilson's not wrong, either. A bunch of those boats got sold on the black market instead of being scrapped. Any asshole with money could be driving this thing."

George's nose wrinkled. "I think a nation state is far more likely, sir."

"I'd hope so, but you know what they say about hope not being a military course of action." Alex pulled a piece of candy out of his pocket and popped it in his mouth; chewing helped him think. "All right, whoever this is, we need to avoid them. So let's go deep. Maggie, make your depth nine hundred feet. If he or she is just here for the scenery, they're not going to follow us."

"And if they do?" George asked, talking over Maggie's orders to the diving officer.

"Then we've got eight torpedo tubes with their names on them." Alex bared his teeth as George flinched.

It wasn't like he'd actually shoot eight torpedoes at once. That would be a waste, particularly at a diesel boat so small *one* Mark 84 would crack it open like an Easter Surprise. But it was a nice thought.

"Got any action for me and my team on this one, Captain?" Paul asked.

"If we do, we're in real trouble." Alex chuckled as his friend deflated. "Sorry, but surfacing is *bad* in our game, man."

Paul harrumphed. "I guess I can live with that."

"Colonel, now is hardly the time—" George's mouth snapped shut when Alex held up a hand.

Talk about now not being the time. How the hell was he supposed to think tactics with George and his love of ceremony at his hip? Alex wanted to scream. "XO, can you see to some battle messing? I think we're going to be at battle stations for a while, and I want the crew fed and fresh."

"Of course, sir." George bustled out, ignoring—or not seeing—the glares various watchstanders pointed at his back.

"You think you could be a little less obvious about sending him away?" Paul muttered in his ear.

"Oh, shut up. *You* don't have to work right now," Alex hissed. "I need to think."

Jimmy Carter's deck sloped as she dove beneath the layer; Maggie, on point as usual, heard Alex's earlier comment and transformed it into reality. Meanwhile, Alex watched the plot to see what their visitor did. Slowly, the yellow icon representing the unknown submarine blinked from an unsteady track to a solid "known" position. Then two other tracks appeared on the display.

"Conn, Sonar, new surface tracks, designated tracks 4079 and

4080. Unknown types, probably military. Both are twin screwed. Neither was moving until about thirty seconds ago."

Alex's head snapped up. "They were lying in wait."

"If so, they're out of position," Maggie said. "All three of them are to port."

"You assume they're all working together?" Paul asked.

"No reason why three military-type targets would move together otherwise," Alex replied. Judging the ranges, he did some math. "Our best silent speed is twenty-two knots, Maggie. Let's come up to eighteen."

"Even if it takes us straight at the submerged target?" she asked.

"Better the one in our territory than the other two." Alex grinned. "Besides, if he's a diesel, he's slower than we are. By a lot."

"You got it, Captain." Maggie turned to the helm. "All ahead full for eighteen knots."

"Ahead full for twenty-two knots, aye. My engines are ahead full for eighteen knots."

Maggie nodded as *Jimmy Carter* trembled under their feet. "Very well."

Chapter 24

Playing Chicken

26 September 2039, the Taiwan Strait

Two hours later, *Jimmy Carter* was still playing chicken. The submerged contact faded in and out as it paralleled their course, and the two surface contacts were racing to intercept *Jimmy Carter*—badly. They clearly couldn't track her on sonar, which left them taking direction from their submerged friend, who couldn't quite keep up.

Unfortunately, the submerged contact was to the inside of the port turn *Jimmy Carter* had to make to get out of the South China Sea, leaving Alex with a decision: go behind them or in front of them. Neither was a great choice, since he wasn't sure if the mystery submarine would shoot at him or not.

"Captain, we need to talk about the SOM," George hissed in his ear.

Alex jumped. How had he let his mother hen of an XO sneak up on him? George was usually as subtle as a two-by-four to the face. "This really isn't the time, XO."

"Sir, there's a *battle* coming up there."

"Well, I guess that'll be excellent cover. These guys first." Alex gestured at the plot as George's jaw dropped. "SOM later."

He couldn't let himself forget the three military-type contacts. Not when the sub was skillfully cutting the corner to stay in range of *Jimmy Carter*. His new destination would let the sub stay in range longer, too, now that he couldn't make that south turn. Alex shook himself and turned to the bitch box.

"Sonar, Conn, any updated class types on our friends?"

"Conn, Sonar, submerged contact is eighty percent likely a type two-one-four U-Boat. Track four-zero-seven-nine is tentatively ID'd as a corvette, likely Russian-built *Nanuchka*-class. They don't have those anymore, so it belongs to someone not Russia," Wilson replied. "And the computer's not real sure on the last one, but I'm betting it's a Chinese type fifty-three or fifty-four frigate. They've sold bunches of both of them, so also likely owned by someone else."

"I don't like *bets*," George muttered, but Alex didn't let him get close enough to the speaker to lecture Wilson.

At least he knew Wilson hadn't gotten off the boat on Red Tiger Station. The kid wasn't drunk—but was he *right*? Alex wished he could trust him.

"Captain, we're getting a call on underwater standard. It's broadband, but it's definitely directed at us," the radio watch said.

"Shit." So much for stealth; Admiral Hamilton was going to murder him. Alex swallowed. "Put it on speaker."

The radio crackled; underwater transmissions via "Gertrude" weren't terribly clear, but Alex could hear the slight accent in the speaker's voice—and the confidence:

"Attention, American submarine. You have been surrounded by surface and submerged assets. Surrender immediately or be fired upon."

"Really?" Alex cocked his head. "Going straight to threats without even telling us who they are. Lame."

George almost choked; Paul hooted with laughter.

Maggie snickered. "Odds are they don't have a track on us if they're talking like that, sir."

"That's what I'm thinking. Still, let's confuse them a little. Come right twenty degrees and slow to fourteen knots."

Maggie passed the orders along as Alex tried not to grimace. He hated slowing, but he couldn't speed up without being detected. *Jimmy Carter's* theoretical maximum silent speed was four knots faster than they were going...but Alex's boat was old. There was no telling if she would stay silent at twenty-two knots. Eighteen was a solid speed, and quiet. Unfortunately, that meant the only way to screw up someone else's target motion analysis was to decrease speed.

"Sir, are you sure we should ignore these people?" George finally whispered. "They sound...unfriendly."

"I don't think there's a friendly soul out here, XO." Alex tried to smile; it came out lopsided. But he didn't have time for more reassurance. "Sonar, Conn, do you have a track on this joker?"

"You bet your ass I do, sir. And the more the idiot talks, the better it'll get," Wilson replied.

In the background, Chief Bradley's muttered, "Goddamn it, Wilson," was audible before the younger sonar operator took his foot off the *talk* pedal. Alex tried not to laugh.

"Conn, Sonar, track seven-zero-eight-one on your display," Chief Bradley said.

"Conn, aye," Alex replied.

He blinked. Chief Bradley was apparently an enterprising soul, too; he'd made the track red and hostile on the plot. Then again, the mystery sub *had* threatened to shoot them.

"Pity our ROE isn't enough to let us take the first shot when they've been overtly threatening," Alex muttered.

"Captain?" George's voice was a squeak. "You can't be thinking of *shooting!* Our orders are to maintain stealth!"

"Yeah, and that's working out for us real well right now." Alex shook his head. "But no, I'm not going to shoot anyone we're not supposed to. Sneaking is the mission."

"Damn shame. These guys are asking for it," Paul said.

Alex threw a half-hearted glare at him. "Don't tempt me, you big lug."

Paul laughed.

The speaker crackled again. *"American submarine, we have your position. We know you are carrying the Fogborne Research Team from Pulsar Power. Surface immediately and hand them over or be sunk."*

"You want to keep ignoring them, Captain?" the radio watch asked. She looked awfully young and pale, twirling a lock of hair between her fingers.

"Let 'em rot."

"Why do *pirates* want us?" another voice, young and quiet, asked from just inside the control room hatch.

Alex spun to face Ning Tang as she made a face. Damn. He hadn't realized she'd sneaked into control. George was responsible for telling their guests to stay put when the boat went to battle stations. Had she not listened?

"I mean, I know we've made a breakthrough everyone and their grandmother wants to get rich off of. And I was almost kidnapped on the station. Not to mention the bribes." Ning grimaced. "But how pirates know?"

"News got out. No idea how," Paul rumbled. "Those bribery-loving ass nuggets on the station obviously got the same memo."

Ning scuffed her toes against the deck. "What are they going to do if they get us?" she whispered. She looked up, her brown eyes wide and reminding Alex of his daughters. "Pirates have taken every sub to leave Red Tiger Station for the last four months."

Alex grinned. "They haven't tangled with an attack submarine before."

"I don't know." Her eyes flicked left and right. "Everything in here looks older than I am."

"Some of it might be." Alex forced himself to shrug, ignoring the sting that came when someone mocked his boat's age. "*Jimmy Carter* is the oldest attack boat in the navy…but she was also built from the keel up as a spy submarine. This is the shit we're good at."

"It's *really* a pity you can't just shoot the fuckers. No one would miss a few pirates," Paul grumbled. "Come to think of it, the three or four Chinas might thank you for it."

"Five Chinas," George said.

"Maybe they'd like it. But then they'd know we were here, wouldn't they?" Alex wrinkled his nose. "You and I might have a love of pirate hunting, but stealth's the name of the game today. Stealth and plausible deniability."

"People are going to notice we're not on Red Tiger anymore," Ning said. "That's hard to plausibly deny."

"Sure, but they can wonder how it happened. Meanwhile—"

"*American submarine, this is your last chance. Surface immediately or be depth charged.*"

"Ooh, threaten me like it's 1945." Alex rolled his eyes.

Maggie giggled. "Captain, you don't have to make it sound like they're coming onto you."

"No surer way to tell us they don't know where we are than threaten to depth charge us." Alex shrugged and glanced at his crew. "Might as well settle in, folks. We're going to be playing hide and seek for a while."

A while turned out to be another three hours; now *Jimmy Carter* had the entire length of the South China Sea to transit and couldn't escape with a hard left turn that let them sneak around the north end of the Philippines. No, Alex's boat had to go the long way, past all of China, the contested Spratly Islands, Vietnam, and the Gulf of Thailand before they could sneak around the corner into the Singapore Strait.

The pirates seemed determined to stick with them, although their guess of *Jimmy Carter's* position was off. The corvette lobbed some depth charges in the water almost a mile to port of Alex's submarine, and they exploded too far away for Alex to even feel the vibrations. After wasting a dozen depth charges, the pirates stopped dropping them, made another radio threat, and then just continued dogging *Jimmy Carter* as she sailed through the South China Sea.

Damn, it was going to be a long sixteen-hundred-mile transit. Just thinking about it gave Alex a headache. How long would the pirates follow? They didn't know exactly where he was, but they had a shrewd guess where he was going. All three pirate units were headed southwest, almost parallel to *Jimmy Carter's* track.

"Conn, Sonar, new contact bearing one-niner-three, range approximately twenty-two thousand yards. Faint contact, submerged, tonals match *Hai Jiao*-class SSP," Chief Bradley's voice reported.

George beat Alex to the intercom. "Sonar, Conn, have they detected us?"

There was a pause before Bradley replied: "No way to tell, sir. Their estimated speed is one-zero knots, course undetermined."

"Conn, Sonar, doppler says inbound," Wilson added.

"Conn, aye." George looked constipated; Alex studied the plot. "Captain..."

"Yeah?"

"This isn't good. We're practically trapped between them after our turn." George wiped his hands on his coveralls. "We have to do something."

"Remaining undetected is our best defense," Alex replied, trying to keep his voice even. Shaking his XO would not do. "It always has been. This is the same game you and I trained for our entire careers." He turned to Maggie. "OOD, slow to eight knots."

"Officer of the Deck, aye." Her crisp voice contrasted deeply with George's wavering tone.

"But if a Taiwanese boat hears us..." George gulped. "They'll certainly complain to the U.N."

"They'd have to prove we were here." Alex pinched the bridge of his nose and wished for painkillers, but asking for them would make his crew question his decisions. George's sweaty brow was bad enough for morale. "And as long as we stay in stealth, they'll have a damn hard time doing that."

"What if, I don't know, the pirates tell them?" Tang asked.

Alex laughed, wishing he'd sent her out of control earlier. But now Doctor Leifsson was with her, both crammed into a corner, trying to look more fascinated than scared. "That *Hai Jao* will sink the shit out of these pirates if they get a whiff of them," he said. "I expect our piratical friends will be *very* quiet now that there's another warship about. They don't know we won't make a friendly call and build a pirate hunting alliance."

"Can't we?" Doctor Leifsson asked.

"Unfortunately, the U.N. declared the South China Sea—north of the Paracel Islands—a no-sail zone for warships. The Taiwanese obviously aren't obeying that because a, this is their front yard, and b, they're in the middle of a war in China. But *we*, as in the U.S. government, agreed to abide by that."

Leifsson frowned. "Then why were you sent for us?"

"Someone thought your research was more important than following the rules."

The two scientists exchanged a look. "It is." Tang crossed her arms. "Fusion is coming, and the reactor we built is small enough to fit in a submarine." She glanced around. "Definitely newer than this antique shit."

"*Ning*," Leifsson hissed.

"What? Half of it's older than I am, and I'm not half as young as people usually think I am." She looked around. "Maybe three-quarters."

"You can't possibly have miniaturized a *fusion* reactor that much," George said. "Research indicates we're a generation away from that breakthrough."

Tang grinned. "My generation, you mean?"

George scoffed. "Every submariner is a trained nuclear engineer. Don't try to sandbag me. I know what's possible."

"We had a few fortuitous breakthroughs." Leifsson put a hand on Ning's arm. "And some very smart engineers. As you captain said, *someone* thought our work was important enough to send you out here."

"Probably because Pulsar bribed a senator." George rolled his eyes.

"Actually, it was Admiral Hamilton," Alex said, and George's head whipped around.

Everyone in the sub community knew Admiral Freddie Hamilton meant business. Hers was the guiding hand that kept them manned, trained, and equipped—and deployed against the growing Russian threat in the North Atlantic. Marco Rodriquez was the Pac-Indio face of the war, but Freddie Hamilton was hardly in his shadow.

"She believes this?" George scowled.

"She called me herself."

"You didn't tell me?" George looked like a kicked puppy, and a pang of guilt made Alex's throat tight. He hadn't wanted to add stress to the life of someone already operating at capacity...but maybe he should've shared that. His best captains hadn't kept secrets from their XOs.

"I should have," he said. "I think I got caught up in events. I apologize."

George's jaw worked like he didn't know what to say to that; he nodded roughly and turned back to the scientists. "I hope you're worth the risk," he said.

"Me, too," Leifsson replied, scuffing her toes against the metal deck.

Alex returned his attention to the plot. Their track on the Taiwanese boat was firming up, and it was about twenty nautical miles away, crossing their bow from left to right. Now that *Jimmy Carter* had slowed, their closest point of approach would be about twelve miles. Alex grimaced.

Way too close.

"I wish I'd streamed the tail earlier," he muttered.

"There was no time," George replied. "Someone would've heard it. And we can't risk high-speed maneuvers with it out—or someone shooting it off."

Alex shook his head. "I'd rather risk the tail than the boat, but nothing we can do about it now. This cat's close enough that he'll definitely detect it." Sighing, he popped another candy in his mouth. "Maggie, what's the depth here?"

"About twelve thousand feet, give or take a couple thousand."

"Damn." Alex scowled. "So much for that idea."

"What were you thinking, Captain?" Maggie asked.

"I was thinking this was a great time to break out the skegs and bottom the boat, but that's not going to happen now. Let's slow to hover, see if we can let this cat pass by a bigger CPA."

"Aye sir." Maggie gave the orders. Within a few minutes, she reported: "Commenced hovering, Captain."

"Very well." Alex took a deep breath. "Maybe they'll all pass us, and we can just go home without further incident."

"You mean Diego Garcia, sir," George said.

"Same thing, at this point."

The Indian Ocean, north of Diego Garcia

"This is risky, Captain," Lieutenant Commander Patricia Abercrombie said as *Razorback* disconnected from what John hoped was their final videoconference.

Razorback's captain and XO were alone in the wardroom, sitting together at the end of the blue plastic–covered table. The fake wood paneling in the room felt oppressive right now; were those pre-battle jitters? John hoped not. He'd seen enough combat now that his hands no longer tried to shake, but this *was* the most ambitious tactic he'd ever attempted.

"High risk, high reward." He spread his hands. "We're about to go into the proverbial shooting gallery, but it only works if they don't know we're there." He pointed at the sweeping entrance to the Strait of Malacca, less than a thousand miles away. "We know they have a sub or two lurking in there, but they're bound to be diesel boats. Who would waste a nuc when you've got shallow waters and ports right there to support it?"

Pat crossed her arms. "I follow that logic, Captain. But I think that trying to sneak *under* two alert warships and leaving them for the surface weenies to kill maybe more risk than we want to take."

"If we can pull it off, we'll be deep in their belly before they have any idea we're there. Odds are we can even sink one of those diesel boats before they get word out. *Then* we can go after their other surface craft with torpedoes at close range, and they have shit for room to maneuver in there." John swallowed, suddenly far away, remembering the most terrifying day of his life. He shook himself. "Ask me how I know."

"We're going to have that same handicap, sir."

John pulled himself out of that dark place with an effort, refusing to think of sunken carriers and lost friends. "We're not going to try to maneuver," he said. "We're going to be the bull in the goddamn China shop, boring our way into the strait and sinking one ship after another like they're pins in a bowling alley."

"Don't try that mixed metaphor on Admiral Anderson." Pat snickered. "It won't fly far."

"I'm not going to. We don't work for her. We work for Admiral Rodriquez."

"He's bought off on this crazy plan of yours?" she asked.

John grinned. "You bet he has."

"Why am I not surprised?" Pat asked the overhead. "So we drive under the first two destroyers and then sink everything in our path for as long as the torpedoes hold out?"

"Satellite imagery shows five more destroyers, two frigates, and a patrol craft in the Strait after those first two. That's sixteen torpedoes if we shoot two fish each. Add however many subs to that…and we may come home with an empty weapons room. But with *Bluefish* guarding the back door, I think we'll be all right."

"It's a long walk back to Perth."

"Longer if we don't go through the SOM."

"I can't deny that, sir." Pat sighed. "Shoot or die, huh?"

John chuckled. "You think I should use that as my motivational speech to the crew before we go in?"

"Good morning, Captain, the *Hai Jiao* has changed course northward." Maggie covered her yawn as Alex walked back into control. "Sonar holds her on the lateral array, sixty-plus miles and opening, still outbound. We've only got her on bottom bounce, odds she doesn't have us."

"Thank you." Alex cocked his head. "What are you doing up? I thought Benji had the watch."

After another hour of creeping along, waiting to lose their Taiwanese friend, Alex called an audible. He sent his watchstanders into a rotation, letting half the crew sleep while the others stood a reduced battle stations watch. It wasn't perfect, but it let his people rest while they slunk away. Alex even alternated with George to get four hours of shuteye in the intervening twelve hours.

"He needed the little boys' room, and I was awake."

"You don't look it."

Maggie rubbed her eyes. "That's because I'm a glorious morning person, Captain."

"I can tell. How far are we from the Paracel Islands?"

Maggie grimaced. "Three hundred and nine miles. Not that I'm counting."

Alex laughed. "You want to sink these pirates?"

"Doesn't *everyone* want to sink pirates, sir?" She shoved curly hair out of her face, bending over the chart. "But I'm not sure it's going to happen. I'd bet these guys know about the no-sail zone and don't want to set one foot outside it. They want the Fogborne peeps—and maybe us, if they'd like a serving of extra dumb sauce—but they've got to know we'll come after them with both barrels the moment we don't have to pretend."

"I'm not sure our orders are vague enough to let me shoot them without them firing first, even if they're dumb enough to cross that imaginary line," Alex admitted. Re-reading those orders hadn't helped, and it wasn't like he was going to break comms silence to ask questions. He rubbed the back of his neck. "The idea of letting them go so they can prey on someone else chaps my ass, but if they don't shoot..."

"And you people keep asking me why I don't want to stick around for command." Maggie stuck out her tongue. "I'd rather analyze someone else's choices, thanks."

Alex laughed. "Well, in that light, let's kick it up to twenty knots and see if we can't shake these assholes. Doing the job is more important than sinking pirates, no matter how much I *want* to burn those fuckers to the ground."

"You got it, sir."

"I think I have something on sonar, boss." Jenny's tongue darted out between her teeth as she squinted in concentration. "Maybe...maybe bearing two-zero-four. Range undetermined. Computer can't correlate yet, but closer than we were."

"Well, it's nice to know I was right." Diego Reyes sat back in his chair. He'd contemplated capturing the Taiwanese submarine but resisted the urge. It was an AIP diesel, like his own boat, which meant it would be a much easier target...but the American boat was a bigger prize.

Instead, he let that damn Taiwanese sub wander across his course and sped up, closing the range between his boat and the nuclear attack sub that could otherwise outrun *Destroyer*. He'd read their playbook, though. The Americans were so predictable. Someone might detect you? Go slow. Someone might shoot you? Hide. Even war didn't change them.

This was something he could take advantage of.

"Come up to twenty knots," Diego ordered. "And tell *Weirwood* to get right on top of where you think they are. I want to get in close so they know we can ream them with torpedoes *and* depth charges."

"Our battery will only last us another twenty hours if we increase to twenty knots, Captain," his helm operator said.

"We'll be able to recharge long before then." Diego waved a hand. "I want these assholes."

---

27 September 2039, the South China Sea

Midnight local rolled by, and Alex's eyes burned.

"Sonar, Conn, they still back there?" he asked.

"Same as last time you asked, Captain," Wilson replied.

"Wilson!" Lieutenant (j.g.) Vincentelli's voice could be heard without the intercom, and he sounded so horrified that Alex briefly wondered if the sonar operator had started streaking.

No, that'd be too interesting for this slow-as-molasses chase.

He suppressed a smile. "Thanks, Sonar. Let me know if there's a change."

"Sonar, aye." That was Vincentelli, of course. The poor kid was spelling Chief Bradley as Sonar Supervisor—they were too short-handed to take Wilson's ears off the contact—and he was still a stickler for details, even after all these months.

Not laughing at him was hard, but good captains didn't laugh at their division officers. It was bad for morale.

Alex rubbed his face and popped another piece of candy. He was running low, but Diego Garcia was less than two weeks away. There he could buy several cases to store in every random corner of his stateroom. He'd always enjoyed long hunts; they were part of being a submarine captain. But being the *prey*... Yeah. Fuck that.

These pirates were determined, even if common sense said they should be terrified of his submarine. They wanted a fight? It was time to change the rules.

"Officer of the Deck, let's slow to five knots," Alex said.

Benji turned to look at him, brow scrunched. "You want them to gain on us, Captain?"

"These jokers want to play, so let's join the game." Alex shoved his hands in his pockets. "They're in for a world more of hurt than they think they are if they catch us, so let's just stop running."

"I like the sound of that, Captain." Benji grinned. "Sure as hell beats this creeping around like we're hoping they'll go away."

"Now that we don't have a Taiwanese witness around to tell people we were here, the rules change." Alex studied the plot, letting his mind wing through possibilities. He was still constrained by their rules of engagement...but what kind of torpedoes could a pirate get their hands on?

How much of their threats were bluffs? The muscle might be the surface ships, and surface ships were just targets for *Jimmy Carter*.

"You want to go back to battle stations, sir?" Master Chief Morton asked from his elbow. He didn't know where the COB materialized from, but that wasn't new.

Alex nodded. "Make it happen."

Alex was done being prey for pirates. It was time to turn the tables.

Chapter 25

The Destroyers

27 September 2039, the South China Sea

"Captain, I'm not sure we should break stealth." George swallowed, his Adam's apple bobbing up and down. "Our orders say to remain *undetected* no matter what."

"They already know we're here, XO." Alex had wrestled with those same orders until he'd come to that inevitable conclusion. "They've been following us for sixteen hours."

"Just because they can guess what direction we're moving doesn't mean they have a track on us. And that's all the more reason to stay in stealth." George's eyes flicked wildly around control, where the quiet hum of activity had returned. *Jimmy Carter* was at battle stations once more, strung like a taut bowstring ready to fire. "And that's what our orders *say*."

"Well, it wouldn't be the first time I disobeyed an order." Alex shrugged. "Admiral's Mast sucked, but they pay me to use my judgment."

"Captain..."

"I understand your objections, George. You're not even wrong. But we can't exactly transit the SOM with these assholes following us, can we? Those cats on the surface will give our positions away in a heartbeat."

George sighed, his shoulders slumping. "Tell me you're not planning on shooting first, sir. Our orders explicitly forbid that."

"No, I'm not. But I'm not crazy enough to let them take more than one shot, either, so we're damn well going to be ready to send them to whatever hell pirates go to," Alex replied. "You good with that?"

"I...I can live with it, sir." George's nod was a little shaky, but he took his station with the fire-control team on steady feet.

Okay. One obstacle was dealt with, and knowing George, he was the toughest enemy Alex would face today.

His stomach rumbled, reminding him he'd skipped breakfast and eaten candy instead. Nancy would get after him about his sugar intake if she knew, but Nancy was off fighting the war on a destroyer. Alex popped another hard candy and sucked it to help himself think.

"All right, folks, here's what we do. We've slowed down to suck these lovely people in, and now we'll rig for silent running so they can't have a hope of tracking us. But the ball's still in their court. Once they realize we're *somewhere* close by, I expect they'll do something threatening, and then we'll give them a good old American hello." Alex grinned. "From two tubes at a time."

His crew laughed, and Alex could feel the tension eking out of them. Pirates weren't really a threat, were they? *Jimmy Carter* could deal with these three antiques with one arm tied behind her back. For once, Alex's submarine wasn't the oldest warship in the game, and that felt nice.

Now he just had to wait for the pirates to act like pirates.

"Cap, they've slowed down. A lot. Maybe five, eight knots?" Jenny looked tired, and Diego couldn't blame her.

Destroyer had a small technical crew married to lots of muscle. That meant he didn't have much of a bench to spell Jenny when she got tired. Jenny could run navigation or sonar—or both at once, when things were quiet—and Adrian was Diego's best sonar operator. When one or both of them went down to sleep, he was out of choices.

He was the fool who'd let this chase go on for too long, but what kind of idiot didn't surrender when surrounded? He didn't *really* want to sink the American submarine with the Fogborne team on board. They were worth ten *million* dollars! So he had to force the boat to surface, and if he could do that, he might as well steal the damned thing. Diego Reyes was sure as shit going to get a good payday out of all this work.

"You think they broke something?" he asked.

Jenny made a face. "Maybe. Probably not. System says they're turning toward us."

"Oh, really?" Diego turned to his radio watch. "Tell *Siren* and *Weirwood* to get into position. This guy's finally made a mistake, and I want them there to catch him."

"You got it, Cap," the radio gal said.

"And then when you're done with that, let's tell them how much we appreciate them." Diego bared his teeth.

"American submarine, this is the submarine Destroyer *of Diego's Destroyers. You are surrounded by our warships. Surface immediately and surrender the Fogborne Research Team, and you will be allowed to go on your way."*

"Does anyone believe that?" Alex snorted. "We'll be allowed to 'go on our way.' Yeah, right."

Maggie snickered. "It sounds like these people are too used to playing with gullible civilians, sir."

"Or they have something worse up their sleeve than we've already seen," George said. "What if they're privateers and have state-of-the-art weapons?"

That made Alex hesitate. Privateers were sanctioned and supported by a nation, and they *might* have much better weapons than Alex bet these pirates could purchase on the black market. *Unless that sub of theirs came fully armed, you jackass*, he thought.

"Privateers are legally required to identify themselves," Benji said. "International law requires it."

Maggie cocked her head. "Leave it to you to know legal trivia."

"Hey, just because I'm a rebel and refused when my mom wanted me to be a lawyer doesn't mean I don't find law *interesting*." Benji spread his hands. "I just don't tell her that."

Alex chuckled. "Your family drama never ceases to amaze me."

The radio squawked again. *"American submarine, we will not warn you again. Surface and surrender the Fogborne Research Team* now *or we will start depth charging you!"*

"They should've used that threat *before* they started missing," Benji muttered.

Maggie grinned and ordered a course change.

"You want to answer these guys, Captain?" Master Chief Morton scratched at the stubble growing on his chin. "I know you've enjoyed letting them stew, but it's probably time to tell them to fuck off."

"I'm inclined to make them wait longer." Alex popped another piece of candy in his mouth without looking at the wrapper and then grimaced when he realized it was flavored grape. Ugh. His least favorite. "Just to make them dumber."

"Desperate ain't a good look, especially on pirates," Morton said quietly.

"You know, I have to agree with the COB here," Paul said. He looked rosy-cheeked and well rested, having wandered off for the boring stuff and just now returned when things were getting interesting. "You and I have met desperate pirates, Rook Buddy, and good decisions they do not make."

"I hate it when you're right." Sighing, Alex picked up the handset for the underwater radio. "Maggie, make another course change as soon as I'm done talking, please."

"Aye, Captain."

Steeling himself to talk on the radio was an old habit, but somehow it didn't get any easier. Alex hated himself for his fear of public speaking, but it just wouldn't go away, no matter how hard he worked. Thank goodness it didn't make him turn into a quivering mess *every* time he talked to his own crew. Or at least it didn't now that he knew them.

"Pirate submarine, this is U.S. Navy Warship," Alex said. "We do not recognize your authority and are not inclined to follow your orders, over."

Alex made a conscious decision not to identify his boat by hull number; there was only one SSN-23 out there, and *Jimmy Carter* had one huge advantage over the attack boat classes that came after her: she had eight torpedo tubes to a *Cero* or *Virginia's* four.

That meant she could take all three pirates out in one attack and still have a pair of torpedoes left in case some other idiot came by.

"*U.S. Navy warship, that is a very foolish choice,*" the voice on the other end of the radio said. Alex couldn't pinpoint the accent, only that each word grew sharper as the man's anger grew. "*We will give you two minutes to make a better one. Out.*"

"Weps, make tubes one through eight ready in all respects, including opening the outer doors." Alex did not smile. "That should be answer enough."

The article broke online that evening in the United States, a day behind Alex Coleman in the South China Sea thanks to the International Date Line. It would go out in the papers the next morning, but by now, the internet was the king of the twenty-four-hour news cycle. *The New York Times* hadn't stayed in the action by being slow off the mark.

PRACTICAL FUSION ACHIEVED. NOW WHAT?

Parker Sechrist, New York Times

September 26, 2039—Workable fusion reactors smaller than a football field have been the impossible dream of nuclear scientists for generations. Fusion, not to be confused with its more volatile counterpart, *fission*, is a stable nuclear reaction that generates almost no radioactive waste and eliminates the risk of a runaway reaction. And it seemed always out of reach.

Until now.

Pulsar Power, Ltd. has confirmed that one of their many research teams has made multiple fusion breakthroughs in the past three years, up to and including miniaturizing a reactor into a size small enough to power a ship, submarine, or power plant. And according to Pulsar Power, these reactors are powerful.

"While we cannot yet provide technical specifications, we assure the public that the specifics will be provided in due course," Amanda Cannon, Pulsar Public Relations, said yesterday. "However, the reactor design *has* been tested and Pulsar will roll it into production within the next year. We have named the reactor Fogborne, in honor of the team that designed it."

The scientific community is already clamoring for access to the reactor specs, with a few calling Pulsar out for misleading the public. Doctor Nathan Carr, a troubadour who can always be counted on to speak his mind, has made several videos accusing Pulsar of lying. His claim is that the reactor design doesn't exist at all, or if it does, it's far bigger than Pulsar has advertised.

Pulsar denies these claims; however, proof has yet to be provided. This article will be updated when more information comes to light.

Pearl Harbor, Hawaii

"Fuck."

Marco almost threw his stapler after reading the article, but why break a poor stapler when he had actual people to yell at? Not that it would make him feel better.

On the bright side, it sure as shit looked like Freddie was wrong. The leak wasn't on *Jimmy Carter*; someone at Pulsar was blabbing like there was a knife to their blasted throat. So then Pulsar went public with the news, putting *Jimmy Carter*, the Fogborne Team, and the entire damn future of nuclear engineering in danger.

Yep. Great fucking day to be in the navy.

"COS!" he bellowed, and like magic, his chief of staff shot through the door. It was almost the end of the workday, but in war time, no one went home at sixteen hundred. Particularly not if you worked for Marco.

"Admiral?" Captain Tim Blake was a decent sort. He was shorter than Marco, quick on his feet, and generally worked hard. But he wasn't Tanya, either.

"Shoot off a warning message to *Jimmy Carter* like right the fuck yesterday. They're going to be in deep shit if people realize the future of fucking nuclear fusion is on board that submarine."

Blake blinked. "Has something happened, sir?"

"Do you not dick around and read the internet at work, son? The *New York Times* just broke the news of fusion in our lifetimes, and it's on board that fucking antique death trap we somehow call an attack submarine. So fucking tell them they're in danger!"

"Yes, sir!"

Grumbling more obscenities, Marco picked up the phone, punched in a number, and waited for the squawking and squeaking to finish as the secure line dialed in. Once that rigmarole was finished, it took forever and a day for the *Lexington* watch officer to pick up.

"USS *Lexington* CIC, this is a secure line. Combat Information Center Watch Officer Speaking. How may I help you?" an impossibly youthful voice said.

"This is Vice Admiral Rodriquez. Please tell Rear Admiral Anderson that I would like to speak to her at her earliest convenience," Marco growled. "Which means right the fuck now, if you please."

"I'll have her called to CIC right now, sir."

"Thank you." Marco settled in to wait, reaching for his computer mouse and a screwdriver.

It took too long. He had the mouse disassembled and had started on his keyboard, using the tip of the screwdriver to fling the keys across the room. His aide would have kittens over it, but hey, Marco had another keyboard. And if he got bored and broke that one, well, that's why he had a tablet.

"This is Admiral Anderson."

"Kristi, it's Marco Rodriquez, COMSUBPAC," Marco said. Then he paused, the enormity of what he was up to hitting him. He outranked Anderson, but she sure as shit didn't work for him. Exactly *one* of her units, *Razorback*, was in any way his responsibility. He just happened to be her predecessor with Task Force Two-Three, which she'd boringly renamed the *Lexington* Strike Group when she started camping on the carrier.

"What can I do for you, sir?" Anderson sounded wary, as well she probably should be. Marco was definitely pissing in her Wheaties.

"I just got some intel that indicates an op we're trying very hard to protect may be compromised. The submarine in question should transit the SOM on or about the fourth of October, and there's reason to believe that all our enemies are going to be *very* interested in them."

"You're aware of my operational schedule, I take it? The fourth shouldn't be a problem."

"I'm more concerned about them making it *to* the SOM." Marco managed not to say something cutting about Anderson's last attempt to take that critical little stream. The SOM hadn't been kind to America in the war, and that probably wasn't Anderson's fault. He broke the spacebar off the keyboard. "You read all these articles about nuclear fusion?"

"Can't say I have. It's not my area of expertise," Anderson replied.

"Well, it is mine. Let's just say that the holy fucking grail of nuclear engineering has been realized, and I've got a boat with all the goodies on board creeping up your way. Pretty soon, India's going to catch the hell on and close that strait up so tight a starfish couldn't squeak through. I need a distraction big time, Kristi. And you need to get in before they slam the safe door shut."

"You're telling me that your goddamned nuclear Easter egg hunt is going to ruin my chances of taking the SOM?" Something scraped against metal; was that Anderson coming out of her chair? "What the hell are you playing at? Sir."

"I'm not trying to play at anything. God's fucking honest with you here. This was not my plan. But now we're both up shit creek, so it would be goddamned nice if we *paddled together*, wouldn't it?"

Her sigh was explosive even across several thousand miles of satellite uplinks. "You're asking me to push my operational schedule up."

"Damn right I am." No use beating around the bush. "Might help if the Indians have cottoned onto you, anyway. Catch 'em with their pants down and on the shitter."

"That's not a mental image I needed," she replied. "I'll think about it."

"That's all I can ask." Not reaching through the line to strangle her was so damned hard, but Marco made himself smile. He'd once read that smiles could be heard over the phone. "Thank you for your time, Admiral. Please keep me advised of changes. I need to let my boat know."

"As if *Razorback* won't tell you." She snorted. "I know you have your little spy along."

Marco laughed. "If you think I'm holding Dalton's dick all day long, believe me, I've got better things to do. He's too competent for that. You might not like him, but the guy's a pro. He'll lead you through *and* cut the enemy down to size for you."

"I'm sure he will. Thank you for the call, sir. I must be going."

She didn't wait for him to say goodbye before she hung up, but Marco didn't care. Had he given *Jimmy Carter* a chance to get through before the Indians slammed the door shut? Maybe.

He hated maybes, but in this war, sometimes maybes were the best you had.

"Cap, I've finally got contact on the American. Bearing is...either one-eight-eight or zero-zero-two. Range ten nautical mile—oh, *shit*, I've got definite sounds of tubes opening!"

"Tubes?" Captain Diego Reyes, comfortable and a little sleepy in his chair, jolted upright. Making threats was part of his daily routine, so he hadn't bothered to get up—or put his tablet game down—to talk to his prey. Now, however, the tablet tumbled to the deck, and the game made a sad little sound while his character died. "*Torpedo* tubes?"

"Definite air bubbles and tubes flooding."

"Flood our tubes!" He jumped to his feet. "And tell *Weirwood* to drop depth charges off their bow!"

An unwelcome cold chill stole up Diego's spine. Victims weren't supposed to turn around and bare their teeth. Sure, a few tried to fight back, but they were meant to be *frightened* after he stalked them for so long.

Jenny twisted to look at him, dark circles under her eyes and her voice ragged. "Which bearing?"

Adrian was back at sonar, which freed Jenny up for navigation and communications. She was more or less Diego's second-in-command, as much as he wanted to have one. Which he usually didn't. Now, however, she wanted answers he didn't have. And now he was angry, angry at himself for getting in this situation and angry as the damned American submarine for not cooperating.

They'd come too far to lose this prey now.

"The closer one!" he snapped. That one was more dangerous, both to *Destroyer* and *Weirwood*. Thinking tactically was hard when he was shaking with fury.

"Relaying now." Jenny listened on her headset for a moment. "*Weirwood* launching."

Diego grinned. "Now let's see how fast these assholes become 'inclined to follow our orders.'"

"Conn, Sonar, splashes!" Wilson's voice blared through the speaker. "Splashes off the starboard bow, range approximate but at least a couple thousand yards. Nowhere close."

"Splashes?" George reared up from Benji's side, his face white. "Are they *depth charging* us?"

"And missing. The gall is impressive." Alex felt strangely calm—and very glad he'd changed course after talking to these people. "Sonar, Conn, you have a bearing and range to the ship that launched them?"

"Sir, I thought you'd never ask. Formerly track four-zero-seven-en-nine, now designated hostile and track seven-zero-seven-nine."

Alex's eyes snapped to the plot. That was the closer of the two surface ships, the one the computer identified as a type 053 or type 054 Chinese frigate. It was a genuine warship, one that *had* belonged to the nation his boat was supposed to hide from...but China decommissioned the last of them more than a decade ago.

"Captain, that's a Chinese frigate..." George said, weaving across control back to his side.

"*Former* Chinese," Alex said. "That's an important distinction out here."

"Conn, Sonar, two explosions at medium range," Chief Bradley reported. "Whatever these pirates bought, it's not rocket-propelled depth charges. These might not be Second World War vintage, but it sure sounds like they're kicking them right off the stern and using old-fashioned detonation timers."

"Conn, aye." Alex chewed his candy thoughtfully. Pirates could drive relatively new ships, but could they find modern weapons...?

"Sir, engaging them goes against the spirit of our orders, if not the letter."

"I understand your concerns, XO, but we don't have time for a debate," Alex replied and then raised his voice. "Firing point procedures, tubes one and three, track seven-zero-seven-nine."

"Firing point procedures, track seven-zero-seven-nine, Weps, aye," Benji replied. Less than twenty seconds passed before he added: "Solution ready."

"Ship ready!" Chief Stevens sang out.

George, clearly torn between arguing and duty, swayed back and forth for a moment before scurrying back to Benji's side to double-check the firing solution. Reluctantly, he nodded.

Alex didn't wait for additional confirmation. "Tubes one and three, fire!"

Chapter 26

Smart Pirates

"Tubes one and three fired electronically," Chief Stevens reported.

"Conn, Sonar, two fish running hot, straight, and normal."

"Very well," Alex replied, trying to hide the way his heart raced. Thank God his hands were in his pockets so no one could see his palms sweating. Still, he'd spent years training for this, and he knew what to do, even if his imagination wanted to run wild. "Cut the wires, close the outer doors, and reload both tubes. Officer of the Deck, come right to zero-three-five."

"Come right to zero-three-five, OOD, aye," Maggie replied, relaying the orders. The new course split the difference between the two enemies who hadn't fired.

"You really want to cut the wires so soon, Captain?" Benji leaned forward. "That's a fairly advanced frigate up there."

"They're dead in the water and using old-school depth charges. These cats aren't going to get up enough speed to dodge a pair of Mark 84s fast enough, and I don't want to be chained to them."

"Cutting the wires and closing the outer doors, aye." Benji hit the buttons himself.

"Thank you, Weps."

Alex didn't mind questions; hell, he didn't even mind George's incessant worry that they'd violate the spirit of their always-stay-in-stealth *unless fired upon* orders. Sure, those depth charges were a thousand yards away and not a genuine threat, but someone *meant* them to be dangerous, and Alex wasn't paid to give people a second shot at his submarine.

"Now that we've started shooting, we pretty much have to take all these pirates out so they can't say we were here, don't we?" George's jaw trembled.

"You read my mind, XO." Alex didn't smile; his eyes were on the plot, waiting for that pirate U-Boat to realize what was going on.

"Conn, Sonar, more splashes, now to port. Bearing is changing as we turn, range over a thousand yards," Wilson reported.

"Conn, aye." Alex turned to Benji. "What's the runtime on the torps?"

"Twenty seconds to impact, Captain."

"Damn, those Mark 84s are fast." Alex grinned. "It's nice to have the newest toys for once, isn't it?"

Benji's laugh sounded a little strangled, like he surprised himself with it. "Yes, sir, it is. Just try not to use them all—I don't know when they'll give us more, okay?"

Alex chuckled. "I'll try."

"Conn, Sonar, track seven-zero-seven-nine is maneuvering! Big kick up in screw RPM, like she just woke up and smelled the coffee! She's trying to turn, but it ain't going to do her shit—"

"Wilson!" Bradley shouted.

"Torpedo sonar has a hard lock on the target. Five seconds," Benji said.

"Maggie, make your depth twelve hundred feet," Alex ordered.

"Impact!"

"Cap, *Weirwood* says she has torpedoes inbound!"

"What the fuck?" Diego leaned forward over Jenny's chair, as if staring at her display would get him answers faster. "Where are they, Adrian?"

"I don't know—I lost them after they opened their outer doors." Adrian's boyish face was pale and panicked. "The depth charges have mucked up everything underwater, and the computers can't hear *anything*."

"I thought German sonar computers were the best in the world?"

"They are!" Adrian jerked back, staring at his console with wide eyes.

"What? What is it?" Diego stalked over to the other side of his submarine's control room, only to see the unbelievable on the sonar display: *Weirwood* had been hit.

He was no sonar expert, but he didn't need to be with

state-of-the-art systems. Adrian had helpfully paused the feed at the right moment, and the giant plume of sound was right there, in stark glowing green and blue, for anyone with eyes to see.

"Find me that American so I can *kill them*," he hissed from behind gritted teeth.

The Northern Indian Ocean, approaching the Strait of Malacca

The knock on John's door woke him up from a dead sleep.

Pat walked in from their shared head without waiting for him to reply. "Captain, we just got a message from Admiral Anderson."

"Do I want to know?" John rolled over to face her, staying in bed until Pat told him he had to move. It was warm under the covers, and he was a man who liked sleep.

"We have the go order for Operation Sandicast. It's T-plus-twenty-four hours until the advance force enters the SOM."

"What?" John rolled out of bed so fast he ended up sitting on the deck. He scrambled to his feet, not caring about a captain's dignity. "We've still got six days!"

"Not now we don't."

"Shit." John shook himself and grabbed his coveralls. "Call the navigator and let's meet in control. We need to review the nav plan now and turn and burn so we can beat everyone there." He scratched his head, doing quick math. "What's the task force speed of advance?"

"Thirty knots."

"Then we'll have to make an average of forty-five if we're going to beat them by eight hours. Depending on how liberal I want to be while sprinting and drifting." John pulled his shoes on. "Agreed?"

"The numbers check out." Pat grimaced. "You know, I really thought this thing was supposed to be better planned."

John shrugged. "Maybe the Indians got wind of our planned day and we're going early. Maybe the president has a speech scheduled. Who knows? Either way, it's nice to stop sitting around and start doing the damned job."

"You can say that again, Captain."

Jimmy Carter's deck sloped downward as she headed for deeper water. Far beneath the thermodynamic layer, they couldn't feel *Weirwood's* explosion, but Wilson's whoop from sonar gave it away.

"Conn, Sonar, two good hits! Got them with both barrels!"

"Conn, aye." Alex chuckled. "Now we've got to do this twice more, as the XO pointed out."

"Why from twelve hundred feet, Captain?" Maggie turned from watching the depth gauge a little too closely. "I know we tested the boat down to thirteen hundred during trials, but we haven't done it since."

"That Chinese frigate is—or maybe was," he corrected himself, and watched grins blossom on his crew's faces, "a lot newer than the weapons she threw at us. Which has me thinking that might be a lot easier for a pirate to buy or steal a mostly modern warship than it is to get modern weapons."

"You don't think their depth charges will go this deep?" George perked up.

"Might not." Alex didn't want to mention that he was willing to take the boat down to *Jimmy Carter's* rated crush depth of nineteen hundred feet, which was calculated based on her age and their pre-deployment sea trials. Or he would take her down that far *if* he thought it would keep them away from enemy weapons.

Nineteen hundred feet was deeper than any other American fast attack submarine could dive, which meant any pirate with a copy of *Jane's* probably wouldn't guess *Jimmy Carter* could go so deep. Worst case, Alex *might* be brave enough to try his boat's original crush depth of two thousand feet.

Maybe.

"There's no use giving them free pot shots at us," he continued. "Besides, the Mark 84 will shoot from over two thousand feet, courtesy of our friends at Lazark and AIB. Might as well take advantage of that."

Even George's face ticked into a smile. Apparently, he liked the idea of shooting without getting shot at.

Who didn't?

"Sonar, Conn, I've got motion from our submerged friend, now designated track seven-zero-seven-eight on your display. They're driving toward where the last spread of depth charges detonated, moving from right to left, speed eight knots."

"Conn aye, break, range?"

"About twenty thousand yards counting the drop from our depth, sir," Chief Bradley replied. "Got a real good read on them now, and tonals match the South Korean *Sohn Won-yil*. Their naval registrar has her listed as a Type 214, decommissioned six years ago and sold."

"Well, it's nice to know who we're up against, isn't it?" Alex chewed the last of that damn grape candy, thinking.

"Designating them hostile might be a bit premature, Captain?" George fidgeted like he didn't know the answer to his own question. "The submarine didn't fire on us."

"With respect, XO, they threatened to and then their friends tried to drop depth charges on our heads," Master Chief Morton said before Alex could reply. The COB stood with arms crossed across his skinny chest, his dark eyes narrowed in the universal *chiefs-know-best* look. "Even a peacetime navy would find their actions hostile unless they were backing away, screamin' apologies and prayers to the fucking lord." He leaned forward to speak into the intercom. "Sonar, COB, are the U-Boat's outer doors open?"

"COB, Sonar, like they're flashing us on a hot summer day," Wilson replied.

Morton snorted out a laugh. "COB, aye." Then he twisted to look at the XO. "Good enough for hostile intent, sir?"

George flushed.

"Weps, firing point procedures, tubes two and four, track seven-zero-seven-eight," Alex ordered.

"Firing point procedures, tubes two and four for track seven-zero-seven-eight, Weps, aye!"

"Where the fuck are they, Adrian?" Diego wanted to pace, but the knot in his stomach kept him rooted to the floor.

"I don't know! There's too much churn in the water. I could go active—"

"And then they'd know where we are!"

"It won't matter if we shoot first." Adrian's jaw set as he glared. "We go active, we sink the bastards, and then we go help *Weirwood*."

Jenny shook her head. "Won't matter, Cap. They're abandoning ship."

"*What?*" Diego's heart did a painful pitter-patter, like it wanted to stop cold.

He'd *never* lost a ship. Not in six years as a pirate—six *plentiful* and profitable years as a pirate. Diego prided himself on being smart, on never biting off more than he could chew, and there was no way in hell *one* attack submarine should be more than a match for his three ships! The top-of-the-line German technology on *Destroyer* should've sniffed them out long before the Americans could ever find them, and to think that a *Virginia*-class boat had the utter gall to shoot at *Weirwood* when they were just throwing out warning charges?

"Marticia says they have progressive flooding." Jenny cringed. "Sounds like the keel is broken."

"Fuck." Diego slumped against the back of Adrian's chair and then shook himself, feeling like a boxer on round seven of a losing fight. "Find them, Adrian. Find them so we can kill them."

"Let's do this thing before someone changes their mind."

Razorback leaped forward, burning holes in the water at fifty-five knots. It wasn't actually her top speed. Improved *Ceros* like *Razorback* were some of the fastest submarines in the world, and John had never *quite* pushed his boat to her limits. Still, sprinting like this would give John's boat a twenty-knot advantage over the surface ships trailing behind her, which meant he could get to the Strait a full eight hours before the advance group.

Then *Razorback* would have ample time to slip into the shallow waters between Indonesia and Malaysia before the enemy realized she might be creeping among them.

Pouring on speed was risky, but the current plan left them little choice. So that left the old submarine tactic of sprinting and drifting—driving hard and then slowing to listen to their surroundings. Theoretically, that would ensure that the sound damping software in *Razorback's* sonar system wasn't overwhelmed. The manufacturer claimed that the software could factor out the *Razorback's* noise and waterflow at any speed, but no one really believed that.

Except maybe Admiral Anderson, who'd given John zero time to plan.

John glanced at the clock as the deck vibrated slightly under his feet. *Fifteen hours.* He'd done well so far in command of *Razorback*, but he'd never felt pressure like this.

"I think I've got something!" Adrian sang out. "Bearing...two-nine-zeroish, around eight miles. They must be closing with us for a better shot after taking *Weirwood* out."

Diego didn't need to be told twice. No, he needed distraction from the image of *Weirwood* breaking up on the surface that Marticia, the frigate's *former* captain, had messaged him. *Weirwood* was gone, and he damned well was going to spook these Americans into surrendering.

He wanted them dead. Salivated for it. But smart pirates checked their email and saw that the ransom for the Fogborne Research Team was up to twenty million dollars.

Smart pirates could kill one or two American submariners afterward, like their weapons officer and captain.

Accidents happened.

"Fire a warning shot across their bow!" he snarled.

"Torpedo in the water! Torpedo in the water bearing...three-one-five?" Wilson sounded confused. "Conn, Sonar, I say again, torpedo in the water bearing three-one-five, not inbound own ship."

Alex blinked. "What the hell are they shooting at?"

"If you want me to answer that, Captain, I need to go sit a few minutes on that other boat and ask the assholes." Master Chief Morton grinned. "But best guess? You've got them spooked, and they just blew their wad at a sonar ghost."

Alex snickered.

Alex snickered. Laughter was a strange feeling with a torpedo in the water, but it wasn't aimed at his boat, and Alex had a five hundred–long Swiss army knife of a submarine with which to respond.

"Part of me wants to sit here and see how many torpedoes they'll pickle off in the wrong direction." He scratched the back of his neck. "But that's not very smart, is it?"

"I would recommend against it, Captain." George had his serious face on. Was Alex being too blithe?

"From where I'm sitting, it's always good tactics to let the enemy waste rounds on something that isn't you," Paul said. The giant marine had crammed himself into a corner again, and now he grinned at Alex. "How many torpedoes do those U-Boats hold, anyway?"

"Export version?" Master Chief Morton asked. "The Type 214s have eight tubes and room for twelve more weapons. When a country owns them, that's a mix of missiles and torpedoes, total of twenty. But how many torps a pirate can afford is the magic question."

"Probably not twenty." Paul cocked his head. "Then again, if they can afford a submarine on the black market…"

"Torpedoes expire," Alex said. "Submarines…as long as the pressure hull is good, we're okay."

No one mentioned that *Jimmy Carter* was rated for a lifespan of forty years from the day her keel was laid down in 1998. Submariners were good at math.

The Gertrude crackled. *"American submarine, that is the only warning shot you will get,"* the same accented—but now angry—voice said. A buzz almost ate his next words: *"Surface now and surrender the Fogborne Team, or you will all die!"*

"Sir, we should probably talk to them." George clasped his hands like he was trying not to grab the handset.

Alex almost wished he would. The idea of having to come up with something pithy and smart to say on a radio circuit *anyone could hear* tied his stomach into more knots than being shot at did.

He rubbed his eyes, suddenly very tired. What the hell was wrong with him? All these years of talking on comms circuits should've gotten him over his fear of public speaking, yet here he was, hating the way his own crew stared at him expectantly. Alex swallowed.

"You're probably right, XO."

"I can handle it if you need me to, sir," Maggie said quietly. Her dark eyes were a little wide and her hair was getting frizzy again, but she looked calmer than he felt.

"No." He shook his head. "It's my damned job."

Alex refused to be like Chris goddamned Kennedy and sluff his job off on other people just because he was a little bit of a coward about talking on the stupid radio. Licking his lips, he grabbed the handset.

Why was this easier earlier? Was it because he hadn't stopped to think about it?

"Weps, dial in tubes five and seven on track seven-zero-eight-zero. If either of them twitches a weapon in our direction, I want to send one at them first," Alex ordered.

Was he trying to buy himself time? Sure. He didn't want to engage in public speaking. But it was still a smart order to give.

"Weps, aye! Solution ready." Benji grinned; his team had kept the firing solution on the pirate corvette updated since the beginning of their little stalk.

"Ship ready," Chief Stevens echoed.

"American submarine, we will not warn you again! You have one minute to begin surfacing. If we do not detect motion toward the surface, you are going to the bottom."

Shaking himself, Alex lifted the handset. "Pirate submarine, this is U.S. Navy Warship. Your compatriot has engaged in hostile action against the United States Navy. Your verbal statements—recorded by our logs—have indicated you are eager to do the same. Surrender now and stand by to be boarded by my marines. If you do not indicate your immediate willingness to do so, I will assume you intend to continue your attack and meet that with the precision and violence characteristic of the U.S. Navy, over."

"Shit, Captain, that sounded badass," Maggie whispered.

"Nav!" George hissed as Alex flushed.

"Do I get to board them? Please?" Paul rubbed his hands together. "I'd love to give you a pirate submarine for Christmas."

"It's September, Paul."

"Hey, a smart marine starts early."

"American submarine, you are outnumbered two to one. Don't be stupid. Turn over the Fogborne team and you can go free."

"My ass," Alex muttered before he could stop himself. "Yeah, just surface and get vulnerable. Then everything will be hunky fucking dory and we'll be nice. Promise."

"Sir, shouldn't we pursue all peaceful avenues?" George asked.

"Not if it involves violating our orders or handing *innocent people* to pirates," Alex replied, aghast.

"Besides," Paul rumbled, his smile gone, "we're at war, Commander Kirkland. These idiots may not be the enemies who've declared war upon us, but they're worked pretty damned hard at putting a target on their backs. It is *not* our job to take the fucking thing off once they put it on."

George flinched. "I didn't mean that we should, Colonel." He crossed his arms. "Only that as these pirates are *not* combatants in the war, we should not automatically treat them as such."

"Gentlemen, this is a fascinating theoretical discussion, but given that these assholes have shot at us and seem willing to do it again, I'm going to err on the side of shooting them first," Alex said. He held up a hand when George opened his mouth to object. "I'll give them one last chance to suffer an attack of common sense."

One last deep breath. Alex let his annoyance with George put an edge in his voice as he said: "Pirate Submarine, the U.S. Navy does not negotiate with pirates. I have both your vessels in my sights. Surface now. Out."

"No way they surface." Paul slumped. "Pity. You squids get all the fun."

"Not sorry."

"Pfft."

"Conn, Sonar, torpedo in the water!" Wilson's voice sang through the intercom. "Two torpedoes in the water, bearing zero-one-five and zero-one-four. Range eighteen thousand yards, torpedo speed...fifty knots. Tonals match the LIG Tiger Shark Heavyweight Torp across the board. Looks like the South Koreans sold some fish with her when they chucked the boat."

"Weps, match bearings and shoot, tubes two and four for track seven-zero-eight-zero!"

Benji's hand slapped down. "Tubes two and four fired electronically."

"Two fish running hot, straight, and normal," Chief Bradley reported.

"Conn, Sonar, incoming fish are in a search pattern," Wilson added. "They're better shots than the last one, but they're not barreling straight at us. I don't think they have a good fix on us, sir."

"And here I thought me talking so much gave us away." Alex forced a smile despite the lump in his throat. "Sonar, Conn, what depth are the torps searching at?"

"Sir, if you want, I can take a walk outside to check, but ain't no way for sure to tell that by listening. Least not when their torpedo sonar *isn't* hitting us for me to use," Wilson replied. "I mean, you *could* do something and let them find us, then I can tell you if they're diving down to our depth. But I could also tell you that I love trivia and the Tiger Shark is rated to three hundred meters."

"Which is nine hundred and eighty-four feet." Alex laughed. "I know."

Every eye in control swiveled to look at Alex.

Except those looking at the depth gauge that read *1200* in glowing red numbers.

Three hundred feet above *Jimmy Carter*, the pirates' torpedoes kept circling, looking for a target they couldn't find. Meanwhile, American torpedoes closed with their closer enemy.

Chaos reigned on board *Destroyer* as the U-Boat ran. A French, Indian, or Russian submarine would have had practice evading a torpedo. But a pirate?

Diego Reyes and his crew were not accustomed to enemies who fought back. Angry as he was, Diego's mind had been on the big payday he could earn from capturing the Fogborne Team—and the extra bonus he could pick up from one of America's enemies if he delivered an intact attack submarine. He never realized he'd bitten off more than he could chew.

A Mark 84 Advanced Spearfish Variant's maximum speed was eighty-seven knots. By the time *Destroyer* sped up to her maximum submerged speed of twenty knots, *Jimmy Carter's* torpedoes had already crossed almost twelve thousand yards, or six nautical miles. *Destroyer* turned away from the torpedoes, running for her life, but the turn cost her speed, as well—and AIP diesel submarines were not built for evasion.

Now it was a stern chase, and both ASVs had sixty-seven knots of overtake. They needed less than three minutes to cross that last six thousand yards.

"Two more good hits!" Wilson sounded like he wanted to throw a party. "Hot damn, I've got multiple secondary explosions. Ouch! No one's making it off that puppy."

Alex tried not to swallow. He should feel ecstatic—two shots, two kills! Instead, the voice of a now-dead pirate echoed in his mind. Who was he to end lives like that?

No. He shook himself. This was the job, and whoever was on that U-Boat preyed on innocents. It wasn't his fault they'd gone after a hard target.

"Conn, Sonar, the corvette is turning to run," Chief Bradley said.

Shit, Alex had almost forgotten them. "Weps, match bearings and shoot, tubes five and seven, track seven-zero-eight-one."

"Captain, are you sure we shouldn't—" George started, but Benji talked right over him.

"Match bearings and shoot, track seven-zero-eight-one aye. Tubes five and seven fired electrically!"

"Conn, Sonar, two fish running—belay that, *one* fish running hot, straight, and normal. The second motor didn't kick on," Bradley reported.

Alex leaned forward, his heart suddenly racing like a car gone out of control. "Sonar, Conn, say again."

"Sir, the fish out of tube five is dropping like the U-Boat. No motor, nada. It wants to be an anchor," Wilson replied.

"Torp out of tube seven is on target," Bradley said.

Alex looked over at Benji, who was bent over the fire control team's consoles as his sailors worked furiously. As if sensing his eyes, the weapons officer turned to him. "Looks like it's a dud, sir. Torpedo's not responding, even though we haven't cut the wire."

"Cut it now. Like Wilson said, if it has aspirations to be an anchor, I don't want to drag it around."

Benji cringed. "Anchors bearing warheads. No thanks."

"You want to fire tube one, sir?" Chief Stevens asked. "Reload will be done in thirty seconds."

Alex shook his head. "Hold that one for a snapshot if needed. We shouldn't *need* more than one to crack a corvette open—but just in case, let's not cut the wire to the tube seven torp. Drive this one in."

Stevens grinned. "You got it, Captain. Wire cut on five, guiding torp seven in."

"Very well."

Squaring his shoulders, Alex glanced around control. The dragging feeling of *uselessness* had vanished. Instead, his crew was buoyed by the chance to finally *do* something—even if it was just sinking pirates.

"Thanks for not selling us out," Ning Tang whispered from his left, hugging herself.

Alex jumped. Had she been in control the entire time?

"It was never an option," he said.

"Torp in final acquisition," Chief Stevens reported. "Ten seconds to impact."

His eyes flicked to the plot, watching without guilt as the final torpedo hit the patrol corvette. It was a small ship, meant for coastal patrols more than open ocean pirating, not designed to withstand anything like the warhead on a Mark 84 ASV heavyweight torpedo. It cracked her open like an egg. The initial explosion shattered her keel and killed a third of her crew; many of the others were thrown overboard.

They were the fortunate few.

Less than two minutes later, *Siren* joined her piratical comrades beneath the waves. *Jimmy Carter's* crew listened to the secondary explosions curiously. Was that it? Were they finished?

Two or three long minutes ticked by before Alex asked: "Conn, Sonar, any other contacts?"

"Negative, sir. Nothing in range." Chief Bradley sounded subdued. Was he thinking the same thing, too? Was this it?

Alex glanced at Ning Tang, still standing quietly against the bulkhead, her face still pale but her eyes fierce. Perhaps this was the only difference *Jimmy Carter* could make, but they'd damned well get the Fogborne Team to safety. Maybe their technology would change the world. Maybe it wouldn't.

Maybe *Jimmy Carter* would just go back to escorting convoys.

Chapter 27

Vanguard

28 September 2029, the Strait of Malacca

Bluefish had settled into a standard search pattern by the time *Razorback* entered the Strait of Malacca. Hundreds of miles away and unbeknownst to Commander Peterson's watchstanders, *Razorback* slowed an hour out from the SOM, creeping her way in at ten knots and sneaking right under the two destroyers guarding the entrance. Meanwhile, *Bluefish* went to battle stations and plowed along on her own search pattern, crawling along at a lazy eight knots and just waiting for someone to barge in and oppose the *Lexington* Strike Grosup.

They missed the squadron of Indian destroyers that slipped into the Strait three hours before their arrival. Operating in complete silence and emitting no radars or communications, the destroyers were on a final shakedown cruise before their first wartime deployment. They had no idea *Lexington* and her cohorts were on their way—days earlier than intelligence indicated they would be—but *Bluefish* didn't know they were there, either.

Bobby had been OOD for the last hour, ever since *Bluefish* had gone to battle stations. It would be a long watch, particularly since Commander Peterson didn't believe in spelling off his crew when things were slow. *Bluefish's* mission was remain in position until the *Lexington* Strike Group had successfully cleared out opposition in the Strait, shooting anyone who tried to join the party. For Bobby, that meant over twelve consecutive hours in control, supervising a whole lot of dangerous nothing.

Every one of those hours gave Commander Peterson another opportunity to glare unhappily at the back of his head, too. Bobby wasn't great at standing still to begin with; having his CO glower at him only made his own anxiety grow like poison ivy.

Still, there had to be some benefits to staring at the chart long enough. Unfortunately, the idea that struck him wasn't good—in fact, it was downright terrifying. A few seconds thinking about it knotted Bobby's stomach into a solid ball of festering lead.

After a few moments of trying, he caught the XO's eye, and Vanderbilt ambled over. He was probably glad for the distraction; there were only so many minutes you could stare at a blank fire control plot before going insane. *Bluefish* wasn't tracking anything; the surrounding seas were unnaturally still.

"What's on your mind, Nav?" Vanderbilt asked, guiding Bobby away from the corner of control where Peterson stewed.

Not glancing at his CO took a Herculean effort. Bobby gestured at the electronic chart. "I was just staring at our projected course like a good OOD." He shifted from his left foot to his right. All this standing still made him stiff. "And then I remembered the mine warfare module back at the sub school."

"Okay...?"

Maybe this wasn't such a good idea. Bobby swallowed. Still, he was committed, so he fidgeted and continued.

"Well, sir, I was just thinking that this looks like the ideal bottom type for mines," he said. "And I remember from the intel download that the Indians haven't been using many mines in the last couple months."

The XO frowned. "Didn't that same intel download speculate that Alliance forces might have inadvertently destroyed a few thousand mines in transit from Mumbai to Jakarta?"

"But what if they didn't?" Bobby *knew* something was wrong. "Speculation isn't fact. And we're heading into shallower water now, which only increases the mine danger."

"No kidding," Vanderbilt breathed. Then he gave Bobby a hard look. "You should have brought that to the captain's attention, you know."

Bobby turned a look on his XO that he knew resembled a deer caught in the headlights. Vanderbilt's shoulders slumped.

"I know. I'll talk to him."

It was the XO's job to take that gut shot, but Bobby felt guilty as he watched Vanderbilt head over to where Peterson was frowning over the sailor on the helm. They spoke quietly for several moments before Peterson twisted to look at Bobby. The captain's gray eyes bored in on him, and Bobby tried to pretend he didn't notice. Doing his *job* correctly shouldn't have created an attack of performance anxiety, but the longer he was on *Bluefish*, the more fretful he got. He was tired of being berated for trying to do the right thing.

"Nav."

The sound of the captain's voice made him jump like a targeted rabbit. "Yes, sir?"

"Join us."

"Yes, sir."

The captain and the XO stood over by the chart table Bobby had abandoned earlier. Bobby noticed Peterson had zoomed in to study the same area Bobby and Vanderbilt had discussed. Even after Bobby moved to the captain's side, Peterson said nothing for several long moments, leaving Bobby to stew, his stomach churning. Man, he should've drank less coffee.

Bluefish edged into the shallows. The conning officer, one of the junior officers assigned to Bobby's watch at battle stations, was keeping the submarine directly on the track Peterson had laid out, not daring to vary more than a handful of yards right or left of it. Most boats streamlined their watch organizations and combined the watches of OOD and conning officer, but Peterson was a stickler for details, so *Bluefish* kept them separate.

Bobby wouldn't have cared if Ensign D'Angelo hadn't been so darn new and inexperienced, but D'Angelo required more effort to supervise than driving the boat himself would have taken. D'Angelo could be trusted to steer *Bluefish* on any prearranged course, but when it came to tactical maneuvering, he was hopeless.

That meant D'Angelo blindly followed that programmed track when it wandered into the most dangerous area for bottom mines...and *Bluefish* was there now. Yeah, Bobby would stick mines here if he wanted to ruin someone's day. The ocean floor was less than three hundred feet below the keel of the submarine, perfect for moored mines *and* bottom mines.

Bobby licked his lips. Did he try to speak out again? He'd already argued against trying to patrol this area, only to be shot down. Twice.

"The XO tells me you're concerned about mines in this area," Peterson finally said, his disapproving sneer still in place.

"Well, um." Bobby shrugged, trying to look casual. "It seems logical, sir. I mean, if I was going to stick some mines out here to annoy enemy visitors, this is where I'd put them."

"It's a good point," Peterson said, making Bobby's head jerk up in surprise. "Intelligence disagrees with you, but it's still smart to keep an eye out. Good thinking, Mister O'Kane."

Bobby blinked. "Thank you, Captain?" He wasn't sure when he'd last heard Peterson praise someone. "Do you want to head for deeper water, then?"

"Not at this time." Peterson scowled. "We need to remain on station."

Bobby managed not to groan. Why was it that the captain picked *now* to be courageous?

Ninety minutes into the SOM and *Razorback* had already sunk two Indian *Scorpenes*. The first had been waiting just south of the destroyers guarding the mouth of the Strait, snorkeling to charge her batteries. John knew why; the Indians weren't stupid and they owned quite a few satellites. Everyone and their drunk grandfather knew the *Lexington* Strike Group was coming. They might've been caught off guard by their early move, but by now, every satellite focused on the area had spotted the ships. Hell, the Indians probably even knew how far ahead the advance group was, despite efforts to conceal it.

But no one knew about *Razorback*.

That diesel boat's captain probably thought he was being proactive and that he had a couple hours to prepare. John torpedoed him without a moment's hesitation, putting two Mark 84 torpedoes into the snorkeling submarine before the enemy ever detected him.

His first victim didn't have time to get a transmission off and warn its fellows, which made sinking the second one even easier. That *Scorpene* was lurking in slightly deeper water, not shallow enough to snorkel but clearly in communications with its higher headquarters. The newer *Scorpenes* had pretty good communications suites, John knew, and the odds of this sub notifying others of his attack were high.

Razorback slammed a pair of torpedoes into this one as well and then headed further into the SOM, cruising along at fifteen knots.

"Conn, Sonar, you're not gonna to believe this, Captain," John's leading sonar tech said fifteen minutes after they'd sent the second sub to the bottom.

"I don't know about that. You all know that I've got a pretty active imagination." John leaned into the speaker with a grin.

The atmosphere on *Razorback* had been tense when they'd first gone to battle stations. Everyone knew that heading into the Strait of Malacca ahead of the main force was a suicide mission in all but name. But the first two kills came so damn *easy*. No one said anything, but now they were all starting to believe that they might survive. So the answering smile from the senior chief manning sonar was genuine.

"I've got four contacts incoming at high speed, two surface, two subsurface. But they're not coming as a combined force—they're staggered out. I can get good reads on all of them."

John's heart did a backflip. Would they really come at him one at a time? A team of ships and subs might track *Razorback* and kill her with relative ease, but if they came in separately...

"What kind of spacing are we looking at?"

"Seems like six to eight thousand yards, sir," was the immediate response. "Separation of six minutes plus at the speed they're moving. Maybe more."

"We've got system IDs, Captain," another sonar tech said. "The destroyers are French, but the subs aren't. They're both *Akulas*. The trailer is Indian...and I'm pretty sure the lead one is Russian."

Hot damn. John forced himself to speak lightly. "Well, I suppose they had to get sick of beating up on the Japanese at some point."

The single best submariner in the world might have been French, but John was smart enough to fear the Russian Navy. Thought dead and buried at the beginning of the century, the Russians' unexpected resurgence in the late 2020s was unnerving. A few pointless local wars sharpened their teeth, and then their navy exploded almost overnight. Then, through the 2030s, they rediscovered a dangerously professional core.

Their surface forces were still working out the kinks, but the sub fleet was an entirely different beast. Russian submarines had almost singlehandedly destroyed the Japanese fleet. Although most American submariners had yet to encounter their Russian counterparts, many of those who did failed to survive the experience. There were troubles up north, near Alaska, that John's superiors didn't admit to—but John heard the rumors.

A chill ran down John's spine. The Russians might be good, but this one had made a mistake. He or she was rushing into the fight, probably eager to beat the Indians or the French to the punch. But the *Akula's* CO had either misjudged *Razorback's* location or was overly optimistic concerning how quiet his own submarine was at thirty-seven knots. *Probably the former.*

What the Russian was thinking really didn't matter. The lead *Akula* was racing straight into the jaws of death, and John would do nothing to dissuade the bastard.

"Dial the first two in, Weps," he ordered. "Two torps each, please."

"Yes, sir!"

His weapons officer sounded excited, but John couldn't blame her. Assignment to clear the SOM had been a terrifying proposition, but if the enemy was going to be so obliging...

"Solutions ready," Weps reported.

"Ship ready." Patricia shot John a thumbs-up.

John grinned and then glanced at the plot. Damn it if all four enemy ships weren't still burning holes in the water right toward him. They couldn't know that *Razorback* was there. No professional naval officer should be so stupid. Moments ticked by without change.

"Range?" he asked one more time, just to be sure.

"Sixteen thousand yards."

Given the current situation, it was the perfect range for a down-the-throat shot. John took a deep breath.

"Tubes one and two...*fire!*"

Diego Garcia, British Indian Ocean Territory

"The sub's gone in," Julia said quietly, gesturing at the large screen displays in *Belleau Wood's* CIC.

Diego Garcia was close enough to the Strait of Malacca to catch a satellite Link connection with the *Lexington* Strike Group, so Rear Admiral Rosario pulled rank and connected her former cruiser to the Link picture. Besides, *Belleau Wood* and *Fletcher* were on hot standby to be support if everything went wrong.

Nancy didn't want to think about how much had gone wrong in the First Battle of the SOM...or the help they'd needed afterward. Would the Indians let them collect survivors this time if the battle turned into a massacre? Nancy shivered, imagining John Dalton and a dozen other friends as prisoners of war.

The Link picture was only a sanitized look at what tracks were where. Each icon was color-coded for friend or foe, with foes diamond shaped and friends circular. Recent airborne reconnaissance gave the strike group a good idea of what enemy ships were present in the SOM, and recent ship movements meant that the Freedom Union outnumbered the Alliance...despite Admiral Anderson's best efforts. Her decision to divide her force in two only made the odds worse, but her formations showed no sign of changing.

That meant it was up to the lone submarine out front to even the odds.

Nancy Coleman sat by her boss's side, outwardly composed but with acidic butterflies eating at her insides. "That's John Dalton, you know."

"Is it?" Julia sat up straight. "Screw whatever asshole sent him back in there after last time. He saved us when McNally shat the bed and got a carrier sunk out from under him for his reward."

"I don't know if I ever told you he married my college roommate." Nancy's smile was crooked. "They're my younger daughter's godparents."

"Damn. No, you didn't." Julia curled up in the admiral's chair, seemingly not caring that twenty or thirty of *Belleau Wood's* crew—including ten officers—were also in CIC, watching the displays and whispering amongst themselves. "I hope he's as good in a sub as he was with a strike group."

"From what my husband says, John's better in a boat." Nancy pushed her worry for Alex aside; at least *he* wasn't in the SOM. She didn't much like the idea of him on some secret mission he couldn't talk about, but Alex was doing his job. And at least it wasn't *there*.

"I hope he's right," Julia whispered. "Because he's going to have to be if they want *anyone* to come home from that battle."

Nancy had read the pre-battle briefs. Anderson expected seven destroyers, two frigates, and a corvette in the strait, along with an unknown number of submarines. She viewed the shore-based missiles as the real threat, which was what her advance group, SAG Alpha, was supposed to deal with. Then the carrier would take out the aircraft and the airfield. Simple.

Except now there were *thirteen* destroyers in the SOM, and Nancy knew from experience how many missiles an Indian destroyer brought to the party. She rubbed her arms for warmth. If the Indian-French force coordinated their fire...

"What the—" The CIC watch officer clapped her hand over her mouth.

"There go two French destroyers." Julia crossed two off the crude checklist she'd written on her console in grease pencil. "Ten destroyers to go—I wonder if he left the two in the mouth of the Strait on purpose?"

"I bet he did." Nancy grinned. "Told you he was good."

"When I joked about running out of torpedoes, I didn't actually mean it," John said as the sounds of a frigate breaking up filled *Razorback's* control room.

Was having it on speaker dumb? Maybe. But using the dying ship to hide was a time-honored sub tactic, and there were two destroyers out there hunting for John's boat. No one knew better than a submariner how useless active sonar was in waters disturbed by a sinking ship suffering secondary explosions and implosions as her watertight bulkheads collapsed. Those destroyers could ping away all day and not find him here.

"We'd be in better shape if we hadn't shot two duds at that frigate," Pat said. "But do you want to ration torps this early, Captain? We're still ten miles shy of the halfway point."

"Want?" John grimaced and resisted the urge to kick something. Every available surface was metal, and his foot would lose. "Need...?"

Improved *Cero*-class submarines like *Razorback* could carry thirty weapons in their torpedo room and four more in the tubes. Usually, captains chose to carry eight Harpoon III anti-ship missiles—eight being the most any weapons depot would give you—and twenty-six torpedoes. For this mission, however, John rejected the missiles and loaded thirty-four torpedoes.

Unfortunately, *Razorback* had already shot fifteen of those, including two duds.

"Judging from the number of ships we've already encountered, our pre-battle intel was wrong," John said quietly. "I think we have to plan for the worst."

Pat's eyes went a little wide, but she was as seasoned as him by now, and she only nodded. "One torpedo per target it is," she said. "And here's hoping for no more duds."

"Lazark's current stats say it's one out of every thirty," John said. He knew that number because his retired admiral mother was an advisor to the secretary of defense, and SecDef didn't appreciate reports of torpedoes flunking out before they could kill the enemy.

"Well, then we've hit our fair share." Pat's smile was wry. "Someone should tell them that."

"Let's save it for after the battle." John glanced right. "Weps, make sure we save the data on the bad torps, will you? I want to give it to Admiral Rodriquez so he can bludgeon Lazark with it."

"On it, sir."

John took a deep breath, not liking the creeping feeling walking up his spine. "XO, let's stream the comms wire. This not knowing what's coming for us is so twentieth century. I want to come up in Link 18 with the strike group." He turned to the comms watch. "But Link only please, gentlemen. I'm too busy to take calls right now, so let's just not dial into any comms bands and give the admiral ideas, all right?"

His sailors grinned. "Yes, sir."

"All right, then." John glanced at the clock. "The advance force should enter the SOM in twenty minutes. In the meantime, let's go be the bull in the proverbial China shop."

"You've got an idea?" Pat asked.

"Oh, yeah. These destroyers are focused on sub hunting right now. They expect us to shoot at them, and they're going to *keep* sub hunting until they're certain we're dead, right?"

"That's generally how it works."

"Then let's leave them to it. We'll sneak right under them and pass targeting info straight to *Parramatta*. I bet Commander Goddard can figure out what to do with that."

Pat cocked her head, studying the developing Link picture. "It's too far for a Harpoon shot, sir."

"But not for LRASM." John grinned.

Entering the Strait of Malacca, Lexington Strike Group—SAG Alpha

"Link picture updating, Captain," a watch keeper reported, and Commander Fletch Goddard turned away from his conversation with his Ops officer to study the display.

"So *Razorback* decided to join the party." He scratched his chin. "Bloody hell. I didn't expect them to be halfway in already."

"They're actually fifteen miles shy of the halfway point, Captain," his Ops officer said.

"Close enough," Fletch grunted. "Damned good work so far, but if they dance with those destroyers too long, the next group will catch up with them..."

The thought hit him like lightning just as he started to wonder why *Razorback* would choose *now* to come up in Link. They could've done it early on, when streaming their comms wire—a potentially noisy evolution—wouldn't have a high chance of two highly motivated enemies detecting them.

Fletch grabbed a nearby phone and dialed the bridge.

"XO," Charlie Markey said.

"Charlie, how many LRASMs does *Jason Dunham* carry?"

"Eight. She got an entire VLS cell of them." There was no hesitation; Charlie was great at details.

"And the range on those darlings is over three hundred nautical miles, correct?"

"Yes, sir." He could hear Charlie's grin. "I like the way you think."

"I bet *Razorback* will, too." Fletch hung that phone up and pulled on a headset. One stop of his foot pedal, and he was live on the strike group command circuit. "*Jason Dunham*, this is *Parramatta* Actual. Launch two LSRAMs each at track seven-seven-one-four and seven-seven-one-five, over."

The AGM-158C LRASM (Long Range Anti-Ship Missile) was a relatively new missile, and *Jason Dunham* was the only ship in Fletch's advance force that carried it. From what Fletch understood, *Dunham* only had those missiles thanks to a lost bet between the weapons depot and *Dunham's* XO, but he didn't much give a damn how the aging destroyer got the new missiles. Their range was *twelve times* that of the Evolved Sea Sparrow Missiles *Parramatta* carried.

Even better, the LRASM was a stealthy, sea-skimming missile. It would take almost thirty minutes reach the Indian destroyers...but they would never see it coming.

"This is *Jason Dunham*, roger, break, spin up and launch will take two mikes, over."

"*Parramatta*, roger out."

Fletch turned back to his Ops officer as excitement vibrated through *Parramatta's* entire Ops Center. "Let's find someone else for *Dunham* to kill on our way in, shall we?

"All stations, SUWC, bulldogs away!" *Jason Dunham's* Surface Warfare Coordinator reported on the internal communications net.

"Bridge, aye." Lieutenant Commander Stephanie Gomez turned to the officer of the deck and grinned. "I guess that bet paid off, huh?"

Lieutenant (junior grade) Angelina Darnell snickered. Laughing made her one-eyed face look vaguely evil, a fact she traded on with officers more junior than her. "Ma'am, I'm going to miss you when you move on."

"Who said anything about going anywhere?" Steph asked.

"Promotions lists come out in November, and I bet you're going to be on it." Angelina shrugged. "That'll mean you're too senior to stay XO on a lowly and aging destroyer."

"Well, if our counterparts didn't keep getting sunk, *Dunham* wouldn't be working her way toward being the oldest destroyer in the fleet." Steph shuddered.

She loved this ship. She did. After almost a year and a half on board—through three captains, two collisions, multiple other disasters, and countless battles won or lost—the crew was like family. But Steph was also ready to move on. She burned for her own command, for her own chance to make a difference. *Dunham* had been in a lot of battles, but she was usually stuck in the back...or sent to fight for secondary objectives.

Not today, though. Today, *Dunham* sailed just three hundred yards off *Parramatta's* port beam, and *they* were the first of SAG Alpha to fire. Even as the newer destroyers in the group fired their Harpoon-IIIs at the two destroyers guarding the SOM entrance—*Dunham* was left out of that fight, but now Steph didn't mind—they were on track to matter.

After being stuck between an advancing French force and jack shit for resources back on Armistice Station at the war's start, that was all Steph wanted. To *matter*.

Today, *Jason Dunham* might finally shake her bad-luck reputation.

BOOM!

Bluefish jerked out from under his feet and threw herself to port, rolling through ten, twenty, thirty, and then forty degrees before ponderously righting herself. Lights flickered and sailors slammed into equipment before the submarine finally crept back onto an even keel. Bobby could hear Rose swearing viciously as the master fire-control computer arced and sparked as watchstanders yelped and jumped clear.

Boom!

The second concussion was more distant, but *Bluefish* still jumped like a wounded animal, bucking and creaking in protest. For several moments, no one spoke—even Rose stopped swearing—and everyone waited anxiously as one of the techs leaped over to secure the power to the fire-control panel, which extinguished the electrical fire.

"Officer of the Deck, I've got indications of flooding in the sonar dome," the sonar supervisor reported. "I have a complete loss of sonar forward."

"OOD, aye," Bobby replied. His brain went to autopilot, reaching back into his prewar training. "Diving Officer, make your depth one hundred feet."

He hadn't bothered to ask the captain, but no one contradicted him.

"Dear God," someone whispered. "What happened?"

A long moment of silence stretched out before Master Chief Baker said what no one else would: "Must've been a mine. But we weren't right a top of the fucker; if we were, we'd be in shredded pieces on the bottom."

"Fuck." Rose grabbed Bobby's arm and squeezed; he could feel her wanting to say it, but no one would.

What did you say when the captain had driven them straight into a minefield? Nothing, that was what. Bobby's first priority was getting *Bluefish* closer to the surface as soon as possible.

"Make my depth one hundred feet, aye, sir." The diving officer sounded relieved to have something to do.

"Commence hover once we reach one hundred feet." Bobby's mind worked furiously. He knew there were no mines *here*, but ahead of them? To port and starboard? How far into a minefield could they have wandered?

Commander Peterson was pale and frozen when Bobby finally remembered to glance his way, staring with hollow eyes at the chart. He couldn't believe it, could he? Bobby shifted slightly, hoping to get his attention.

No joy.

"Conn, DCA, repair parties heading forward," the voice of *Bluefish's* damage control assistant said on the comm.

Bobby steeled himself; Peterson still said nothing.

"Conn, aye." He sucked in a ragged breath. "We've had an electrical fire up here, DCA."

"DCA, aye. Electrician in route."

I hate being right. Hate. Hate. Hate. Hate. Bobby swallowed, trying to screw up the courage to say something or stop wiggling. Either would work. Fortunately, someone else got in first.

"Captain, I recommend going active on the low-frequency mine-hunting sonar until we're clear of the minefield," the XO said. Vanderbilt was bleeding from a cut on his forehead and swaying more than Bobby. Bobby's heart sank. Did he have a concussion?

Peterson shook his head convulsively. "Not while we're half blind. Someone might hear..."

"Sir, if we hit another mine, it won't matter what they hear," Vanderbilt said, his voice slurring like a drunk who was a six-pack into a great weekend.

Definitely a concussion, Bobby decided. Vanderbilt was usually more subtle.

"We damned well *better* not," Peterson snapped. "If we do—"

The speaker on the bulkhead crackled, cutting him off. "Conn, Maneuvering Room."

"Go ahead." Peterson got there before Bobby could, sounding waspish.

Lou's disembodied voice was eerily calm. "Sir, preliminary damage assessment as follows: major flooding in the dome through a hole on the starboard side forward. Pumps online and are maintaining three feet of water on deck. Flooding in the torpedo room from burst seawater service piping with eight inches of water on deck. Patch in progress. Multiple class-charlie fires reported on the starboard side. Breakers tripping from shock damage throughout the boat. Investigation in progress."

"Can I maneuver?" Peterson demanded.

"Yes, sir," Lou replied after a moment. "Engineering recommends remaining below five knots to minimize changes of pressure in the dome. Shallow water maneuvering is better."

"Captain, aye." Bobby almost decided that Peterson was starting to sound normal again, but before he could complete the thought, his captain turned to face him with burning eyes. "Get us out of here, Nav," he snarled. "Now that you've gotten us into this mess."

Bobby reeled back as if struck, eyes going wide. He stuttered: "Captain, I—"

"I don't want to hear it."

Stung, Bobby could only stare. He'd *tried* to tell Peterson that they were entering a mine danger area, only to be ignored—and now it was *his* fault? Peterson was the captain. He could paint this however he wanted, and there was no use arguing with him. Besides, Bobby's mouth opened and closed several times, but he couldn't come up with a coherent objection. The captain had always been prickly, but he'd never been so blatantly unfair as this.

"Get us out of this infernal minefield, Mister O'Kane," Peterson repeated. "I need to report to Commodore Banks."

"Aye, sir," Bobby managed as Peterson stalked out.

The trip back to Perth was going to be a long one.

Chapter 28

The Early Bird Gets the Worm

28 September 2029, the Strait of Malacca—SAG Alpha

Parramatta shuddered, launching a pair of Evolved Sea Sparrow Missiles at the incoming threat. The missiles burst out of her launch cells, flaring into the air with brilliant abandon and then burning away from the ship at Mach 4. Fletch, sitting in the frigate's Ops Room, tried to appear calm, but he was a sub hunter at heart—and so was his ship. Air threats were not his area of expertise, yet seniority had put him in command of the advance group.

Sometimes, he wondered if Admiral Anderson put an Australian in command of the SAG Alpha precisely so that there would not be a successful *American* with whom to compete. It was a dirty thought but hard to escape when you associated with someone as blatantly ambitious as Kristi Anderson.

Fletch drummed his fingers against his console and decided he was glad she wasn't in *his* navy.

"All stations, Air, track seven-one-niner-niner killed with birds," his air warfare coordinator reported.

"Captain, aye. Well done, people," Fletch said into the internal comms net. "That's two Indian destroyers down, and the doorway to the Strait of Malacca is open. Let's keep our eyes open for shore-based missiles while we march through."

Parramatta wasn't made for this fight, but Fletch would damned well fight it.

"All Stations, Lima Alpha, launching chicks in one-five mikes for tac air cover," the staff watch on board *Lexington* reported.

Fletch glanced at his plot. *Parramatta* and her formation were roaring into the strait at thirty knots, past the flaming wreckage of two Indian destroyers. Cruise missile sites to both port and starboard had been destroyed in their first barrage of missiles, though a few leakers got through—one of which hit *Sam Nuun*, the newer of Fletch's two American destroyers. Fortunately, the damage was relatively minor; *Sam Nuun's* helicopters had both been taken out by the missile, which went straight through her helicopter hangar before exploding.

But this wasn't a battle where helicopters mattered much, or at least it wouldn't be if *Razorback* did her job and cleared the subs out of the strait.

And in fifteen minutes, American F-35s would scream overhead and take out a few more of those annoying cruise missile sites...hopefully before they targeted Fletch's ships.

"One torpedo running—damn it, sir, we got another dud!" Chief Anton Kruger swore in a language John didn't know and wasn't going to ask about.

"Snapshot tube three, track seven-seven-one-six!" John ordered. "Cut that dead torp loose! All ahead flank!"

Razorback surged forward, her propulsor chewing into the water as she clawed her way up to her top speed of sixty-three knots. John almost never reached for speed, but with an angry frigate on his tail, today was a day to run.

"Conn, Sonar, splashes!" Sonar reported. "Splashes aft."

"Brace for impact!" John snapped. "Right standard rudder."

"Right standard rudder, aye, my rudder is right fifteen degrees, no new course given," the diving officer replied. "Captain, we are at flank speed."

"Very well." John grabbed for the overhead as his submarine leaned into the turn, trembling. Pre-war thinking said not to use over five to eight degrees of rudder at flank speed. Anything more might shear sound-absorbing tiles off the boat's exterior...or break something vital.

Somehow, John thought they'd forgive him, provided he didn't sink the entire damned submarine.

"Tube three fired electrically!" Weps reported. "One fish running hot, straight, and normal."

"Thank God," John whispered before he could stop himself. Then he looked over at Pat. "I could drop one of those duds on the Lazark CEO's house right about now. Fuck their thirty percent failure rate."

"Maybe we got a bad batch, sir."

"Let's hope not." John turned back toward the plot, but the depth charges exploding muddied the picture up so much that tracks were jumping all over the place. Computers were brilliant, but so-called *optimized automatic passive sonar tracking* worked like crap when there was a lot of noise in the water. John hit the talk switch on the box to his right. "Sonar, Conn, what's our friend doing?"

"Conn, Sonar, bottom bounce says he's right outside the mess and staying where he can fling rocket-propelled depth charges at us."

"You hear that, Weps?" John twisted around.

"Yes, sir. Chief Kruger is driving this fish personally, and it's going under the gunk to find something special on the other side."

"Good. Steady as she goes." John liked his current course; it was right on the edge of the cloud of explosions the Indian frigate was causing with their constant depth charging. *Razorback* was close enough that they could occasionally feel a tremor through her hull but far enough away for nothing to hurt her.

"Steady as she goes, aye. My course is zero-two-seven, Captain," the diving officer reported.

"Very well." John eyed the chart. They were almost at the SOM's narrowest point, where it was only about forty nautical miles wide. He couldn't keep racing around right here, not if he didn't want to run right up onto the coast of Malaysia. Running into islands tended to bad for submarines, so it was time to be a responsible adult. "All ahead standard for fifteen knots."

"All ahead standard for fifteen knots, aye. My engines are ahead standard."

"Very well."

"Torpedo in final acquisition. Time to impact...thirty seconds."

"Conn, Sonar, target is maneuvering, turning away and dropping noisemakers."

"Conn, aye." John glanced at the plot one more time; the frigate's track was clearer now, and he could see them turning away. John imagined the frigate was pushing for flank speed and doing their torpedo evasion maneuvers. Unfortunately for the Indians, those maneuvers were all designed to work against the old CBASS torpedo...*and* this torpedo still had a human brain telling it not to fall for noisemakers or other tricks.

Besides, the ASV was more than twice as fast as that frigate.

"Impact!"

No one cheered, though most of the watchstanders in control smiled. John just turned to Pat. "Find me the next one."

"Vampire, vampire, vampire! Vampire track 7654, inbound own sector! Engaging with birds!"

A flash split the air, followed by the whooshing roar of a missile leaving *Jason Dunham's* vertical launch system. It was a spectacular sight from the bridge, and Steph remembered staring in awe during training exercises back when she was a division officer. Back when they launched maybe a missile or two a year.

Another fireball roared out from astern as the second missile in the pair launched. Standard doctrine was to shoot two missiles at any incoming threat, and *Jason Dunham's* air warfare coordinator had done just that when a Brahmos NG missile from one of the shore batteries to the west targeted them.

Steph swallowed and tried to keep her eyes on the horizon, searching for surface threats. But it was damned hard when the battle was an air battle. Missiles crossed in the air, coming from both shores and raining down on SAG Alpha's five ships. Being stuck in a crossfire like this was nerve rattling, even when it was part of the battle plan. And Steph was no admiral, so who was she to question the sanity of the people who put them here?

She knew their air defense was carefully coordinated by the watch on board *Sam Nunn*, whose SPY radar was the newest and most powerful. Their backup was the Australian destroyer HMAS *Sydney*, who was built with the same Aegis weapons system Stephanie's own destroyer possessed. Together, the three Aegis ships were responsible for the outer rings of air defense, while *Parramatta* and the littoral combat ship *Billings* handled leakers with their short-range Sea Sparrow and Enhanced Sea Sparrow missiles.

If planning had been in Steph's hands, she wouldn't have sent either *Parramatta* or *Billings* in with the advance group. Neither was good at air defense by design! But no one asked her. In fact,

Admiral Anderson seemed distinctly unwilling to take *any* input...so here they were.

Jason Dunham's internal net crackled with energy. "Leaker, leaker, leaker, leaker track seven-six-five-niner and seven-six-five-one, inbound *Sam Nuun!*"

Instinctively, Steph looked at the ship just ahead of them in the formation. Missile hatches opened on *Dunham's* younger sister's aft missile deck, but a long moment passed with nothing happening.

"Christ, I think they have a hang fire," Angelina breathed.

Moments later, two of *Jason Dunham's* forward missile hatches slammed open, and her own short-ranged ESSMs spat out. Evolved Sea Sparrow Missiles were shorter ranged than standard missiles, but they were faster, too. A quartet of them had the best chance of covering *Sam Nuun*—but they were a split second too late.

Steph watched in horror as the missiles crossed in the sky, the ESSMs arcing just feet above the missiles they intended to kill. Losing lock, they tumbled into the ocean uselessly.

Then the pair of shore-launched BrahMos missiles slammed into *Sam Nuun's* midsection, and their two hundred–kilogram warheads exploded together.

"Shit, I think *Sam Nuun* went down," Rear Admiral Julia Rosario whispered.

Nancy's head jerked up in time to see the flashing Link track representing the American destroyer vanish. She swallowed. "I don't suppose everyone could've lost radar contact on her at once?"

Sometimes, all you had were forlorn hopes.

"I wish." Julia rubbed her face. "I didn't feel bad about not going back, but now I'm starting to."

"Was that when the air attack hit the main group, or just now?"

"Both."

Nancy's eyes flicked back to the plot on *Belleau Wood's* large-screen displays. "Looks like *Sydney* won't be far behind her. Anderson never should've stuck her up front—she got hammered hard."

"Those *Hobarts* are pretty tough customers. I think whoever was up there solo would've gotten the ax," Julia replied.

"But you wouldn't have put someone up there alone." Nancy glanced at her boss, remembering her own experiences fighting off an unexpected air attack in the Strait of Malacca—and the woman whose level-headed tactics saved her ship.

"No. Not against BrahMos missiles. Those damn things are just too fast." Julia shook her head. "The air-launched ones are even worse than the ship-launched versions, because you've got less time to get a lock on them. Poor bastards."

Watching from an electronically aided distance was torture. The advance group was almost at the midpoint of the Strait now, with the main force less than an hour behind them. The ships out front were doing okay against shore-based cruise missiles—minus *Sam Nunn's* recent loss—but *Lexington* and her escorts had been hit hard by air attacks.

Reports in chat indicated that the cruiser *Anzio* was on fire, the littoral combat ship *Oakland* had exploded after two hits, and *Lexington* herself had been hit, too. It wasn't a great start for Admiral Anderson's "unbeatable" plan, for sure.

"I'm trying to distract myself by reading the news," Nancy said after several moments of heavy silence. "It's all about fusion, since the press hasn't caught wind of this battle yet."

"If the universe is kind, they'll wait for the press release."

Nancy snorted. "You know it won't be. Easley will be all over this shit, starting with the number of Americans dead."

"Don't burst my bubble. Anything interesting about fusion?"

"Blah blah blah going to change the world blah," she said. "I'll share the link, if you want."

"Sure."

Nancy wasn't just reading articles, however. She didn't have to be a genius to add two and two together and figure out Alex's current mission. Sure, article after article talked about *finally cracking the fusion code* and what that meant for humanity. She'd already read six. Most didn't mention what fusion could do for the war effort; she figured those would come out tomorrow.

But a lot talked about a mysterious research group on an underwater station in the South China Sea. Some even mentioned Red Tiger Station. And while Alex hadn't told Nancy where he was going, he had mentioned a secret mission that was outside the normal scope of the war. Given the details she now had, she could only think of one place the navy's former spy sub would go where they were out of comms for such a long time.

The fact that he'd be in Diego Garcia in a few days confirmed her suspicions. Nancy could do time-distance just as well as when she'd been a navigator in her division officer days, and the timing for some secret mission in the Indian Ocean just didn't add up.

Julia whistled. "The navy that gets this in a submarine first is going to have a hell of an advantage, aren't they?"

"You're asking the wrong Commander Coleman." Nancy's grin was brief as her stomach tried to twist itself into worried knots. "My husband's the nuc."

"I know enough to be dangerous in a coffee shop convo," Julia said. "And enough to understand that navies who *aren't* already shooting will go to war for this tech, too. Safe nuclear power for your ships and subs? Not to mention stable power on the home front? Everyone's going to be gunning for this Fogborne Team. I hope to hell we get to them first."

Nancy swallowed. "Me, too."

"You want to head back toward the middle of the strait, Captain?" Pat asked after the frigate finished breaking up and *Razorback* turned southeast once more.

Their previous sprint had deposited the attack sub in the shallow waters along Malaysia's coast, a place where most nuclear power boats avoided out of habit. John studied the chart. It wasn't *too* shallow here—he still had six hundred feet of water to play with. And who cared if he was in Malaysian territorial waters? Malaysia had chosen their side in the war, and it wasn't the Alliance.

"I like this spot. Let's make like a diesel for a bit and see if we can flush one or two out while we're at it," John replied.

Pat arched an eyebrow. "You think there are any left in here?"

"Maybe." John shrugged. "It doesn't hurt to look, and now we know we have more surface targets coming at us. So it pays to be where they won't expect us."

"Hooray for satellites, I guess." Pat frowned. "I'm still nervous about torpedo consumption, sir. We're down to fifteen, and who knows how many of those might be duds?"

"I hear you. Fifteen's not the number I'd like to have when we know there's another eight destroyers coming at us, along with whatever other boats they can scrape up."

"I'm more worried about the subs now that SAG Alpha is in action."

"They've lost one." John gestured at the plot. "*Sam Nuun* is either out of the action or going down. Hopefully, the main group can pick up her survivors, but that's one Aegis destroyer down from SAG Alpha. That's going to make air defense harder for them."

"You say so, sir. That skimmer stuff really isn't my thing."

John chuckled. "Not mine, either, but I learned a lot when I was on *Enterprise*." Thinking about the First Battle of the SOM still threatened to drag him into a dark place, but John shook it off. "Helps that I've got a good friend who is a SWO, too."

"And that you want to be an admiral someday?" Pat grinned.

"Well, my parents would be pretty disappointed if I didn't," John replied. "But that's a topic for another day. Let's survive today first."

"I second that." Pat flicked the intercom switch. "Sonar, Conn, you got anything for us?"

"Link tracks on the destroyers are still too far for sonar in current conditions, but we've got a sniff of something submerged in the shallows. Bearing about one-two-niner, range fourteen thousand yards. Whoever it is, they're trying to hide in under the layer."

"There's our next customer!" John said, feeling his heart race in the best way. Damn it all if he didn't have the best crew—did he really have to leave them in just a few months? "Set up on him, Weps."

"Weps, aye."

Razorback's crew responded with well-oiled precision, and soon, another *Scorpene* joined her fellows on the bottom. Like the others, this one never knew *Razorback* was even there...though it was safe to say that *someone* on the Indian side had figured it out.

Twenty minutes later, the destroyer squadron launched helicopters and started some serious anti-submarine warfare.

John smiled to himself, kept hugging the shallows, and watched those helicopters concentrate on the deep water American submarines were known to operate in.

"The strike group has reached *Sam Nuun's* survivors, Captain," Charlie said.

Fletch was glad they were on the phone and his XO couldn't see his ashen-white face. He felt a little sick; one of his ships had sunk, and he hadn't been able to do a damned thing to help her people. "Please tell me they're picking them up."

"*Northumberland* has slowed."

"Thank God." Fletch sank back in his chair in *Parramatta's* ops center, allowing himself ten seconds to savor his relief. Then he forced his mind back to work. "Thank you, Charlie."

"Anytime, sir."

Fletch hung up the phone and turned back to his Ops officer. But he didn't get a chance to speak before the strike group command circuit crackled. "*Parramatta* Actual, this is Lima Alpha. Your request for *Anzio* to engage tracks seven-six-eight-eight and company with LSRASM is approved, over."

"All stations, *Anzio*, launching long-range bulldogs, over."

Fletch felt a giddy feeling curl up in his stomach. "This is *Parramatta*, roger, very many thanks, out." He grinned. "Let's see if we can't help our submerged friend by thinning out these next six targets."

"Not to mention ourselves, eh, sir?" his Ops officer replied. "It'd be nice not to get hammered again."

"We've still got cruise missile batteries to face yet," Fletch replied grimly. "The rest of the strike group can't help much with those, since we don't know where the bloody things are until they shoot at us. We've just got to endure and kill them before they kill us."

"We'll beat them, Captain."

"We damned well better. I'm a wretched swimmer."

"Conn, Sonar, two solid hits. Sounds of secondary implosions."

"Conn, aye." John hadn't been counting his kills—he thought it was kind of a crass thing to do before writing his patrol report—but knowing his team had nailed three *Scorpenes* among so many other enemies was gratifying.

The only thing that kept him from grinning from ear-to-ear were those eight destroyers rolling through the SOM toward him. Frowning, John glanced at the plot, pulling up data from *Razorback's* integrated combat system and doing the calculations again.

"No matter what way we play it, it's bad math." He sighed. "Thirteen torps left and six targets. Even if we have zero duds, that only leaves us one fish for anything else lurking around..."

Pat made a face. "And the entire trip back to Perth. That's like asking someone to sink us."

"Yeah, let's not hang that sign on the door." John scratched the stubble on his chin. "*Anzio* launched eight long-range strike missiles at the destroyer squadron, but with only eight missiles to saturate their defenses, they're going to be just fine."

"Eight missiles seem like a lot to me," Pat said.

"It's only halfway to terrible if you're used to fending off bigger waves." John shivered, trying not think about wave after wave of Brahmos missiles crashing into *Enterprise* as the carrier and her escorts desperately fought them off.

"So do we time our torpedoes to arrive at the same time? We have Link tracks on the missiles and can see their time on top."

"That's a good idea, but I was thinking of launching our Harpoons at them."

Pat's eyebrows flew up. "It's a dead giveaway for our position."

"Only if we stay there."

Razorback carried eight Harpoon-III sub-to-surface launched missiles in her vertical launch cells. They were older missiles, slower and easier for the enemy to track than the sea-skimming LRASM, but the submarine version of the LRASM's production had been delayed pre-war, and now no one knew when they would see the light of day.

The latest version of the Harpoon was still a fire-and-forget weapon, however, which meant John's submarine could launch all eight, dive deep, and get the hell out of Dodge.

"Odds are high they'll see the Harpoons coming," Pat pointed out.

"And maybe not notice the LRASMs." John's smile was tight. "Better than wasting torpedoes as a distraction."

"Less likely to throw a dud, too," his weapons officer pointed out. "At least the Harpoon's tried and true, unlike these Mark 84 chucklefucks."

"At least they're fast chucklefucks, ma'am," Chief Kruger muttered.

John chuckled. "Set up the Harpoon engagement," he ordered. "Time it to match *Anzio's* missile time on top, and then I'll know when I need to get near the surface."

"You got it, Captain."

Pat leaned in close to John while the fire-control team worked. "You know, we could ask *Bluefish* to range forward a little and help out."

"Good idea. I'm senior to what's-his-name over there—Peterson? Patterson? Something like that—so make it more of an order than a suggestion."

John glanced at the plot. *Bluefish* had reliably held the back door closed, patrolling a box at the bottom of the strait near Singapore. But she hadn't shown an iota of initiative, either, and John didn't miss the fact that those six destroyers must've snuck by her.

"Where the hell *is* she?" John zoomed in on the bottom of the strait, but it didn't provide answers. *Bluefish* was gone.

"The commodore has redirected us to Christmas Island for repairs." Peterson appeared in the wardroom with a satisfied sneer on his face. "The sub tender *Nereus* is waiting for us there."

Bobby looked up from the navigation plan he was building on a laptop. "I'll rework the track, sir."

How long ago had Peterson called the commodore to report their damage? Probably right after he'd come up with a sufficiently ass-covering story, which meant he'd let Bobby get an hour into creating their all-too-slow track to Perth before he bothered to tell him they were going somewhere else.

The only good news was that Christmas Island was a hell of a lot closer than Perth.

"And what are *you* doing here, Mr. Cooper?" Peterson eyed Bobby's silent companion like he wanted to grow lasers in his eyeballs and murder him.

"Consulting with the navigator about his planned track, sir." Somehow, Lieutenant Lou Cooper managed to sound normal. He hefted his mug. "Also grabbing some more coffee. We're out in Maneuvering."

Peterson scowled. "And your *repairs?*"

"The patch in the torpedo room is holding and dewatering is complete. All fires reported throughout the boat are out with deranged equipment checklists complete. Pressure in the sonar dome is still variable; pumps are keeping up, but we won't be able to patch the hole until we hit port," Lou replied. "Good news is that launching a UUV showed that the damage is above the waterline. We should be able to repair it without a drydock."

"And *who* exactly authorized launching that UUV?" Unlike Lou, who pronounced UUV the normal navy way of "you-vee," Peterson drawled out every individual letter like the damned thing was a useful piece of equipment.

"The XO did, sir. He said you were not to be disturbed," Bobby replied. Having top cover was nice, for once. Vanderbilt must be feeling charitable, because of course he was going to get reamed for this.

Creativity was not the way. Not on *Bluefish*.

Peterson sniffed. "Very well. How long until I can increase speed and get us out of this death trap?"

"I wouldn't go over eight to ten knots with that hole in the dome, sir," Lou said. "We want the pumps to keep up."

"Can't we just flood the dome completely and compensate with ballast?" Bobby asked. "I know it's bad for the sensors, but I remember reading about *South Carolina* doing that a few months ago."

"*South Carolina* is a *Virginia*-class boat, Mister O'Kane." Peterson's eyes narrowed. "What works for her would *not* necessarily work for a *much* newer class of submarine. I appreciate your enthusiasm, but it is entirely misplaced."

"I don't know, Captain. I think I could make it work. We do have a procedure for waterproofing the dome interior, though it's obviously on Weps's don't-try-if-you-have-another-option list." Lou scratched his chin. "We'd still lose some speed having to ballast the boat to compensate, but I could get you a top speed of twenty-five, maybe thirty knots. I'd have to check."

"Don't be ridiculous, Mister Cooper!" Peterson snapped. "And I'm sure you're needed in engineering by now. Return to your station."

Lou deflated. "Aye, sir."

Bluefish's engineering officer didn't argue, and he didn't offer alternative ideas, either. He just left silently. Bobby watched, guilt twisting in his gut. Why was he the idiot who had to bring that up? Now Lou was in trouble, and Peterson was angrier than usual. Great.

"Officer of the Deck, make your depth one hundred feet."

Gently, *Razorback* edged her way toward the surface of the Strait of Malacca, coming to a hover just shallow enough to launch missiles out of her vertical launch system. Like all *Cero-I* submarines, she had twenty total VLS cells, twelve of which held tomahawk land-attack missiles, which were useless today. The other eight held Harpoon IIIs.

Harpoon IIIs were a faster and smarter successor to the missile originally built in the 1970s. However, this design was rushed into service before the war, so they faced limitations brought around by using the same missile body and warhead. Limited to a range of just eighty-two nautical miles, the newest version of the Harpoon was slower than the LRASMs *Anzio* fired from much further away, which meant *Razorback* had to fire them early enough that *Anzio's* missiles could catch up.

Calculating precision massed fire was an art that submariners were not usually gifted at. But Patricia Abercrombie was the type of math whiz who won competitions as a kid.

"Time minus thirty seconds," she announced.

"Weps, now's your chance to object," John said.

"Flight plans locked in. Missile cells one through eight ready to launch, Captain," Weps replied.

"Very well." John's eyes flicked to the countdown clock. It was precisely timed to the launch of the *first* missile, which would hesitate before its rocket booster ignited, waiting for the other seven.

The time ticked down slowly, and John's eyes flicked to the plot. *Razorback* was vulnerable here, hovering almost motionless near the surface. If he'd missed any submerged contacts in the SOM...

"Time," Pat said.

"Begin launch sequence!" John ordered.

"Missile one away!"

Missile launches were silent and invisible for a submarine. In peacetime conditions, John would've put the periscope up and watched his missiles fly, but this was war and stealth was paramount. He *might* give his boat's position away with launching missiles, but popping the scope up increased the likelihood of detection tenfold.

No one liked to talk about how most submarines were spotted visually. The urge to sneak a look around at the world was strong when you spent weeks or months driving around in the dark, but every peek came at a cost.

John wanted to go *home* after this damned mission. He loved his wife, and he had career goals to accomplish. Besides, the SOM would be a miserable place to die.

"Launch cycle complete. Re-pressurizing launch cells," the weapons officer reported.

"Very well. OOD, kick it up to ten knots and do a couple of turns to get away from this position in case anyone back traces the missile tracks, please," John said.

"Officer of the Deck, aye! Helm, come right to zero-five-nine. Ahead two-thirds."

John tuned out the repeat backs of the orders and turned to Pat. "All right. We've done our damnedest to stack the deck against these guys—now let's see if *Anzio* can get the kill."

"It's going to be a long twenty-minute wait."

"I know." John sighed. "Missiles are so damned boring."

Chapter 29

Turnover

28 September 2039, the South China Sea

A quick check of the mail did nothing to improve Alex's day.

It was a day that needed improving, that was for sure. It started well enough, with the junior officers allying with the two youngest Fogborne members to prank the XO. Unfortunately, George took the joke—a realistically dressed medical dummy appearing out of the ether and landing in his rack—with predictable bad grace. Then, when he confronted young Doctor Tang about it, she called him a dumb ape who was afraid of his own shadow and wouldn't understand fusion if it smacked him in the face.

Doctor Leifsson tried to smooth things over, and from there it only got worse. Most of *Jimmy Carter's* officers were fascinated by the concept of a working fusion reactor, which gave the Fogborne team a lot of leeway, but the pranks turned George into a one-man army determined to shut fusion down.

That didn't go as George planned, either. Paul tried all too obviously not to mock him, and that almost ended in a shouting match.

Sneaking up to periscope depth and downloading the mail packet—just to make sure their orders hadn't changed *again*—only resulted in the gift of another six articles about the Fogborne team. Part of Alex still couldn't bring himself to believe in a working fusion reactor smaller than a football field, but if it was real, the possibilities were endless.

Alex let himself fantasize for a few minutes after *Jimmy Carter* dove to the safety of deeper water, settling in on his rack with a good book. He didn't have a lot of chances to take a break, but if everyone was occupied by the news and email downloads, he might steal a few minutes.

Five minutes into his thriller, the phone in his stateroom rang. Alex groaned, praying that Paul hadn't found another way to antagonize George. "Captain."

"Good afternoon, sir, it's the officer of the deck," Elena Alvaro said. "Sonar reports multiple tracks, likely military on an inbound course from what looks like the Spratly Islands."

Alex's heart leaped into his throat. "How many contacts?"

"At least six, possibly more. Range is over sixty nautical miles and sonar is still classifying. They're moving in formation at twenty-five knots."

"Shit." The word escaped before Alex could stop himself. That made for a closure rate of almost fifty knots, which meant *Jimmy Carter* barely had an hour before their tracks would cross. "They're probably Chinese. I'll be right up."

"OOD, aye."

Alex reached control in under two minutes, and that included pulling on his sneakers. When he arrived, the atmosphere was tense, and Wilson was actually outside sonar, standing with Elena Alvaro at the chart table.

"It looks like they're coming from the Spratlys toward...well, nothing normal, unless they're taking a wonky-ass course that asks for trouble." Wilson pointed at the projected course for the new contacts. "Then again, they *could* be heading for Taiwan, just begging for a fight, but why go to the Spratlys first if they want that?"

"I'm not paid enough to speculate on what the Chinese are doing." Alvaro made a face.

Wilson laughed. "Ma'am, half my job is speculation, but they sure as shit don't pay me enough."

"Don't let Vincentelli hear you say that."

"So what are you speculating now, Wilson?" Alex asked and grinned when the sonar operator jumped.

But Wilson never lost his lazy grin. "Sir, I'd bet good money that these guys"—his finger stabbed the plot—"are Chinese. Ain't gonna guess *which* of the four Chinas they are, except to say they're probably not Taiwanese, since Taiwan's never been into the Spratly Islands." He shrugged. "But you don't have to be a fancy navigator type to see that they're on a least-time course straight to Red Tiger Station."

Ice water filled Alex's veins. He wanted to argue, but when he looked at the nav plot, Wilson's theory was spot on.

"Looks like someone read the news." Alex swallowed. "Good thing they're a little late."

"Unless they're hoping to find us along the way, sir," Alvaro said quietly.

"Unfortunately, that's the theory we've got to work with," he said. "And our orders are plain, even if this isn't a coincidence. We can't allow ourselves to be noticed."

Worry rolled in Alex's gut; what if Alvaro and Wilson were right, and the Chinese were after the Fogborne team? What would he do if *they* tried to engage him?

His orders didn't cover this, and his instincts told him to do everything his orders said he couldn't.

"Conn, Sonar, I've got aircraft engines at range. Doppler says inbound, maybe fifty nautical miles? Sounds like a Y-8 at low altitude," Boxer's voice reported through the speaker.

Wilson's head snapped up. "Well, aren't they industrious fuckeroos?"

"That they are." Alex laughed. "How deep's the layer?"

"About three hundred feet," Wilson replied. "Shallow here, but the water's deep."

Alex scowled. "I don't think that's going to do it. OOD, take her low and slow. Make your depth twelve hundred feet."

"Officer of the Deck, aye." Alvaro turned away from the chart table to give the orders, her voice crisp and professional.

Alex watched her for a moment, proud to see her blossoming. Elena Alvaro had come a long way from the closed-off and hesitant junior officer she'd been when he arrived. She had always been the best he had, but now she was damned near ready to be a department head.

That meant he'd lose her soon, but another sub would win. And that was the way the navy worked, even in wartime.

"Conn, Sonar, got tentative IDs on the contacts. Three Type 55 *Renhai*-class destroyers, a Type 075 *Yushen* LHD, and two Type 54 frigates that the computer *thinks* are *Jiangkai* IIs. Sounds like the *Yushen* has helos up, though I can't make much of them," Boxer reported. "Last TACMEMO indicates that no *Yushens* have gone over to the new Chinas, so it looks like these guys are ChiComms."

"Conn, aye," Alvaro replied.

"That's a good summary," Alex said, scratching his chin.

Wilson's eyebrows waggled. "Boxer's good, sir. Got great ears and a fantastic brain."

"That why you're out here?"

"I'm not on watch. I was bored."

Better than him drinking or finding trouble, Alex didn't say. Wilson was a conundrum. The kid was downright brilliant at sonar. He even seemed to be a good leader *and* an excellent trainer. His future would be bright if he could keep his nose out of the shit pile, but having met Wilson, Alex thought that unlikely.

"Wilson, can you program a UUV as a decoy?"

"Sure, but a torp's easier."

"I don't want to waste one."

Wilson shrugged. "The programming is there, so it's not like we shouldn't. It's part of their operating system, though a torp's got more gas."

"We don't need a lot of gas. What we need is something programed to sound like a *Hai Jiao* so we can distract them with a sub they *want* to hunt."

Wilson's eyebrows shot up. "That's tricky, sir. Maybe even mean."

"Hey, if we have to hide, we might as well do it smartly."

"I'll program the UUV." Wilson grinned. "Vasquez, you got my back?"

Vazquez snorted from her position over at fire control. "Figures you'd want me to do the hard work." She rose, wiping her hands on her coveralls. "I'm a'coming."

Twenty minutes later, *Jimmy Carter* launched one of the U.S. Navy's notoriously unreliable—and horrifically expensive—underwater drones. As the attack sub went deeper, the UUV played the recorded sound signature of an almost-quiet-enough Taiwanese *Hai Jiao*-class submarine. It changed depth to three hundred feet, just beneath the layer, simulating a submarine trying to remain undetected.

Slowly, *Jimmy Carter* turned away from her decoy, creeping along in the depths as the Chinese ships approached. The UUV was quiet, trucking along at ten knots on a course tangentially toward the Chinese. It took the Y-8 almost twenty minutes to find it, and then the aircraft dropped a sea of sonobuoys to localize—and then depth charge—the decoy.

It hit the bottom in pieces, taking a couple million dollars' worth of taxpayer money with it. Still, it was a bargain compared to *Jimmy Carter*.

Relieved, Alex laughed and watched the Chinese ships pass. Still, since he wasn't an idiot, he wanted another six hours before increasing speed to twenty-two knots.

Many hours later, a Chinese admiral and his ships arrived at Red Tiger Station and demanded the station manager turn over the Fogborne Team. Laughing, the station manager kicked his feet up on his desk and thought of the millions of dollars *he* could've gained by keeping them there.

"They're long gone," he said. "Left on an American submarine with a bunch of marines three days ago. I'll say the same thing to you I said to three separate pirate groups: feel free to hunt them down. I'd be glad to see someone take those pretentious assholes down a peg."

The Chinese admiral pursed his lips. "I see."

"Catch 'em if you can, Admiral." The station manager grinned. "There's a hell of a bounty on them, you know."

"All stations, Surface, last group six costal missile site destroyed," *Jason Dunham's* surface warfare coordinator reported over the net. "*Parramatta* is passing instruction for an ASW redeployment."

Lieutenant (junior grade) Angelina Darnel cocked her head. "They don't trust *Razorback* to clean house?"

Steph Gomez shrugged. "Trust but verify, my young Padawan. *Razorback* appears to have massacred the undersea enemy, but it pays to be careful."

Angelina snickered. "I wouldn't mind bagging a diesel or two, that's for sure."

"I'm pretty sure the crew agrees with you," Steph replied. *Dunham* had done well in the Third Battle of the SOM, but she hadn't sparkled. It always felt like the destroyer was on the edge of disaster or waiting for her chance to shine.

"Gladiator, this is Argent." The bridge-to-bridge radio crackled. "Slow to pick up survivors from Magic Carpet and join the main force when rescue is complete, over."

Steph grabbed the radio handset. "This is Gladiator, roger, out."

Gladiator was *Dunham's* call sign, used by her fellow Alliance ships on open circuits so that her exact identity was not known to the enemy. And Magic Carpet was USS *Oakland*, or had been... The littoral combat ship had taken two hits from coastal missile batteries and been torn apart. There were twenty or thirty sailors in the water just astern of Steph's destroyer, less than half *Oakland's* crew, but a decent number considering how fast she went down.

Steph hated herself for doing that math without blinking.

"Bring us around, Angelina," she ordered before turning to the boatswain's mate of the watch. "And Boats, call away the Rescue and Assistance Detail. Standby for recovery."

"Boats, aye!"

Jason Dunham turned away from *Parramatta* and the other ships of the forward group, giving up any chance at further glory. It was worth it, however, to save their fellows in the water.

After all, Steph never knew when she might share their fate.

Anzio's missiles did the trick. Oh, the Harpoons that *Razorback* launched made for a great distraction—two of them even hit their targets—but it was the LRASMs from *Anzio* that slammed into the remaining Indian destroyers. Three went to the bottom, the fourth was left a flaming wreck, and the last two ran, damaged and smoking.

It was a pretty good day's work, if anyone asked Captain John Dalton.

"Where the hell is *Bluefish*?" he asked as *Razorback* circled near what was *supposed* to be *Bluefish's* patrol box at the bottom of the Strait of Malacca. John had ordered his boat shallow, just in case *Bluefish* was running silently and deep, but even an active sonar sweep of the area didn't find the other sub.

They did find a dozen or so mines, however, which made John *really* glad he hadn't aimed for deeper water. The nice thing about having a carrier along, however, was that *Lexington* had helicopters armed with mine-hunting gear. They were on the way, and *Razorback* was inching away from the mines as smoothly as John dared.

"That's a great question," Pat replied. Scowling, she zoomed the

Link picture out, looking at American and Alliance ships that were further away. "She's outbound. Out of the Strait already and headed south."

"What?"

Pat shrugged. "Take a look, Captain."

"It's not that I don't believe you, it's just that I don't believe you." John glanced at the plot, but there she was in all her glory, SSN 843, heading away from the battle they just won. He gaped. "At that speed, she headed out when we were mid-strait."

"Pretty damned unkind of her."

"Tell me about it." John leaned back against the periscope stand, staring blankly at the overhead. Did *Bluefish's* absence matter? Maybe not. But it could have. "Did he get mine damage?"

"If he did, he didn't report it." Pat scowled. "You know *Bluefish's* reputation, sir."

Who was in command of *Bluefish*? Right. Wade Peterson. He didn't know the fellow, but word in the fleet said he was a curmudgeon, slow to change, and even slower to get underway.

God help me if I'm saddled with him for my next mission.

"Have we won?" Pat asked. "The Strait seems empty except for our forces."

"I guess so." John shook himself. It felt anti-climactic; here he was, cruising along at the Singapore end of the SOM, with no targets to shoot at. Weren't battles supposed to end with a bang?

"Bridge, midships, recovery complete." Steph handed a blanket to the last of *Oakland's* survivors.

"Bridge, aye," Angelina Darnell's voice replied over the radio.

The main force was in sight aft of *Jason Dunham*, and Steph felt the destroyer quiver as she picked up speed to find a place in this new formation. There were holes in the main force, too; while the advance group had lost *Sam Nunn* and *Oakland*, Admiral Anderson's main body—tasked with dealing with the fighter aircraft—had lost *Bogan*, *Perth*, and *Termagant*.

A traitorous part of Steph's brain wondered how Anderson managed to lose only non-U.S. ships. Two Australian frigates had been hammered into nothing, and of the *seven* destroyers in their task force, Anderson lost one of the two British ones. *Sydney*, up in the front group, had also taken significant damage. Had she intentionally put them on the threat axis?

No, that was a terrible thought.

"Thanks for picking us up, ma'am," the sailor with the blanket said. His uniform made him a chief petty officer, and a glance at the crowd said he was one of the senior survivors from the shredded littoral combat ship. "We were resigned to floating around for a bit."

"We always take care of our own, Chief." Steph smiled. "Besides, it looks like the shooting's about done, which means there are a lot of recovery ops to do."

"You let me know if I can help. I'm a boatswain's mate, and a couple of my folks survived. We'd all rather work than sit huddled under blankets, if you know what I mean."

"I do." Steph had never taken that long, sad swim, or spent time in a life raft outside of training, but she could imagine what it felt like to get a ship shot out from under you. "And I'm sure we can use you." She turned and called *Jason Dunham's* leading chief boatswain's mate. "Boats!"

"What's up, XO?" Chief Boatswain's Mate Gosney was a tall woman, with hair as dark as her skin and angular cheekbones.

"Chief Carter here is one of your ilk and has offered assistance. I think we'll have a few more recoveries in our future, so I figure we can put him to work. Thoughts?"

"Chief Carter and I go way back, ma'am." Gosney grinned. "We—"

"*Vampire, vampire, vampire!*" The tactical action officer's voice boomed out over the loudspeakers. "*Missiles inbound, starboard side!*"

"Shit!" Steph swore. "Chief, get these people inside the skin of the ship, *now!*"

Sprinting forward, Steph shouted at everyone along the starboard side—the same side they'd done recovery operations on—to get aft and inside. A few sailors were forward on the missile deck, and they fled aft as missile hatches flipped open and alarms sounded.

Steph twisted away, covering her ears and closing her eyes as *Jason Dunham* launched a quartet of SM-6 standard missiles.

But *Dunham* only had a crossing shot at the incoming missiles. The Indian missiles—fired from one last pair of coastal batteries that concealed themselves until now—were aimed at *Lexington*. And the carrier was two miles astern of *Dunham*, whose missiles only had seconds to find and intercept sixteen enemy missiles.

Two of them did.

Anzio, off *Lexington's* port quarter, had a better shot. But she was down to two SM-2s in her launchers, both of which she fired within seconds. Water boiling at her stern, the cruiser sprinted forward to put herself on the threat axis, interposing her two CIWS phalanx guns between the missiles and the carrier.

Meanwhile, the superfast brain of her Aegis Weapons System assigned shots to the rest of the strike group. *Jason Dunham* fired four missiles. *Bull Run*, the other cruiser, put eight in the air. *Morton, Ernest E. Evans,* and *Tyrian* all fired three. *Northumberland* only carried short range Sea Sparrows, as did *Lexington*, but both fired those as the missiles grew closer.

Steph wasn't in CIC to hear the missile counts going out on the net, but she could see their launch trails highlighted in the blue-gray sky. And she knew how few missiles all the ships had left. They weren't *empty*—everyone learned from the first Battle of the SOM—but some were perilously close.

Like *Anzio*, whose position relative to *Lexington* meant she'd taken the brunt of the missiles aimed at the carrier all day.

Steph never could tell how many Brahmos NG missiles got through the task force's coordinated defenses. She didn't have time to get to the bridge, or to CIC, or anywhere to make a difference. She could just stand on *Dunham's* deck, two miles away, and watch in horror as missile after missile slammed into *Anzio*, almost tearing the cruiser in three.

She vanished in a fiery grave within minutes, but *Lexington* steamed on. *Bull Run's* Aegis weapons system took over control of the strike group's fire, and within minutes, more missiles arced into the air, destroying the coastal battery that took *Anzio* out.

Steph sucked in a deep breath and raised her radio. "Bridge, XO. Standing by for more recovery operations."

Three hours after *Anzio's* demise, Admiral Anderson's voice boomed across the strike group command channel.

"All stations, this is Lima Bravo Actual," she said. "Well done to all hands. Marines are landing in Malaysia and are liberating sites the Indians took in Indonesia. Our job here is done! We have reopened the Strait of Malacca for Grand Alliance shipping. New assignments will be passed via chat, over."

John nodded at his radio watch and let them acknowledge the message. He had no time for Anderson's posturing.

"She wants us to stay here," Pat said without looking up from the laptop computer wedged between the fire control and weapons stations.

"We don't work for her," John replied. Frankly, he found Anderson exhausting, but he wasn't going to say that out loud.

"You want to reach out to SUBPAC for orders?" Pat asked.

"Sure, shoot out the standard email." John let himself sigh. "But for now, let's secure from battle stations and settle into a patrol pattern. Give the crew a well-deserved rest—and let's break out some steaks or something. They did damned good."

"I'd say better than good, sir." Pat grinned. "Five subs and three surface ships in one patrol? I think that might be a record."

"I tried not to count them," John admitted. "Seemed smarter."

Pat laughed. "I think we're at the point where counting is okay. We survived and thrived. Can't ask for much better."

"I'll count when we're out of the damned SOM." John didn't want to admit that this place would still give him nightmares. He'd be happiest if he never had to transit the damned strait again—though that was unlikely, given how his future laid on a surface ship.

Two hours later, when he was pretending to sleep in his stateroom, new orders came through. *Razorback* was to make for Perth at best speed. HMS *Galahad* and USS *John Warner* would take over undersea security in the SOM, and *Razorback* was not to wait for their arrival. With the orders came a personal email for John's eyes only.

John,

I know I promised you some time off before your next command—and another go round with your boat—but I need your ass back in Perth. It turns out that Captain Shapiro is pregnant with triplets. Needless to say, we need to get her ass off of Nereus *as fast as possible. No one wants the risk of having a pregnant captain going to war—even an old dinosaur like me.*

Get your ass and your boat back as fast as you can and prepare for a change of command. Your crew will get some time off while I juggle people and get them a new CO sooner than intended.

Well done in the SOM. Good hunting on the way home.

Marco

John stared at that email for a long time, pressing one hand against the hull as he read it. This was it? The patrol made for a good ending, but damn it all…he had thought he'd have more time to prepare.

He took a deep breath. This was what he wanted. Moving up required moving *on*, and John Dalton had stars in his future. That meant having no regrets.

Or at least pretending he had none.

Epilogue

1 October, Rihaakuru Station, occupied by India

Vice Admiral Aadil Khare was thoroughly sick of owning multiple underwater stations. Conquest was exhilarating, but overlordship was *tiring*. The locals weren't difficult, of course; the Maldives were a small nation, and they knew who to suck up to in the growing new world order. But pretending to care about local affairs while the government took months to import a brace of suitable station administrators was tedious.

His place was on a flagship, preferably an aircraft carrier, blasting enemy warships to pieces. Yet his flagship still remained a destroyer—and the admiralty told him to be *grateful?* Khare wanted to scream when he received that message, but proper admirals did not vent their frustration where their subordinates could witness it, so he folded his hands, sipped his tea, and thanked his superiors graciously.

He would not forget. Khare had a long list of people upon which he would visit revenges, be they petty or large, and the current chief of naval operations was a deserving political buffoon. Almost *six months* after he took this group of stations off the Maldives, he was still stuck here, marking time until the next offensive...and waiting for missiles.

Missiles he finally had. A target, however, he did not.

"Admiral, may I interrupt?" Captain Kiara Naidu, his chief of staff, ducked into his office while he ate a late breakfast at his computer.

He beckoned her in. "You have news?"

Kiara was *not* one of the people on his list for vengeance; no, his loyal-but-ambitious right hand would help him rise to the top...so long as she could join him there.

And have a clear path to succeeding him, but Khare did not think that too much to ask. Kiara was not so impatient as not to wait her turn, and Khare was loyal in exchange for loyalty. The relationship served both well.

"My asset on Red Tiger Station has made contact. They were unable to purchase or steal the plans...and an American submarine picked up the Pulsar team. Intelligence suggests they are heading for Diego Garcia."

Khare sat up so fast he spilled his juice and did not notice. He licked his lips. "Really?"

"Yes, sir."

Anticipation shot up his spine like lightning. This was it. This was his chance to change the future of the Indian Navy—and put himself right on top while he was at it. Khare smiled.

"Pass the word to my flag captain that we will get underway tomorrow morning."

4 October 2039, Diego Garcia, British Indian Ocean Territory

Nine days of nail-biting stealth later, *Jimmy Carter* surfaced and pulled into Diego Garcia. Spotting *Fletcher* still tied up alongside *Belleau Wood* was one of the most beautiful sights Alex had ever seen, and he didn't care that his grin stretched from ear to ear.

He didn't even notice the beauty of the small atoll. Diego Garcia should look like paradise after so many days underway, but the thought of his wife was even better. Then again, being *with* his wife on a tropical island...well, this was a pretty good end to the mission, wasn't it?

"That happy to see dry land? I thought you sub dudes were all about being haze gray and underway." Paul laughed.

His mammoth friend had squeezed into the sail with him after *Jimmy Carter* was nestled against the short end of Diego Garcia's last pier. Alex had left driving her in to Elena Alvaro, who needed the experience—and besides, Diego Garcia was an easy transit. It was a nice reward for an excellent young officer, who glowed when

Alex complimented her driving.

Now she was watching the line handlers, with Maggie along to make sure everything went just right. Could Alex finally relax? Maybe.

"Nancy's still here," he replied. "She said she doesn't get underway until the eighth—something about a delay in the rounds for her big gun—but I never believe navy scheduling until I see it in action."

"You can say that again, brother." Paul clapped him on the shoulder. "I'll be glad to see her, too, though I'll only be here today for a quick hello."

"You hear back from your regiment?"

"Yep. Out at first light, heading to do some sneaky shit in Malaysia." Paul grinned. "Finally something I'm *trained* to do, you know?"

Alex swallowed the sudden lump of worry. "Try to be careful while you're humping rifles in the mud, okay?"

"I will try." Paul grinned as he quoted the Norwich University motto.

"Fuck, I walked right into that." Alex chuckled.

"You always do. What's the plan for you fine folks?"

"Two days in port, we pick up some fresh food, drop you and the Fogborne Team off, and then we head out to Samar Station to meet Convoy 57." Alex tried not to sigh. "No rest for the wicked, I guess."

"Not even a thank-you? Your boss is an asshole."

Alex shrugged. "We're not exactly the tip of the spear, and subs are needed for convoy escorts. We do a lot of them. At least this gives me a bit of time with Nancy."

"Well, I hope this one gives you guys a break. You deserve a rest after that hairy-ass transit through the South China Sea," Paul replied. "I thought you were going to have to sink that last *Kilo*."

"It was probably Russian, so I *might* have gotten away with it, but my rules of engagement said not to shoot." Alex scowled. "Better that we crept under them, and they had no idea we were around."

"Anyone ever tell you that you're good at this shit?"

Alex felt his face warm up and fought the urge to stutter. "You're not exactly a pro submariner, Paul."

"No, but I can tell a good crew when I see one. Ain't that hard; leadership's leadership, and this one will follow you through the gates of hell."

"I hope they never have to."

Mid-Indian Ocean—Indian Task Force "Durga"

Assembling a force was the hardest part. Vice Admiral Khare had enough rank to conscript ships to his flag, but he needed *overwhelming* force. That took longer—and politicking.

"The last ships of the strike force will join us tomorrow, and we will be in range of Diego Garcia the day after that," Captain Kiara Naidu reported.

Khare sat on the bridgewing of *Rajput*, his *Kolkata II*-class flagship. The destroyer was a sleek and beautiful warship, even if she wasn't the newest class India had. Still, she would do the job.

She would do the job well.

"What do we have now?" he asked, tipping his head back to watch the sunset.

"We have our original task group of three *Shivalik*-class frigates, another *Kolkata*-class destroyer, and four *Kamorta*-class corvettes. However, Admiral Nagar has been…persuaded to join his force with us for the attack. This gives us another three destroyers—his are *Visakhapatnams*—and one more frigate."

Khare added up the number of missile launchers. "A hundred and twelve surface-to-surface missiles. That will work."

"I believe so. Intelligence reports only one cruiser and one destroyer in Diego Garcia. There is also an attack submarine, but they cannot help with air defense." Kiara's smile was smug.

"You've done well, Captain. Thank you." Khare stroked his beard. "Now, let us be on high alert for any aircraft flying in to remove the Fogborne Research Team. I want them."

"Diego Garcia will not surrender, sir. We may kill them in the crossfire." Kiara worried her lower lip between her teeth. "Then we will lose the secrets of fusion as well."

"Better no one have it than we allow fusion to benefit our enemies."

"As you say, Admiral. We will attack Diego Garcia in two days...and either tear that secret from the Americans or destroy them."

...to be continued in *I Will Try*, available for preorder now!

Thank you so much for reading! As an independent author, every reader means the world to me, and I'm delighted that you've joined the fight in *War of the Submarine*. If you haven't already joined my mailing list, you can do so by going to my website at www.rgrobertswriter.com, where you can get a free short story in this universe, *Pedal to the Medal*. You'll also get early looks at everything I'm working on, as well as fun behind-the-scene tidbits! You can also find access to my Ream there, where you can get exclusive first looks at my works.

If you enjoyed this story, please be kind and leave a review. I'd be so grateful! Reviews help indie authors like me be seen in the vast wasteland of publishing, and every review is a chance for a new reader.

Some Fun Notes

*A**dmiral Dewey's anchor* was dedicated in 1990 to the graduates of Norwich University serving in the Navy and Marine Corps. It is located on Sabine Field, the main football field at "the Wick." The anchor is a standard 30,000-pound Navy stockless anchor made during World War II. The anchor is painted white in honor of Admiral Dewey's flagship the USS *Olympia*.

Dewey Hall at Norwich is also named after the admiral. It was completed in 1901 as a memorial to Admiral of the Fleet George Dewey, the Hero of Manila Bay. Fun fact about Dewey Hall: this is where the code flags for the uniform of the day are hung from. Rooks (Recruits, or freshmen) read these code flags so they can announce to their fellow recruits and upperclassmen cadets what the uniform to wear that day is.

USS *Douglass* is named for what I assume will be the fifty-first or fifty-second state, the State of Washington, Douglass Commonwealth. This is the proposed name for Washington, D.C. if it becomes a state. I assume that by the late 2030s, the U.S. will have admitted both D.C. and Puerto Rico as states. Why? Mostly because I needed another two names for *Virginia*-class submarines, which are always named after states.

Also because it's probably about time. That whole taxation without representation thing is getting old for a lot of folks. I can't really blame them there, given what started our entire Revolution.

Remember that complaint to the Navy inspector general that happens on *Utah*? It's based on a true story of something that happened on one of the ships I was on. Despite the fact that he didn't know who made the complaint, it was specific enough that our captain could guess what division it was from. And what was his reaction? Not to be better. No, it was to hate that specific department head, because it was obviously his fault that one of his sailors felt the captain was abusing his power. (Spoiler: he was). I worked for some *amazing* captains in the navy...but this was not one of my finer commanding officers. In fact, if I ever see him again, it will be too soon. Some of his traits have snuck into two different characters in this series, as have traits from *another* not-so-great captain I served under.

But on the bright side, Alex Coleman did get some motivations and characteristics from one of the *best* officers I ever had the privilege to serve under. If he ever reads this, I'll probably be mortified, because he might just recognize himself!

All of "The Destroyers" ships actually exist today! Obviously, I'm guessing what might or might not be sold on the black market in ten to twenty years, but here they are:

Destroyer, the U-Boat, starts life as he South Korean submarine *Sohn Won-yil*. She is a Type 214 U-Boat built in Germany and specifically designed for export. I am postulating that *Sohn Won-yil* gets sold sometime in the mid-2030s and then a pirate group ends up with her.

Weirwood is Ex-*Wenzhou*, is a Chinese type 054 Frigate. She commissioned in 2005, and (theoretically) decomisioned and was sold in 2035.

Siren is ex-*Passat*, a Russian-built *Nanuchka*-class corvette that commissioned in 1990. She's likely to decommission in the mid-2020s, which is when the pirates buy her. Unlike a lot of Russian ships, she seems to be in serviceable condition (and still in service!), which is why I picked her.

Paul Swanson isn't just an easter egg for my Before the Storm readers; he's going to be in and out of this story a significant amount. He's a favorite character of mine; he and Alex have been pulling a David and Goliath routine off since college.

If you haven't read *Before the Storm*, Paul plays a major role in the prequel novella, where he's leading the team of marines Alex partners with to take on some (prewar) pirates. They're one of my favorite pairs of characters to write, though they do lose out to Alex and Bobby O'Kane, who you *haven't* seen together yet. (But consider this a treat for those who bothered to read my notes!)

***Right now, Bobby O'Kane is the hapless navigator on board the very unhappy submarine* Bluefish.** He's not having a great war, and he's working for the man who might just be the war's worst captain. Fortunately for him, he's got some great friends at his side. We'll see more of Bobby in Book 4, and *much* more of him in Book 5. Unfortunately, that means we'll see some more Commander Peterson, too, but he's a man you have to love to hate. (And if I told you he was based on someone I once served under, can you blame me?)

Bobby, however, is one of my favorite characters. He's always ready with a pop culture quip and isn't always serious, but he's got a good brain and has a last name that is *very* familiar to anyone familiar with the history of the American submarine community. Extra bonus points to anyone who has read this far, recognizes the last name, and pops that gem in a review!

And finally, I'll leave you with a fun fact for *I Will Try* – IWT is named after the motto for my alma mater, Norwich University, which I share with Nancy, Alex, and Paul, who were all classmates there. According to the Recruit Handbook (called "Rook Book" at the Wick), the motto "signifies our willingness to persevere in the face of adversity and recalls the proud heritage of citizen-soldiers and their success as leaders." It was inspired by Colonel James Miller's words at the Battle of Lundy's Lane in the War of 1812; when ordered to make a daunting, night time, frontal assault against a fortified British artillery battery, Miller's response was "I'll try, sir." After two unsuccessful attempts, Miller and the 21st Infantry Regiment took the hill.

Why did I choose this title? Firstly, because I love to use Norwich-themed titles for my books that focus on Norwich alums (we're a creative and ornery bunch, by and large). Secondly, because *I Will Try* fits book 4 perfectly. In book 4, Alex finds himself in a battle that will change both his career and his life...and no matter what he does, he'll never be the same again.

Thank you again for reading, and I hope to see you next time!

Also By the Author

War of the Submarine

Before the Storm
Cardinal Virtues
The War No One Wanted
Fire When Ready
Clean Sweep
I Will Try
Fortune Favors the Bold (Coming Soon!)

War of the Submarine Shorts

Never Take a Recon Marine to a Casino Robbery (subscriber exclusive)
Pedal to the Medal

Age the Legacy

Shade
Shadow (Coming Soon!)
Night Rider
Before the Dawn (Coming Soon!)

Legacy Shorts

Prelude to Conquest (subscriber exclusive)
The First Ride (Exclusive on Ream!)
City of Light (Exclusive on Ream!)

Alternate History

Against the Wind
Caesar's Command

Other Works

Agent of Change (Portal Sci-Fi with an Alternate History Twist)
Fido (Cozy Fantasy Serial, high on humor)
Once Upon a Dragon (Exclusive on Ream!)

About R.G. Roberts

R.G. Roberts is a veteran of the U.S. Navy, currently living in Connecticut and working as a Manufacturing Manager for a major medical device manufacturer. While an officer in the Navy, R.G. Roberts served on three ships, taught at the Surface Warfare Officer's School, and graduated from the U.S. Naval War College with a masters degree in Strategic Studies & National Security, with a concentration in leadership.

She is a multi-genre author, and has published in military thrillers, science fiction, epic fantasy, and alternate history. She rode horses until she joined the Navy (ships aren't very compatible with high-strung jumpers) and fenced (with swords!) in college. Add in the military experience and history degree, and you get A+ anatomy for a fantasy author. However, since she also enjoyed her time in the Navy and loves history, you'll find her in those genres as well.

You can find R.G. Roberts' website at www.rgrobertswriter.com or find all her links at linktr.ee/rgroberts. From there, you can join her newsletter! Joining the newsletter will get you a free novella or short story, set in either the War of the Submarine or Age of the Legacy universes (or both, if you like both genres). Newsletters are a twice-a-month affair, so there won't be a ton of spam in your inbox, but you'll be the first to hear about sales, get sneak peeks of new writing, and get to read free short stories from time to time, too!

R.G. Roberts is also one of the authors trying the new-fangled site known as "Ream." It's like Pateron, but made for authors and readers – and especially for superfans! There you will have access to exclusive first looks at all of her works, including early access to chapters of novels, short stories, and more! You can find her Ream at www.reamstories.com/rgrobertswriter.

Printed in Great Britain
by Amazon